The Wit, Whimsy, and Wisdom of
G. K. Chesterton

Dear Mr & Mrs Galley,

The Napoleon of Notty Hill
is an odd but astoundy book.
Not everyone's sense of humour,
but with a real Christian point.
I hope you enjoy it,

Very best wishes,

Kit

The Wit, Whimsy, and Wisdom of
G. K. Chesterton

Volume I

THE NAPOLEON OF NOTTING HILL

THE FLYING INN

THE TREES OF PRIDE

Coachwhip Publications
Landisville, Pennsylvania

The Wit, Whimsy, and Wisdom of G. K. Chesterton, Volume 1
Copyright © 2009 Coachwhip Publications

ISBN 1-930585-80-2
ISBN-13 978-1-930585-80-5

Cover: 1912 *Vanity Fair* caricature, by Strickland

Coachwhipbooks.com

THE NAPOLEON OF NOTTING HILL

THE TREES OF PRIDE

The Napoleon of Notting Hill

I

INTRODUCTORY REMARKS ON THE ART OF PROPHECY

The human race, to which so many of my readers belong, has been playing at children's games from the beginning, and will probably do it till the end, which is a nuisance for the few people who grow up. And one of the games to which it is most attached is called "Keep to-morrow dark," and which is also named (by the rustics in Shropshire, I have no doubt) "Cheat the Prophet." The players listen very carefully and respectfully to all that the clever men have to say about what is to happen in the next generation. The players then wait until all the clever men are dead, and bury them nicely. They then go and do something else. That is all. For a race of simple tastes, however, it is great fun.

For human beings, being children, have the childish wilfulness and the childish secrecy. And they never have from the beginning of the world done what the wise men have seen to be inevitable. They stoned the false prophets, it is said; but they could have stoned true prophets with a greater and juster enjoyment. Individually, men may present a more or less rational appearance, eating, sleeping, and scheming. But humanity as a whole is changeful, mystical, fickle, delightful. Men are men, but Man is a woman.

But in the beginning of the twentieth century the game of Cheat the Prophet was made far more difficult than it had ever been before. The reason was, that there were so many prophets and so many prophecies, that it was difficult to elude all their ingenuities. When a man did something free and frantic and entirely his own, a horrible thought struck him afterwards; it might have been predicted. Whenever a duke climbed a lamp-post, when a dean got drunk, he could not be really happy, he could not be certain that he was not fulfilling some prophecy. In the beginning of the twentieth century you could not see the ground for clever men. They were so common that a stupid man was quite exceptional, and when they found him, they followed him in crowds down the street and treasured him up and gave him some high post in the State. And all these clever men were at work giving accounts of what would happen in the next age, all quite clear, all quite keen-sighted and ruthless, and all quite different. And it seemed that the good old game of hoodwinking your ancestors could not really be managed this time, because the ancestors neglected meat and sleep and practical politics, so that they might meditate day and night on what their descendants would be likely to do.

But the way the prophets of the twentieth century went to work was this. They took something or other that was certainly going on in their time, and then said that it would go on more and more until something extraordinary happened. And very often they added that in some odd place that extraordinary thing had happened, and that it showed the signs of the times.

Thus, for instance, there were Mr. H. G. Wells and others, who thought that science would take charge of the future; and just as the motor-car was quicker than the coach, so some lovely thing would be quicker than the motor-car; and so on for ever. And there arose from their ashes Dr. Quilp, who said that a man could be sent on his machine so fast round the world that he could keep up a long, chatty conversation in some old-world village by saying a word of a sentence each time he came round. And it was said that the experiment had been tried on an apoplectic old major, who was sent round the world so fast that there seemed to be (to the inhabitants of some other star) a continuous band round the earth of white whiskers, red complexion and tweeds— a thing like the ring of Saturn.

Then there was the opposite school. There was Mr. Edward Carpenter, who thought we should in a very short time return to Nature, and live simply and slowly as the animals do. And Edward Carpenter was followed by James Pickie, D.D. (of Pocohontas College), who said that men were immensely improved by grazing, or taking their food slowly and continuously, after the manner of cows. And he said that he had, with the most encouraging results, turned city men out on all fours in a field covered with veal cutlets. Then Tolstoy and the Humanitarians said that the world was growing more merciful, and therefore no one would ever desire to kill. And Mr. Mick not only became a vegetarian, but at length declared vegetarianism doomed ("shedding," as he called it finely, "the green blood of the silent animals"), and predicted that men in a better age would live on nothing but salt. And then came the pamphlet from Oregon (where the thing was tried), the pamphlet called "Why should Salt suffer?" and there was more trouble.

And on the other hand, some people were predicting that the lines of kinship would become narrower and sterner. There was Mr. Cecil Rhodes, who thought that the one thing of the future was the British Empire, and that there would be a gulf between those who were of the Empire and those who were not, between the Chinaman in Hong Kong and the Chinaman outside, between the Spaniard on the Rock of Gibraltar and the Spaniard off it, similar to the gulf between man and the lower animals. And in the same way his impetuous friend, Dr. Zoppi ("the Paul of Anglo-Saxonism"), carried it yet further, and held that, as a result of this view, cannibalism should be held to mean eating a member of the Empire, not eating one of the subject peoples, who should, he said, be killed without needless pain. His horror at the idea of eating a man in British Guiana showed how they misunderstood his stoicism who thought him devoid of feeling. He was, however, in a hard position; as it was said that he had attempted the experiment, and, living in London, had to subsist entirely on Italian organ-grinders. And his end was terrible, for just when he had begun, Sir Paul Swiller read his great paper at the Royal Society, proving that the savages were not only quite right in eating their enemies, but right on moral and hygienic grounds, since it was true that the qualities of the enemy, when eaten, passed into the eater. The notion that the nature of an Italian organ-man was irrevocably growing and burgeoning inside him was almost more than the kindly old professor could bear.

There was Mr. Benjamin Kidd, who said that the growing note of our race would be the care for and knowledge of the future. His idea was developed more powerfully by William Borker, who wrote that passage which every schoolboy knows by heart, about men in future ages weeping by the graves of their descendants, and tourists being shown over the scene of the historic battle which was to take place some centuries afterwards.

And Mr. Stead, too, was prominent, who thought that England would in the twentieth century be united to America; and his young lieutenant, Graham Podge, who included the states of France, Germany, and Russia in the American Union, the State of Russia being abbreviated to Ra.

There was Mr. Sidney Webb, also, who said that the future would see a continuously increasing order and neatness in the life of the people, and his poor friend Fipps, who went mad and ran about the country with an axe, hacking branches off the trees whenever there were not the same number on both sides.

All these clever men were prophesying with every variety of ingenuity what would happen soon, and they all did it in the same way, by taking something they saw "going strong," as the saying is, and carrying it as far as ever their imagination could stretch. This, they said, was the true and simple way of anticipating the future. "Just as," said Dr. Pellkins, in a fine passage,— "just as when we see a pig in a litter larger than the other pigs, we know that by an unalterable law of the Inscrutable it will some day be larger than an elephant,—just as we know, when we see weeds and dandelions growing more and more thickly in a garden, that they must, in spite of all our efforts, grow taller than the chimney-pots and swallow the house from sight, so we know and reverently acknowledge, that when any power in human politics has shown for any period of time any considerable activity, it will go on until it reaches to the sky."

And it did certainly appear that the prophets had put the people (engaged in the old game of Cheat the Prophet) in a quite unprecedented difficulty. It seemed really hard to do anything without fulfilling some of their prophecies.

But there was, nevertheless, in the eyes of labourers in the streets, of peasants in the fields, of sailors and children, and especially women, a strange look that kept the wise men in a perfect fever of doubt. They could not fathom the motionless mirth in their eyes. They still had something up their sleeve; they were still playing the game of Cheat the Prophet.

Then the wise men grew like wild things, and swayed hither and thither, crying, "What can it be? What can it be? What will London be like a century hence? Is there anything we have not thought of? Houses upside down—more hygienic, perhaps? Men walking on hands—make feet flexible, don't you know? Moon ... motor-cars ... no heads...." And so they swayed and wondered until they died and were buried nicely.

Then the people went and did what they liked. Let me no longer conceal the painful truth. The people had cheated the prophets of the twentieth century. When the curtain goes up on this story, eighty years after the present date, London is almost exactly like what it is now.

II

THE MAN IN GREEN

Very few words are needed to explain why London, a hundred years hence, will be very like it is now, or rather, since I must slip into a prophetic past, why London, when my story opens, was very like it was in those enviable days when I was still alive.

The reason can be stated in one sentence. The people had absolutely lost faith in revolutions. All revolutions are doctrinal—such as the French one, or the one that introduced Christianity. For it stands to common sense that you cannot upset all existing things, customs, and compromises, unless you believe in something outside them, something positive and divine. Now, England, during this century, lost all belief in this. It believed in a thing called Evolution. And it said, "All theoretic changes have ended in blood and ennui. If we change, we must change slowly and safely, as the animals do. Nature's revolutions are the only successful ones. There has been no conservative reaction in favour of tails."

And some things did change. Things that were not much thought of dropped out of sight. Things that had not often happened did not happen at all. Thus, for instance, the actual physical force ruling the country, the soldiers and police, grew smaller and smaller, and at last vanished almost to a point. The people combined could have swept the few policemen away in ten minutes: they did not, because they did not believe it would do them the least good. They had lost faith in revolutions.

Democracy was dead; for no one minded the governing class governing. England was now practically a despotism, but not an hereditary one. Some one in the official class was made King. No one cared how: no one cared who. He was merely an universal secretary.

In this manner it happened that everything in London was very quiet. That vague and somewhat depressed reliance upon things happening as they have always happened, which is with all Londoners a mood, had become an assumed condition. There was really no reason for any man doing anything but the thing he had done the day before.

There was therefore no reason whatever why the three young men who had always walked up to their Government office together should not walk up to it together on this particular wintry and cloudy morning. Everything in that age had become mechanical, and Government clerks especially. All those clerks assembled regularly at their posts. Three of those clerks always walked into town together. All the neighbourhood knew them: two of them were tall and one short. And on this particular morning the short clerk was only a few seconds late to join the other two as they passed his gate: he could have overtaken them in three strides; he could have called after them easily. But he did not.

For some reason that will never be understood until all souls are judged (if they are ever judged; the idea was at this time classed with fetish worship) he did not join his two companions, but walked steadily behind them. The day was dull, their dress was dull, everything was dull; but in some odd impulse he walked through street after street, through district after district, looking at the backs of the two men, who would have swung round at the sound of his voice. Now, there is a law written in the darkest of the Books of Life, and it is this: If you look at a thing nine hundred and ninety-nine times, you are perfectly safe; if you look at it the thousandth time, you are in frightful danger of seeing it for the first time.

So the short Government official looked at the coat-tails of the tall Government officials, and through street after street, and round corner after corner, saw only coat-tails, coat-tails, and again coat-tails—when, he did not in the least know why, something happened to his eyes.

Two black dragons were walking backwards in front of him. Two black dragons were looking at him with evil eyes. The dragons were walking backwards it was true, but they kept their eyes fixed on him none the less. The eyes which he saw were, in truth, only the two buttons at the back of a frock-coat: perhaps some traditional memory of their meaningless character gave this half-witted prominence to their gaze. The slit between the tails was the nose-line of the monster: whenever the tails flapped in the winter wind the dragons licked their lips. It was only a momentary fancy, but the small clerk found it imbedded in his soul ever afterwards. He never could again think of men in frock-coats except as dragons walking backwards. He explained afterwards, quite tactfully and nicely, to his two official friends, that (while feeling an inexpressible regard for each of them) he could not seriously regard the face of either of them as anything but a kind of tail. It was, he admitted, a handsome tail—a tail elevated in the air. But if, he said, any true friend of theirs wished to see their faces, to look into the eyes of their soul, that friend must be allowed to walk reverently round behind them, so as to see them from the rear. There he would see the two black dragons with the blind eyes.

But when first the two black dragons sprang out of the fog upon the small clerk, they had merely the effect of all miracles—they changed the universe. He discovered the fact that all romantics know—that adventures happen on dull days, and not on sunny ones. When the chord of monotony is stretched most tight, then it breaks with a sound like song. He had scarcely noticed the weather before, but with the four dead eyes glaring at him he looked round and realised the strange dead day.

The morning was wintry and dim, not misty, but darkened with that shadow of cloud or snow which steeps everything in a green or copper twilight. The light there is on such a day seems not so much to come from the clear heavens as to be a phosphorescence clinging to the shapes themselves. The load of heaven and the clouds is like a load of waters, and the men move like fishes, feeling that they are on the floor of a sea. Everything in a London street completes the fantasy; the carriages and cabs themselves resemble deep-sea creatures with eyes of flame. He had been startled at first to meet two dragons. Now he found he was among deep-sea dragons possessing the deep sea.

The two young men in front were like the small young man himself, well-dressed. The lines of their frock-coats and silk hats had that luxuriant severity which makes the modern fop, hideous as he is, a favourite exercise of the modern draughtsman; that element which Mr. Max Beerbohm has admirably expressed in speaking of "certain congruities of dark cloth and the rigid perfection of linen."

They walked with the gait of an affected snail, and they spoke at the longest intervals, dropping a sentence at about every sixth lamp-post.

They crawled on past the lamp-posts; their mien was so immovable that a fanciful description might almost say, that the lamp-posts crawled past the men, as in a dream. Then the small man suddenly ran after them and said—

"I want to get my hair cut. I say, do you know a little shop anywhere where they cut your hair properly? I keep on having my hair cut, but it keeps on growing again."

One of the tall men looked at him with the air of a pained naturalist.

"Why, here is a little place," cried the small man, with a sort of imbecile cheerfulness, as the bright bulging window of a fashionable toilet-saloon glowed abruptly out of the foggy twilight. "Do you know, I often find hair-dressers when I walk about London. I'll lunch with you at Cicconani's. You know, I'm awfully fond of hair-dressers' shops. They're miles better than those nasty butchers'." And he disappeared into the doorway.

The man called James continued to gaze after him, a monocle screwed into his eye.

"What the devil do you make of that fellow?" he asked his companion, a pale young man with a high nose.

The pale young man reflected conscientiously for some minutes, and then said—

"Had a knock on his head when he was a kid, I should think."

"No, I don't think it's that," replied the Honourable James Barker. "I've sometimes fancied he was a sort of artist, Lambert."

"Bosh!" cried Mr. Lambert, briefly.

"I admit I can't make him out," resumed Barker, abstractedly; "he never opens his mouth without saying something so indescribably half-witted that to call him a fool seems the very feeblest attempt at characterisation. But there's another thing about him that's rather funny. Do you know that he has the one collection of Japanese lacquer in Europe? Have you ever seen his books? All Greek poets and mediæval French and that sort of thing. Have you ever been in his rooms? It's like being inside an amethyst. And he moves about in all that and talks like—like a turnip."

"Well, damn all books. Your blue books as well," said the ingenuous Mr. Lambert, with a friendly simplicity. "You ought to understand such things. What do you make of him?"

"He's beyond me," returned Barker. "But if you asked me for my opinion, I should say he was a man with a taste for nonsense, as they call it—artistic fooling, and all that kind of thing. And I seriously believe that he has talked nonsense so much that he has half bewildered his own mind and doesn't know the difference between sanity and insanity. He has gone round the mental world, so to speak, and found the place where the East and the West are one, and extreme idiocy is as good as sense. But I can't explain these psychological games."

"You can't explain them to me," replied Mr. Wilfrid Lambert, with candour.

As they passed up the long streets towards their restaurant the copper twilight cleared slowly to a pale yellow, and by the time they reached it they stood discernible in a tolerable winter daylight. The Honourable James Barker, one of the most powerful officials in the English Government (by this time a rigidly official one), was a lean and elegant young man, with a blank handsome face and bleak blue eyes. He had a great amount of intellectual capacity, of that peculiar kind which raises a man from throne to throne and lets him die loaded with honours without having either amused or enlightened the mind of a single man. Wilfrid Lambert, the youth with the nose which appeared to impoverish the rest of his face, had also contributed little to the enlargement of the human spirit, but he had the honourable excuse of being a fool.

Lambert would have been called a silly man; Barker, with all his cleverness, might have been called a stupid man. But mere silliness and stupidity sank into insignificance in the presence of the awful and mysterious treasures of foolishness apparently stored up in the small figure that stood waiting for them outside Cicconani's. The little man, whose name was Auberon Quin, had an appearance compounded of a baby and an owl. His round head, round eyes, seemed to have been designed by nature playfully with a pair of compasses. His flat dark hair and preposterously long frock-coat gave him something of the look of a child's "Noah." When he entered a room of strangers, they mistook him for a small boy, and wanted to take him on their knees, until he spoke, when they perceived that a boy would have been more intelligent.

"I have been waiting quite a long time," said Quin, mildly. "It's awfully funny I should see you coming up the street at last."

"Why?" asked Lambert, staring. "You told us to come here your-self."

"My mother used to tell people to come to places," said the sage.

They were about to turn into the restaurant with a resigned air, when their eyes were caught by something in the street. The weather, though cold and blank, was now quite clear, and across the dull brown of the wood pavement and between the dull grey terraces was moving something not to be seen for miles round—not to be seen perhaps at that time in England—a man dressed in bright colours. A small crowd hung on the man's heels.

He was a tall stately man, clad in a military uniform of brilliant green, splashed with great silver facings. From the shoulder swung a short green furred cloak, somewhat like that of a Hussar, the lining of which gleamed every now and then with a kind of tawny crimson. His breast glittered with medals; round his neck was the red ribbon and star of some foreign order; and a long straight sword, with a blazing hilt, trailed and clattered along the pavement. At this time the pacific and utilitarian development of Europe had relegated all such customs to the Museums. The only remaining force, the small but well-organised police, were attired in a sombre and hygienic manner. But even those who remembered the last Life Guards and Lancers who disappeared in 1912 must have known at a glance that this was not, and never had been, an English uniform; and this conviction would have been height-ened by the yellow aquiline face, like Dante carved in bronze, which rose, crowned with white hair, out of the green military collar, a keen and distinguished, but not an English face.

The magnificence with which the green-clad gentleman walked down the centre of the road would be something difficult to express in human language. For it was an ingrained simplicity and arrogance, something in the mere carriage of the head and body, which made ordinary moderns in the street stare after him; but it had comparatively little to do with actual conscious gestures or expression. In the matter of these merely temporary movements, the man appeared to be rather worried and in-quisitive, but he was inquisitive with the inquisitiveness of a despot and worried as with the responsibilities of a god. The men who lounged and wondered behind him followed partly with an astonishment at his brilliant uniform, that is to say, partly because of that instinct which makes us all follow one who looks like a madman, but far more because of that instinct which makes all men follow (and worship) any one who chooses to behave like a king. He had to so sublime an extent that great quality of royalty—an almost imbecile unconsciousness of everybody, that people went after him as they do after kings—to see what would be the first thing or person he would take notice of. And all the time, as we have said, in spite of his quiet splendour, there was an air about him as if he were looking for somebody; an expression of inquiry.

Suddenly that expression of inquiry vanished, none could tell why, and was replaced by an expression of contentment. Amid the rapt attention of the mob of idlers, the magnificent green gentleman deflected himself from his direct course down the centre of the road and walked to one side of it. He came to a halt opposite to a large poster of Colman's Mustard erected on a wooden hoarding. His spectators almost held their breath.

He took from a small pocket in his uniform a little penknife; with this he made a slash at the stretched paper. Completing the rest of the operation with his fingers, he tore off a strip or rag of paper, yellow in colour and wholly irregular in outline. Then for the first time the great being addressed his adoring onlookers—

"Can any one," he said, with a pleasing foreign accent, "lend me a pin?"

Mr. Lambert, who happened to be nearest, and who carried innumerable pins for the purpose of attaching innumerable buttonholes, lent him one, which was received with extravagant but dignified bows, and hyperboles of thanks.

The gentleman in green, then, with every appearance of being gratified, and even puffed up, pinned the piece of yellow paper to the green silk and silver-lace adornments of his breast. Then he turned his eyes round again, searching and unsatisfied.

"Anything else I can do, sir?" asked Lambert, with the absurd politeness of the Englishman when once embarrassed.

"Red," said the stranger, vaguely, "red."

"I beg your pardon?"

"I beg yours also, Señor," said the stranger, bowing. "I was wondering whether any of you had any red about you."

"Any red about us?—well really—no, I don't think I have—I used to carry a red bandanna once, but—"

"Barker," asked Auberon Quin, suddenly, "where's your red cockatoo? Where's your red cockatoo?"

"What do you mean?" asked Barker, desperately. "What cockatoo? You've never seen me with any cockatoo!"

"I know," said Auberon, vaguely mollified. "Where's it been all the time?"

Barker swung round, not without resentment.

"I am sorry, sir," he said, shortly but civilly, "none of us seem to have anything red to lend you. But why, if one may ask—"

"I thank you, Señor, it is nothing. I can, since there is nothing else, fulfil my own requirements."

And standing for a second of thought with the penknife in his hand, he stabbed his left palm. The blood fell with so full a stream that it struck the stones without dripping. The foreigner pulled out his handkerchief and tore a piece from it with his teeth. The rag was immediately soaked in scarlet.

"Since you are so generous, Señor," he said, "another pin, perhaps."

Lambert held one out, with eyes protruding like a frog's.

The red linen was pinned beside the yellow paper, and the foreigner took off his hat.

"I have to thank you all, gentlemen," he said; and wrapping the remainder of the handkerchief round his bleeding hand, he resumed his walk with an overwhelming stateliness.

While all the rest paused, in some disorder, little Mr. Auberon Quin ran after the stranger and stopped him, with hat in hand. Considerably to everybody's astonishment, he addressed him in the purest Spanish—

"Señor," he said in that language, "pardon a hospitality, perhaps indiscreet, towards one who appears to be a distinguished, but a solitary guest in London. Will you do me and my friends, with whom you have held some conversation, the honour of lunching with us at the adjoining restaurant?"

The man in the green uniform had turned a fiery colour of pleasure at the mere sound of his own language, and he accepted the invitation with that profusion of bows which so often shows, in the case of the Southern races, the falsehood of the notion that ceremony has nothing to do with feeling.

"Señor," he said, "your language is my own; but all my love for my people shall not lead me to deny to yours the possession of so chivalrous an entertainer. Let me say that the tongue is Spanish but the heart English." And he passed with the rest into Cicconani's.

"Now, perhaps," said Barker, over the fish and sherry, intensely polite, but burning with curiosity, "perhaps it would be rude of me to ask why you did that?"

"Did what, Señor?" asked the guest, who spoke English quite well, though in a manner indefinably American.

"Well," said the Englishman, in some confusion, "I mean tore a strip off a hoarding and ... er ... cut yourself ... and...."

"To tell you that, Señor," answered the other, with a certain sad pride, "involves merely telling you who I am. I am Juan del Fuego, President of Nicaragua."

The manner with which the President of Nicaragua leant back and drank his sherry showed that to him this explanation covered all the facts observed and a great deal more. Barker's brow, however, was still a little clouded.

"And the yellow paper," he began, with anxious friendliness, "and the red rag...."

"The yellow paper and the red rag," said Fuego, with indescribable grandeur, "are the colours of Nicaragua."

"But Nicaragua ..." began Barker, with great hesitation, "Nicaragua is no longer a...."

"Nicaragua has been conquered like Athens. Nicaragua has been annexed like Jerusalem," cried the old man, with amazing fire. "The Yankee and the German and the brute powers of modernity have trampled it with the hoofs of oxen. But Nicaragua is not dead. Nicaragua is an idea."

Auberon Quin suggested timidly, "A brilliant idea."

"Yes," said the foreigner, snatching at the word. "You are right, generous Englishman. An idea *brillant*, a burning thought. Señor, you asked me why, in my desire to see the colours of my country, I snatched at paper and blood. Can you not understand the ancient sanctity of colours? The Church has her symbolic colours. And think of what colours mean to us—think of the position of one like myself, who can see nothing but those two colours, nothing but the red and the yellow. To me all shapes are equal, all common and noble things are in a democracy of combination. Wherever there is a field of marigolds and the red cloak of an old woman, there is Nicaragua. Wherever there is a field of poppies and a yellow patch of sand, there is Nicaragua. Wherever there is a lemon and a red sunset, there is my country. Wherever I see a red pillar-box and a yellow sunset, there my heart beats. Blood and a splash of mustard can be my heraldry. If there be yellow mud and red mud in the same ditch, it is better to me than white stars."

"And if," said Quin, with equal enthusiasm, "there should happen to be yellow wine and red wine at the same lunch, you could not confine yourself to sherry. Let me order some Burgundy, and complete, as it were, a sort of Nicaraguan heraldry in your inside."

Barker was fiddling with his knife, and was evidently making up his mind to say something, with the intense nervousness of the amiable Englishman.

"I am to understand, then," he said at last, with a cough, "that you, ahem, were the President of Nicaragua when it made its—er—one must, of course, agree—its quite heroic resistance to—er—"

The ex-President of Nicaragua waved his hand.

"You need not hesitate in speaking to me," he said. "I'm quite fully aware that the whole tendency of the world of to-day is against Nicaragua and against me. I shall not consider it any diminution of your evident courtesy if you say what you think of the misfortunes that have laid my republic in ruins."

Barker looked immeasurably relieved and gratified.

"You are most generous, President," he said, with some hesitation over the title, "and I will take advantage of your generosity to express the doubts which, I must confess, we moderns have about such things as—er—the Nicaraguan independence."

"So your sympathies are," said Del Fuego, quite calmly, "with the big nation which—"

"Pardon me, pardon me, President," said Barker, warmly; "my sympathies are with no nation. You misunderstand, I think, the modern intellect. We do not disapprove of the fire and extravagance of such commonwealths as yours only to become more extravagant on a larger scale. We do not condemn Nicaragua because we think Britain ought to be more Nicaraguan. We do not discourage small nationalities because we wish large nationalities to have all their smallness, all their uniformity of outlook, all their exaggeration of spirit. If I differ with the greatest respect from your Nicaraguan enthusiasm, it is not because a nation or ten nations were against you; it is because civilisation was against you. We moderns believe in a great cosmopolitan civilisation, one which shall include all the talents of all the absorbed peoples—"

"The Señor will forgive me," said the President. "May I ask the Señor how, under ordinary circumstances, he catches a wild horse?"

"I never catch a wild horse," replied Barker, with dignity.

"Precisely," said the other; "and there ends your absorption of the talents. That is what I complain of your cosmopolitanism. When you say you want all peoples to unite, you really mean that you want all peoples to unite to learn the tricks of your people. If the Bedouin Arab does not know how to read, some English missionary or schoolmaster must be sent to teach him to read, but no one ever says, 'This schoolmaster does not know how to ride on a camel; let us pay a Bedouin to teach him.' You say your civilisation will include all talents. Will it? Do you really mean to say that at the moment when the Esquimaux has learnt to vote for a County Council, you will have learnt to spear a walrus? I recur to the example I gave. In Nicaragua we had a way of catching wild horses—by lassooing the fore feet—which was supposed to be the best in South America. If you are going to include all the talents, go and do it. If not, permit me to say what I have always said, that something went from the world when Nicaragua was civilised."

"Something, perhaps," replied Barker, "but that something a mere barbarian dexterity. I do not know that I could chip flints as well as a primeval man, but I know that civilisation can make these knives which are better, and I trust to civilisation."

"You have good authority," answered the Nicaraguan. "Many clever men like you have trusted to civilisation. Many clever Babylonians, many clever Egyptians, many clever men at the end of Rome. Can you tell me, in a world that is flagrant with the failures of civilisation, what there is particularly immortal about yours?"

"I think you do not quite understand, President, what ours is," answered Barker. "You judge it rather as if England was still a poor and pugnacious island; you have been long out of Europe. Many things have happened."

"And what," asked the other, "would you call the summary of those things?"

"The summary of those things," answered Barker, with great animation, "is that we are rid of the superstitions, and in becoming so we have not merely become rid of the superstitions which have been most frequently and most enthusiastically so described. The superstition of big nationalities is bad, but the superstition of small nationalities is worse. The superstition of reverencing our own country is bad, but the superstition of reverencing other people's countries is worse. It is so everywhere, and in a hundred ways. The superstition of monarchy is bad, and the superstition of aristocracy is bad, but the superstition of democracy is the worst of all."

The old gentleman opened his eyes with some surprise.

"Are you, then," he said, "no longer a democracy in England?"

Barker laughed.

"The situation invites paradox," he said. "We are, in a sense, the purest democracy. We have become a despotism. Have you not noticed how continually in history democracy becomes despotism? People call it the decay of democracy. It is simply its fulfilment. Why take the trouble to number and register and enfranchise all the innumerable John Robinsons, when you can take one John Robinson with the same intellect or lack of intellect as all the rest, and have done with it? The old idealistic republicans used to found democracy on the idea that all men were equally intelligent. Believe me, the sane and enduring democracy is founded on the fact that all men are equally idiotic. Why should we not choose out of them one as much as another. All that we want for Government is a man not criminal and insane, who can rapidly look over some petitions and sign some proclamations. To think what time was wasted in arguing about the House of Lords, Tories saying it ought to be preserved because it was clever, and Radicals saying it ought to be destroyed because it was stupid, and all the time no one saw that it was right because it was stupid, because that chance mob of ordinary men thrown there by accident of blood, were a great democratic protest against the Lower House, against the eternal insolence of the aristocracy of talents. We have established now in England, the thing towards which all systems have dimly groped, the dull popular despotism without illusions. We want one man at the head of our State, not because he is brilliant or virtuous, but because he is one man and not a chattering crowd. To avoid the possible chance of hereditary diseases or such things, we have abandoned hereditary monarchy. The King of England is chosen like a juryman upon an official rotation list. Beyond that the whole system is quietly despotic, and we have not found it raise a murmur."

"Do you really mean," asked the President, incredulously, "that you choose any ordinary man that comes to hand and make him despot— that you trust to the chance of some alphabetical list...."

"And why not?" cried Barker. "Did not half the historical nations trust to the chance of the eldest sons of eldest sons, and did not half of them get on tolerably well? To have a perfect system is impossible; to have a system is indispensable. All hereditary monarchies were a matter of luck: so are alphabetical monarchies. Can you find a deep philosophical meaning in the difference between the Stuarts and the Hanoverians? Believe me, I will undertake to find a deep philosophical meaning in the contrast between the dark tragedy of the A's, and the solid success of the B's."

"And you risk it?" asked the other. "Though the man may be a tyrant or a cynic or a criminal."

"We risk it," answered Barker, with a perfect placidity. "Suppose he is a tyrant—he is still a check on a hundred tyrants. Suppose he is a cynic, it is to his interest to govern well. Suppose he is a criminal—by removing poverty and substituting power, we put a check on his criminality. In short, by substituting despotism we have put a total check on one criminal and a partial check on all the rest."

The Nicaraguan old gentleman leaned over with a queer expression in his eyes.

"My church, sir," he said, "has taught me to respect faith. I do not wish to speak with any disrespect of yours, however fantastic. But do you really mean that you will trust to the ordinary man, the man who may happen to come next, as a good despot?"

"I do," said Barker, simply. "He may not be a good man. But he will be a good despot. For when he comes to a mere business routine of government he will endeavour to do ordinary justice. Do we not assume the same thing in a jury?"

The old President smiled.

"I don't know," he said, "that I have any particular objection in detail to your excellent scheme of Government. My only objection is a quite personal one. It is, that if I were asked whether I would belong to it, I should ask first of all, if I was not permitted, as an alternative, to be a toad in a ditch. That is all. You cannot argue with the choice of the soul."

"Of the soul," said Barker, knitting his brows, "I cannot pretend to say anything, but speaking in the interests of the public—"

Mr. Auberon Quin rose suddenly to his feet.

"If you'll excuse me, gentlemen," he said, "I will step out for a moment into the air."

"I'm so sorry, Auberon," said Lambert, good-naturedly; "do you feel bad?"

"Not bad exactly," said Auberon, with self-restraint; "rather good, if anything. Strangely and richly good. The fact is, I want to reflect a little on those beautiful words that have just been uttered. 'Speaking,' yes, that was the phrase, 'speaking in the interests of the public.' One cannot get the honey from such things without being alone for a little."

"Is he really off his chump, do you think?" asked Lambert.

The old President looked after him with queerly vigilant eyes.

"He is a man, I think," he said, "who cares for nothing but a joke. He is a dangerous man."

Lambert laughed in the act of lifting some maccaroni to his mouth.

"Dangerous!" he said. "You don't know little Quin, sir!"

"Every man is dangerous," said the old man without moving, "who cares only for one thing. I was once dangerous myself."

And with a pleasant smile he finished his coffee and rose, bowing profoundly, passed out into the fog, which had again grown dense and sombre. Three days afterwards they heard that he had died quietly in lodgings in Soho.

Drowned somewhere else in the dark sea of fog was a little figure shaking and quaking, with what might at first sight have seemed terror or ague: but which was really that strange malady, a lonely laughter. He was repeating over and over to himself with a rich accent— "But speaking in the interests of the public...."

III
THE HILL OF HUMOUR

"In a little square garden of yellow roses, beside the sea," said Auberon Quin, "there was a Nonconformist minister who had never been to Wimbledon. His family did not understand his sorrow or the strange look in his eyes. But one day they repented their neglect, for they heard that a body had been found on the shore, battered, but wearing patent leather boots. As it happened, it turned out not to be the minister at all. But in the dead man's pocket there was a return ticket to Maidstone."

There was a short pause as Quin and his friends Barker and Lambert went swinging on through the slushy grass of Kensington Gardens. Then Auberon resumed.

"That story," he said reverently, "is the test of humour."

They walked on further and faster, wading through higher grass as they began to climb a slope.

"I perceive," continued Auberon, "that you have passed the test, and consider the anecdote excruciatingly funny; since you say nothing. Only coarse humour is received with pot-house applause. The great anecdote is received in silence, like a benediction. You felt pretty benedicted, didn't you, Barker?"

"I saw the point," said Barker, somewhat loftily.

"Do you know," said Quin, with a sort of idiot gaiety, "I have lots of stories as good as that. Listen to this one."

And he slightly cleared his throat.

"Dr. Polycarp was, as you all know, an unusually sallow bimetallist. 'There,' people of wide experience would say, 'There goes the sallowest bimetallist in Cheshire.' Once this was said so that he overheard it: it was said by an actuary, under a sunset of mauve and grey. Polycarp turned upon him. 'Sallow!' he cried fiercely, 'sallow! *Quis tulerit Gracchos de seditione querentes.*' It was said that no actuary ever made game of Dr. Polycarp again."

Barker nodded with a simple sagacity. Lambert only grunted.

"Here is another," continued the insatiable Quin. "In a hollow of the grey-green hills of rainy Ireland, lived an old, old woman, whose uncle was always Cambridge at the Boat Race. But in her grey-green hollows, she knew nothing of this: she didn't know that there was a Boat Race. Also she did not know that she had an uncle. She had heard of nobody at all, except of George the First, of whom she had heard (I know not why), and in whose historical memory she put her simple trust. And by and by in God's good time, it was discovered that this uncle of hers was not really her uncle, and they came and told her so. She smiled through her tears, and said only, 'Virtue is its own reward.'"

Again there was a silence, and then Lambert said—

"It seems a bit mysterious."

"Mysterious!" cried the other. "The true humour is mysterious. Do you not realise the chief incident of the nineteenth and twentieth centuries?"

"And what's that?" asked Lambert, shortly.

"It is very simple," replied the other. "Hitherto it was the ruin of a joke that people did not see it. Now it is the sublime victory of a joke that people do not see it. Humour, my friends, is the one sanctity remaining to mankind. It is the one thing you are thoroughly afraid of. Look at that tree."

His interlocutors looked vaguely towards a beech that leant out towards them from the ridge of the hill.

"If," said Mr. Quin, "I were to say that you did not see the great truths of science exhibited by that tree, though they stared any man of intellect in the face, what would you think or say? You would merely regard me as a pedant with some unimportant theory about vegetable cells. If I were to say that you did not see in that tree the vile mismanagement of local politics, you would dismiss me as a Socialist crank with some particular fad about public parks. If I were to say that you were guilty of the supreme blasphemy of looking at that tree and not seeing in it a new religion, a special revelation of God, you would simply say I was a mystic, and think no more about me. But if"—and he lifted a pontifical hand— "if I say that you cannot see the humour of that tree, and that I see the humour of it—my God! you will roll about at my feet."

He paused a moment, and then resumed.

"Yes; a sense of humour, a weird and delicate sense of humour, is the new religion of mankind! It is towards that men will strain themselves with the asceticism of saints. Exercises, spiritual exercises, will be set in it. It will be asked, 'Can you see the humour of this iron railing?' or 'Can you see the humour of this field of corn? Can you see the humour of the stars? Can you see the humour of the sunsets?' How often I have laughed myself to sleep over a violet sunset."

"Quite so," said Mr. Barker, with an intelligent embarrassment.

"Let me tell you another story. How often it happens that the M.P.'s for Essex are less punctual than one would suppose. The least punctual Essex M.P., perhaps, was James Wilson, who said, in the very act of plucking a poppy—"

Lambert suddenly faced round and struck his stick into the ground in a defiant attitude.

"Auberon," he said, "chuck it. I won't stand it. It's all bosh."

Both men stared at him, for there was something very explosive about the words, as if they had been corked up painfully for a long time.

"You have," began Quin, "no—"

"I don't care a curse," said Lambert, violently, "whether I have 'a delicate sense of humour' or not. I won't stand it. It's all a confounded fraud. There's no joke in those infernal tales at all. You know there isn't as well as I do."

"Well," replied Quin, slowly, "it is true that I, with my rather gradual mental processes, did not see any joke in them. But the finer sense of Barker perceived it."

Barker turned a fierce red, but continued to stare at the horizon.

"You ass," said Lambert; "why can't you be like other people? Why can't you say something really funny, or hold your tongue? The man who sits on his hat in a pantomime is a long sight funnier than you are."

Quin regarded him steadily. They had reached the top of the ridge and the wind struck their faces.

"Lambert," said Auberon, "you are a great and good man, though I'm hanged if you look it. You are more. You are a great revolutionist or deliverer of the world, and I look forward to seeing you carved in marble between Luther and Danton, if possible in your present attitude, the hat slightly on one side. I said as I came up the hill that the new humour was the last of the religions. You have made it the last of the superstitions. But let me give you a very serious warning. Be careful how you ask me to do anything *outré*, to imitate the man in the pantomime, and to sit on my hat. Because I am a man whose soul has been emptied of all pleasures but folly. And for twopence I'd do it."

"Do it, then," said Lambert, swinging his stick impatiently. "It would be funnier than the bosh you and Barker talk."

Quin, standing on the top of the hill, stretched his hand out towards the main avenue of Kensington Gardens.

"Two hundred yards away," he said, "are all your fashionable acquaintants with nothing on earth to do but to stare at each other and at us. We are standing upon an elevation under the open sky, a peak as it were of fantasy, a Sinai of humour. We are in a great pulpit or platform, lit up with sunlight, and half London can see us. Be careful how you suggest things to me. For there is in me a madness which goes beyond martyrdom, the madness of an utterly idle man."

"I don't know what you are talking about," said Lambert, contemptuously. "I only know I'd rather you stood on your silly head, than talked so much."

"Auberon! for goodness' sake ..." cried Barker, springing forward; but he was too late.

Faces from all the benches and avenues were turned in their direction. Groups stopped and small crowds collected; and the sharp sunlight picked out the whole scene in blue, green and black, like a picture in a child's toy-book.

And on the top of the small hill Mr. Auberon Quin stood with considerable athletic neatness upon his head, and waved his patent-leather boots in the air.

"For God's sake, Quin, get up, and don't be an idiot," cried Barker, wringing his hands; "we shall have the whole town here."

"Yes, get up, get up, man," said Lambert, amused and annoyed. "I was only fooling; get up."

Auberon did so with a bound, and flinging his hat higher than the trees, proceeded to hop about on one leg with a serious expression. Barker stamped wildly.

"Oh, let's get home, Barker, and leave him," said Lambert; "some of your proper and correct police will look after him. Here they come!"

Two grave-looking men in quiet uniforms came up the hill towards them. One held a paper in his hand.

"There he is, officer," said Lambert, cheerfully; "we ain't responsible for him."

The officer looked at the capering Mr. Quin with a quiet eye.

"We have not come, gentlemen," he said, "about what I think you are alluding to. We have come from head-quarters to announce the selection of His Majesty the King. It is the rule, inherited from the old *régime*, that the news should be brought to the new Sovereign immediately, wherever he is; so we have followed you across Kensington Gardens."

Barker's eyes were blazing in his pale face. He was consumed with ambition throughout his life. With a certain dull magnanimity of the intellect he had really believed in the chance method of selecting despots. But this sudden suggestion, that the selection might have fallen upon him, unnerved him with pleasure.

"Which of us," he began, and the respectful official interrupted him.

"Not you, sir, I am sorry to say. If I may be permitted to say so, we know your services to the Government, and should be very thankful if it were. The choice has fallen...."

"God bless my soul!" said Lambert, jumping back two paces. "Not me. Don't say I'm autocrat of all the Russias."

"No, sir," said the officer, with a slight cough and a glance towards Auberon, who was at that moment putting his head between his legs and making a noise like a cow; "the gentleman whom we have to congratulate seems at the moment—er—er—occupied."

"Not Quin!" shrieked Barker, rushing up to him; "it can't be. Auberon, for God's sake pull yourself together. You've been made King!"

With his head still upside down between his legs, Mr. Quin answered modestly—

"I am not worthy. I cannot reasonably claim to equal the great men who have previously swayed the sceptre of Britain. Perhaps the only peculiarity that I can claim is that I am probably the first monarch that ever spoke out his soul to the people of England with his head and body in this position. This may in some sense give me, to quote a poem that I wrote in my youth—

> A nobler office on the earth
> Than valour, power of brain, or birth
> Could give the warrior kings of old.

The intellect clarified by this posture—"

Lambert and Barker made a kind of rush at him.

"Don't you understand?" cried Lambert. "It's not a joke. They've really made you King. By gosh! they must have rum taste."

"The great Bishops of the Middle Ages," said Quin, kicking his legs in the air, as he was dragged up more or less upside down, "were in the habit of refusing the honour of election three times and then accepting it. A mere matter of detail separates me from those great men. I will accept the post three times and refuse it afterwards. Oh! I will toil for you, my faithful people! You shall have a banquet of humour."

By this time he had been landed the right way up, and the two men were still trying in vain to impress him with the gravity of the situation.

"Did you not tell me, Wilfrid Lambert," he said, "that I should be of more public value if I adopted a more popular form of humour? And when should a popular form of humour be more firmly riveted upon me than now, when I have become the darling of a whole people? Officer," he continued, addressing the startled messenger, "are there no ceremonies to celebrate my entry into the city?"

"Ceremonies," began the official, with embarrassment, "have been more or less neglected for some little time, and—"

Auberon Quin began gradually to take off his coat.

"All ceremony," he said, "consists in the reversal of the obvious. Thus men, when they wish to be priests or judges, dress up like women. Kindly help me on with this coat." And he held it out.

"But, your Majesty," said the officer, after a moment's bewilderment and manipulation, "you're putting it on with the tails in front."

"The reversal of the obvious," said the King, calmly, "is as near as we can come to ritual with our imperfect apparatus. Lead on."

The rest of that afternoon and evening was to Barker and Lambert a nightmare, which they could not properly realise or recall. The King, with his coat on the wrong way, went towards the streets that were awaiting him, and the old Kensington Palace which was the Royal residence. As he passed small groups of men, the groups turned into crowds, and gave forth sounds which seemed strange in welcoming an autocrat. Barker walked behind, his brain reeling, and, as the crowds grew thicker and thicker, the sounds became more and more unusual. And when he had reached the great market-place opposite the church, Barker knew that he had reached it, though he was roods behind, because a cry went up such as had never before greeted any of the kings of the earth.

Book II

I

The Charter of the Cities

Lambert was standing bewildered outside the door of the King's apartments amid the scurry of astonishment and ridicule. He was just passing out into the street, in a dazed manner, when James Barker dashed by him.

"Where are you going?" he asked.

"To stop all this foolery, of course," replied Barker; and he disappeared into the room.

He entered it headlong, slamming the door, and slapping his incomparable silk hat on the table. His mouth opened, but before he could speak, the King said—

"Your hat, if you please."

Fidgetting with his fingers, and scarcely knowing what he was doing, the young politician held it out.

The King placed it on his own chair, and sat on it.

"A quaint old custom," he explained, smiling above the ruins. "When the King receives the representatives of the House of Barker, the hat of the latter is immediately destroyed in this manner. It represents the absolute finality of the act of homage expressed in the removal of it. It declares that never until that hat shall once more appear upon your head (a contingency which I firmly believe to be remote) shall the House of Barker rebel against the Crown of England."

Barker stood with clenched fist, and shaking lip.

"Your jokes," he began, "and my property—" and then exploded with an oath, and stopped again.

"Continue, continue," said the King, waving his hands.

"What does it all mean?" cried the other, with a gesture of passionate rationality. "Are you mad?"

"Not in the least," replied the King, pleasantly. "Madmen are always serious; they go mad from lack of humour. You are looking serious yourself, James."

"Why can't you keep it to your own private life?" expostulated the other. "You've got plenty of money, and plenty of houses now to play the fool in, but in the interests of the public—"

"Epigrammatic," said the King, shaking his finger sadly at him. "None of your daring scintillations here. As to why I don't do it in private, I rather fail to understand your question. The answer is of comparative limpidity. I don't do it in private, because it is funnier to do it in public. You appear to think that it would be amusing to be dignified in the banquet hall and in the street, and at my own fireside (I could procure a fireside) to keep the company in a roar. But that is what every one does. Every one is grave in public, and funny in private. My sense of humour suggests the reversal of this; it suggests that one should be funny in public, and solemn in private. I desire to make the State functions, parliaments, coronations, and so on, one roaring old-fashioned pantomime. But, on the other hand, I shut myself up alone in a small store-room for two hours a day, where I am so dignified that I come out quite ill."

By this time Barker was walking up and down the room, his frock coat flapping like the black wings of a bird.

"Well, you will ruin the country, that's all," he said shortly.

"It seems to me," said Auberon, "that the tradition of ten centuries is being broken, and the House of Barker is rebelling against the Crown of England. It would be with regret (for I admire your appearance) that I should be obliged forcibly to decorate your head with the remains of this hat, but—"

"What I can't understand," said Barker flinging up his fingers with a feverish American movement, "is why you don't care about anything else but your games."

The King stopped sharply in the act of lifting the silken remnants, dropped them, and walked up to Barker, looking at him steadily.

"I made a kind of vow," he said, "that I would not talk seriously, which always means answering silly questions. But the strong man will always be gentle with politicians.

'The shape my scornful looks deride
Required a God to form;'

if I may so theologically express myself. And for some reason I cannot in the least understand, I feel impelled to answer that question of yours, and to answer it as if there were really such a thing in the world as a serious subject. You ask me why I don't care for anything else. Can you tell me, in the name of all the gods you don't believe in, why I should care for anything else?"

"Don't you realise common public necessities?" cried Barker. "Is it possible that a man of your intelligence does not know that it is every one's interest—"

"Don't you believe in Zoroaster? Is it possible that you neglect Mumbo-Jumbo?" returned the King, with startling animation. "Does a man of your intelligence come to me with these damned early Victorian ethics? If, on studying my features and manner, you detect any particular resemblance to the Prince Consort, I assure you you are mistaken. Did Herbert Spencer ever convince you—did he ever convince anybody—did he ever for one mad moment convince himself—that it must be to the interest of the individual to feel a public spirit? Do you believe that, if you rule your department badly, you stand any more chance, or one half of the chance, of being guillotined, that an angler stands of being pulled into the river by a strong pike? Herbert Spencer refrained from theft for the same reason that he refrained from wearing feathers in his hair, because he was an English gentleman with different tastes. I am an English gentleman with different tastes. He liked philosophy. I like art. He liked writing ten books on the nature of human society. I like to see the Lord Chamberlain walking in front of me with a piece of paper pinned to his coat-tails. It is my humour. Are you answered? At any rate, I have said my last serious word to-day, and my last serious word I trust for the remainder of my life in this Paradise of Fools. The remainder of my conversation with you to-day, which I trust will be long and stimulating, I propose to conduct in a new language of my own by means of rapid and symbolic movements of the left leg." And he began to pirouette slowly round the room with a preoccupied expression.

Barker ran round the room after him, bombarding him with demands and entreaties. But he received no response except in the new language. He came out banging the door again, and sick like a man coming on shore. As he strode along the streets he found himself suddenly opposite Cicconani's restaurant, and for some reason there rose up before him the green fantastic figure of the Spanish General, standing, as he had seen him last, at the door, with the words on his lips, "You cannot argue with the choice of the soul."

The King came out from his dancing with the air of a man of business legitimately tired. He put on an overcoat, lit a cigar, and went out into the purple night.

"I will go," he said, "and mingle with the people."

He passed swiftly up a street in the neighbourhood of Notting Hill, when suddenly he felt a hard object driven into his waistcoat. He paused, put up his single eye-glass, and beheld a boy with a wooden sword and a paper cocked hat, wearing that expression of awed satisfaction with which a child contemplates his work when he has hit some one very hard. The King gazed thoughtfully for some time at his assailant, and slowly took a note-book from his breast-pocket.

"I have a few notes," he said, "for my dying speech;" and he turned over the leaves. "Dying speech for political assassination; ditto, if by former friend—h'm, h'm. Dying speech for death at hands of injured husband (repentant). Dying speech for same (cynical). I am not quite sure which meets the present...."

"I'm the King of the Castle," said the boy, truculently, and very pleased with nothing in particular.

The King was a kind-hearted man, and very fond of children, like all people who are fond of the ridiculous.

"Infant," he said, "I'm glad you are so stalwart a defender of your old inviolate Notting Hill. Look up nightly to that peak, my child, where it lifts itself among the stars so ancient, so lonely, so unutterably Notting. So long as you are ready to die for the sacred mountain, even if it were ringed with all the armies of Bayswater—"

The King stopped suddenly, and his eyes shone.

"Perhaps," he said, "perhaps the noblest of all my conceptions. A revival of the arrogance of the old mediæval cities applied to our glorious suburbs. Clapham with a city guard. Wimbledon with a city wall. Surbiton tolling a bell to raise its citizens. West Hampstead going into battle with its own banner. It shall be done. I, the King, have said it."

And, hastily presenting the boy with half a crown, remarking, "For the war-chest of Notting Hill," he ran violently home at such a rate of speed that crowds followed him for miles. On reaching his study, he ordered a cup of coffee, and plunged into profound meditation upon the project. At length he called his favourite Equerry, Captain Bowler, for whom he had a deep affection, founded principally upon the shape of his whiskers.

"Bowler," he said, "isn't there some society of historical research, or something of which I am an honorary member?"

"Yes, sir," said Captain Bowler, rubbing his nose, "you are a member of 'The Encouragers of Egyptian Renaissance,' and 'The Teutonic Tombs Club,' and 'The Society for the Recovery of London Antiquities,' and—"

"That is admirable," said the King. "The London Antiquities does my trick. Go to the Society for the Recovery of London Antiquities and speak to their secretary, and their sub-secretary, and their president, and their vice-president, saying, 'The King of England is proud, but the honorary member of the Society for the Recovery of London Antiquities is prouder than kings. I should like to tell you of certain discoveries I have made touching the neglected traditions of the London boroughs. The revelations may cause some excitement, stirring burning memories and touching old wounds in Shepherd's Bush and Bayswater, in Pimlico and South Kensington. The King hesitates, but the honorary member is firm. I approach you invoking the vows of my initiation, the Sacred Seven Cats, the Poker of Perfection, and the Ordeal of the Indescribable Instant (forgive me if I mix you up with the Clan-na-Gael or some other club I belong to), and ask you to permit me to read a paper at your next meeting on the "Wars of the London Boroughs."' Say all this to the Society, Bowler. Remember it very carefully, for it is most important, and I have forgotten it altogether, and send me another cup of coffee and some of the cigars that we keep for vulgar and successful people. I am going to write my paper."

The Society for the Recovery of London Antiquities met a month after in a corrugated iron hall on the outskirts of one of the southern suburbs of London. A large number of people had collected there under the coarse and flaring gas-jets when the King arrived, perspiring and genial. On taking off his great-coat, he was perceived to be in evening dress, wearing the Garter. His appearance at the small table, adorned only with a glass of water, was received with respectful cheering.

The chairman (Mr. Huggins) said that he was sure that they had all been pleased to listen to such distinguished lecturers as they had heard for some time past (hear, hear). Mr. Burton (hear, hear), Mr. Cambridge, Professor King (loud and continued cheers), our old friend Peter Jessop, Sir William White (loud laughter), and other eminent men, had done honour to their little venture (cheers). But there were other circumstances which lent a certain unique quality to the present occasion (hear, hear). So far as his recollection went, and in connection with the Society for the Recovery of London Antiquities it went very far (loud cheers), he did not remember that any of their lecturers had borne the title of King. He would therefore call upon King Auberon briefly to address the meeting.

The King began by saying that this speech might be regarded as the first declaration of his new policy for the nation. "At this supreme hour of my life I feel that to no one but the members of the Society for the Recovery of London Antiquities can I open my heart (cheers). If the world turns upon my policy, and the storms of popular hostility begin to rise (no, no), I feel that it is here, with my brave Recoverers around me, that I can best meet them, sword in hand" (loud cheers).

His Majesty then went on to explain that, now old age was creeping upon him, he proposed to devote his remaining strength to bringing about a keener sense of local patriotism in the various municipalities of London. How few of them knew the legends of their own boroughs! How many there were who had never heard of the true origin of the Wink of Wandsworth! What a large proportion of the younger generation in Chelsea neglected to perform the old Chelsea Chuff! Pimlico no longer pumped the Pimlies. Battersea had forgotten the name of Blick.

There was a short silence, and then a voice said "Shame!"

The King continued: "Being called, however unworthily, to this high estate, I have resolved that, so far as possible, this neglect shall cease. I desire no military glory. I lay claim to no constitutional equality with Justinian or Alfred. If I can go down to history as the man who saved from extinction a few old English customs, if our descendants can say it was through this man, humble as he was, that the Ten Turnips are still eaten in Fulham, and the Putney parish councillor still shaves one half of his head, I shall look my great fathers reverently but not fearfully in the face when I go down to the last house of Kings."

The King paused, visibly affected, but collecting himself, resumed once more.

"I trust that to very few of you, at least, I need dwell on the sublime origins of these legends. The very names of your boroughs bear witness to them. So long as Hammersmith is called Hammersmith, its people will live in the shadow of that primal hero, the Blacksmith, who led the democracy of the Broadway into battle till he drove the chivalry of Kensington before him and overthrew them at that place which in honour of the best blood of the defeated aristocracy is still called Kensington Gore. Men of Hammersmith will not fail to remember that the very name of Kensington originated from the lips of their hero. For at the great banquet of reconciliation held after the war, when the disdainful oligarchs declined to join in the songs of the men of the Broadway (which are to this day of a rude and popular character), the great Republican leader, with his rough humour, said the words which are written in gold upon his monument, 'Little birds that can sing and won't sing, must be made to sing.' So that the Eastern Knights were called Cansings or Kensings ever afterwards. But you also have great memories, O men of Kensington! You showed that you could sing, and sing great war-songs. Even after the dark day of Kensington Gore, history will not forget those three Knights who guarded your disordered retreat from Hyde Park (so called from your hiding there), those three Knights after whom Knightsbridge is named. Nor will it forget the day of your re-emergence, purged in the fire of calamity, cleansed of your oligarchic corruptions, when, sword in hand, you drove the Empire of Hammersmith back mile by mile, swept it past its own Broadway, and broke it at last in a battle so long and bloody that the birds of prey have left their name upon it. Men have called it, with austere irony, the Ravenscourt. I shall not, I trust, wound the patriotism of Bayswater, or the lonelier pride of Brompton, or that of any other historic township, by taking these two special examples. I select them, not because they are more glorious than the rest, but partly from personal association (I am myself descended from one of the three heroes of Knightsbridge), and partly from the consciousness that I am an amateur antiquarian, and cannot presume to deal with times and places more remote and more mysterious. It is not for me to settle the question between two such men as Professor Hugg and Sir William Whisky as to whether Notting Hill means Nutting Hill (in allusion to the rich woods which no longer cover it), or whether it is a corruption of Nothing-ill, referring to its reputation among the ancients as an Earthly Paradise. When a Podkins and a Jossy confess themselves doubtful about the boundaries of West Kensington (said to have been traced in the blood of Oxen), I need not be ashamed to confess a similar doubt. I will ask you to excuse me from further history, and to assist me with your encouragement in dealing with the problem which faces us to-day. Is this ancient spirit of the London townships to die out? Are our omnibus conductors and policemen to lose altogether that light which we see so often in their eyes, the dreamy light of

> 'Old unhappy far-off things
> And battles long ago'

—to quote the words of a little-known poet who was a friend of my youth? I have resolved, as I have said, so far as possible, to preserve the eyes of policemen and omnibus conductors in their present dreamy state. For what is a state without dreams? And the remedy I propose is as follows:—

"To-morrow morning at twenty-five minutes past ten, if Heaven spares my life, I purpose to issue a Proclamation. It has been the work of my life, and is about half finished. With the assistance of a whisky and soda, I shall conclude the other half to-night, and my people will receive it to-morrow. All these boroughs where you were born, and hope to lay your bones, shall be reinstated in their ancient magnificence,— Hammersmith, Kensington, Bayswater, Chelsea, Battersea, Clapham, Balham, and a hundred others. Each shall immediately build a city wall with gates to be closed at sunset. Each shall have a city guard, armed to the teeth. Each shall have a banner, a coat-of-arms, and, if convenient, a gathering cry. I will not enter into the details now, my heart is too full. They will be found in the proclamation itself. You will all, however, be subject to enrolment in the local city guards, to be summoned together by a thing called the Tocsin, the meaning of which I am studying in my researches into history. Personally, I believe a tocsin to be some kind of highly paid official. If, therefore, any of you happen to have such a thing as a halberd in the house, I should advise you to practise with it in the garden."

Here the King buried his face in his handkerchief and hurriedly left the platform, overcome by emotions.

The members of the Society for the Recovery of London Antiquities rose in an indescribable state of vagueness. Some were purple with indignation; an intellectual few were purple with laughter; the great majority found their minds a blank. There remains a tradition that one pale face with burning blue eyes remained fixed upon the lecturer, and after the lecture a red-haired boy ran out of the room.

The Council of the Provosts

The King got up early next morning and came down three steps at a time like a schoolboy. Having eaten his breakfast hurriedly, but with an appetite, he summoned one of the highest officials of the Palace, and presented him with a shilling. "Go and buy me," he said, "a shilling paint-box, which you will get, unless the mists of time mislead me, in a shop at the corner of the second and dirtier street that leads out of Rochester Row. I have already requested the Master of the Buckhounds to provide me with cardboard. It seemed to me (I know not why) that it fell within his department."

The King was happy all that morning with his cardboard and his paint-box. He was engaged in designing the uniforms and coats-of-arms for the various municipalities of London. They gave him deep and no inconsiderable thought. He felt the responsibility.

"I cannot think," he said, "why people should think the names of places in the country more poetical than those in London. Shallow romanticists go away in trains and stop in places called Hugmy-in-the-Hole, or Bumps-on-the-Puddle. And all the time they could, if they liked, go and live at a place with the dim, divine name of St. John's Wood. I have never been to St. John's Wood. I dare not. I should be afraid of the innumerable night of fir trees, afraid to come upon a blood-red cup and the beating of the wings of the Eagle. But all these things can be imagined by remaining reverently in the Harrow train."

And he thoughtfully retouched his design for the head-dress of the halberdier of St. John's Wood, a design in black and red, compounded of a pine tree and the plumage of an eagle. Then he turned to another card. "Let us think of milder matters," he said. "Lavender Hill! Could

any of your glebes and combes and all the rest of it produce so fragrant an idea? Think of a mountain of lavender lifting itself in purple
poignancy into the silver skies and filling men's nostrils with a new
breath of life—a purple hill of incense. It is true that upon my few
excursions of discovery on a halfpenny tram I have failed to hit the
precise spot. But it must be there; some poet called it by its name. There
is at least warrant enough for the solemn purple plumes (following the
botanical formation of lavender) which I have required people to wear
in the neighbourhood of Clapham Junction. It is so everywhere, after
all. I have never been actually to Southfields, but I suppose a scheme
of lemons and olives represent their austral instincts. I have never visited Parson's Green, or seen either the Green or the Parson, but surely
the pale-green shovel-hats I have designed must be more or less in the
spirit. I must work in the dark and let my instincts guide me. The great
love I bear to my people will certainly save me from distressing their
noble spirit or violating their great traditions."

As he was reflecting in this vein, the door was flung open, and an
official announced Mr. Barker and Mr. Lambert.

Mr. Barker and Mr. Lambert were not particularly surprised to find
the King sitting on the floor amid a litter of water-colour sketches.
They were not particularly surprised because the last time they had called
on him they had found him sitting on the floor, surrounded by a litter
of children's bricks, and the time before surrounded by a litter of wholly
unsuccessful attempts to make paper darts. But the trend of the royal
infant's remarks, uttered from amid this infantile chaos, was not quite
the same affair.

For some time they let him babble on, conscious that his remarks
meant nothing. And then a horrible thought began to steal over the
mind of James Barker. He began to think that the King's remarks did
not mean nothing.

"In God's name, Auberon," he suddenly volleyed out, startling the
quiet hall, "you don't mean that you are really going to have these city
guards and city walls and things?"

"I am, indeed," said the infant, in a quiet voice. "Why shouldn't I have
them? I have modelled them precisely on your political principles. Do you
know what I've done, Barker? I've behaved like a true Barkerian. I've ... but
perhaps it won't interest you, the account of my Barkerian conduct."

"Oh, go on, go on," cried Barker.

"The account of my Barkerian conduct," said Auberon, calmly, "seems not only to interest, but to alarm you. Yet it is very simple. It merely consists in choosing all the provosts under any new scheme by the same principle by which you have caused the central despot to be appointed. Each provost, of each city, under my charter, is to be appointed by rotation. Sleep, therefore, my Barker, a rosy sleep."

Barker's wild eyes flared.

"But, in God's name, don't you see, Quin, that the thing is quite different? In the centre it doesn't matter so much, just because the whole object of despotism is to get some sort of unity. But if any damned parish can go to any damned man—"

"I see your difficulty," said King Auberon, calmly. "You feel that your talents may be neglected. Listen!" And he rose with immense magnificence. "I solemnly give to my liege subject, James Barker, my special and splendid favour, the right to override the obvious text of the Charter of the Cities, and to be, in his own right, Lord High Provost of South Kensington. And now, my dear James, you are all right. Good day."

"But—" began Barker.

"The audience is at an end, Provost," said the King, smiling.

How far his confidence was justified, it would require a somewhat complicated description to explain. "The Great Proclamation of the Charter of the Free Cities" appeared in due course that morning, and was posted by bill-stickers all over the front of the Palace, the King assisting them with animated directions, and standing in the middle of the road, with his head on one side, contemplating the result. It was also carried up and down the main thoroughfares by sandwichmen, and the King was, with difficulty, restrained from going out in that capacity himself, being, in fact, found by the Groom of the Stole and Captain Bowler, struggling between two boards. His excitement had positively to be quieted like that of a child.

The reception which the Charter of the Cities met at the hands of the public may mildly be described as mixed. In one sense it was popular enough. In many happy homes that remarkable legal document was read aloud on winter evenings amid uproarious appreciation, when everything had been learnt by heart from that quaint but immortal old classic,

Mr. W. W. Jacobs. But when it was discovered that the King had every intention of seriously requiring the provisions to be carried out, of insisting that the grotesque cities, with their tocsins and city guards, should really come into existence, things were thrown into a far angrier confusion. Londoners had no particular objection to the King making a fool of himself, but they became indignant when it became evident that he wished to make fools of them; and protests began to come in.

The Lord High Provost of the Good and Valiant City of West Kensington wrote a respectful letter to the King, explaining that upon State occasions it would, of course, be his duty to observe what formalities the King thought proper, but that it was really awkward for a decent householder not to be allowed to go out and put a post-card in a pillar-box without being escorted by five heralds, who announced, with formal cries and blasts of a trumpet, that the Lord High Provost desired to catch the post.

The Lord High Provost of North Kensington, who was a prosperous draper, wrote a curt business note, like a man complaining of a railway company, stating that definite inconvenience had been caused him by the presence of the halberdiers, whom he had to take with him everywhere. When attempting to catch an omnibus to the City, he had found that while room could have been found for himself, the halberdiers had a difficulty in getting in to the vehicle—believe him, theirs faithfully.

The Lord High Provost of Shepherd's Bush said his wife did not like men hanging round the kitchen.

The King was always delighted to listen to these grievances, delivering lenient and kingly answers, but as he always insisted, as the absolute *sine qua non*, that verbal complaints should be presented to him with the fullest pomp of trumpets, plumes, and halberds, only a few resolute spirits were prepared to run the gauntlet of the little boys in the street.

Among these, however, was prominent the abrupt and business-like gentleman who ruled North Kensington. And he had before long, occasion to interview the King about a matter wider and even more urgent than the problem of the halberdiers and the omnibus. This was the great question which then and for long afterwards brought a stir to the blood and a flush to the cheek of all the speculative builders and house agents from Shepherd's Bush to the Marble Arch, and from Westbourne Grove to High Street, Kensington. I refer to the great affair of the improvements in Notting Hill. The scheme was conducted chiefly by Mr. Buck, the abrupt North Kensington magnate, and by Mr. Wilson, the Provost of Bayswater. A great thoroughfare was to be driven through three boroughs, through West Kensington, North Kensington and Notting Hill, opening at one end into Hammersmith Broadway, and at the other into Westbourne Grove. The negotiations, buyings, sellings, bullying and bribing took ten years, and by the end of it Buck, who had conducted them almost single-handed, had proved himself a man of the strongest type of material energy and material diplomacy. And just as his splendid patience and more splendid impatience had finally brought him victory, when workmen were already demolishing houses and walls along the great line from Hammersmith, a sudden obstacle appeared that had neither been reckoned with nor dreamed of, a small and strange obstacle, which, like a speck of grit in a great machine, jarred the whole vast scheme and brought it to a stand-still, and Mr. Buck, the draper, getting with great impatience into his robes of office and summoning with indescribable disgust his halberdiers, hurried over to speak to the King.

Ten years had not tired the King of his joke. There were still new faces to be seen looking out from the symbolic head-gears he had designed, gazing at him from amid the pastoral ribbons of Shepherd's Bush or from under the sombre hoods of the Blackfriars Road. And the interview which was promised him with the Provost of North Kensington he anticipated with a particular pleasure, for "he never really enjoyed," he said, "the full richness of the mediæval garments unless the people compelled to wear them were very angry and business-like."

Mr. Buck was both. At the King's command the door of the audience-chamber was thrown open and a herald appeared in the purple colours of Mr. Buck's commonwealth emblazoned with the Great Eagle which the King had attributed to North Kensington, in vague reminiscence of Russia, for he always insisted on regarding North Kensington as some kind of semi-arctic neighbourhood. The herald announced that the Provost of that city desired audience of the King.

"From North Kensington?" said the King, rising graciously. "What news does he bring from that land of high hills and fair women? He is welcome."

The herald advanced into the room, and was immediately followed by twelve guards clad in purple, who were followed by an attendant bearing the banner of the Eagle, who was followed by another attendant bearing the keys of the city upon a cushion, who was followed by Mr. Buck in a great hurry. When the King saw his strong animal face and steady eyes, he knew that he was in the presence of a great man of business, and consciously braced himself.

"Well, well," he said, cheerily coming down two or three steps from a daïs, and striking his hands lightly together, "I am glad to see you. Never mind, never mind. Ceremony is not everything."

"I don't understand your Majesty," said the Provost, stolidly.

"Never mind, never mind," said the King, gaily. "A knowledge of Courts is by no means an unmixed merit; you will do it next time, no doubt."

The man of business looked at him sulkily from under his black brows and said again without show of civility—

"I don't follow you."

"Well, well," replied the King, good-naturedly, "if you ask me I don't mind telling you, not because I myself attach any importance to these forms in comparison with the Honest Heart. But it is usual—it is usual—that is all, for a man when entering the presence of Royalty to lie down on his back on the floor and elevating his feet towards heaven (as the source of Royal power) to say three times 'Monarchical institutions improve the manners.' But there, there—such pomp is far less truly dignified than your simple kindliness."

The Provost's face was red with anger, and he maintained silence.

"And now," said the King, lightly, and with the exasperating air of a man softening a snub; "what delightful weather we are having! You must find your official robes warm, my Lord. I designed them for your own snow-bound land."

"They're as hot as hell," said Buck, briefly. "I came here on business."

"Right," said the King, nodding a great number of times with quite unmeaning solemnity; "right, right, right. Business, as the sad glad old Persian said, is business. Be punctual. Rise early. Point the pen to the shoulder. Point the pen to the shoulder, for you know not whence you come nor why. Point the pen to the shoulder, for you know not when you go nor where."

The Provost pulled a number of papers from his pocket and savagely flapped them open.

"Your Majesty may have heard," he began, sarcastically, "of Hammersmith and a thing called a road. We have been at work ten years buying property and getting compulsory powers and fixing compensation and squaring vested interests, and now at the very end, the thing is stopped by a fool. Old Prout, who was Provost of Notting Hill, was a business man, and we dealt with him quite satisfactorily. But he's dead, and the cursed lot has fallen on a young man named Wayne, who's up to some game that's perfectly incomprehensible to me. We offer him a better price than any one ever dreamt of, but he won't let the road go through. And his Council seems to be backing him up. It's midsummer madness."

The King, who was rather inattentively engaged in drawing the Provost's nose with his finger on the window-pane, heard the last two words.

"What a perfect phrase that is!" he said. "'Midsummer madness'!"

"The chief point is," continued Buck, doggedly, "that the only part that is really in question is one dirty little street—Pump Street—a street with nothing in it but a public-house and a penny toy-shop, and that sort of thing. All the respectable people of Notting Hill have accepted our compensation. But the ineffable Wayne sticks out over Pump Street. Says he's Provost of Notting Hill. He's only Provost of Pump Street."

"A good thought," replied Auberon. "I like the idea of a Provost of Pump Street. Why not let him alone?"

"And drop the whole scheme!" cried out Buck, with a burst of brutal spirit. "I'll be damned if we do. No. I'm for sending in workmen to pull down without more ado."

"Strike for the purple Eagle!" cried the King, hot with historical associations.

"I'll tell you what it is," said Buck, losing his temper altogether. "If your Majesty would spend less time in insulting respectable people with your silly coats-of-arms, and more time over the business of the nation—"

The King's brow wrinkled thoughtfully.

"The situation is not bad," he said; "the haughty burgher defying the King in his own Palace. The burgher's head should be thrown back and the right arm extended; the left may be lifted towards Heaven, but that I leave to your private religious sentiment. I have sunk back in this chair, stricken with baffled fury. Now again, please."

Buck's mouth opened like a dog's, but before he could speak another herald appeared at the door.

"The Lord High Provost of Bayswater," he said, "desires an audience."

"Admit him," said Auberon. "This *is* a jolly day."

The halberdiers of Bayswater wore a prevailing uniform of green, and the banner which was borne after them was emblazoned with a green bay-wreath on a silver ground, which the King, in the course of his researches into a bottle of champagne, had discovered to be the quaint old punning cognisance of the city of Bayswater.

"It is a fit symbol," said the King, "your immortal bay-wreath. Fulham may seek for wealth, and Kensington for art, but when did the men of Bayswater care for anything but glory?"

Immediately behind the banner, and almost completely hidden by it, came the Provost of the city, clad in splendid robes of green and silver with white fur and crowned with bay. He was an anxious little man with red whiskers, originally the owner of a small sweet-stuff shop.

"Our cousin of Bayswater," said the King, with delight; "what can we get for you?" The King was heard also distinctly to mutter, "Cold beef, cold 'am, cold chicken," his voice dying into silence.

"I came to see your Majesty," said the Provost of Bayswater, whose name was Wilson, "about that Pump Street affair."

"I have just been explaining the situation to his Majesty," said Buck, curtly, but recovering his civility. "I am not sure, however, whether his Majesty knows how much the matter affects you also."

"It affects both of us, yer see, yer Majesty, as this scheme was started for the benefit of the 'ole neighbourhood. So Mr. Buck and me we put our 'eads together—"

The King clasped his hands.

"Perfect!" he cried in ecstacy. "Your heads together! I can see it! Can't you do it now? Oh, do do it now!"

A smothered sound of amusement appeared to come from the halberdiers, but Mr. Wilson looked merely bewildered, and Mr. Buck merely diabolical.

"I suppose," he began bitterly, but the King stopped him with a gesture of listening.

"Hush," he said, "I think I hear some one else coming. I seem to hear another herald, a herald whose boots creak."

As he spoke another voice cried from the doorway—

"The Lord High Provost of South Kensington desires an audience."

"The Lord High Provost of South Kensington!" cried the King. "Why, that is my old friend James Barker! What does he want, I wonder? If the tender memories of friendship have not grown misty, I fancy he wants something for himself, probably money. How are you, James?"

Mr. James Barker, whose guard was attired in a splendid blue, and whose blue banner bore three gold birds singing, rushed, in his blue and gold robes, into the room.

Despite the absurdity of all the dresses, it was worth noticing that he carried his better than the rest, though he loathed it as much as any of them. He was a gentleman, and a very handsome man, and could not help unconsciously wearing even his preposterous robe as it should be worn. He spoke quickly, but with the slight initial hesitation he always showed in addressing the King, due to suppressing an impulse to address his old acquaintance in the old way.

"Your Majesty—pray forgive my intrusion. It is about this man in Pump Street. I see you have Buck here, so you have probably heard what is necessary. I—"

The King swept his eyes anxiously round the room, which now blazed with the trappings of three cities.

"There is one thing necessary," he said.

"Yes, your Majesty," said Mr. Wilson of Bayswater, a little eagerly. "What does yer Majesty think necessary?"

"A little yellow," said the King, firmly. "Send for the Provost of West Kensington."

Amid some materialistic protests he was sent for, and arrived with his yellow halberdiers in his saffron robes, wiping his forehead with a handkerchief. After all, placed as he was, he had a good deal to say on the matter.

"Welcome, West Kensington," said the King. "I have long wished to see you touching that matter of the Hammersmith land to the south of the Rowton House. Will you hold it feudally from the Provost of Hammersmith? You have only to do him homage by putting his left arm in his overcoat and then marching home in state."

"No, your Majesty; I'd rather not," said the Provost of West Kensington, who was a pale young man with a fair moustache and whiskers, who kept a successful dairy.

The King struck him heartily on the shoulder.

"The fierce old West Kensington blood," he said; "they are not wise who ask it to do homage."

Then he glanced again round the room. It was full of a roaring sunset of colour, and he enjoyed the sight, possible to so few artists— the sight of his own dreams moving and blazing before him. In the foreground the yellow of the West Kensington liveries outlined itself against the dark blue draperies of South Kensington. The crests of these again brightened suddenly into green as the almost woodland colours of Bayswater rose behind them. And over and behind all, the great purple plumes of North Kensington showed almost funereal and black.

"There is something lacking," said the King— "something lacking. What can—Ah, there it is! there it is!"

In the doorway had appeared a new figure, a herald in flaming red. He cried in a loud but unemotional voice—

"The Lord High Provost of Notting Hill desires an audience."

III

Enter a Lunatic

The King of the Fairies, who was, it is to be presumed, the godfather of King Auberon, must have been very favourable on this particular day to his fantastic godchild, for with the entrance of the guard of the Provost of Notting Hill there was a certain more or less inexplicable addition to his delight. The wretched navvies and sandwich-men who carried the colours of Bayswater or South Kensington, engaged merely for the day to satisfy the Royal hobby, slouched into the room with a comparatively hang-dog air, and a great part of the King's intellectual pleasure consisted in the contrast between the arrogance of their swords and feathers and the meek misery of their faces. But these Notting Hill halberdiers in their red tunics belted with gold had the air rather of an absurd gravity. They seemed, so to speak, to be taking part in the joke. They marched and wheeled into position with an almost startling dignity and discipline.

They carried a yellow banner with a great red lion, named by the King as the Notting Hill emblem, after a small public-house in the neighbourhood, which he once frequented.

Between the two lines of his followers there advanced towards the King a tall, red-haired young man, with high features and bold blue eyes. He would have been called handsome, but that a certain indefinable air of his nose being too big for his face, and his feet for his legs, gave him a look of awkwardness and extreme youth. His robes were red, according to the King's heraldry, and, alone among the Provosts, he was girt with a great sword. This was Adam Wayne, the intractable Provost of Notting Hill.

The King flung himself back in his chair, and rubbed his hands.

"What a day, what a day!" he said to himself. "Now there'll be a row. I'd no idea it would be such fun as it is. These Provosts are so very indignant, so very reasonable, so very right. This fellow, by the look in his eyes, is even more indignant than the rest. No sign in those large blue eyes, at any rate, of ever having heard of a joke. He'll remonstrate with the others, and they'll remonstrate with him, and they'll all make themselves sumptuously happy remonstrating with me."

"Welcome, my Lord," he said aloud. "What news from the Hill of a Hundred Legends? What have you for the ear of your King? I know that troubles have arisen between you and these others, our cousins, but these troubles it shall be our pride to compose. And I doubt not, and cannot doubt, that your love for me is not less tender, no less ardent, than theirs."

Mr. Buck made a bitter face, and James Barker's nostrils curled; Wilson began to giggle faintly, and the Provost of West Kensington followed in a smothered way. But the big blue eyes of Adam Wayne never changed, and he called out in an odd, boyish voice down the hall—

"I bring homage to my King. I bring him the only thing I have—my sword."

And with a great gesture he flung it down on the ground, and knelt on one knee behind it.

There was a dead silence.

"I beg your pardon," said the King, blankly.

"You speak well, sire," said Adam Wayne, "as you ever speak, when you say that my love is not less than the love of these. Small would it be if it were not more. For I am the heir of your scheme—the child of the great Charter. I stand here for the rights the Charter gave me, and I swear, by your sacred crown, that where I stand, I stand fast."

The eyes of all five men stood out of their heads.

Then Buck said, in his jolly, jarring voice: "Is the whole world mad?"

The King sprang to his feet, and his eyes blazed.

"Yes," he cried, in a voice of exultation, "the whole world is mad, but Adam Wayne and me. It is true as death what I told you long ago, James Barker, seriousness sends men mad. You are mad, because you care for politics, as mad as a man who collects tram tickets. Buck is mad, because he cares for money, as mad as a man who lives on opium.

Wilson is mad, because he thinks himself right, as mad as a man who thinks himself God Almighty. The Provost of West Kensington is mad, because he thinks he is respectable, as mad as a man who thinks he is a chicken. All men are mad but the humorist, who cares for nothing and possesses everything. I thought that there was only one humorist in England. Fools!—dolts!—open your cows' eyes; there are two! In Notting Hill—in that unpromising elevation—there has been born an artist! You thought to spoil my joke, and bully me out of it, by becoming more and more modern, more and more practical, more and more bustling and rational. Oh, what a feast it was to answer you by becoming more and more august, more and more gracious, more and more ancient and mellow! But this lad has seen how to bowl me out. He has answered me back, vaunt for vaunt, rhetoric for rhetoric. He has lifted the only shield I cannot break, the shield of an impenetrable pomposity. Listen to him. You have come, my Lord, about Pump Street?"

"About the city of Notting Hill," answered Wayne, proudly, "of which Pump Street is a living and rejoicing part."

"Not a very large part," said Barker, contemptuously.

"That which is large enough for the rich to covet," said Wayne, drawing up his head, "is large enough for the poor to defend."

The King slapped both his legs, and waved his feet for a second in the air.

"Every respectable person in Notting Hill," cut in Buck, with his cold, coarse voice, "is for us and against you. I have plenty of friends in Notting Hill."

"Your friends are those who have taken your gold for other men's hearthstones, my Lord Buck," said Provost Wayne. "I can well believe they are your friends."

"They've never sold dirty toys, anyhow," said Buck, laughing shortly.

"They've sold dirtier things," said Wayne, calmly: "they have sold themselves."

"It's no good, my Buckling," said the King, rolling about on his chair. "You can't cope with this chivalrous eloquence. You can't cope with an artist. You can't cope with the humorist of Notting Hill. Oh, *Nunc dimittis*—that I have lived to see this day! Provost Wayne, you stand firm?"

"Let them wait and see," said Wayne. "If I stood firm before, do you think I shall weaken now that I have seen the face of the King? For

I fight for something greater, if greater there can be, than the hearth-stones of my people and the Lordship of the Lion. I fight for your royal vision, for the great dream you dreamt of the League of the Free Cities. You have given me this liberty. If I had been a beggar and you had flung me a coin, if I had been a peasant in a dance and you had flung me a favour, do you think I would have let it be taken by any ruffians on the road? This leadership and liberty of Notting Hill is a gift from your Majesty, and if it is taken from me, by God! it shall be taken in battle, and the noise of that battle shall be heard in the flats of Chelsea and in the studios of St. John's Wood."

"It is too much—it is too much," said the King. "Nature is weak. I must speak to you, brother artist, without further disguise. Let me ask you a solemn question. Adam Wayne, Lord High Provost of Notting Hill, don't you think it splendid?"

"Splendid!" cried Adam Wayne. "It has the splendour of God."

"Bowled out again," said the King. "You will keep up the pose. Funnily, of course, it is serious. But seriously, isn't it funny?"

"What?" asked Wayne, with the eyes of a baby.

"Hang it all, don't play any more. The whole business—the Charter of the Cities. Isn't it immense?"

"Immense is no unworthy word for that glorious design."

"Oh, hang you! But, of course, I see. You want me to clear the room of these reasonable sows. You want the two humorists alone to-gether. Leave us, gentlemen."

Buck threw a sour look at Barker, and at a sullen signal the whole pageant of blue and green, of red, gold, and purple, rolled out of the room, leaving only two in the great hall, the King sitting in his seat on the daïs, and the red-clad figure still kneeling on the floor before his fallen sword.

The King bounded down the steps and smacked Provost Wayne on the back.

"Before the stars were made," he cried, "we were made for each other. It is too beautiful. Think of the valiant independence of Pump Street. That is the real thing. It is the deification of the ludicrous."

The kneeling figure sprang to his feet with a fierce stagger.

"Ludicrous!" he cried, with a fiery face.

"Oh, come, come," said the King, impatiently, "you needn't keep it up with me. The augurs must wink sometimes from sheer fatigue of the eyelids. Let us enjoy this for half an hour, not as actors, but as dramatic critics. Isn't it a joke?"

Adam Wayne looked down like a boy, and answered in a constrained voice—

"I do not understand your Majesty. I cannot believe that while I fight for your royal charter your Majesty deserts me for these dogs of the gold hunt."

"Oh, damn your—But what's this? What the devil's this?"

The King stared into the young Provost's face, and in the twilight of the room began to see that his face was quite white and his lip shaking.

"What in God's name is the matter?" cried Auberon, holding his wrist.

Wayne flung back his face, and the tears were shining on it.

"I am only a boy," he said, "but it's true. I would paint the Red Lion on my shield if I had only my blood."

King Auberon dropped the hand and stood without stirring, thunderstruck.

"My God in Heaven!" he said; "is it possible that there is within the four seas of Britain a man who takes Notting Hill seriously?"

"And my God in Heaven!" said Wayne passionately; "is it possible that there is within the four seas of Britain a man who does not take it seriously?"

The King said nothing, but merely went back up the steps of the daïs, like a man dazed. He fell back in his chair again and kicked his heels.

"If this sort of thing is to go on," he said weakly, "I shall begin to doubt the superiority of art to life. In Heaven's name, do not play with me. Do you really mean that you are—God help me!—a Notting Hill patriot; that you are—?"

Wayne made a violent gesture, and the King soothed him wildly.

"All right—all right—I see you are; but let me take it in. You do really propose to fight these modern improvers with their boards and inspectors and surveyors and all the rest of it?"

"Are they so terrible?" asked Wayne, scornfully.

The King continued to stare at him as if he were a human curiosity.

"And I suppose," he said, "that you think that the dentists and small tradesmen and maiden ladies who inhabit Notting Hill, will rally with war-hymns to your standard?"

"If they have blood they will," said the Provost.

"And I suppose," said the King, with his head back among the cushions, "that it never crossed your mind that"—his voice seemed to lose itself luxuriantly— "never crossed your mind that any one ever thought that the idea of a Notting Hill idealism was—er—slightly—slightly ridiculous?"

"Of course they think so," said Wayne.

"What was the meaning of mocking the prophets?"

"Where," asked the King, leaning forward— "where in Heaven's name did you get this miraculously inane idea?"

"You have been my tutor, Sire," said the Provost, "in all that is high and honourable."

"Eh?" said the King.

"It was your Majesty who first stirred my dim patriotism into flame. Ten years ago, when I was a boy (I am only nineteen), I was playing on the slope of Pump Street, with a wooden sword and a paper helmet, dreaming of great wars. In an angry trance I struck out with my sword, and stood petrified, for I saw that I had struck you, Sire, my King, as you wandered in a noble secrecy, watching over your people's welfare. But I need have had no fear. Then was I taught to understand Kingliness. You neither shrank nor frowned. You summoned no guards. You invoked no punishments. But in august and burning words, which are written in my soul, never to be erased, you told me ever to turn my sword against the enemies of my inviolate city. Like a priest pointing to the altar, you pointed to the hill of Notting. 'So long,' you said, 'as you are ready to die for the sacred mountain, even if it were ringed with all the armies of Bayswater.' I have not forgotten the words, and I have reason now to remember them, for the hour is come and the crown of your prophecy. The sacred hill is ringed with the armies of Bayswater, and I am ready to die."

The King was lying back in his chair, a kind of wreck.

"Oh, Lord, Lord, Lord," he murmured, "what a life! what a life! All my work! I seem to have done it all. So you're the red-haired boy that hit me in the waistcoat. What have I done? God, what have I done? I thought I would have a joke, and I have created a passion. I tried to compose a burlesque, and it seems to be turning halfway through into an epic. What is to be done with such a world? In the Lord's name, wasn't the joke broad and bold enough? I abandoned my subtle humour to amuse you, and I seem to have brought tears to your eyes. What's to be done with people when you write a pantomime for them—call the sausages classic festoons, and the policeman cut in two a tragedy of public duty? But why am I talking? Why am I asking questions of a nice young gentleman who is totally mad? What is the good of it? What is the good of anything? Oh, Lord! Oh, Lord!"

Suddenly he pulled himself upright.

"Don't you really think the sacred Notting Hill at all absurd?"

"Absurd?" asked Wayne, blankly. "Why should I?"

The King stared back equally blankly.

"I beg your pardon," he said.

"Notting Hill," said the Provost, simply, "is a rise or high ground of the common earth, on which men have built houses to live, in which they are born, fall in love, pray, marry, and die. Why should I think it absurd?"

The King smiled.

"Because, my Leonidas—" he began, then suddenly, he knew not how, found his mind was a total blank. After all, why was it absurd? Why was it absurd? He felt as if the floor of his mind had given way. He felt as all men feel when their first principles are hit hard with a question. Barker always felt so when the King said, "Why trouble about politics?"

The King's thoughts were in a kind of rout; he could not collect them.

"It is generally felt to be a little funny," he said vaguely.

"I suppose," said Adam, turning on him with a fierce suddenness— "I suppose you fancy crucifixion was a serious affair?"

"Well, I—" began Auberon— "I admit I have generally thought it had its graver side."

"Then you are wrong," said Wayne, with incredible violence. "Crucifixion is comic. It is exquisitely diverting. It was an absurd and obscene kind of impaling reserved for people who were made to be laughed at—for slaves and provincials, for dentists and small tradesmen, as you would say. I have seen the grotesque gallows-shape, which the little Roman gutter-boys scribbled on walls as a vulgar joke, blazing on the pinnacles of the temples of the world. And shall I turn back?"

The King made no answer.

Adam went on, his voice ringing in the roof.

"This laughter with which men tyrannise is not the great power you think it. Peter was crucified, and crucified head downwards. What could be funnier than the idea of a respectable old Apostle upside down? What could be more in the style of your modern humour? But what was the good of it? Upside down or right side up, Peter was Peter to mankind. Upside down he stills hangs over Europe, and millions move and breathe only in the life of his Church."

King Auberon got up absently.

"There is something in what you say," he said. "You seem to have been thinking, young man."

"Only feeling, sire," answered the Provost. "I was born, like other men, in a spot of the earth which I loved because I had played boys' games there, and fallen in love, and talked with my friends through nights that were nights of the gods. And I feel the riddle. These little gardens where we told our loves. These streets where we brought out our dead. Why should they be commonplace? Why should they be absurd? Why should it be grotesque to say that a pillar-box is poetic when for a year I could not see a red pillar-box against the yellow evening in a certain street without being wracked with something of which God keeps the secret, but which is stronger than sorrow or joy? Why should any one be able to raise a laugh by saying 'the Cause of Notting Hill'?— Notting Hill where thousands of immortal spirits blaze with alternate hope and fear."

Auberon was flicking dust off his sleeve with quite a new seriousness on his face, distinct from the owlish solemnity which was the pose of his humour.

"It is very difficult," he said at last. "It is a damned difficult thing. I see what you mean; I agree with you even up to a point—or I should like to agree with you, if I were young enough to be a prophet and poet. I feel a truth in everything you say until you come to the words 'Notting Hill.' And then I regret to say that the old Adam awakes roaring with laughter and makes short work of the new Adam, whose name is Wayne."

For the first time Provost Wayne was silent, and stood gazing dreamily at the floor. Evening was closing in, and the room had grown darker.

"I know," he said, in a strange, almost sleepy voice, "there is truth in what you say, too. It is hard not to laugh at the common names—I only say we should not. I have thought of a remedy; but such thoughts are rather terrible."

"What thoughts?" asked Auberon.

The Provost of Notting Hill seemed to have fallen into a kind of trance; in his eyes was an elvish light.

"I know of a magic wand, but it is a wand that only one or two may rightly use, and only seldom. It is a fairy wand of great fear, stronger than those who use it—often frightful, often wicked to use. But whatever is touched with it is never again wholly common; whatever is touched with it takes a magic from outside the world. If I touch, with this fairy wand, the railways and the roads of Notting Hill, men will love them, and be afraid of them for ever."

"What the devil are you talking about?" asked the King.

"It has made mean landscapes magnificent, and hovels outlast cathedrals," went on the madman. "Why should it not make lamp-posts fairer than Greek lamps; and an omnibus-ride like a painted ship? The touch of it is the finger of a strange perfection."

"What is your wand?" cried the King, impatiently.

"There it is," said Wayne; and pointed to the floor, where his sword lay flat and shining.

"The sword!" cried the King; and sprang up straight on the daïs.

"Yes, yes," cried Wayne, hoarsely. "The things touched by that are not vulgar; the things touched by that—"

King Auberon made a gesture of horror.

"You will shed blood for that!" he cried. "For a cursed point of view—"

"Oh, you kings, you kings!" cried out Adam, in a burst of scorn. "How humane you are, how tender, how considerate! You will make war for a frontier, or the imports of a foreign harbour; you will shed blood for the precise duty on lace, or the salute to an admiral. But for the things that make life itself worthy or miserable—how humane you are! I say here, and I know well what I speak of, there were never any necessary wars but the religious wars. There were never any just wars but the religious wars. There were never any humane wars but the religious wars. For these men were fighting for something that claimed, at least, to be the happiness of a man, the virtue of a man. A Crusader thought, at least, that Islam hurt the soul of every man, king or tinker, that it could really capture. I think Buck and Barker and these rich vultures hurt the soul of every man, hurt every inch of the ground, hurt every brick of the houses, that they can really capture. Do you think I have no right to fight for Notting Hill, you whose English Government has so often fought for tomfooleries? If, as your rich friends say, there are no gods, and the skies are dark above us, what should a man fight for, but the place where he had the Eden of childhood and the short heaven of first love? If no temples and no scriptures are sacred, what is sacred if a man's own youth is not sacred?"

The King walked a little restlessly up and down the daïs.

"It is hard," he said, biting his lips, "to assent to a view so desperate—so responsible..."

As he spoke, the door of the audience chamber fell ajar, and through the aperture came, like the sudden chatter of a bird, the high, nasal, but well-bred voice of Barker.

"I said to him quite plainly—the public interests—"

Auberon turned on Wayne with violence.

"What the devil is all this? What am I saying? What are you saying? Have you hypnotised me? Curse your uncanny blue eyes! Let me go. Give me back my sense of humour. Give it me back—give it me back, I say!"

"I solemnly assure you," said Wayne, uneasily, with a gesture, as if feeling all over himself, "that I haven't got it."

The King fell back in his chair, and went into a roar of Rabelaisian laughter.

"I don't think you have," he cried.

BOOK III

I

THE MENTAL CONDITION OF ADAM WAYNE

A little while after the King's accession a small book of poems appeared, called "Hymns on the Hill." They were not good poems, nor was the book successful, but it attracted a certain amount of attention from one particular school of critics. The King himself, who was a member of the school, reviewed it in his capacity of literary critic to "Straight from the Stables," a sporting journal. They were known as the Hammock School, because it had been calculated malignantly by an enemy that no less than thirteen of their delicate criticisms had begun with the words, "I read this book in a hammock: half asleep in the sleepy sunlight, I ..."; after that there were important differences. Under these conditions they liked everything, but especially everything silly. "Next to authentic goodness in a book," they said— "next to authentic goodness in a book (and that, alas! we never find) we desire a rich badness." Thus it happened that their praise (as indicating the presence of a rich badness) was not universally sought after, and authors became a little disquieted when they found the eye of the Hammock School fixed upon them with peculiar favour.

The peculiarity of "Hymns on the Hill" was the celebration of the poetry of London as distinct from the poetry of the country. This sentiment or affectation was, of course, not uncommon in the twentieth century, nor was it, although sometimes exaggerated, and sometimes artificial, by any means without a great truth at its root, for there is one respect in which a town must be more poetical than the country, since it is closer to the spirit of man; for London, if it be not one of the masterpieces of man, is at least one of his sins. A street is really more poetical than a meadow, because a street has a secret. A street is going somewhere, and a meadow nowhere. But, in the case of the book called "Hymns on the Hill," there was another peculiarity, which the King pointed out with great acumen in his review. He was naturally interested in the matter, for he had himself published a volume of lyrics about London under his pseudonym of "Daisy Daydream."

This difference, as the King pointed out, consisted in the fact that, while mere artificers like "Daisy Daydream" (on whose elaborate style the King, over his signature of "Thunderbolt," was perhaps somewhat too severe) thought to praise London by comparing it to the country—using nature, that is, as a background from which all poetical images had to be drawn—the more robust author of "Hymns on the Hill" praised the country, or nature, by comparing it to the town, and used the town itself as a background. "Take," said the critic, "the typically feminine lines, 'To the Inventor of The Hansom Cab'—

> 'Poet, whose cunning carved this amorous shell,
> Where twain may dwell.'"

"Surely," wrote the King, "no one but a woman could have written those lines. A woman has always a weakness for nature; with her art is only beautiful as an echo or shadow of it. She is praising the hansom cab by theme and theory, but her soul is still a child by the sea, picking up shells. She can never be utterly of the town, as a man can; indeed, do we not speak (with sacred propriety) of 'a man about town'? Who ever spoke of a woman about town? However much, physically, 'about town' a woman may be, she still models herself on nature; she tries to carry nature with her; she bids grasses to grow on her head, and furry beasts to bite her about the throat. In the heart of a dim city, she models her hat on a flaring cottage garden of flowers. We, with our nobler civic sentiment, model ours on a chimney pot; the ensign of civilisation. And rather than be without birds, she will commit massacre, that she may turn her head into a tree, with dead birds to sing on it."

This kind of thing went on for several pages, and then the critic remembered his subject, and returned to it.

> "Poet, whose cunning carved this amorous shell,
> Where twain may dwell."

"The peculiarity of these fine though feminine lines," continued "Thunderbolt," "is, as we have said, that they praise the hansom cab by comparing it to the shell, to a natural thing. Now, hear the author of 'Hymns on the Hill,' and how he deals with the same subject. In his fine nocturne, entitled 'The Last Omnibus' he relieves the rich and poignant melancholy of the theme by a sudden sense of rushing at the end—

> 'The wind round the old street corner
> Swung sudden and quick as a cab.'

"Here the distinction is obvious. 'Daisy Daydream' thinks it a great compliment to a hansom cab to be compared to one of the spiral chambers of the sea. And the author of 'Hymns on the Hill' thinks it a great compliment to the immortal whirlwind to be compared to a hackney coach. He surely is the real admirer of London. We have no space to speak of all his perfect applications of the idea; of the poem in which, for instance, a lady's eyes are compared, not to stars, but to two perfect street-lamps guiding the wanderer. We have no space to speak of the fine lyric, recalling the Elizabethan spirit, in which the poet, instead of saying that the rose and the lily contend in her complexion, says, with a purer modernism, that the red omnibus of Hammersmith and the white omnibus of Fulham fight there for the mastery. How perfect the image of two contending omnibuses!"

Here, somewhat abruptly, the review concluded, probably because the King had to send off his copy at that moment, as he was in some want of money. But the King was a very good critic, whatever he may have been as King, and he had, to a considerable extent, hit the right nail on the head. "Hymns on the Hill" was not at all like the poems originally published in praise of the poetry of London. And the reason was that it was really written by a man who had seen nothing else but London, and who regarded it, therefore, as the universe. It was written by a raw, red-headed lad of seventeen, named Adam Wayne, who had been born in Notting Hill. An accident in his seventh year prevented his being taken away to the seaside, and thus his whole life had been passed in his own Pump Street, and in its neighbourhood. And the consequence was, that he saw the street-lamps as things quite as eternal as the stars; the two fires were mingled. He saw the houses as things enduring, like the mountains, and so he wrote about them as one would write about mountains. Nature puts on a disguise when she speaks to every man; to this man she put on the disguise of Notting Hill. Nature would mean to a poet born in the Cumberland hills, a stormy sky-line and sudden rocks. Nature would mean to a poet born in the Essex flats, a waste of splendid waters and splendid sunsets. So nature meant to this man Wayne a line of violet roofs and lemon lamps, the chiaroscuro of the town. He did not think it clever or funny to praise the shadows and colours of the town; he had seen no other shadows or colours, and so he praised them—because they were shadows and colours. He saw all this because he was a poet, though in practice a bad poet. It is too often forgotten that just as a bad man is nevertheless a man, so a bad poet is nevertheless a poet.

Mr. Wayne's little volume of verse was a complete failure; and he submitted to the decision of fate with a quite rational humility, went back to his work, which was that of a draper's assistant, and wrote no more. He still retained his feeling about the town of Notting Hill, because he could not possibly have any other feeling, because it was the back and base of his brain. But he does not seem to have made any particular attempt to express it or insist upon it.

He was a genuine natural mystic, one of those who live on the border of fairyland. But he was perhaps the first to realise how often the boundary of fairyland runs through a crowded city. Twenty feet from him (for he was very short-sighted) the red and white and yellow suns of the gas-lights thronged and melted into each other like an orchard of fiery trees, the beginning of the woods of elf-land.

But, oddly enough, it was because he was a small poet that he came to his strange and isolated triumph. It was because he was a failure in literature that he became a portent in English history. He was one of those to whom nature has given the desire without the power of artistic expression. He had been a dumb poet from his cradle. He might have been so to his grave, and carried unuttered into the darkness a treasure of new and sensational song. But he was born under the lucky star of a single coincidence. He happened to be at the head of his dingy municipality at the time of the King's jest, at the time when all municipalities were suddenly commanded to break out into banners and flowers. Out of the long procession of the silent poets, who have been passing since the beginning of the world, this one man found himself in the midst of an heraldic vision, in which he could act and speak and live lyrically. While the author and the victims alike treated the whole matter as a silly public charade, this one man, by taking it seriously, sprang suddenly into a throne of artistic omnipotence. Armour, music, standards, watch-fires, the noise of drums, all the theatrical properties were thrown before him. This one poor rhymster, having burnt his own rhymes, began to live that life of open air and acted poetry of which all the poets of the earth have dreamed in vain; the life for which the Iliad is only a cheap substitute.

Upwards from his abstracted childhood, Adam Wayne had grown strongly and silently in a certain quality or capacity which is in modern cities almost entirely artificial, but which can be natural, and was primarily almost brutally natural in him, the quality or capacity of patriotism. It exists, like other virtues and vices, in a certain undiluted reality. It is not confused with all kinds of other things. A child speaking of his country or his village may make every mistake in Mandeville or tell every lie in Munchausen, but in his statement there will be no psychological lies any more than there can be in a good song. Adam Wayne, as a boy, had for his dull streets in Notting Hill the ultimate and ancient sentiment that went out to Athens or Jerusalem. He knew the secret of the passion, those secrets which make real old national songs sound so strange to our civilisation. He knew that real patriotism tends to sing about sorrows and forlorn hopes much more than about victory. He knew that in proper names themselves is half the poetry of all national poems. Above all, he knew the supreme psychological fact about patriotism, as certain in connection with it as that a fine shame comes to all lovers, the fact that the patriot never under any circumstances boasts of the largeness of his country, but always, and of necessity, boasts of the smallness of it.

All this he knew, not because he was a philosopher or a genius, but because he was a child. Any one who cares to walk up a side slum like Pump Street, can see a little Adam claiming to be king of a paving-stone. And he will always be proudest if the stone is almost too narrow for him to keep his feet inside it.

It was while he was in such a dream of defensive battle, marking out some strip of street or fortress of steps as the limit of his haughty

claim, that the King had met him, and, with a few words flung in mockery, ratified for ever the strange boundaries of his soul. Thenceforward
the fanciful idea of the defence of Notting Hill in war became to him a
thing as solid as eating or drinking or lighting a pipe. He disposed his
meals for it, altered his plans for it, lay awake in the night and went
over it again. Two or three shops were to him an arsenal; an area was to
him a moat; corners of balconies and turns of stone steps were points
for the location of a culverin or an archer. It is almost impossible to
convey to any ordinary imagination the degree to which he had trans-
mitted the leaden London landscape to a romantic gold. The process
began almost in babyhood, and became habitual like a literal madness.
It was felt most keenly at night, when London is really herself, when
her lights shine in the dark like the eyes of innumerable cats, and the
outline of the dark houses has the bold simplicity of blue hills. But for
him the night revealed instead of concealing, and he read all the blank
hours of morning and afternoon, by a contradictory phrase, in the light
of that darkness. To this man, at any rate, the inconceivable had happened. The artificial city had become to him nature, and he felt the
curbstones and gas-lamps as things as ancient as the sky.

One instance may suffice. Walking along Pump Street with a friend,
he said, as he gazed dreamily at the iron fence of a little front garden,
"How those railings stir one's blood!"

His friend, who was also a great intellectual admirer, looked at them
painfully, but without any particular emotion. He was so troubled about
it that he went back quite a large number of times on quiet evenings
and stared at the railings, waiting for something to happen to his blood,
but without success. At last he took refuge in asking Wayne himself. He
discovered that the ecstacy lay in the one point he had never noticed
about the railings even after his six visits—the fact that they were, like
the great majority of others—in London, shaped at the top after the
manner of a spear. As a child, Wayne had half unconsciously compared
them with the spears in pictures of Lancelot and St. George, and had
grown up under the shadow of the graphic association. Now, whenever
he looked at them, they were simply the serried weapons that made a
hedge of steel round the sacred homes of Notting Hill. He could not
have cleansed his mind of that meaning even if he tried. It was not a
fanciful comparison, or anything like it. It would not have been true to

say that the familiar railings reminded him of spears; it would have been far truer to say that the familiar spears occasionally reminded him of railings.

A couple of days after his interview with the King, Adam Wayne was pacing like a caged lion in front of five shops that occupied the upper end of the disputed street. They were a grocer's, a chemist's, a barber's, an old curiosity shop and a toy-shop that sold also newspapers. It was these five shops which his childish fastidiousness had first selected as the essentials of the Notting Hill campaign, the citadel of the city. If Notting Hill was the heart of the universe, and Pump Street was the heart of Notting Hill, this was the heart of Pump Street. The fact that they were all small and side by side realised that feeling for a formidable comfort and compactness which, as we have said, was the heart of his patriotism, and of all patriotism. The grocer (who had a wine and spirit licence) was included because he could provision the garrison; the old curiosity shop because it contained enough swords, pistols, partisans, cross-bows, and blunderbusses to arm a whole irregular regiment; the toy and paper shop because Wayne thought a free press an essential centre for the soul of Pump Street; the chemist's to cope with outbreaks of disease among the besieged; and the barber's because it was in the middle of all the rest, and the barber's son was an intimate friend and spiritual affinity.

It was a cloudless October evening settling down through purple into pure silver around the roofs and chimneys of the steep little street, which looked black and sharp and dramatic. In the deep shadows the gas-lit shop fronts gleamed like five fires in a row, and before them, darkly outlined like a ghost against some purgatorial furnaces, passed to and fro the tall bird-like figure and eagle nose of Adam Wayne.

He swung his stick restlessly, and seemed fitfully talking to himself.

"There are, after all, enigmas," he said "even to the man who has faith. There are doubts that remain even after the true philosophy is completed in every rung and rivet. And here is one of them. Is the normal human need, the normal human condition, higher or lower than those special states of the soul which call out a doubtful and dangerous glory? those special powers of knowledge or sacrifice which are made possible only by the existence of evil? Which should come first to our affections, the enduring sanities of peace or the half-maniacal virtues of battle? Which should come first, the man great in the daily round or the man great in emergency? Which should come first, to return to the enigma before me, the grocer or the chemist? Which is more certainly the stay of the city, the swift chivalrous chemist or the benignant all-providing grocer? In such ultimate spiritual doubts it is only possible to choose a side by the higher instincts, and to abide the issue. In any case, I have made my choice. May I be pardoned if I choose wrongly, but I choose the grocer."

"Good morning, sir," said the grocer, who was a middle-aged man, partially bald, with harsh red whiskers and beard, and forehead lined with all the cares of the small tradesman. "What can I do for you, sir?"

Wayne removed his hat on entering the shop, with a ceremonious gesture, which, slight as it was, made the tradesman eye him with the beginnings of wonder.

"I come, sir," he said soberly, "to appeal to your patriotism."

"Why, sir," said the grocer, "that sounds like the times when I was a boy and we used to have elections."

"You will have them again," said Wayne, firmly, "and far greater things. Listen, Mr. Mead. I know the temptations which a grocer has to a too cosmopolitan philosophy. I can imagine what it must be to sit all day as you do surrounded with wares from all the ends of the earth, from strange seas that we have never sailed and strange forests that we could not even picture. No Eastern king ever had such argosies or such cargoes coming from the sunrise and the sunset, and Solomon in all his glory was not enriched like one of you. India is at your elbow," he cried, lifting his voice and pointing his stick at a drawer of rice, the grocer making a movement of some alarm, "China is before you, Demerara is behind you, America is above your head, and at this very moment, like some old Spanish admiral, you hold Tunis in your hands."

Mr. Mead dropped the box of dates which he was just lifting, and then picked it up again vaguely.

Wayne went on with a heightened colour, but a lowered voice,

"I know, I say, the temptations of so international, so universal a vision of wealth. I know that it must be your danger not to fall like many tradesmen into too dusty and mechanical a narrowness, but rather to be too broad, to be too general, too liberal. If a narrow nationalism be the danger of the pastry-cook, who makes his own wares under his own heavens, no less is cosmopolitanism the danger of the grocer. But I come to you in the name of that patriotism which no wanderings or enlightenments should ever wholly extinguish, and I ask you to remember Notting Hill. For, after all, in this cosmopolitan magnificence, she has played no small part. Your dates may come from the tall palms of Barbary, your sugar from the strange islands of the tropics, your tea from the secret villages of the Empire of the Dragon. That this room might be furnished, forests may have been spoiled under the Southern Cross, and leviathans speared under the Polar Star. But you yourself—surely no inconsiderable treasure—you yourself, the brain that wields these vast interests—you yourself, at least, have grown to strength and wisdom between these grey houses and under this rainy sky. This city which made you, and thus made your fortunes, is threatened with war. Come forth and tell to the ends of the earth this lesson. Oil is from the North and fruits from the South; rices are from India and spices from Ceylon; sheep are from New Zealand and men from Notting Hill."

The grocer sat for some little while, with dim eyes and his mouth open, looking rather like a fish. Then he scratched the back of his head, and said nothing. Then he said—

"Anything out of the shop, sir?"

Wayne looked round in a dazed way. Seeing a pile of tins of pine-apple chunks, he waved his stick generally towards them.

"Yes," he said; "I'll take those."

"All those, sir?" said the grocer, with greatly increased interest.

"Yes, yes; all those," replied Wayne, still a little bewildered, like a man splashed with cold water.

"Very good, sir; thank you, sir," said the grocer with animation. "You may count upon my patriotism, sir."

"I count upon it already," said Wayne, and passed out into the gathering night.

The grocer put the box of dates back in its place.

"What a nice fellow he is!" he said. "It's odd how often they are nice. Much nicer than those as are all right."

Meanwhile Adam Wayne stood outside the glowing chemist's shop, unmistakably wavering.

"What a weakness it is!" he muttered. "I have never got rid of it from childhood—the fear of this magic shop. The grocer is rich, he is romantic, he is poetical in the truest sense, but he is not—no, he is not supernatural. But the chemist! All the other shops stand in Notting Hill, but this stands in Elf-land. Look at those great burning bowls of colour. It must be from them that God paints the sunsets. It is superhuman, and the superhuman is all the more uncanny when it is beneficent. That is the root of the fear of God. I am afraid. But I must be a man and enter."

He was a man, and entered. A short, dark young man was behind the counter with spectacles, and greeted him with a bright but entirely business-like smile.

"A fine evening, sir," he said.

"Fine indeed, strange Father," said Adam, stretching his hands somewhat forward. "It is on such clear and mellow nights that your shop is most itself. Then they appear most perfect, those moons of green and gold and crimson, which from afar oft guide the pilgrim of pain and sickness to this house of merciful witchcraft."

"Can I get you anything?" asked the chemist.

"Let me see," said Wayne, in a friendly but vague manner. "Let me have some sal volatile."

"Eightpence, tenpence, or one and sixpence a bottle?" said the young man, genially.

"One and six—one and six," replied Wayne, with a wild submissiveness. "I come to ask you, Mr. Bowles, a terrible question."

He paused and collected himself.

"It is necessary," he muttered— "it is necessary to be tactful, and to suit the appeal to each profession in turn."

"I come," he resumed aloud, "to ask you a question which goes to the roots of your miraculous toils. Mr. Bowles, shall all this witchery cease?" And he waved his stick around the shop.

Meeting with no answer, he continued with animation—

"In Notting Hill we have felt to its core the elfish mystery of your profession. And now Notting Hill itself is threatened."

"Anything more, sir?" asked the chemist.

"Oh," said Wayne, somewhat disturbed— "oh, what is it chemists sell? Quinine, I think. Thank you. Shall it be destroyed? I have met these men of Bayswater and North Kensington—Mr. Bowles, they are materialists. They see no witchery in your work, even when it is wrought within their own borders. They think the chemist is commonplace. They think him human."

The chemist appeared to pause, only a moment, to take in the insult, and immediately said—

"And the next article, please?"

"Alum," said the Provost, wildly. "I resume. It is in this sacred town alone that your priesthood is reverenced. Therefore, when you fight for us you fight not only for yourself, but for everything you typify. You fight not only for Notting Hill, but for Fairyland, for as surely as Buck and Barker and such men hold sway, the sense of Fairyland in some strange manner diminishes."

"Anything more, sir?" asked Mr. Bowles, with unbroken cheerfulness.

"Oh yes, jujubes—Gregory powder—magnesia. The danger is imminent. In all this matter I have felt that I fought not merely for my own city (though to that I owe all my blood), but for all places in which these great ideas could prevail. I am fighting not merely for Notting Hill, but for Bayswater itself; for North Kensington itself. For if the gold-hunters prevail, these also will lose all their ancient sentiments and all the mystery of their national soul. I know I can count upon you."

"Oh yes, sir," said the chemist, with great animation; "we are always glad to oblige a good customer."

Adam Wayne went out of the shop with a deep sense of fulfilment of soul.

"It is so fortunate," he said, "to have tact, to be able to play upon the peculiar talents and specialities, the cosmopolitanism of the grocer and the world-old necromancy of the chemist. Where should I be without tact?"

II

THE REMARKABLE MR. TURNBULL

After two more interviews with shopmen, however, the patriot's confidence in his own psychological diplomacy began vaguely to wane. Despite the care with which he considered the peculiar rationale and the peculiar glory of each separate shop, there seemed to be something unresponsive about the shopmen. Whether it was a dark resentment against the uninitiate for peeping into their masonic magnificence, he could not quite conjecture.

His conversation with the man who kept the shop of curiosities had begun encouragingly. The man who kept the shop of curiosities had, indeed, enchanted him with a phrase. He was standing drearily at the door of his shop, a wrinkled man with a grey pointed beard, evidently a gentleman who had come down in the world.

"And how does your commerce go, you strange guardian of the past?" said Wayne, affably.

"Well, sir, not very well," replied the man, with that patient voice of his class which is one of the most heart-breaking things in the world. "Things are terribly quiet."

Wayne's eyes shone suddenly.

"A great saying," he said, "worthy of a man whose merchandise is human history. Terribly quiet; that is in two words the spirit of this age, as I have felt it from my cradle. I sometimes wondered how many other people felt the oppression of this union between quietude and terror. I see blank well-ordered streets and men in black moving about inoffensively, sullenly. It goes on day after day, day after day, and nothing happens; but to me it is like a dream from which I might wake screaming. To me the straightness of our life is the straightness of a thin cord stretched tight. Its stillness is terrible. It might snap with a noise like thunder. And you who sit, amid the *débris* of the great wars, you who sit, as it were, upon a battlefield, you know that war was less terrible than this evil peace; you know that the idle lads who carried those swords under Francis or Elizabeth, the rude Squire or Baron who swung that mace about in Picardy or Northumberland battles, may have been terribly noisy, but were not like us, terribly quiet."

Whether it was a faint embarrassment of conscience as to the original source and date of the weapons referred to, or merely an engrained depression, the guardian of the past looked, if anything, a little more worried.

"But I do not think," continued Wayne, "that this horrible silence of modernity will last, though I think for the present it will increase. What a farce is this modern liberality! Freedom of speech means practically, in our modern civilisation, that we must only talk about unimportant things. We must not talk about religion, for that is illiberal; we must not talk about bread and cheese, for that is talking shop; we must not talk about death, for that is depressing; we must not talk about birth, for that is indelicate. It cannot last. Something must break this strange indifference, this strange dreamy egoism, this strange loneliness of millions in a crowd. Something must break it. Why should it not be you and I? Can you do nothing else but guard relics?"

The shopman wore a gradually clearing expression, which would have led those unsympathetic with the cause of the Red Lion to think that the last sentence was the only one to which he had attached any meaning.

"I am rather old to go into a new business," he said, "and I don't quite know what to be, either."

"Why not," said Wayne, gently having reached the crisis of his delicate persuasion— "why not be a colonel?"

It was at this point, in all probability, that the interview began to yield more disappointing results. The man appeared inclined at first to regard the suggestion of becoming a colonel as outside the sphere of immediate and relevant discussion. A long exposition of the inevitable war of independence, coupled with the purchase of a doubtful sixteenth-century sword for an exaggerated price, seemed to resettle matters. Wayne left the shop, however, somewhat infected with the melancholy of its owner.

That melancholy was completed at the barber's.

"Shaving, sir?" inquired that artist from inside his shop.

"War!" replied Wayne, standing on the threshold.

"I beg your pardon," said the other, sharply.

"War!" said Wayne, warmly. "But not for anything inconsistent with the beautiful and the civilised arts. War for beauty. War for society. War for peace. A great chance is offered you of repelling that slander which, in defiance of the lives of so many artists, attributes poltroonery to those who beautify and polish the surface of our lives. Why should not hairdressers be heroes? Why should not—"

"Now, you get out," said the barber, irascibly. "We don't want any of your sort here. You get out."

And he came forward with the desperate annoyance of a mild person when enraged.

Adam Wayne laid his hand for a moment on the sword, then dropped it.

"Notting Hill," he said, "will need her bolder sons;" and he turned gloomily to the toy-shop.

It was one of those queer little shops so constantly seen in the side streets of London, which must be called toy-shops only because toys upon the whole predominate; for the remainder of goods seem to consist of almost everything else in the world—tobacco, exercise-books, sweet-stuff, novelettes, halfpenny paper clips, halfpenny pencil sharpeners, bootlaces, and cheap fireworks. It also sold newspapers, and a row of dirty-looking posters hung along the front of it.

"I am afraid," said Wayne, as he entered, "that I am not getting on with these tradesmen as I should. Is it that I have neglected to rise to the full meaning of their work? Is there some secret buried in each of these shops which no mere poet can discover?"

He stepped to the counter with a depression which he rapidly conquered as he addressed the man on the other side of it,—a man of short stature, and hair prematurely white, and the look of a large baby.

"Sir," said Wayne, "I am going from house to house in this street of ours, seeking to stir up some sense of the danger which now threatens our city. Nowhere have I felt my duty so difficult as here. For the toy-shop keeper has to do with all that remains to us of Eden before the first wars began. You sit here meditating continually upon the wants of that wonderful time when every staircase leads to the stars, and every garden-path to the other end of nowhere. Is it thoughtlessly, do you think, that I strike the dark old drum of peril in the paradise of children? But consider a moment; do not condemn me hastily. Even that paradise itself contains the rumour or beginning of that danger, just as the Eden that was made for perfection contained the terrible tree. For judge childhood, even by your own arsenal of its pleasures. You keep bricks; you make yourself thus, doubtless, the witness of the constructive instinct older than the destructive. You keep dolls; you make yourself the priest of that divine idolatry. You keep Noah's Arks; you perpetuate the memory of the salvation of all life as a precious, an irreplaceable thing. But do you keep only, sir, the symbols of this prehistoric sanity, this childish rationality of the earth? Do you not keep more terrible things? What are those boxes, seemingly of lead soldiers, that I see in that glass case? Are they not witnesses to that terror and beauty, that desire for a lovely death, which could not be excluded even from the immortality of Eden? Do not despise the lead soldiers, Mr. Turnbull."

"I don't," said Mr. Turnbull, of the toy-shop, shortly, but with great emphasis.

"I am glad to hear it," replied Wayne. "I confess that I feared for my military schemes the awful innocence of your profession. How, I thought to myself, will this man, used only to the wooden swords that give pleasure, think of the steel swords that give pain? But I am at least partly reassured. Your tone suggests to me that I have at least the entry of a gate of your fairyland—the gate through which the soldiers enter, for it cannot be denied—I ought, sir, no longer to deny, that it is of soldiers that I come to speak. Let your gentle employment make you merciful towards the troubles of the world. Let your own silvery experience tone down our sanguine sorrows. For there is war in Notting Hill."

The little toy-shop keeper sprang up suddenly, slapping his fat hands like two fans on the counter.

"War?" he cried. "Not really, sir? Is it true? Oh, what a joke! Oh, what a sight for sore eyes!"

Wayne was almost taken aback by this outburst.

"I am delighted," he stammered. "I had no notion—"

He sprang out of the way just in time to avoid Mr. Turnbull, who took a flying leap over the counter and dashed to the front of the shop.

"You look here, sir," he said; "you just look here."

He came back with two of the torn posters in his hand which were flapping outside his shop.

"Look at those, sir," he said, and flung them down on the counter. Wayne bent over them, and read on one—

"Last Fighting.
Reduction of the Central Dervish City.
Remarkable, Etc."

On the other he read—

"Last Small Republic Annexed.
Nicaraguan Capital Surrenders After A Month's Fighting.
Great Slaughter."

Wayne bent over them again, evidently puzzled; then he looked at the dates. They were both dated in August fifteen years before.

"Why do you keep these old things?" he said, startled entirely out of his absurd tact of mysticism. "Why do you hang them outside your shop?"

"Because," said the other, simply, "they are the records of the last war. You mentioned war just now. It happens to be my hobby."

Wayne lifted his large blue eyes with an infantile wonder.

"Come with me," said Turnbull, shortly, and led him into a parlour at the back of the shop.

In the centre of the parlour stood a large deal table. On it were set rows and rows of the tin and lead soldiers which were part of the shopkeeper's stock. The visitor would have thought nothing of it if it had not been for a certain odd grouping of them, which did not seem either entirely commercial or entirely haphazard.

"You are acquainted, no doubt," said Turnbull, turning his big eyes upon Wayne— "you are acquainted, no doubt, with the arrangement of the American and Nicaraguan troops in the last battle;" and he waved his hand towards the table.

"I am afraid not," said Wayne. "I—"

"Ah! you were at that time occupied too much, perhaps, with the Dervish affair. You will find it in this corner." And he pointed to a part of the floor where there was another arrangement of children's soldiers grouped here and there.

"You seem," said Wayne, "to be interested in military matters."

"I am interested in nothing else," answered the toy-shop keeper, simply.

Wayne appeared convulsed with a singular, suppressed excitement.

"In that case," he said, "I may approach you with an unusual degree of confidence. Touching the matter of the defence of Notting Hill, I—"

"Defence of Notting Hill? Yes, sir. This way, sir," said Turnbull, with great perturbation. "Just step into this side room;" and he led Wayne into another apartment, in which the table was entirely covered with an arrangement of children's bricks. A second glance at it told Wayne that the bricks were arranged in the form of a precise and perfect plan of Notting Hill. "Sir," said Turnbull, impressively, "you have, by a kind of accident, hit upon the whole secret of my life. As a boy, I grew up among the last wars of the world, when Nicaragua was taken and the dervishes wiped out. And I adopted it as a hobby, sir, as you might adopt astronomy or bird-stuffing. I had no ill-will to any one, but I was interested in war as a science, as a game. And suddenly I was bowled out. The big Powers of the world, having swallowed up all the small ones, came to that confounded agreement, and there was no more war. There was nothing more for me to do but to do what I do now—to read the old campaigns in dirty old newspapers, and to work them out with tin soldiers. One other thing had occurred to me. I thought it an amusing fancy to make a plan of how this district or ours ought to be defended if it were ever attacked. It seems to interest you too."

"If it were ever attacked," repeated Wayne, awed into an almost mechanical enunciation. "Mr. Turnbull, it is attacked. Thank Heaven, I am bringing to at least one human being the news that is at bottom the only good news to any son of Adam. Your life has not been useless. Your work has not been play. Now, when the hair is already grey on your head, Turnbull, you shall have your youth. God has not destroyed, He has only deferred it. Let us sit down here, and you shall explain to

me this military map of Notting Hill. For you and I have to defend
Notting Hill together."

Mr. Turnbull looked at the other for a moment, then hesitated, and
then sat down beside the bricks and the stranger. He did not rise again
for seven hours, when the dawn broke.

The headquarters of Provost Adam Wayne and his Commander-in-
Chief consisted of a small and somewhat unsuccessful milk-shop at
the corner of Pump Street. The blank white morning had only just begun to break over the blank London buildings when Wayne and Turnbull
were to be found seated in the cheerless and unswept shop. Wayne had
something feminine in his character; he belonged to that class of persons who forget their meals when anything interesting is in hand. He
had had nothing for sixteen hours but hurried glasses of milk, and,
with a glass standing empty beside him, he was writing and sketching
and dotting and crossing out with inconceivable rapidity with a pencil
and a piece of paper. Turnbull was of that more masculine type in which
a sense of responsibility increases the appetite, and with his sketch-
map beside him he was dealing strenuously with a pile of sandwiches in
a paper packet, and a tankard of ale from the tavern opposite, whose
shutters had just been taken down. Neither of them spoke, and there
was no sound in the living stillness except the scratching of Wayne's
pencil and the squealing of an aimless-looking cat. At length Wayne
broke the silence by saying—

"Seventeen pounds eight shillings and ninepence."

Turnbull nodded and put his head in the tankard.

"That," said Wayne, "is not counting the five pounds you took yesterday. What did you do with it?"

"Ah, that is rather interesting!" replied Turnbull, with his mouth
full. "I used that five pounds in a kindly and philanthropic act."

Wayne was gazing with mystification in his queer and innocent eyes.

"I used that five pounds," continued the other, "in giving no less
than forty little London boys rides in hansom cabs."

"Are you insane?" asked the Provost.

"It is only my light touch," returned Turnbull. "These hansom-cab
rides will raise the tone—raise the tone, my dear fellow—of our London youths, widen their horizon, brace their nervous system, make them

acquainted with the various public monuments of our great city. Education, Wayne, education. How many excellent thinkers have pointed out that political reform is useless until we produce a cultured populace. So that twenty years hence, when these boys are grown up—"

"Mad!" said Wayne, laying down his pencil; "and five pounds gone!"

"You are in error," explained Turnbull. "You grave creatures can never be brought to understand how much quicker work really goes with the assistance of nonsense and good meals. Stripped of its decorative beauties, my statement was strictly accurate. Last night I gave forty half-crowns to forty little boys, and sent them all over London to take hansom cabs. I told them in every case to tell the cabman to bring them to this spot. In half an hour from now the declaration of war will be posted up. At the same time the cabs will have begun to come in, you will have ordered out the guard, the little boys will drive up in state, we shall commandeer the horses for cavalry, use the cabs for barricade, and give the men the choice between serving in our ranks and detention in our basements and cellars. The little boys we can use as scouts. The main thing is that we start the war with an advantage unknown in all the other armies—horses. And now," he said, finishing his beer, "I will go and drill the troops."

And he walked out of the milk-shop, leaving the Provost staring.

A minute or two afterwards, the Provost laughed. He only laughed once or twice in his life, and then he did it in a queer way as if it were an art he had not mastered. Even he saw something funny in the preposterous coup of the half-crowns and the little boys. He did not see the monstrous absurdity of the whole policy and the whole war. He enjoyed it seriously as a crusade, that is, he enjoyed it far more than any joke can be enjoyed. Turnbull enjoyed it partly as a joke, even more perhaps as a reversion from the things he hated—modernity and monotony and civilisation. To break up the vast machinery of modern life and use the fragments as engines of war, to make the barricade of omnibuses and points of vantage of chimney-pots, was to him a game worth infinite risk and trouble. He had that rational and deliberate preference which will always to the end trouble the peace of the world, the rational and deliberate preference for a short life and a merry one.

III

The Experiment of Mr. Buck

An earnest and eloquent petition was sent up to the King signed with the names of Wilson, Barker, Buck, Swindon, and others. It urged that at the forthcoming conference to be held in his Majesty's presence touching the final disposition of the property in Pump Street, it might be held not inconsistent with political decorum and with the unutterable respect they entertained for his Majesty if they appeared in ordinary morning dress, without the costume decreed for them as Provosts. So it happened that the company appeared at that council in frockcoats and that the King himself limited his love of ceremony to appearing (after his not unusual manner), in evening dress with one order—in this case not the Garter, but the button of the Club of Old Clipper's Best Pals, a decoration obtained (with difficulty) from a halfpenny boy's paper. Thus also it happened that the only spot of colour in the room was Adam Wayne, who entered in great dignity with the great red robes and the great sword.

"We have met," said Auberon, "to decide the most arduous of modern problems. May we be successful." And he sat down gravely.

Buck turned his chair a little, and flung one leg over the other.

"Your Majesty," he said, quite good-humouredly, "there is only one thing I can't understand, and that is why this affair is not settled in five minutes. Here's a small property which is worth a thousand to us and is not worth a hundred to any one else. We offer the thousand. It's not business-like, I know, for we ought to get it for less, and it's not reasonable and it's not fair on us, but I'm damned if I can see why it's difficult."

"The difficulty may be very simply stated," said Wayne. "You may offer a million and it will be very difficult for you to get Pump Street."

"But look here, Mr. Wayne," cried Barker, striking in with a kind of cold excitement. "Just look here. You've no right to take up a position like that. You've a right to stand out for a bigger price, but you aren't doing that. You're refusing what you and every sane man knows to be a splendid offer simply from malice or spite—it must be malice or spite. And that kind of thing is really criminal; it's against the public good. The King's Government would be justified in forcing you."

With his lean fingers spread on the table, he stared anxiously at Wayne's face, which did not move.

"In forcing you ... it would," he repeated.

"It shall," said Buck, shortly, turning to the table with a jerk. "We have done our best to be decent."

Wayne lifted his large eyes slowly.

"Was it my Lord Buck," he inquired, "who said that the King of England 'shall' do something?"

Buck flushed and said testily—

"I mean it must—it ought to. As I say, we've done our best to be generous; I defy any one to deny it. As it is, Mr. Wayne, I don't want to say a word that's uncivil. I hope it's not uncivil to say that you can be, and ought to be, in gaol. It is criminal to stop public works for a whim. A man might as well burn ten thousand onions in his front garden or bring up his children to run naked in the street, as do what you say you have a right to do. People have been compelled to sell before now. The King could compel you, and I hope he will."

"Until he does," said Wayne, calmly, "the power and government of this great nation is on my side and not yours, and I defy you to defy it."

"In what sense," cried Barker, with his feverish eyes and hands, "is the Government on your side?"

With one ringing movement Wayne unrolled a great parchment on the table. It was decorated down the sides with wild water-colour sketches of vestrymen in crowns and wreaths.

"The Charter of the Cities," he began.

Buck exploded in a brutal oath and laughed.

"That tomfool's joke. Haven't we had enough—"

"And there you sit," cried Wayne, springing erect and with a voice like a trumpet, "with no argument but to insult the King before his face."

Buck rose also with blazing eyes.

"I am hard to bully," he began—and the slow tones of the King struck in with incomparable gravity—

"My Lord Buck, I must ask you to remember that your King is present. It is not often that he needs to protect himself among his subjects."

Barker turned to him with frantic gestures.

"For God's sake don't back up the madman now," he implored. "Have your joke another time. Oh, for Heaven's sake—"

"My Lord Provost of South Kensington," said King Auberon, steadily, "I do not follow your remarks, which are uttered with a rapidity unusual at Court. Nor do your well-meant efforts to convey the rest with your fingers materially assist me. I say that my Lord Provost of North Kensington, to whom I spoke, ought not in the presence of his Sovereign to speak disrespectfully of his Sovereign's ordinances. Do you disagree?"

Barker turned restlessly in his chair, and Buck cursed without speaking. The King went on in a comfortable voice—

"My Lord Provost of Notting Hill, proceed."

Wayne turned his blue eyes on the King, and to every one's surprise there was a look in them not of triumph, but of a certain childish distress.

"I am sorry, your Majesty," he said; "I fear I was more than equally to blame with the Lord Provost of North Kensington. We were debating somewhat eagerly, and we both rose to our feet. I did so first, I am ashamed to say. The Provost of North Kensington is, therefore, comparatively innocent. I beseech your Majesty to address your rebuke chiefly, at least, to me. Mr. Buck is not innocent, for he did no doubt, in the heat of the moment, speak disrespectfully. But the rest of the discussion he seems to me to have conducted with great good temper."

Buck looked genuinely pleased, for business men are all simpleminded, and have therefore that degree of communion with fanatics. The King, for some reason, looked, for the first time in his life, ashamed.

"This very kind speech of the Provost of Notting Hill," began Buck, pleasantly, "seems to me to show that we have at least got on to a friendly footing. Now come, Mr. Wayne. Five hundred pounds have been offered to you for a property you admit not to be worth a hundred. Well, I am a rich man and I won't be outdone in generosity. Let us say fifteen hundred pounds, and have done with it. And let us shake hands;" and he rose, glowing and laughing.

"Fifteen hundred pounds," whispered Mr. Wilson of Bayswater; "can we do fifteen hundred pounds?"

"I'll stand the racket," said Buck, heartily. "Mr. Wayne is a gentleman and has spoken up for me. So I suppose the negotiations are at an end."

Wayne bowed.

"They are indeed at an end. I am sorry I cannot sell you the property."

"What?" cried Mr. Barker, starting to his feet.

"Mr. Buck has spoken correctly," said the King.

"I have, I have," cried Buck, springing up also; "I said—"

"Mr. Buck has spoken correctly," said the King; "the negotiations are at an end."

All the men at the table rose to their feet; Wayne alone rose without excitement.

"Have I, then," he said, "your Majesty's permission to depart? I have given my last answer."

"You have it," said Auberon, smiling, but not lifting his eyes from the table. And amid a dead silence the Provost of Notting Hill passed out of the room.

"Well?" said Wilson, turning round to Barker— "well?"

Barker shook his head desperately.

"The man ought to be in an asylum," he said. "But one thing is clear—we need not bother further about him. The man can be treated as mad."

"Of course," said Buck, turning to him with sombre decisiveness. "You're perfectly right, Barker. He is a good enough fellow, but he can be treated as mad. Let's put it in simple form. Go and tell any twelve men in any town, go and tell any doctor in any town, that there is a man offered fifteen hundred pounds for a thing he could sell commonly for four hundred, and that when asked for a reason for not accepting it he pleads the inviolate sanctity of Notting Hill and calls it the Holy Mountain. What would they say? What more can we have on our side than the common sense of everybody? On what else do all laws rest? I'll tell you, Barker, what's better than any further discussion. Let's send in workmen on the spot to pull down Pump Street. And if old Wayne says a word, arrest him as a lunatic. That's all."

Barker's eyes kindled.

"I always regarded you, Buck, if you don't mind my saying so, as a very strong man. I'll follow you."

"So, of course, will I," said Wilson.

Buck rose again impulsively.

"Your Majesty," he said, glowing with popularity, "I beseech your Majesty to consider favourably the proposal to which we have committed ourselves. Your Majesty's leniency, our own offers, have fallen in vain on that extraordinary man. He may be right. He may be God. He may be the devil. But we think it, for practical purposes, more probable that he is off his head. Unless that assumption were acted on, all human affairs would go to pieces. We act on it, and we propose to start operations in Notting Hill at once."

The King leaned back in his chair.

"The Charter of the Cities ...," he said with a rich intonation.

But Buck, being finally serious, was also cautious, and did not again make the mistake of disrespect.

"Your Majesty," he said, bowing, "I am not here to say a word against anything your Majesty has said or done. You are a far better educated man than I, and no doubt there were reasons, upon intellectual grounds, for those proceedings. But may I ask you and appeal to your common good-nature for a sincere answer? When you drew up the Charter of the Cities, did you contemplate the rise of a man like Adam Wayne? Did you expect that the Charter—whether it was an experiment, or a scheme of decoration, or a joke—could ever really come to this—to stopping a vast scheme of ordinary business, to shutting up a road, to spoiling the chances of cabs, omnibuses, railway stations, to disorganising half a city, to risking a kind of civil war? Whatever were your objects, were they that?"

Barker and Wilson looked at him admiringly; the King more admiringly still.

"Provost Buck," said Auberon, "you speak in public uncommonly well. I give you your point with the magnanimity of an artist. My scheme did not include the appearance of Mr. Wayne. Alas! would that my poetic power had been great enough."

"I thank your Majesty," said Buck, courteously, but quickly. "Your Majesty's statements are always clear and studied; therefore I may draw a deduction. As the scheme, whatever it was, on which you set your heart did not include the appearance of Mr. Wayne, it will survive his removal. Why not let us clear away this particular Pump Street, which does interfere with our plans, and which does not, by your Majesty's own statement, interfere with yours."

"Caught out!" said the King, enthusiastically and quite impersonally, as if he were watching a cricket match.

"This man Wayne," continued Buck, "would be shut up by any doctors in England. But we only ask to have it put before them. Meanwhile no one's interests, not even in all probability his own, can be really damaged by going on with the improvements in Notting Hill. Not our interests, of course, for it has been the hard and quiet work of ten years. Not the interests of Notting Hill, for nearly all its educated inhabitants desire the change. Not the interests of your Majesty, for you say, with characteristic sense, that you never contemplated the rise of the lunatic at all. Not, as I say, his own interests, for the man has a kind heart and many talents, and a couple of good doctors would probably put him righter than all the free cities and sacred mountains in creation. I therefore assume, if I may use so bold a word, that your Majesty will not offer any obstacle to our proceeding with the improvements."

And Mr. Buck sat down amid subdued but excited applause among the allies.

"Mr. Buck," said the King, "I beg your pardon, for a number of beautiful and sacred thoughts, in which you were generally classified as a fool. But there is another thing to be considered. Suppose you send in your workmen, and Mr. Wayne does a thing regrettable indeed, but of which, I am sorry to say, I think him quite capable—knocks their teeth out?"

"I have thought of that, your Majesty," said Mr. Buck, easily, "and I think it can simply be guarded against. Let us send in a strong guard of, say, a hundred men—a hundred of the North Kensington Halberdiers" (he smiled grimly), "of whom your Majesty is so fond. Or say a hundred and fifty. The whole population of Pump Street, I fancy, is only about a hundred."

"Still they might stand together and lick you," said the King, dubiously.

"Then say two hundred," said Buck, gaily.

"It might happen," said the King, restlessly, "that one Notting Hiller fought better than two North Kensingtons."

"It might," said Buck, coolly; "then say two hundred and fifty."

The King bit his lip.

"And if they are beaten too?" he said viciously.

"Your Majesty," said Buck, and leaned back easily in his chair, "suppose they are. If anything be clear, it is clear that all fighting matters are mere matters of arithmetic. Here we have a hundred and fifty, say, of Notting Hill soldiers. Or say two hundred. If one of them can fight two of us—we can send in, not four hundred, but six hundred, and smash him. That is all. It is out of all immediate probability that one of them could fight four of us. So what I say is this. Run no risks. Finish it at once. Send in eight hundred men and smash him—smash him almost without seeing him. And go on with the improvements."

And Mr. Buck pulled out a bandanna and blew his nose.

"Do you know, Mr. Buck," said the King, staring gloomily at the table, "the admirable clearness of your reason produces in my mind a sentiment which I trust I shall not offend you by describing as an aspiration to punch your head. You irritate me sublimely. What can it be in me? Is it the relic of a moral sense?"

"But your Majesty," said Barker, eagerly and suavely, "does not refuse our proposals?"

"My dear Barker, your proposals are as damnable as your manners. I want to have nothing to do with them. Suppose I stopped them altogether. What would happen?"

Barker answered in a very low voice— "Revolution."

The King glanced quickly at the men round the table. They were all looking down silently: their brows were red.

He rose with a startling suddenness, and an unusual pallor.

"Gentlemen," he said, "you have overruled me. Therefore I can speak plainly. I think Adam Wayne, who is as mad as a hatter, worth more than a million of you. But you have the force, and, I admit, the common sense, and he is lost. Take your eight hundred halberdiers and smash him. It would be more sportsmanlike to take two hundred."

"More sportsmanlike," said Buck, grimly, "but a great deal less humane. We are not artists, and streets purple with gore do not catch our eye in the right way."

"It is pitiful," said Auberon. "With five or six times their number, there will be no fight at all."

"I hope not," said Buck, rising and adjusting his gloves. "We desire no fight, your Majesty. We are peaceable business men."

"Well," said the King, wearily, "the conference is at an end at last." And he went out of the room before any one else could stir.

Forty workmen, a hundred Bayswater Halberdiers, two hundred from South, and three from North Kensington, assembled at the foot of Holland Walk and marched up it, under the general direction of Barker, who looked flushed and happy in full dress.

At the end of the procession a small and sulky figure lingered like an urchin. It was the King.

"Barker," he said at length, appealingly, "you are an old friend of mine—you understand my hobbies as I understand yours. Why can't you let it alone? I hoped that such fun might come out of this Wayne business. Why can't you let it alone? It doesn't really so much matter to you—what's a road or so? For me it's the one joke that may save me from pessimism. Take fewer men and give me an hour's fun. Really and truly, James, if you collected coins or humming-birds, and I could buy one with the price of your road, I would buy it. I collect incidents—those rare, those precious things. Let me have one. Pay a few pounds for it. Give these Notting Hillers a chance. Let them alone."

"Auberon," said Barker, kindly, forgetting all royal titles in a rare moment of sincerity, "I do feel what you mean. I have had moments when these hobbies have hit me. I have had moments when I have sympathised with your humours. I have had moments, though you may not easily believe it, when I have sympathised with the madness of Adam Wayne. But the world, Auberon, the real world, is not run on these hobbies. It goes on great brutal wheels of facts—wheels on which you are the butterfly; and Wayne is the fly on the wheel."

Auberon's eyes looked frankly at the other's.

"Thank you, James; what you say is true. It is only a parenthetical consolation to me to compare the intelligence of flies somewhat favourably with the intelligence of wheels. But it is the nature of flies to die soon, and the nature of wheels to go on for ever. Go on with the wheel. Good-bye, old man."

And James Barker went on, laughing, with a high colour, slapping his bamboo on his leg.

The King watched the tail of the retreating regiment with a look of genuine depression, which made him seem more like a baby than ever. Then he swung round and struck his hands together.

"In a world without humour," he said, "the only thing to do is to eat. And how perfect an exception! How can these people strike dignified attitudes, and pretend that things matter, when the total ludicrousness of life is proved by the very method by which it is supported? A man strikes the lyre, and says, 'Life is real, life is earnest,' and then goes into a room and stuffs alien substances into a hole in his head. I think Nature was indeed a little broad in her humour in these matters. But we all fall back on the pantomime, as I have in this municipal affair. Nature has her farces, like the act of eating or the shape of the kangaroo, for the more brutal appetite. She keeps her stars and mountains for those who can appreciate something more subtly ridiculous." He turned to his equerry. "But, as I said 'eating,' let us have a picnic like two nice little children. Just run and bring me a table and a dozen courses or so, and plenty of champagne, and under these swinging boughs, Bowler, we will return to Nature."

It took about an hour to erect in Holland Lane the monarch's simple repast, during which time he walked up and down and whistled, but still with an unaffected air of gloom. He had really been done out of a pleasure he had promised himself, and had that empty and sickened feeling which a child has when disappointed of a pantomime. When he and the equerry had sat down, however, and consumed a fair amount of dry champagne, his spirits began mildly to revive.

"Things take too long in this world," he said. "I detest all this Barkerian business about evolution and the gradual modification of things. I wish the world had been made in six days, and knocked to pieces again in six more. And I wish I had done it. The joke's good enough in a broad way, sun and moon and the image of God, and all that, but they keep it up so damnably long. Did you ever long for a miracle, Bowler?"

"No, sir," said Bowler, who was an evolutionist, and had been carefully brought up.

"Then I have," answered the King. "I have walked along a street with the best cigar in the cosmos in my mouth, and more Burgundy inside me than you ever saw in your life, and longed that the lamp-post would turn into an elephant to save me from the hell of blank existence. Take my word for it, my evolutionary Bowler, don't you believe people when they tell you that people sought for a sign, and believed in miracles because they were ignorant. They did it because they were wise, filthily, vilely wise—too wise to eat or sleep or put on their boots with patience. This seems delightfully like a new theory of the origin of Christianity, which would itself be a thing of no mean absurdity. Take some more wine."

The wind blew round them as they sat at their little table, with its white cloth and bright wine-cups, and flung the tree-tops of Holland Park against each other, but the sun was in that strong temper which turns green into gold. The King pushed away his plate, lit a cigar slowly, and went on—

"Yesterday I thought that something next door to a really entertaining miracle might happen to me before I went to amuse the worms. To see that red-haired maniac waving a great sword, and making speeches to his incomparable followers, would have been a glimpse of that Land of Youth from which the Fates shut us out. I had planned some quite delightful things. A Congress of Knightsbridge with a treaty, and myself in the chair, and perhaps a Roman triumph, with jolly old Barker led in chains. And now these wretched prigs have gone and stamped out the exquisite Mr. Wayne altogether, and I suppose they will put him in a private asylum somewhere in their damned humane way. Think of the treasures daily poured out to his unappreciative keeper! I wonder whether they would let me be his keeper. But life is a vale. Never forget at any moment of your existence to regard it in the light of a vale. This graceful habit, if not acquired in youth—"

The King stopped, with his cigar lifted, for there had slid into his eyes the startled look of a man listening. He did not move for a few moments; then he turned his head sharply towards the high, thin, and lath-like paling which fenced certain long gardens and similar spaces from the lane. From behind it there was coming a curious scrambling and scraping noise, as of a desperate thing imprisoned in this box of thin wood. The King threw away his cigar, and jumped on to the table. From this position he saw a pair of hands hanging with a hungry clutch on the top of the fence. Then the hands quivered with a convulsive effort, and a head shot up between them—

the head of one of the Bayswater Town Council, his eyes and whiskers wild with fear. He swung himself over, and fell on the other side on his face, and groaned openly and without ceasing. The next moment the thin, taut wood of the fence was struck as by a bullet, so that it reverberated like a drum, and over it came tearing and cursing, with torn clothes and broken nails and bleeding faces, twenty men at one rush. The King sprang five feet clear off the table on to the ground. The moment after the table was flung over, sending bottles and glasses flying, and the *débris* was literally swept along the ground by that stream of men pouring past, and Bowler was borne along with them, as the King said in his famous newspaper article, "like a captured bride." The great fence swung and split under the load of climbers that still scaled and cleared it. Tremendous gaps were torn in it by this living artillery; and through them the King could see more and more frantic faces, as in a dream, and more and more men running. They were as miscellaneous as if some one had taken the lid off a human dustbin. Some were untouched, some were slashed and battered and bloody, some were splendidly dressed, some tattered and half naked, some were in the fantastic garb of the burlesque cities, some in the dullest modern dress. The King stared at all of them, but none of them looked at the King. Suddenly he stepped forward.

"Barker," he said, "what is all this?"

"Beaten," said the politician— "beaten all to hell!" And he plunged past with nostrils shaking like a horse's, and more and more men plunged after him.

Almost as he spoke, the last standing strip of fence bowed and snapped, flinging, as from a catapult, a new figure upon the road. He wore the flaming red of the halberdiers of Notting Hill, and on his weapon there was blood, and in his face victory. In another moment masses of red glowed through the gaps of the fence, and the pursuers, with their halberds, came pouring down the lane. Pursued and pursuers alike swept by the little figure with the owlish eyes, who had not taken his hands out of his pockets.

The King had still little beyond the confused sense of a man caught in a torrent—the feeling of men eddying by. Then something happened which he was never able afterwards to describe, and which we cannot describe for him. Suddenly in the dark entrance, between the broken gates of a garden, there appeared framed a flaming figure.

Adam Wayne, the conqueror, with his face flung back, and his mane like a lion's, stood with his great sword point upwards, the red raiment of his office flapping round him like the red wings of an archangel. And the King saw, he knew not how, something new and overwhelming. The great green trees and the great red robes swung together in the wind. The sword seemed made for the sunlight. The preposterous masquerade, born of his own mockery, towered over him and embraced the world. This was the normal, this was sanity, this was nature; and he himself, with his rationality and his detachment and his black frock-coat, he was the exception and the accident—a blot of black upon a world of crimson and gold.

BOOK IV

THE BATTLE OF THE LAMPS

Mr. Buck, who, though retired, frequently went down to his big drapery stores in Kensington High Street, was locking up those premises, being the last to leave. It was a wonderful evening of green and gold, but that did not trouble him very much. If you had pointed it out, he would have agreed seriously, for the rich always desire to be artistic.

He stepped out into the cool air, buttoning up his light yellow coat, and blowing great clouds from his cigar, when a figure dashed up to him in another yellow overcoat, but unbuttoned and flying behind him.

"Hullo, Barker!" said the draper. "Any of our summer articles? You're too late. Factory Acts, Barker. Humanity and progress, my boy."

"Oh, don't chatter," cried Barker, stamping. "We've been beaten."

"Beaten—by what?" asked Buck, mystified.

"By Wayne."

Buck looked at Barker's fierce white face for the first time, as it gleamed in the lamplight.

"Come and have a drink," he said.

They adjourned to a cushioned and glaring buffet, and Buck established himself slowly and lazily in a seat, and pulled out his cigar-case.

"Have a smoke," he said.

Barker was still standing, and on the fret, but after a moment's hesitation, he sat down as if he might spring up again the next minute. They ordered drinks in silence.

"How did it happen?" asked Buck, turning his big bold eyes on him.

"How the devil do I know?" cried Barker. "It happened like—like a dream. How can two hundred men beat six hundred? How can they?"

"Well," said Buck, coolly, "how did they? You ought to know."

"I don't know; I can't describe," said the other, drumming on the table. "It seemed like this. We were six hundred, and marched with those damned poleaxes of Auberon's—the only weapons we've got. We marched two abreast. We went up Holland Walk, between the high palings which seemed to me to go straight as an arrow for Pump Street. I was near the tail of the line, and it was a long one. When the end of it was still between the high palings, the head of the line was already crossing Holland Park Avenue. Then the head plunged into the network of narrow streets on the other side, and the tail and myself came out on the great crossing. When we also had reached the northern side and turned up a small street that points, crookedly as it were, towards Pump Street, the whole thing felt different. The streets dodged and bent so much that the head of our line seemed lost altogether: it might as well have been in North America. And all this time we hadn't seen a soul."

Buck, who was idly dabbing the ash of his cigar on the ash-tray, began to move it deliberately over the table, making feathery grey lines, a kind of map.

"But though the little streets were all deserted (which got a trifle on my nerves), as we got deeper and deeper into them, a thing began to happen that I couldn't understand. Sometimes a long way ahead—three turns or corners ahead, as it were—there broke suddenly a sort of noise, clattering, and confused cries, and then stopped. Then, when it happened, something, I can't describe it—a kind of shake or stagger went down the line, as if the line were a live thing, whose head had been struck, or had been an electric cord. None of us knew why we were moving, but we moved and jostled. Then we recovered, and went on through the little dirty streets, round corners, and up twisted ways. The little crooked streets began to give me a feeling I can't explain—as if it were a dream. I felt as if things had lost their reason, and we should never get out of the maze. Odd to hear me talk like that, isn't it? The streets were quite well-known streets, all down on the map. But the fact remains. I wasn't afraid of something happening. I was afraid of nothing ever happening—nothing ever happening for all God's eternity."

He drained his glass and called for more whisky. He drank it, and went on. "And then something did happen. Buck, it's the solemn truth, that nothing has ever happened to you in your life. Nothing had ever happened to me in my life."

"Nothing ever happened!" said Buck, staring. "What do you mean?"

"Nothing has ever happened," repeated Barker, with a morbid obstinacy. "You don't know what a thing happening means? You sit in your office expecting customers, and customers come; you walk in the street expecting friends, and friends meet you; you want a drink, and get it; you feel inclined for a bet, and make it. You expect either to win or lose, and you do either one or the other. But things happening!" and he shuddered ungovernably.

"Go on," said Buck, shortly. "Get on."

"As we walked wearily round the corners, something happened. When something happens, it happens first, and you see it afterwards. It happens of itself, and you have nothing to do with it. It proves a dreadful thing—that there are other things besides one's self. I can only put it in this way. We went round one turning, two turnings, three turnings, four turnings, five. Then I lifted myself slowly up from the gutter where I had been shot half senseless, and was beaten down again by living men crashing on top of me, and the world was full of roaring, and big men rolling about like nine-pins."

Buck looked at his map with knitted brows.

"Was that Portobello Road?" he asked.

"Yes," said Barker— "yes; Portobello Road. I saw it afterwards; but, my God, what a place it was! Buck, have you ever stood and let a six foot of man lash and lash at your head with six feet of pole with six pounds of steel at the end? Because, when you have had that experience, as Walt Whitman says, 'you re-examine philosophies and religions.'"

"I have no doubt," said Buck. "If that was Portobello Road, don't you see what happened?"

"I know what happened exceedingly well. I was knocked down four times; an experience which, as I say, has an effect on the mental attitude. And another thing happened, too. I knocked down two men. After the fourth fall (there was not much bloodshed—more brutal rushing and throwing—for nobody could use their weapons), after the fourth fall, I say, I got up like a devil, and I tore a poleaxe out of a man's hand and struck where I saw the scarlet of Wayne's fellows, struck again and again. Two of them went over, bleeding on the stones, thank God; and I laughed and found myself sprawling in the gutter again, and got up again, and struck again, and broke my halberd to pieces. I hurt a man's head, though."

Buck set down his glass with a bang, and spat out curses through his thick moustache.

"What is the matter?" asked Barker, stopping, for the man had been calm up to now, and now his agitation was far more violent than his own.

"The matter?" said Buck, bitterly; "don't you see how these maniacs have got us? Why should two idiots, one a clown and the other a screaming lunatic, make sane men so different from themselves? Look here, Barker; I will give you a picture. A very well-bred young man of this century is dancing about in a frock-coat. He has in his hands a nonsensical seventeenth-century halberd, with which he is trying to kill men in a street in Notting Hill. Damn it! don't you see how they've got us? Never mind how you felt—that is how you looked. The King would put his cursed head on one side and call it exquisite. The Provost of Notting Hill would put his cursed nose in the air and call it heroic. But in Heaven's name what would you have called it—two days before?"

Barker bit his lip.

"You haven't been through it, Buck," he said. "You don't understand fighting—the atmosphere."

"I don't deny the atmosphere," said Buck, striking the table. "I only say it's their atmosphere. It's Adam Wayne's atmosphere. It's the atmosphere which you and I thought had vanished from an educated world for ever."

"Well, it hasn't," said Barker; "and if you have any lingering doubts, lend me a poleaxe, and I'll show you."

There was a long silence, and then Buck turned to his neighbour and spoke in that good-tempered tone that comes of a power of looking facts in the face—the tone in which he concluded great bargains.

"Barker," he said, "you are right. This old thing—this fighting, has come back. It has come back suddenly and taken us by surprise. So it is first blood to Adam Wayne. But, unless reason and arithmetic and everything else have gone crazy, it must be next and last blood to us. But when an issue has really arisen, there is only one thing to do—to study that issue as such and win in it. Barker, since it is fighting, we must understand fighting. I must understand fighting as coolly and completely as I understand drapery; you must understand fighting as coolly and completely as you understand politics. Now, look at the facts. I stick without hesitation to my original formula. Fighting, when we have the stronger force, is only a matter of arithmetic. It must be. You asked me just now how two hundred men could defeat six hundred. I can tell you. Two hundred men can defeat six hundred when the six hundred behave like fools. When they forget the very conditions they are fighting in; when they fight in a swamp as if it were a mountain; when they fight in a forest as if it were a plain; when they fight in streets without remembering the object of streets."

"What is the object of streets?" asked Barker.

"What is the object of supper?" cried Buck, furiously. "Isn't it obvious? This military science is mere common sense. The object of a street is to lead from one place to another; therefore all streets join; therefore street fighting is quite a peculiar thing. You advanced into that hive of streets as if you were advancing into an open plain where you could see everything. Instead of that, you were advancing into the bowels of a fortress, with streets pointing at you, streets turning on you, streets jumping out at you, and all in the hands of the enemy. Do you know what Portobello Road is? It is the only point on your journey where two side streets run up opposite each other. Wayne massed his men on the two sides, and when he had let enough of your line go past, cut it in two like a worm. Don't you see what would have saved you?"

Barker shook his head.

"Can't your 'atmosphere' help you?" asked Buck, bitterly. "Must I attempt explanations in the romantic manner? Suppose that, as you were fighting blindly with the red Notting Hillers who imprisoned you on both sides, you had heard a shout from behind them. Suppose, oh, romantic Barker! that behind the red tunics you had seen the blue and gold of South Kensington taking them in the rear, surrounding them in their turn and hurling them on to your halberds."

"If the thing had been possible," began Barker, cursing.

"The thing would have been as possible," said Buck, simply, "as simple as arithmetic. There are a certain number of street entries that lead to Pump Street. There are not nine hundred; there are not nine million. They do not grow in the night. They do not increase like mushrooms. It must be possible, with such an overwhelming force as we have, to advance by all of them at once. In every one of the arteries, or approaches, we can put almost as many men as Wayne can put into the field altogether. Once do that, and we have him to demonstration. It is like a proposition of Euclid."

"You think that is certain?" said Barker, anxious, but dominated delightfully.

"I'll tell you what I think," said Buck, getting up jovially. "I think Adam Wayne made an uncommonly spirited little fight; and I think I am confoundedly sorry for him."

"Buck, you are a great man!" cried Barker, rising also. "You've knocked me sensible again. I am ashamed to say it, but I was getting romantic. Of course, what you say is adamantine sense. Fighting, being physical, must be mathematical. We were beaten because we were neither mathematical nor physical nor anything else—because we deserved to be beaten. Hold all the approaches, and with our force we must have him. When shall we open the next campaign?"

"Now," said Buck, and walked out of the bar.

"Now!" cried Barker, following him eagerly. "Do you mean now? It is so late."

Buck turned on him, stamping.

"Do you think fighting is under the Factory Acts?" he said; and he called a cab. "Notting Hill Gate Station," he said; and the two drove off.

A genuine reputation can sometimes be made in an hour. Buck, in the next sixty or eighty minutes, showed himself a really great man of action. His cab carried him like a thunderbolt from the King to Wilson, from Wilson to Swindon, from Swindon to Barker again; if his course was jagged, it had the jaggedness of the lightning. Only two things he carried with him—his inevitable cigar and the map of North Kensington and Notting Hill. There were, as he again and again pointed out, with every variety of persuasion and violence, only nine possible ways of approaching Pump Street within a quarter of a mile round it; three out of Westbourne Grove, two out of Ladbroke Grove, and four out of Notting Hill High Street. And he had detachments of two hundred each, stationed at every one of the entrances before the last green of that strange sunset had sunk out of the black sky.

The sky was particularly black, and on this alone was one false protest raised against the triumphant optimism of the Provost of North Kensington. He overruled it with his infectious common sense.

"There is no such thing," he said, "as night in London. You have only to follow the line of street lamps. Look, here is the map. Two hundred purple North Kensington soldiers under myself march up Ossington Street, two hundred more under Captain Bruce, of the North Kensington Guard, up Clanricarde Gardens.[1] Two hundred yellow West Kensingtons under Provost Swindon attack from Pembridge Road. Two hundred more of my men from the eastern streets, leading away from Queen's Road. Two detachments of yellows enter by two roads from Westbourne Grove. Lastly, two hundred green Bayswaters come down from the North through Chepstow Place, and two hundred more under Provost Wilson himself, through the upper part of Pembridge Road. Gentlemen, it is mate in two moves. The enemy must either mass in Pump Street and be cut to pieces; or they must retreat past the Gaslight & Coke Co., and rush on my four hundred; or they must retreat past St. Luke's Church, and rush on the six hundred from the West. Unless we are all mad, it's plain. Come on. To your quarters and await Captain Brace's signal to advance. Then you have only to walk up a line of gas-lamps and smash this nonsense by pure mathematics. To-morrow we shall all be civilians again."

His optimism glowed like a great fire in the night, and ran round the terrible ring in which Wayne was now held helpless. The fight was already over. One man's energy for one hour had saved the city from war.

For the next ten minutes Buck walked up and down silently beside the motionless clump of his two hundred. He had not changed his appearance in any way, except to sling across his yellow overcoat a case with a revolver in it. So that his light-clad modern figure showed up oddly beside the pompous purple uniforms of his halberdiers, which darkly but richly coloured the black night.

At length a shrill trumpet rang from some way up the street; it was the signal of advance. Buck briefly gave the word, and the whole purple line, with its dimly shining steel, moved up the side alley. Before it was a slope of street, long, straight, and shining in the dark. It was a sword pointed at Pump Street, the heart at which nine other swords were pointed that night.

[1] Clanricarde Gardens at this time was no longer a *cul-de-sac*, but was connected by Pump Street to Pembridge Square.

A quarter of an hour's silent marching brought them almost within earshot of any tumult in the doomed citadel. But still there was no sound and no sign of the enemy. This time, at any rate, they knew that they were closing in on it mechanically, and they marched on under the lamplight and the dark without any of that eerie sense of ignorance which Barker had felt when entering the hostile country by one avenue alone.

"Halt—point arms!" cried Buck, suddenly, and as he spoke there came a clatter of feet tumbling along the stones. But the halberds were levelled in vain. The figure that rushed up was a messenger from the contingent of the North.

"Victory, Mr. Buck!" he cried, panting; "they are ousted. Provost Wilson of Bayswater has taken Pump Street."

Buck ran forward in his excitement.

"Then, which way are they retreating? It must be either by St. Luke's to meet Swindon, or by the Gas Company to meet us. Run like mad to Swindon, and see that the yellows are holding the St. Luke's Road. We will hold this, never fear. We have them in an iron trap. Run!"

As the messenger dashed away into the darkness, the great guard of North Kensington swung on with the certainty of a machine. Yet scarcely a hundred yards further their halberd-points again fell in line gleaming in the gaslight; for again a clatter of feet was heard on the stones, and again it proved to be only the messenger.

"Mr. Provost," he said, "the yellow West Kensingtons have been holding the road by St. Luke's for twenty minutes since the capture of Pump Street. Pump Street is not two hundred yards away; they cannot be retreating down that road."

"Then they are retreating down this," said Provost Buck, with a final cheerfulness, "and by good fortune down a well-lighted road, though it twists about. Forward!"

As they moved along the last three hundred yards of their journey, Buck fell, for the first time in his life, perhaps, into a kind of philosophical reverie, for men of his type are always made kindly, and as it were melancholy, by success.

"I am sorry for poor old Wayne, I really am," he thought. "He spoke up splendidly for me at that Council. And he blacked old Barker's eye with considerable spirit. But I don't see what a man can expect when he fights against arithmetic, to say nothing of civilisation. And what a wonderful hoax all this military genius is! I suspect I've just discovered what Cromwell discovered, that a sensible tradesman is the best general, and that a man who can buy men and sell men can lead and kill them. The thing's simply like adding up a column in a ledger. If Wayne has two hundred men, he can't put two hundred men in nine places at once. If they're ousted from Pump Street they're flying somewhere. If they're not flying past the church they're flying past the Works. And so we have them. We business men should have no chance at all except that cleverer people than we get bees in their bonnets that prevent them from reasoning properly—so we reason alone. And so I, who am comparatively stupid, see things as God sees them, as a vast machine. My God, what's this?" and he clapped his hands to his eyes and staggered back.

Then through the darkness he cried in a dreadful voice—

"Did I blaspheme God? I am struck blind."

"What?" wailed another voice behind him, the voice of a certain Wilfred Jarvis of North Kensington.

"Blind!" cried Buck; "blind!"

"I'm blind too!" cried Jarvis, in an agony.

"Fools, all of you," said a gross voice behind them; "we're all blind. The lamps have gone out."

"The lamps! But why? where?" cried Buck, turning furiously in the darkness. "How are we to get on? How are we to chase the enemy? Where have they gone?"

"The enemy went—" said the rough voice behind, and then stopped doubtfully.

"Where?" shouted Buck, stamping like a madman.

"They went," said the gruff voice, "past the Gas Works, and they've used their chance."

"Great God!" thundered Buck, and snatched at his revolver; "do you mean they've turned out—"

But almost before he had spoken the words, he was hurled like a stone from catapult into the midst of his own men.

"Notting Hill! Notting Hill!" cried frightful voices out of the darkness, and they seemed to come from all sides, for the men of North Kensington, unacquainted with the road, had lost all their bearings in the black world of blindness.

"Notting Hill! Notting Hill!" cried the invisible people, and the invaders were hewn down horribly with black steel, with steel that gave no glint against any light.

Buck, though badly maimed with the blow of a halberd, kept an angry but splendid sanity. He groped madly for the wall and found it. Struggling with crawling fingers along it, he found a side opening and retreated into it with the remnants of his men. Their adventures during that prodigious night are not to be described. They did not know whether they were going towards or away from the enemy. Not knowing where they themselves were, or where their opponents were, it was mere irony to ask where was the rest of their army. For a thing had descended upon them which London does not know—darkness, which was before the stars were made, and they were as much lost in it as if they had been made before the stars. Every now and then, as those frightful hours wore on, they buffeted in the darkness against living men, who struck at them and at whom they struck, with an idiot fury. When at last the grey dawn came, they found they had wandered back to the edge of the Uxbridge Road. They found that in those horrible eyeless encounters, the North Kensingtons and the Bayswaters and the West Kensingtons had again and again met and butchered each other, and they heard that Adam Wayne was barricaded in Pump Street.

II

THE CORRESPONDENT OF THE COURT JOURNAL

Journalism had become, like most other such things in England under the cautious government and philosophy represented by James Barker, somewhat sleepy and much diminished in importance. This was partly due to the disappearance of party government and public speaking, partly to the compromise or dead-lock which had made foreign wars impossible, but mostly, of course, to the temper of the whole nation which was that of a people in a kind of back-water. Perhaps the most well known of the remaining newspapers was the *Court Journal*, which was published in a dusty but genteel-looking office just out of Kensington High Street. For when all the papers of a people have been for years growing more and more dim and decorous and optimistic, the dimmest and most decorous and most optimistic is very likely to win. In the journalistic competition which was still going on at the beginning of the twentieth century, the final victor was the *Court Journal*.

For some mysterious reason the King had a great affection for hanging about in the *Court Journal* office, smoking a morning cigarette and looking over files. Like all ingrainedly idle men, he was very fond of lounging and chatting in places where other people were doing work. But one would have thought that, even in the prosaic England of his day, he might have found a more bustling centre.

On this particular morning, however, he came out of Kensington Palace with a more alert step and a busier air than usual. He wore an extravagantly long frock-coat, a pale-green waistcoat, a very full and *dégagé* black tie, and curious yellow gloves. This was his uniform as Colonel of a regiment of his own creation, the 1st Decadents Green. It was a beautiful sight to see him drilling them. He walked quickly across the

Park and the High Street, lighting his cigarette as he went, and flung open the door of the *Court Journal* office.

"You've heard the news, Pally—you've heard the news?" he said.

The Editor's name was Hoskins, but the King called him Pally, which was an abbreviation of Paladium of our Liberties.

"Well, your Majesty," said Hoskins, slowly (he was a worried, gentlemanly looking person, with a wandering brown beard)— "well, your Majesty, I have heard rather curious things, but I—"

"You'll hear more of them," said the King, dancing a few steps of a kind of negro shuffle. "You'll hear more of them, my blood-and-thunder tribune. Do you know what I am going to do for you?"

"No, your Majesty," replied the Paladium, vaguely.

"I'm going to put your paper on strong, dashing, enterprising lines," said the King. "Now, where are your posters of last night's defeat?"

"I did not propose, your Majesty," said the Editor, "to have any posters exactly—"

"Paper, paper!" cried the King, wildly; "bring me paper as big as a house. I'll do you posters. Stop, I must take my coat off." He began removing that garment with an air of set intensity, flung it playfully at Mr. Hoskins' head, entirely enveloping him, and looked at himself in the glass. "The coat off," he said, "and the hat on. That looks like a sub-editor. It is indeed the very essence of sub-editing. Well," he continued, turning round abruptly, "come along with that paper."

The Paladium had only just extricated himself reverently from the folds of the King's frock-coat, and said bewildered—

"I am afraid, your Majesty—"

"Oh, you've got no enterprise," said Auberon. "What's that roll in the corner? Wall-paper? Decorations for your private residence? Art in the home, Pally? Fling it over here, and I'll paint such posters on the back of it that when you put it up in your drawing-room you'll paste the original pattern against the wall." And the King unrolled the wallpaper, spreading it over the whole floor. "Now give me the scissors," he cried, and took them himself before the other could stir.

He slit the paper into about five pieces, each nearly as big as a door. Then he took a big blue pencil, and went down on his knees on the dusty oil-cloth and began to write on them, in huge letters—

"FROM THE FRONT.
GENERAL BUCK DEFEATED.
DARKNESS, DANGER, AND DEATH.
WAYNE SAID TO BE IN PUMP STREET.
FEELING IN THE CITY."

He contemplated it for some time, with his head on one side, and got up, with a sigh.

"Not quite intense enough," he said— "not alarming. I want the *Court Journal* to be feared as well as loved. Let's try something more hard-hitting." And he went down on his knees again. After sucking the blue pencil for some time, he began writing again busily. "How will this do?" he said—

"WAYNE'S WONDERFUL VICTORY."

"I suppose," he said, looking up appealingly, and sucking the pencil— "I suppose we couldn't say 'wictory'— 'Wayne's wonderful wictory'? No, no. Refinement, Pally, refinement. I have it."

"WAYNE WINS.
ASTOUNDING FIGHT IN THE DARK.
The gas-lamps in their courses fought against Buck."

"(Nothing like our fine old English translation.) What else can we say? Well, anything to annoy old Buck;" and he added, thoughtfully, in smaller letters—

"RUMOURED COURT-MARTIAL ON GENERAL BUCK."

"Those will do for the present," he said, and turned them both face downwards. "Paste, please."

The Paladium, with an air of great terror, brought the paste out of an inner room.

The King slabbed it on with the enjoyment of a child messing with treacle. Then taking one of his huge compositions fluttering in each hand, he ran outside, and began pasting them up in prominent positions over the front of the office.

"And now," said Auberon, entering again with undiminished vivacity— "now for the leading article."

He picked up another of the large strips of wall-paper, and, laying it across a desk, pulled out a fountain-pen and began writing with feverish intensity, reading clauses and fragments aloud to himself, and rolling them on his tongue like wine, to see if they had the pure journalistic flavour.

"The news of the disaster to our forces in Notting Hill, awful as it is—awful as it is—(no, *distressing* as it is), may do some good if it draws attention to the what's-his-name inefficiency (scandalous inefficiency, of course) of the Government's preparations. In our present state of information, it would be premature (what a jolly word!)—it would be premature to cast any reflections upon the conduct of General Buck, whose services upon so many stricken fields (ha, ha!), and whose honourable scars and laurels, give him a right to have judgment upon him at least suspended. But there is one matter on which we must speak plainly. We have been silent on it too long, from feelings, perhaps of mistaken caution, perhaps of mistaken loyalty. This situation would never have arisen but for what we can only call the indefensible conduct of the King. It pains us to say such things, but, speaking as we do in the public interests (I plagiarise from Barker's famous epigram), we shall not shrink because of the distress we may cause to any individual, even the most exalted. At this crucial moment of our country, the voice of the People demands with a single tongue, 'Where is the King?' What is he doing while his subjects tear each other in pieces in the streets of a great city? Are his amusements and his dissipations (of which we cannot pretend to be ignorant) so engrossing that he can spare no thought for a perishing nation? It is with a deep sense of our responsibility that we warn that exalted person that neither his great position nor his incomparable talents will save him in the hour of delirium from the fate of all those who, in the madness of luxury or tyranny, have met the English people in the rare day of its wrath."

"I am now," said the King, "going to write an account of the battle by an eye-witness." And he picked up a fourth sheet of wall-paper. Almost at the same moment Buck strode quickly into the office. He had a bandage round his head.

"I was told," he said, with his usual gruff civility, "that your Majesty was here."

"And of all things on earth," cried the King, with delight, "here is an eye-witness! An eye-witness who, I regret to observe, has at present only one eye to witness with. Can you write us the special article, Buck? Have you a rich style?"

Buck, with a self-restraint which almost approached politeness, took no notice whatever of the King's maddening geniality.

"I took the liberty, your Majesty," he said shortly, "of asking Mr. Barker to come here also."

As he spoke, indeed, Barker came swinging into the office, with his usual air of hurry.

"What is happening now?" asked Buck, turning to him with a kind of relief.

"Fighting still going on," said Barker. "The four hundred from West Kensington were hardly touched last night. They hardly got near the place. Poor Wilson's Bayswater men got cut about, though. They fought confoundedly well. They took Pump Street once. What mad things do happen in the world. To think that of all of us it should be little Wilson with the red whiskers who came out best."

The King made a note on his paper—

"*Romantic Conduct of Mr. Wilson.*"

"Yes," said Buck; "it makes one a bit less proud of one's *h*'s."

The King suddenly folded or crumpled up the paper, and put it in his pocket.

"I have an idea," he said. "I will be an eye-witness. I will write you such letters from the Front as will be more gorgeous than the real thing. Give me my coat, Paladium. I entered this room a mere King of England. I leave it, Special War Correspondent of the *Court Journal.* It is useless to stop me, Pally; it is vain to cling to my knees, Buck; it is hopeless, Barker, to weep upon my neck. 'When duty calls'—the remainder of the sentiment escapes me. You will receive my first article this evening by the eight-o'clock post."

And, running out of the office, he jumped upon a blue Bayswater omnibus that went swinging by.

"Well," said Barker, gloomily, "well."

"Barker," said Buck, "business may be lower than politics, but war is, as I discovered last night, a long sight more like business. You politicians are such ingrained demagogues that even when you have a despotism you think of nothing but public opinion. So you learn to tack and run, and are afraid of the first breeze. Now we stick to a thing and get it. And our mistakes help us. Look here! at this moment we've beaten Wayne."

"Beaten Wayne," repeated Barker.

"Why the dickens not?" cried the other, flinging out his hands. "Look here. I said last night that we had them by holding the nine entrances. Well, I was wrong. We should have had them but for a singular event— the lamps went out. But for that it was certain. Has it occurred to you, my brilliant Barker, that another singular event has happened since that singular event of the lamps going out?"

"What event?" asked Barker.

"By an astounding coincidence, the sun has risen," cried out Buck, with a savage air of patience. "Why the hell aren't we holding all those approaches now, and passing in on them again? It should have been done at sunrise. The confounded doctor wouldn't let me go out. You were in command."

Barker smiled grimly.

"It is a gratification to me, my dear Buck, to be able to say that we anticipated your suggestions precisely. We went as early as possible to reconnoitre the nine entrances. Unfortunately, while we were fighting each other in the dark, like a lot of drunken navvies, Mr. Wayne's friends were working very hard indeed. Three hundred yards from Pump Street, at every one of those entrances, there is a barricade nearly as high as the houses. They were finishing the last, in Pembridge Road, when we arrived. Our mistakes," he cried bitterly, and flung his cigarette on the ground. "It is not we who learn from them."

There was a silence for a few moments, and Barker lay back wearily in a chair. The office clock ticked exactly in the stillness.

At length Barker said suddenly—

"Buck, does it ever cross your mind what this is all about? The Hammersmith to Maida Vale thoroughfare was an uncommonly good speculation. You and I hoped a great deal from it. But is it worth it? It will cost us thousands to crush this ridiculous riot. Suppose we let it alone?"

"And be thrashed in public by a red-haired madman whom any two doctors would lock up?" cried out Buck, starting to his feet. "What do you propose to do, Mr. Barker? To apologise to the admirable Mr. Wayne? To kneel to the Charter of the Cities? To clasp to your bosom the flag of the Red Lion? To kiss in succession every sacred lamp-post that saved Notting Hill? No, by God! My men fought jolly well—they were beaten by a trick. And they'll fight again."

"Buck," said Barker, "I always admired you. And you were quite right in what you said the other day."

"In what?"

"In saying," said Barker, rising quietly, "that we had all got into Adam Wayne's atmosphere and out of our own. My friend, the whole territorial kingdom of Adam Wayne extends to about nine streets, with barricades at the end of them. But the spiritual kingdom of Adam Wayne extends, God knows where—it extends to this office, at any rate. The red-haired madman whom any two doctors would lock up is filling this room with his roaring, unreasonable soul. And it was the red-haired madman who said the last word you spoke."

Buck walked to the window without replying. "You understand, of course," he said at last, "I do not dream of giving in."

The King, meanwhile, was rattling along on the top of his blue omnibus. The traffic of London as a whole had not, of course, been greatly disturbed by these events, for the affair was treated as a Notting Hill riot, and that area was marked off as if it had been in the hands of a gang of recognised rioters. The blue omnibuses simply went round as they would have done if a road were being mended, and the omnibus on which the correspondent of the *Court Journal* was sitting swept round the corner of Queen's Road, Bayswater.

The King was alone on the top of the vehicle, and was enjoying the speed at which it was going.

"Forward, my beauty, my Arab," he said, patting the omnibus encouragingly, "fleetest of all thy bounding tribe. Are thy relations with thy driver, I wonder, those of the Bedouin and his steed? Does he sleep side by side with thee—"

His meditations were broken by a sudden and jarring stoppage. Looking over the edge, he saw that the heads of the horses were being held by men in the uniform of Wayne's army, and heard the voice of an officer calling out orders.

King Auberon descended from the omnibus with dignity. The guard or picket of red halberdiers who had stopped the vehicle did not number more than twenty, and they were under the command of a short, dark, clever-looking young man, conspicuous among the rest as being clad in an ordinary frock-coat, but girt round the waist with a red sash and a long seventeenth-century sword. A shiny silk hat and spectacles completed the outfit in a pleasing manner.

"To whom have I the honour of speaking?" said the King, endeavouring to look like Charles I., in spite of personal difficulties.

The dark man in spectacles lifted his hat with equal gravity.

"My name is Bowles," he said. "I am a chemist. I am also a captain of O company of the army of Notting Hill. I am distressed at having to incommode you by stopping the omnibus, but this area is covered by our proclamation, and we intercept all traffic. May I ask to whom I have the honour—Why, good gracious, I beg your Majesty's pardon. I am quite overwhelmed at finding myself concerned with the King."

Auberon put up his hand with indescribable grandeur.

"Not with the King," he said; "with the special war correspondent of the *Court Journal*."

"I beg your Majesty's pardon," began Mr. Bowles, doubtfully.

"Do you call me Majesty? I repeat," said Auberon, firmly, "I am a representative of the press. I have chosen, with a deep sense of responsibility, the name of Pinker. I should desire a veil to be drawn over the past."

"Very well, sir," said Mr. Bowles, with an air of submission, "in our eyes the sanctity of the press is at least as great as that of the throne. We desire nothing better than that our wrongs and our glories should be widely known. May I ask, Mr. Pinker, if you have any objection to being presented to the Provost and to General Turnbull?"

"The Provost I have had the honour of meeting," said Auberon, easily. "We old journalists, you know, meet everybody. I should be most delighted to have the same honour again. General Turnbull, also, it would be a gratification to know. The younger men are so interesting. We of the old Fleet Street gang lose touch with them."

"Will you be so good as to step this way?" said the leader of O company.

"I am always good," said Mr. Pinker. "Lead on."

III

The Great Army of South Kensington

The article from the special correspondent of the *Court Journal* arrived in due course, written on very coarse copy-paper in the King's arabesque of handwriting, in which three words filled a page, and yet were illegible. Moreover, the contribution was the more perplexing at first, as it opened with a succession of erased paragraphs. The writer appeared to have attempted the article once or twice in several journalistic styles. At the side of one experiment was written, "Try American style," and the fragment began— "The King must go. We want gritty men. Flapdoodle is all very ...;" and then broke off, followed by the note, "Good sound journalism safer. Try it."

The experiment in good sound journalism appeared to begin—

"The greatest of English poets has said that a rose by any ..."

This also stopped abruptly. The next annotation at the side was almost undecipherable, but seemed to be something like—

"How about old Steevens and the *mot juste?* E.g. ..."

"Morning winked a little wearily at me over the curt edge of Campden Hill and its houses with their sharp shadows. Under the abrupt black cardboard of the outline, it took some little time to detect colours; but at length I saw a brownish yellow shifting in the obscurity, and I knew that it was the guard of Swindon's West Kensington army. They are being held as a reserve, and lining the whole ridge above the Bayswater Road. Their camp and their main force is under the great Waterworks Tower on Campden Hill. I forgot to say that the Waterworks Tower looked swart.

"As I passed them and came over the curve of Silver Street, I saw the blue cloudy masses of Barker's men blocking the entrance to the high-road like a sapphire smoke (good). The disposition of the allied troops, under the general management of Mr. Wilson, appears to be as follows: The Yellow army (if I may so describe the West Kensingtonians) lies, as I have said, in a strip along the ridge, its furthest point westward being the west side of Campden Hill Road, its furthest point eastward the beginning of Kensington Gardens. The Green army of Wilson lines the Notting Hill High Road itself from Queen's Road to the corner of Pembridge Road, curving round the latter, and extending some three hundred yards up towards Westbourne Grove. Westbourne Grove it-self is occupied by Barker of South Kensington. The fourth side of this rough square, the Queen's Road side, is held by some of Buck's Purple warriors.

"The whole resembles some ancient and dainty Dutch flower-bed. Along the crest of Campden Hill lie the golden crocuses of West Kensington. They are, as it were, the first fiery fringe of the whole. Northward lies our hyacinth Barker, with all his blue hyacinths. Round to the south-west run the green rushes of Wilson of Bayswater, and a line of violet irises (aptly symbolised by Mr. Buck) complete the whole. The argent exterior ... (I am losing the style. I should have said 'Curving with a whisk' instead of merely 'Curving.' Also I should have called the hyacinths 'sudden.' I cannot keep this up. War is too rapid for this style of writing. Please ask office-boy to insert *mots justes*.)

"The truth is that there is nothing to report. That commonplace element which is always ready to devour all beautiful things (as the Black Pig in the Irish Mythology will finally devour the stars and gods); that commonplace element, as I say, has in its Black Piggish way devoured finally the chances of any romance in this affair; that which once con-sisted of absurd but thrilling combats in the streets, has degenerated into something which is the very prose of warfare—it has degenerated into a siege. A siege may be defined as a peace plus the inconvenience of war. Of course Wayne cannot hold out. There is no more chance of help from anywhere else than of ships from the moon. And if old Wayne had stocked his street with tinned meats till all his garrison had to sit on them, he couldn't hold out for more than a month or two. As a matter of melancholy fact, he has done something rather like this. He has stocked his street with food until there must be uncommonly little room to turn round. But what is the good? To hold out for all that time and then to give in of necessity, what does it mean? It means waiting until your victories are forgotten, and then taking the trouble to be defeated. I cannot understand how Wayne can be so inartistic.

"And how odd it is that one views a thing quite differently when one knows it is defeated! I always thought Wayne was rather fine. But now, when I know that he is done for, there seem to be nothing else but Wayne. All the streets seem to point at him, all the chimneys seem to lean towards him. I suppose it is a morbid feeling; but Pump Street seems to be the only part of London that I feel physically. I suppose, I say, that it is morbid. I suppose it is exactly how a man feels about his heart when his heart is weak. 'Pump Street'—the heart is a pump. And I am drivelling.

"Our finest leader at the front is, beyond all question, General Wilson. He has adopted alone among the other Provosts the uniform of his own halberdiers, although that fine old sixteenth-century garb was not originally intended to go with red side-whiskers. It was he who, against a most admirable and desperate defence, broke last night into Pump Street and held it for at least half an hour. He was afterwards expelled from it by General Turnbull, of Notting Hill, but only after desperate fighting and the sudden descent of that terrible darkness which proved so much more fatal to the forces of General Buck and General Swindon.

"Provost Wayne himself, with whom I had, with great good fortune, a most interesting interview, bore the most eloquent testimony to the conduct of General Wilson and his men. His precise words are as follows: 'I have bought sweets at his funny little shop when I was four years old, and ever since. I never noticed anything, I am ashamed to say, except that he talked through his nose, and didn't wash himself particularly. And he came over our barricade like a devil from hell.' I repeated this speech to General Wilson himself, with some delicate improvements, and he seemed pleased with it. He does not, however, seem pleased with anything so much just now as he is with the wearing of a sword. I have it from the front on the best authority that General Wilson was not completely shaved yesterday. It is believed in military circles that he is growing a moustache....

"As I have said, there is nothing to report. I walk wearily to the pillar-box at the corner of Pembridge Road to post my copy. Nothing whatever has happened, except the preparations for a particularly long and feeble siege, during which I trust I shall not be required to be at the Front. As I glance up Pembridge Road in the growing dusk, the aspect of that road reminds me that there is one note worth adding. General Buck has suggested, with characteristic acumen, to General Wilson that, in order to obviate the possibility of such a catastrophe as overwhelmed the allied forces in the last advance on Notting Hill (the catastrophe, I mean, of the extinguished lamps), each soldier should have a lighted lantern round his neck. This is one of the things which I really admire about General Buck. He possesses what people used to mean by 'the humility of the man of science,' that is, he learns steadily from his mistakes. Wayne may score off him in some other way, but not in that way. The lanterns look like fairy lights as they curve round the end of Pembridge Road.

"*Later.*—I write with some difficulty, because the blood will run down my face and make patterns on the paper. Blood is a very beautiful thing; that is why it is concealed. If you ask why blood runs down my face, I can only reply that I was kicked by a horse. If you ask me what horse, I can reply with some pride that it was a war-horse. If you ask me how a war-horse came on the scene in our simple pedestrian warfare, I am reduced to the necessity, so painful to a special correspondent, of recounting my experiences.

"I was, as I have said, in the very act of posting my copy at the pillar-box, and of glancing as I did so up the glittering curve of Pembridge Road, studded with the lights of Wilson's men. I don't know what made me pause to examine the matter, but I had a fancy that the line of lights, where it melted into the indistinct brown twilight, was more indistinct than usual. I was almost certain that in a certain stretch of the road where there had been five lights there were now only four. I strained my eyes; I counted them again, and there were only three. A moment after there were only two; an instant after only one; and an instant after that the lanterns near to me swung like jangled bells, as if struck suddenly. They flared and fell; and for the moment the fall of them was like the fall of the sun and stars out of heaven. It left everything in a primal blindness. As a matter of fact, the road was not yet legitimately dark. There were still red rays of a sunset in the sky, and the brown gloaming was still warmed, as it were, with a feeling as of firelight. But for three seconds after the lanterns swung and sank, I saw in front of me a blackness blocking the sky. And with the fourth second I knew that this blackness which blocked the sky was a man on a great horse; and I was trampled and tossed aside as a swirl of horsemen swept round the corner. As they turned I saw that they were not black, but scarlet; they were a sortie of the besieged, Wayne riding ahead.

"I lifted myself from the gutter, blinded with blood from a very slight skin-wound, and, queerly enough, not caring either for the blindness or for the slightness of the wound. For one mortal minute after that amazing cavalcade had spun past, there was dead stillness on the empty road. And then came Barker and all his halberdiers running like devils in the track of them. It had been their business to guard the gate by which the sortie had broken out; but they had not reckoned, and small blame to them, on cavalry. As it was, Barker and his men made a perfectly splendid run after them, almost catching Wayne's horses by the tails.

"Nobody can understand the sortie. It consists only of a small number of Wayne's garrison. Turnbull himself, with the vast mass of it, is undoubtedly still barricaded in Pump Street. Sorties of this kind are natural enough in the majority of historical sieges, such as the siege of Paris in 1870, because in such cases the besieged are certain of some support outside. But what can be the object of it in this case? Wayne knows (or if he is too mad to know anything, at least Turnbull knows) that there is not, and never has been, the smallest chance of support for him outside; that the mass of the sane modern inhabitants of London regard his farcical patriotism with as much contempt as they do the original idiocy that gave it birth—the folly of our miserable King. What Wayne and his horsemen are doing nobody can even conjecture. The general theory round here is that he is simply a traitor, and has abandoned the besieged. But all such larger but yet more soluble riddles are as nothing compared to the one small but unanswerable riddle: Where did they get the horses?

"*Later.*—I have heard a most extraordinary account of the origin of the appearance of the horses. It appears that that amazing person, General Turnbull, who is now ruling Pump Street in the absence of

Wayne, sent out, on the morning of the declaration of war, a vast number of little boys (or cherubs of the gutter, as we pressmen say), with half-crowns in their pockets, to take cabs all over London. No less than a hundred and sixty cabs met at Pump Street; were commandeered by the garrison. The men were set free, the cabs used to make barricades, and the horses kept in Pump Street, where they were fed and exercised for several days, until they were sufficiently rapid and efficient to be used for this wild ride out of the town. If this is so, and I have it on the best possible authority, the method of the sortie is explained. But we have no explanation of its object. Just as Barker's Blues were swinging round the corner after them, they were stopped, but not by an enemy; only by the voice of one man, and he a friend. Red Wilson of Bayswater ran alone along the main road like a madman, waving them back with a halberd snatched from a sentinel. He was in supreme command, and Barker stopped at the corner, staring and bewildered. We could hear Wilson's voice loud and distinct out of the dusk, so that it seemed strange that the great voice should come out of the little body. 'Halt, South Kensington! Guard this entry, and prevent them returning. I will pursue. Forward, the Green Guards!'

"A wall of dark blue uniforms and a wood of pole-axes was between me and Wilson, for Barker's men blocked the mouth of the road in two rigid lines. But through them and through the dusk I could hear the clear orders and the clank of arms, and see the green army of Wilson marching by towards the west. They were our great fighting-men. Wilson had filled them with his own fire; in a few days they had become veterans. Each of them wore a silver medal of a pump, to boast that they alone of all the allied armies had stood victorious in Pump Street.

"I managed to slip past the detachment of Barker's Blues, who are guarding the end of Pembridge Road, and a sharp spell of running brought me to the tail of Wilson's green army as it swung down the road in pursuit of the flying Wayne. The dusk had deepened into almost total darkness; for some time I only heard the throb of the marching pace. Then suddenly there was a cry, and the tall fighting men were flung back on me, almost crushing me, and again the lanterns swung and jingled, and the cold nozzles of great horses pushed into the press of us. They had turned and charged us.

"'You fools!' came the voice of Wilson, cleaving our panic with a splendid cold anger. 'Don't you see? the horses have no riders!'

"It was true. We were being plunged at by a stampede of horses with empty saddles. What could it mean? Had Wayne met some of our men and been defeated? Or had he flung these horses at us as some kind of ruse or mad new mode of warfare, such as he seemed bent on inventing? Or did he and his men want to get away in disguise? Or did they want to hide in houses somewhere?

"Never did I admire any man's intellect (even my own) so much as I did Wilson's at that moment. Without a word, he simply pointed the halberd (which he still grasped) to the southern side of the road. As you know, the streets running up to the ridge of Campden Hill from the main road are peculiarly steep, they are more like sudden flights of stairs. We were just opposite Aubrey Road, the steepest of all; up that it would have been far more difficult to urge half-trained horses than to run up on one's feet.

"'Left wheel!' hallooed Wilson. 'They have gone up here,' he added to me, who happened to be at his elbow.

"'Why?' I ventured to ask.

"'Can't say for certain,' replied the Bayswater General. 'They've gone up here in a great hurry, anyhow. They've simply turned their horses loose, because they couldn't take them up. I fancy I know. I fancy they're trying to get over the ridge to Kensingston or Hammersmith, or somewhere, and are striking up here because it's just beyond the end of our line. Damned fools, not to have gone further along the road, though. They've only just shaved our last outpost. Lambert is hardly four hundred yards from here. And I've sent him word.'

"'Lambert!' I said. 'Not young Wilfrid Lambert—my old friend.'

"'Wilfrid Lambert's his name,' said the General; 'used to be a "man about town;" silly fellow with a big nose. That kind of man always volunteers for some war or other; and what's funnier, he generally isn't half bad at it. Lambert is distinctly good. The yellow West Kensingtons I always reckoned the weakest part of the army; but he has pulled them together uncommonly well, though he's subordinate to Swindon, who's a donkey. In the attack from Pembridge Road the other night he showed great pluck.'

"'He has shown greater pluck than that,' I said. 'He has criticised my sense of humour. That was his first engagement.'

"This remark was, I am sorry to say, lost on the admirable commander of the allied forces. We were in the act of climbing the last half of Aubrey Road, which is so abrupt a slope that it looks like an old-fashioned map leaning up against the wall. There are lines of little trees, one above the other, as in the old-fashioned map.

"We reached the top of it, panting somewhat, and were just about to turn the corner by a place called (in chivalrous anticipation of our wars of sword and axe) Tower Creçy, when we were suddenly knocked in the stomach (I can use no other term) by a horde of men hurled back upon us. They wore the red uniform of Wayne; their halberds were broken; their foreheads bleeding; but the mere impetus of their retreat staggered us as we stood at the last ridge of the slope.

"'Good old Lambert!' yelled out suddenly the stolid Mr. Wilson of Bayswater, in an uncontrollable excitement. 'Damned jolly old Lambert! He's got there already! He's driving them back on us! Hurrah! hurrah! Forward, the Green Guards!'

"We swung round the corner eastwards, Wilson running first, brandishing the halberd—

"Will you pardon a little egotism? Every one likes a little egotism, when it takes the form, as mine does in this case, of a disgraceful confession. The thing is really a little interesting, because it shows how the merely artistic habit has bitten into men like me. It was the most intensely exciting occurrence that had ever come to me in my life; and I was really intensely excited about it. And yet, as we turned that corner, the first impression I had was of something that had nothing to do with the fight at all. I was stricken from the sky as by a thunderbolt, by the height of the Waterworks Tower on Campden Hill. I don't know whether Londoners generally realise how high it looks when one comes out, in this way, almost immediately under it. For the second it seemed to me that at the foot of it even human war was a triviality. For the second I felt as if I had been drunk with some trivial orgie, and that I had been sobered by the shock of that shadow. A moment afterwards, I realised that under it was going on something more enduring than stone, and something wilder than the dizziest height—the agony of man. And I knew that, compared to that, this overwhelming tower was itself a triviality; it was a mere stalk of stone which humanity could snap like a stick.

"I don't know why I have talked so much about this silly old Water-works Tower, which at the very best was only a tremendous background. It was that, certainly, a sombre and awful landscape, against which our figures were relieved. But I think the real reason was, that there was in my own mind so sharp a transition from the tower of stone to the man of flesh. For what I saw first when I had shaken off, as it were, the shadow of the tower, was a man, and a man I knew.

"Lambert stood at the further corner of the street that curved round the tower, his figure outlined in some degree by the beginning of moon-rise. He looked magnificent, a hero; but he looked something much more interesting than that. He was, as it happened, in almost precisely the same swaggering attitude in which he had stood nearly fifteen years ago, when he swung his walking-stick and struck it into the ground, and told me that all my subtlety was drivel. And, upon my soul, I think he required more courage to say that than to fight as he does now. For then he was fighting against something that was in the ascendant, fashionable, and victorious. And now he is fighting (at the risk of his life, no doubt) merely against something which is already dead, which is impossible, futile; of which nothing has been more impossible and fu-tile than this very sortie which has brought him into contact with it. People nowadays allow infinitely too little for the psychological sense of victory as a factor in affairs. Then he was attacking the degraded but undoubtedly victorious Quin; now he is attacking the interesting but totally extinguished Wayne.

"His name recalls me to the details of the scene. The facts were these. A line of red halberdiers, headed by Wayne, were marching up the street, close under the northern wall, which is, in fact, the bottom of a sort of dyke or fortification of the Waterworks. Lambert and his yellow West Kensingtons had that instant swept round the corner and had shaken the Waynites heavily, hurling back a few of the more timid, as I have just described, into our very arms. When our force struck the tail of Wayne's, every one knew that all was up with him. His favourite military barber was struck down. His grocer was stunned. He himself was hurt in the thigh, and reeled back against the wall. We had him in a trap with two jaws. 'Is that you?' shouted Lambert, genially, to Wilson, across the hemmed-in host of Notting Hill. 'That's about the ticket,' replied General Wilson; 'keep them under the wall.'

"The men of Notting Hill were falling fast. Adam Wayne threw up his long arms to the wall above him, and with a spring stood upon it; a gigantic figure against the moon. He tore the banner out of the hands of the standard-bearer below him, and shook it out suddenly above our heads, so that it was like thunder in the heavens.

"'Round the Red Lion!' he cried. 'Swords round the Red Lion! Halberds round the Red Lion! They are the thorns round rose.'

"His voice and the crack of the banner made a momentary rally, and Lambert, whose idiotic face was almost beautiful with battle, felt it as by an instinct, and cried—

"'Drop your public-house flag, you footler! Drop it!'

"'The banner of the Red Lion seldom stoops,' said Wayne, proudly, letting it out luxuriantly on the night wind.

"The next moment I knew that poor Adam's sentimental theatricality had cost him much. Lambert was on the wall at a bound, his sword in his teeth, and had slashed at Wayne's head before he had time to draw his sword, his hands being busy with the enormous flag. He stepped back only just in time to avoid the first cut, and let the flag-staff fall, that the spear-blade at the end of it pointed to Lambert.

"'The banner stoops,' cried Wayne, in a voice that must have startled streets. 'The banner of Notting Hill stoops to a hero.' And with the words he drove the spear-point and half the flag-staff through Lambert's body and dropped him dead upon the road below, a stone upon the stones of the street.

"'Notting Hill! Notting Hill!' cried Wayne, in a sort of divine rage. 'Her banner is all the holier for the blood of a brave enemy! Up on the wall, patriots! Up on the wall! Notting Hill!'

"With his long strong arm he actually dragged a man up on to the wall to be silhouetted against the moon, and more and more men climbed up there, pulled themselves and were pulled, till clusters and crowds of the half-massacred men of Pump Street massed upon the wall above us.

"'Notting Hill! Notting Hill!' cried Wayne, unceasingly.

"'Well, what about Bayswater?' said a worthy working-man in Wilson's army, irritably. 'Bayswater for ever!'

"'We have won!' cried Wayne, striking his flag-staff in the ground. 'Bayswater for ever! We have taught our enemies patriotism!'

"'Oh, cut these fellows up and have done with it!' cried one of Lambert's lieutenants, who was reduced to something bordering on madness by the responsibility of succeeding to the command.

"'Let us by all means try,' said Wilson, grimly; and the two armies closed round the third.

"I simply cannot describe what followed. I am sorry, but there is such a thing as physical fatigue, as physical nausea, and, I may add, as physical terror. Suffice it to say that the above paragraph was written about 11 p.m., and that it is now about 2 a.m., and that the battle is not finished, and is not likely to be. Suffice it further to say that down the steep streets which lead from the Waterworks Tower to the Notting Hill High Road, blood has been running, and is running, in great red serpents, that curl out into the main thoroughfare and shine in the moon.

"*Later.*—The final touch has been given to all this terrible futility. Hours have passed; morning has broken; men are still swaying and fight-ing at the foot of the tower and round the corner of Aubrey Road; the fight has not finished. But I know it is a farce.

"News has just come to show that Wayne's amazing sortie, followed by the amazing resistance through a whole night on the wall of the Waterworks, is as if it had not been. What was the object of that strange exodus we shall probably never know, for the simple reason that every one who knew will probably be cut to pieces in the course of the next two or three hours.

"I have heard, about three minutes ago, that Buck and Buck's meth-ods have won after all. He was perfectly right, of course, when one comes to think of it, in holding that it was physically impossible for a street to defeat a city. While we thought he was patrolling the eastern gates with his Purple army; while we were rushing about the streets and waving halberds and lanterns; while poor old Wilson was scheming like Moltke and fighting like Achilles to entrap the wild Provost of Notting Hill—Mr. Buck, retired draper, has simply driven down in a hansom cab and done something about as plain as butter and about as useful and nasty. He has gone down to South Kensington, Brompton, and Fulham, and by spending about four thousand pounds of his private means, has raised an army of nearly as many men; that is to say, an army big enough to beat, not only Wayne, but Wayne and all his present enemies put together. The army, I understand, is encamped along High Street, Kensington, and fills it from the Church to Addison Road Bridge. It is to advance by ten different roads uphill to the north.

"I cannot endure to remain here. Everything makes it worse than it need be. The dawn, for instance, has broken round Campden Hill; splendid spaces of silver, edged with gold, are torn out of the sky. Worse still, Wayne and his men feel the dawn; their faces, though bloody and pale, are strangely hopeful ... insupportably pathetic. Worst of all, for the moment they are winning. If it were not for Buck and the new army they might just, and only just, win.

"I repeat, I cannot stand it. It is like watching that wonderful play of old Maeterlinck's (you know my partiality for the healthy, jolly old authors of the nineteenth century), in which one has to watch the quiet conduct of people inside a parlour, while knowing that the very men are outside the door whose word can blast it all with tragedy. And this is worse, for the men are not talking, but writhing and bleeding and dropping dead for a thing that is already settled—and settled against them. The great grey masses of men still toil and tug and sway hither and thither around the great grey tower; and the tower is still motionless, as it will always be motionless. These men will be crushed before the sun is set; and new men will arise and be crushed, and new wrongs done, and tyranny will always rise again like the sun, and injustice will always be as fresh as the flowers of spring. And the stone tower will always look down on it. Matter, in its brutal beauty, will always look down on those who are mad enough to consent to die, and yet more mad, since they consent to live."

Thus ended abruptly the first and last contribution of the Special Correspondent of the *Court Journal* to that valued periodical.

The Correspondent himself, as has been said, was simply sick and gloomy at the last news of the triumph of Buck. He slouched sadly down the steep Aubrey Road, up which he had the night before run in so unusual an excitement, and strolled out into the empty dawn-lit main road, looking vaguely for a cab. He saw nothing in the vacant space except a blue-and-gold glittering thing, running very fast, which looked at first like a very tall beetle, but turned out, to his great astonishment, to be Barker.

"Have you heard the good news?" asked that gentleman.

"Yes," said Quin, with a measured voice. "I have heard the glad tidings of great joy. Shall we take a hansom down to Kensington? I see one over there."

They took the cab, and were, in four minutes, fronting the ranks of the multitudinous and invincible army. Quin had not spoken a word all the way, and something about him had prevented the essentially impressionable Barker from speaking either.

The great army, as it moved up Kensington High Street, calling many heads to the numberless windows, for it was long indeed—longer than the lives of most of the tolerably young—since such an army had been seen in London. Compared with the vast organisation which was now swallowing up the miles, with Buck at its head as leader, and the King hanging at its tail as journalist, the whole story of our problem was insignificant. In the presence of that army the red Notting Hills and the green Bayswaters were alike tiny and straggling groups. In its presence the whole struggle round Pump Street was like an ant-hill under the hoof of an ox. Every man who felt or looked at that infinity of men knew that it was the triumph of Buck's brutal arithmetic. Whether Wayne was right or wrong, wise or foolish, was quite a fair matter for discussion. But it was a matter of history. At the foot of Church Street, opposite Kensington Church, they paused in their glowing good humour.

"Let us send some kind of messenger or herald up to them," said Buck, turning to Barker and the King. "Let us send and ask them to cave in without more muddle."

"What shall we say to them?" said Barker, doubtfully.

"The facts of the case are quite sufficient," rejoined Buck. "It is the facts of the case that make an army surrender. Let us simply say that our army that is fighting their army, and their army that is fighting our army, amount altogether to about a thousand men. Say that we have four thousand. It is very simple. Of the thousand fighting, they have at the very most, three hundred, so that, with those three hundred, they have now to fight four thousand seven hundred men. Let them do it if it amuses them."

And the Provost of North Kensington laughed.

The herald who was despatched up Church Street in all the pomp of the South Kensington blue and gold, with the Three Birds on his tabard, was attended by two trumpeters.

"What will they do when they consent?" asked Barker, for the sake of saying something in the sudden stillness of that immense army.

"I know my Wayne very well," said Buck, laughing. "When he submits he will send a red herald flaming with the Lion of Notting Hill. Even defeat will be delightful to him, since it is formal and romantic."

The King, who had strolled up to the head of the line, broke silence for the first time.

"I shouldn't wonder," he said, "if he defied you, and didn't send the herald after all. I don't think you do know your Wayne quite so well as you think."

"All right, your Majesty," said Buck, easily; "if it isn't disrespectful, I'll put my political calculations in a very simple form. I'll lay you ten pounds to a shilling the herald comes with the surrender."

"All right," said Auberon. "I may be wrong, but it's my notion of Adam Wayne that he'll die in his city, and that, till he is dead, it will not be a safe property."

"The bet's made, your Majesty," said Buck.

Another long silence ensued, in the course of which Barker alone, amid the motionless army, strolled and stamped in his restless way.

Then Buck suddenly leant forward.

"It's taking your money, your Majesty," he said. "I knew it was. There comes the herald from Adam Wayne."

"It's not," cried the King, peering forward also. "You brute, it's a red omnibus."

"It's not," said Buck, calmly; and the King did not answer, for down the centre of the spacious and silent Church Street was walking, beyond question, the herald of the Red Lion, with two trumpeters.

Buck had something in him which taught him how to be magnanimous. In his hour of success he felt magnanimous towards Wayne, whom he really admired; magnanimous towards the King, off whom he had scored so publicly; and, above all, magnanimous towards Barker, who was the titular leader of this vast South Kensington army, which his own talent had evoked. "General Barker," he said, bowing, "do you propose now to receive the message from the besieged?"

Barker bowed also, and advanced towards the herald.

"Has your master, Mr. Adam Wayne, received our request for surrender?" he asked.

The herald conveyed a solemn and respectful affirmative.

Barker resumed, coughing slightly, but encouraged.

"What answer does your master send?"

The herald again inclined himself submissively, and answered in a kind of monotone.

"My message is this. Adam Wayne, Lord High Provost of Notting Hill, under the charter of King Auberon and the laws of God and all mankind, free and of a free city, greets James Barker, Lord High Provost of South Kensington, by the same rights free and honourable, leader of the army of the South. With all friendly reverence, and with all constitutional consideration, he desires James Barker to lay down his arms, and the whole army under his command to lay down their arms also."

Before the words were ended the King had run forward into the open space with shining eyes. The rest of the staff and the forefront of the army were literally struck breathless. When they recovered they began to laugh beyond restraint; the revulsion was too sudden.

"The Lord High Provost of Notting Hill," continued the herald, "does not propose, in the event of your surrender, to use his victory for any of those repressive purposes which others have entertained against him. He will leave you your free laws and your free cities, your flags and your governments. He will not destroy the religion of South Kensington, or crush the old customs of Bayswater."

An irrepressible explosion of laughter went up from the forefront of the great army.

"The King must have had something to do with this humour," said Buck, slapping his thigh. "It's too deliciously insolent. Barker, have a glass of wine."

And in his conviviality he actually sent a soldier across to the restaurant opposite the church and brought out two glasses for a toast.

When the laughter had died down, the herald continued quite monotonously—

"In the event of your surrendering your arms and dispersing under the superintendence of our forces, these local rights of yours shall be carefully observed. In the event of your not doing so, the Lord High Provost of Notting Hill desires to announce that he has just captured the Waterworks Tower, just above you, on Campden Hill, and that within ten minutes from now, that is, on the reception through me of your refusal, he will open the great reservoir and flood the whole valley where you stand in thirty feet of water. God save King Auberon!"

Buck had dropped his glass and sent a great splash of wine over the road.

"But—but—" he said; and then by a last and splendid effort of his great sanity, looked the facts in the face.

"We must surrender," he said. "You could do nothing against fifty thousand tons of water coming down a steep hill, ten minutes hence. We must surrender. Our four thousand men might as well be four. *Vicisti Galilæe!* Perkins, you may as well get me another glass of wine."

In this way the vast army of South Kensington surrendered and the Empire of Notting Hill began. One further fact in this connection is perhaps worth mentioning—the fact that, after his victory, Adam Wayne caused the great tower on Campden Hill to be plated with gold and inscribed with a great epitaph, saying that it was the monument of Wilfrid Lambert, the heroic defender of the place, and surmounted with a statue, in which his large nose was done something less than justice to.

BOOK V

I

THE EMPIRE OF NOTTING HILL

On the evening of the third of October, twenty years after the great victory of Notting Hill, which gave it the dominion of London, King Auberon came, as of old, out of Kensington Palace.

He had changed little, save for a streak or two of grey in his hair, for his face had always been old, and his step slow, and, as it were, decrepit.

If he looked old, it was not because of anything physical or mental. It was because he still wore, with a quaint conservatism, the frock-coat and high hat of the days before the great war. "I have survived the Deluge," he said. "I am a pyramid, and must behave as such."

As he passed up the street the Kensingtonians, in their picturesque blue smocks, saluted him as a King, and then looked after him as a curiosity. It seemed odd to them that men had once worn so elvish an attire.

The King, cultivating the walk attributed to the oldest inhabitant ("Gaffer Auberon" his friends were now confidentially desired to call him), went toddling northward. He paused, with reminiscence in his eye, at the Southern Gate of Notting Hill, one of those nine great gates of bronze and steel, wrought with reliefs of the old battles, by the hand of Chiffy himself.

"Ah!" he said, shaking his head and assuming an unnecessary air of age, and a provincialism of accent— "Ah! I mind when there warn't none of this here."

He passed through the Ossington Gate, surmounted by a great lion, wrought in red copper on yellow brass, with the motto, "Nothing Ill." The guard in red and gold saluted him with his halberd.

It was about sunset, and the lamps were being lit. Auberon paused to look at them, for they were Chiffy's finest work, and his artistic eye never failed to feast on them. In memory of the Great Battle of the Lamps, each great iron lamp was surmounted by a veiled figure, sword in hand, holding over the flame an iron hood or extinguisher, as if ready to let it fall if the armies of the South and West should again show their flags in the city. Thus no child in Notting Hill could play about the streets without the very lamp-posts reminding him of the salvation of his country in the dreadful year.

"Old Wayne was right in a way," commented the King. "The sword does make things beautiful. It has made the whole world romantic by now. And to think people once thought me a buffoon for suggesting a romantic Notting Hill. Deary me, deary me! (I think that is the expression)—it seems like a previous existence."

Turning a corner, he found himself in Pump Street, opposite the four shops which Adam Wayne had studied twenty years before. He entered idly the shop of Mr. Mead, the grocer. Mr. Mead was somewhat older, like the rest of the world, and his red beard, which he now wore with a moustache, and long and full, was partly blanched and discoloured. He was dressed in a long and richly embroidered robe of blue, brown, and crimson, interwoven with an Eastern complexity of pattern, and covered with obscure symbols and pictures, representing his wares passing from hand to hand and from nation to nation. Round his neck was the chain with the Blue Argosy cut in turquoise, which he wore as Grand Master of the Grocers. The whole shop had the sombre and sumptuous look of its owner. The wares were displayed as prominently as in the old days, but they were now blended and arranged with a sense of tint and grouping, too often neglected by the dim grocers of those forgotten days. The wares were shown plainly, but shown not so much as an old grocer would have shown his stock, but rather as an educated virtuoso would have shown his treasures. The tea was stored in great blue and green vases, inscribed with the nine indispensable sayings of the wise men of China. Other vases of a confused orange and purple, less rigid and dominant, more humble and dreamy, stored symbolically the tea of India. A row of caskets of a simple silvery metal contained tinned meats. Each was wrought with some rude but rhythmic form, as a shell, a horn, a fish, or an apple, to indicate what material had been canned in it.

"Your Majesty," said Mr. Mead, sweeping an Oriental reverence. "This is an honour to me, but yet more an honour to the city."

Auberon took off his hat.

"Mr. Mead," he said, "Notting Hill, whether in giving or taking, can deal in nothing but honour. Do you happen to sell liquorice?"

"Liquorice, sire," said Mr. Mead, "is not the least important of our benefits out of the dark heart of Arabia."

And going reverently towards a green and silver canister, made in the form of an Arabian mosque, he proceeded to serve his customer.

"I was just thinking, Mr. Mead," said the King, reflectively, "I don't know why I should think about it just now, but I was just thinking of twenty years ago. Do you remember the times before the war?"

The grocer, having wrapped up the liquorice sticks in a piece of paper (inscribed with some appropriate sentiment), lifted his large grey eyes dreamily, and looked at the darkening sky outside.

"Oh yes, your Majesty," he said. "I remember these streets before the Lord Provost began to rule us. I can't remember how we felt very well. All the great songs and the fighting change one so; and I don't think we can really estimate all we owe to the Provost; but I can remember his coming into this very shop twenty-two years ago, and I remember the things he said. The singular thing is that, as far as I remember, I thought the things he said odd at that time. Now it's the things that I said, as far as I can recall them, that seem to me odd—as odd as a madman's antics."

"Ah!" said the King; and looked at him with an unfathomable quietness.

"I thought nothing of being a grocer then," he said. "Isn't that odd enough for anybody? I thought nothing of all the wonderful places that my goods come from, and wonderful ways that they are made. I did not know that I was for all practical purposes a king with slaves spearing fishes near the secret pool, and gathering fruits in the islands under the world. My mind was a blank on the thing. I was as mad as a hatter."

The King turned also, and stared out into the dark, where the great lamps that commemorated the battle were already flaming.

"And is this the end of poor old Wayne?" he said, half to himself. "To inflame every one so much that he is lost himself in the blaze. Is this his victory that he, my incomparable Wayne, is now only one in a world of Waynes? Has he conquered and become by conquest commonplace? Must Mr. Mead, the grocer, talk as high as he? Lord! what a strange world in which a man cannot remain unique even by taking the trouble to go mad!"

And he went dreamily out of the shop.

He paused outside the next one almost precisely as the Provost had done two decades before.

"How uncommonly creepy this shop looks!" he said. "But yet somehow encouragingly creepy, invitingly creepy. It looks like something in a jolly old nursery story in which you are frightened out of your skin, and yet know that things always end well. The way those low sharp gables are carved like great black bat's wings folded down, and the way those queer-coloured bowls underneath are made to shine like giants' eye-balls. It looks like a benevolent warlock's hut. It is apparently a chemist's."

Almost as he spoke, Mr. Bowles, the chemist, came to his shop door in a long black velvet gown and hood, monastic as it were, but yet with a touch of the diabolic. His hair was still quite black, and his face even paler than of old. The only spot of colour he carried was a red star cut in some precious stone of strong tint, hung on his breast. He belonged to the Society of the Red Star of Charity, founded on the lamps displayed by doctors and chemists.

"A fine evening, sir," said the chemist. "Why, I can scarcely be mistaken in supposing it to be your Majesty. Pray step inside and share a bottle of sal-volatile, or anything that may take your fancy. As it happens, there is an old acquaintance of your Majesty's in my shop carousing (if I may be permitted the term) upon that beverage at this moment."

The King entered the shop, which was an Aladdin's garden of shades and hues, for as the chemist's scheme of colour was more brilliant than the grocer's scheme, so it was arranged with even more delicacy and fancy. Never, if the phrase may be employed, had such a nosegay of medicines been presented to the artistic eye.

But even the solemn rainbow of that evening interior was rivalled or even eclipsed by the figure standing in the centre of the shop. His form, which was a large and stately one, was clad in a brilliant blue velvet, cut in the richest Renaissance fashion, and slashed so as to show gleams and gaps of a wonderful lemon or pale yellow. He had several chains round his neck, and his plumes, which were of several tints of bronze and gold, hung down to the great gold hilt of his long sword. He was drinking a dose of sal-volatile, and admiring its opal tint. The King advanced with a slight mystification towards the tall figure, whose face was in shadow; then he said—

"By the Great Lord of Luck, Barker!"

The figure removed his plumed cap, showing the same dark head and long, almost equine face which the King had so often seen rising out of the high collar of Bond Street. Except for a grey patch on each temple, it was totally unchanged.

"Your Majesty," said Barker, "this is a meeting nobly retrospective, a meeting that has about it a certain October gold. I drink to old days;" and he finished his sal-volatile with simple feeling.

"I am delighted to see you again, Barker," said the King. "It is indeed long since we met. What with my travels in Asia Minor, and my book having to be written (you have read my 'Life of Prince Albert for Children,' of course?), we have scarcely met twice since the Great War. That is twenty years ago."

"I wonder," said Barker, thoughtfully, "if I might speak freely to your Majesty?"

"Well," said Auberon, "it's rather late in the day to start speaking respectfully. Flap away, my bird of freedom."

"Well, your Majesty," replied Barker, lowering his voice, "I don't think it will be so long to the next war."

"What do you mean?" asked Auberon.

"We will stand this insolence no longer," burst out Barker, fiercely. "We are not slaves because Adam Wayne twenty years ago cheated us with a water-pipe. Notting Hill is Notting Hill; it is not the world. We in South Kensington, we also have memories—ay, and hopes. If they fought for these trumpery shops and a few lamp posts, shall we not fight for the great High Street and the sacred Natural History Museum?"

"Great Heavens!" said the astounded Auberon. "Will wonders never cease? Have the two greatest marvels been achieved? Have you turned altruistic, and has Wayne turned selfish? Are you the patriot, and he the tyrant?"

"It is not from Wayne himself altogether that the evil comes," answered Barker. "He, indeed, is now mostly wrapped in dreams, and sits with his old sword beside the fire. But Notting Hill is the tyrant, your Majesty. Its Council and its crowds have been so intoxicated by the spreading over the whole city of Wayne's old ways and visions, that they try to meddle with every one, and rule every one, and civilise every one, and tell every one what is good for him. I do not deny the great impulse which his old war, wild as it seemed, gave to the civic life of our time. It came when I was still a young man, and I admit it enlarged my career. But we are not going to see our own cities flouted and thwarted from day to day because of something Wayne did for us all nearly a quarter of a century ago. I am just waiting here for news upon this very matter. It is rumoured that Notting Hill has vetoed the statue of General Wilson they are putting up opposite Chepstow Place. If that is so, it is a black and white shameless breach of the terms on which we surrendered to Turnbull after the battle of the Tower. We were to keep our own customs and self-government. If that is so—"

"It is so," said a deep voice; and both men turned round.

A burly figure in purple robes, with a silver eagle hung round his neck and moustaches almost as florid as his plumes, stood in the doorway.

"Yes," he said, acknowledging the King's start, "I am Provost Buck, and the news is true. These men of the Hill have forgotten that we fought round the Tower as well as they, and that it is sometimes foolish, as well as base, to despise the conquered."

"Let us step outside," said Barker, with a grim composure.

Buck did so, and stood rolling his eyes up and down the lamp-lit street.

"I would like to have a go at smashing all this," he muttered, "though I am over sixty. I would like—"

His voice ended in a cry, and he reeled back a step, with his hands to his eyes, as he had done in those streets twenty years before.

"Darkness!" he cried— "darkness again! What does it mean?"

For in truth every lamp in the street had gone out, so that they could not see even each other's outline, except faintly. The voice of the chemist came with startling cheerfulness out of the density.

"Oh, don't you know?" he said. "Did they never tell you this is the Feast of the Lamps, the anniversary of the great battle that almost lost and just saved Notting Hill? Don't you know, your Majesty, that on this night twenty-one years ago we saw Wilson's green uniforms charging down this street, and driving Wayne and Turnbull back upon the gas-works, fighting with their handful like fiends from hell? And that then, in that great hour, Wayne sprang through a window of the gas-works, with one blow of his hand brought darkness on the whole city, and then with a cry like a lion's, that was heard through four streets, flew at Wilson's men, sword in hand, and swept them, bewildered as they were, and ignorant of the map, clear out of the sacred street again? And don't you know that upon that night every year all lights are turned out for half an hour while we sing the Notting Hill anthem in the darkness? Hark! there it begins."

Through the night came a crash of drums, and then a strong swell of human voices—

"When the world was in the balance, there was night on Notting
    Hill,
(There was night on Notting Hill): it was nobler than the day;
On the cities where the lights are and the firesides glow,
From the seas and from the deserts came the thing we did not
    know,
Came the darkness, came the darkness, came the darkness on
    the foe,
And the old guard of God turned to bay.
For the old guard of God turns to bay, turns to bay,
And the stars fall down before it ere its banners fall to-day:
For when armies were around us as a howling and a horde,
When falling was the citadel and broken was the sword,
The darkness came upon them like the Dragon of the Lord,
When the old guard of God turned to bay."

The voices were just uplifting themselves in a second verse when they were stopped by a scurry and a yell. Barker had bounded into the street with a cry of "South Kensington!" and a drawn dagger. In less time than a man could blink, the whole packed street was full of curses and struggling. Barker was flung back against the shop-front, but used the second only to draw his sword as well as his dagger, and calling out, "This is not the first time I've come through the thick of you," flung himself again into the press. It was evident that he had drawn blood at last, for a more violent outcry arose, and many other knives and swords were discernible in the faint light. Barker, after having wounded more than one man, seemed on the point of being flung back again, when Buck suddenly stepped out into the street. He had no weapon, for he affected rather the peaceful magnificence of the great burgher, than the pugnacious dandyism which had replaced the old sombre dandyism in Barker. But with a blow of his clenched fist he broke the pane of the next shop, which was the old curiosity shop, and, plunging in his hand, snatched a kind of Japanese scimitar, and calling out, "Kensington! Kensington!" rushed to Barker's assistance.

Barker's sword was broken, but he was laying about him with his dagger. Just as Buck ran up, a man of Notting Hill struck Barker down, but Buck struck the man down on top of him, and Barker sprang up again, the blood running down his face.

Suddenly all these cries were cloven by a great voice, that seemed to fall out of heaven. It was terrible to Buck and Barker and the King, from its seeming to come out the empty skies; but it was more terrible because it was a familiar voice, and one which at the same time they had not heard for so long.

"Turn up the lights," said the voice from above them, and for a moment there was no reply, but only a tumult.

"In the name of Notting Hill and of the great Council of the City, turn up the lights."

There was again a tumult and a vagueness for a moment, then the whole street and every object in it sprang suddenly out of the darkness, as every lamp sprang into life. And looking up they saw, standing upon a balcony near the roof of one of the highest houses, the figure and the face of Adam Wayne, his red hair blowing behind him, a little streaked with grey.

"What is this, my people?" he said. "Is it altogether impossible to make a thing good without it immediately insisting on being wicked? The glory of Notting Hill in having achieved its independence, has been enough for me to dream of for many years, as I sat beside the fire. Is it really not enough for you, who have had so many other affairs to excite and distract you? Notting Hill is a nation. Why should it condescend to be a mere Empire? You wish to pull down the statue of General Wilson, which the men of Bayswater have so rightly erected in Westbourne Grove. Fools! Who erected that statue? Did Bayswater erect it? No. Notting Hill erected it. Do you not see that it is the glory of our achievement that we have infected the other cities with the idealism of Notting Hill? It is we who have created not only our own side, but both sides of this controversy. O too humble fools, why should you wish to destroy your enemies? You have done something more to them. You have created your enemies. You wish to pull down that gigantic silver hammer, which stands, like an obelisk, in the centre of the Broadway of Hammersmith. Fools! Before Notting Hill arose, did any person passing through Hammersmith Broadway expect to see there a gigantic silver hammer? You wish to abolish the great bronze figure of a knight standing upon the artificial bridge at Knightsbridge. Fools! Who would have thought of it before Notting Hill arose? I have even heard, and with deep pain I have heard it, that the evil eye of our imperial envy has been cast towards the remote horizon of the west, and that we have objected to the great black monument of a crowned raven, which commemorates the skirmish of Ravenscourt Park. Who created all these things? Were they there before we came? Cannot you be content with that destiny which was enough for Athens, which was enough for Nazareth? the destiny, the humble purpose, of creating a new world. Is Athens angry because Romans and Florentines have adopted her phraseology for expressing their own patriotism? Is Nazareth angry because as a little village it has become the type of all little villages out of which, as the Snobs say, no good can come? Has Athens asked every one to wear the chlamys? Are all followers of the Nazarene compelled to wear turbans. No! but the soul of Athens went forth and made men drink hemlock, and the soul of Nazareth went forth and made men consent to be crucified. So has the soul of Notting Hill gone forth and made men realise what it is to live in a city. Just as we inaugurated our symbols and ceremonies, so they have inaugurated theirs; and are you so mad as to contend against them? Notting Hill is right; it has always been right. It has moulded itself on its own necessities, its own *sine quâ non*; it has accepted its own ultimatum. Because it is a nation it has created itself; and because it is a nation it can destroy itself. Notting Hill shall always be the judge. If it is your will because of this matter of General Wilson's statue to make war upon Bayswater—"

A roar of cheers broke in upon his words, and further speech was impossible. Pale to the lips, the great patriot tried again and again to speak; but even his authority could not keep down the dark and roaring masses in the street below him. He said something further, but it was not audible. He descended at last sadly from the garret in which he lived, and mingled with the crowd at the foot of the houses. Finding General Turnbull, he put his hand on his shoulder with a queer affection and gravity, and said—

"To-morrow, old man, we shall have a new experience, as fresh as the flowers of spring. We shall be defeated. You and I have been through three battles together, and have somehow or other missed this peculiar delight. It is unfortunate that we shall not probably be able to exchange our experiences, because, as it most annoyingly happens, we shall probably both be dead."

Turnbull looked dimly surprised.

"I don't mind so much about being dead," he said, "but why should you say that we shall be defeated?"

"The answer is very simple," replied Wayne, calmly. "It is because we ought to be defeated. We have been in the most horrible holes before now; but in all those I was perfectly certain that the stars were on our side, and that we ought to get out. Now I know that we ought not to get out; and that takes away from me everything with which I won."

As Wayne spoke he started a little, for both men became aware that a third figure was listening to them—a small figure with wondering eyes.

"Is it really true, my dear Wayne," said the King, interrupting, "that you think you will be beaten to-morrow?"

"There can be no doubt about it whatever," replied Adam Wayne; "the real reason is the one of which I have just spoken. But as a concession to your materialism, I will add that they have an organised army of a hundred allied cities against our one. That in itself, however, would be unimportant."

Quin, with his round eyes, seemed strangely insistent.

"You are quite sure," he said, "that you must be beaten?"

"I am afraid," said Turnbull, gloomily, "that there can be no doubt about it."

"Then," cried the King, flinging out his arms, "give me a halberd! Give me a halberd, somebody! I desire all men to witness that I, Auberon,

King of England, do here and now abdicate, and implore the Provost of Notting Hill to permit me to enlist in his army. Give me a halberd!"

He seized one from some passing guard, and, shouldering it, stamped solemnly after the shouting columns of halberdiers which were, by this time, parading the streets. He had, however, nothing to do with the wrecking of the statue of General Wilson, which took place before morning.

II

The day was cloudy when Wayne went down to die with all his army in Kensington Gardens; it was cloudy again when that army had been swallowed up by the vast armies of a new world. There had been an almost uncanny interval of sunshine, in which the Provost of Notting Hill, with all the placidity of an onlooker, had gazed across to the hostile armies on the great spaces of verdure opposite; the long strips of green and blue and gold lay across the park in squares and oblongs like a proposition in Euclid wrought in a rich embroidery. But the sunlight was a weak and, as it were, a wet sunlight, and was soon swallowed up. Wayne spoke to the King, with a queer sort of coldness and languor, as to the military operations. It was as he had said the night before—that being deprived of his sense of an impracticable rectitude, he was, in effect, being deprived of everything. He was out of date, and at sea in a mere world of compromise and competition, of Empire against Empire, of the tolerably right and the tolerably wrong. When his eye fell on the King, however, who was marching very gravely with a top hat and a halberd, it brightened slightly.

"Well, your Majesty," he said, "you at least ought to be proud to-day. If your children are fighting each other, at least those who win are your children. Other kings have distributed justice, you have distributed life. Other kings have ruled a nation, you have created nations. Others have made kingdoms, you have begotten them. Look at your children, father!" and he stretched his hand out towards the enemy.

Auberon did not raise his eyes.

"See how splendidly," cried Wayne, "the new cities come on—the new cities from across the river. See where Battersea advances over there—under the flag of the Lost Dog; and Putney—don't you see the Man on the White Boar shining on their standard as the sun catches it? It is the coming of a new age, your Majesty. Notting Hill is not a common empire; it is a thing like Athens, the mother of a mode of life, of a manner of living, which shall renew the youth of the world—a thing like Nazareth. When I was young I remember, in the old dreary days, wiseacres used to write books about how trains would get faster, and all the world be one empire, and tram-cars go to the moon. And even as a child I used to say to myself, 'Far more likely that we shall go on the crusades again, or worship the gods of the city.' And so it has been. And I am glad, though this is my last battle."

Even as he spoke there came a crash of steel from the left, and he turned his head.

"Wilson!" he cried, with a kind of joy. "Red Wilson has charged our left. No one can hold him in; he eats swords. He is as keen a soldier as Turnbull, but less patient—less really great. Ha! and Barker is moving. How Barker has improved; how handsome he looks! It is not all having plumes; it is also having a soul in one's daily life. Ha!"

And another crash of steel on the right showed that Barker had closed with Notting Hill on the other side.

"Turnbull is there!" cried Wayne. "See him hurl them back! Barker is checked! Turnbull charges—wins! But our left is broken. Wilson has smashed Bowles and Mead, and may turn our flank. Forward, the Provost's Guard!"

And the whole centre moved forward, Wayne's face and hair and sword flaming in the van. The King ran suddenly forward.

The next instant a great jar that went through it told that it had met the enemy. And right over against them through the wood of their own weapons Auberon saw the Purple Eagle of Buck of North Kensington.

On the left Red Wilson was storming the broken ranks, his little green figure conspicuous even in the tangle of men and weapons, with the flaming red moustaches and the crown of laurel. Bowles slashed at his head and tore away some of the wreath, leaving the rest bloody, and, with a roar like a bull's, Wilson sprang at him, and, after a rattle of fencing, plunged his point into the chemist, who fell, crying, "Notting Hill!" Then the Notting Hillers wavered, and Bayswater swept them back in confusion. Wilson had carried everything before him.

On the right, however, Turnbull had carried the Red Lion banner with a rush against Barker's men, and the banner of the Golden Birds bore up with difficulty against it. Barker's men fell fast. In the centre Wayne and Buck were engaged, stubborn and confused. So far as the fighting went, it was precisely equal. But the fighting was a farce. For behind the three small armies with which Wayne's small army was engaged lay the great sea of the allied armies, which looked on as yet as scornful spectators, but could have broken all four armies by moving a finger.

Suddenly they did move. Some of the front contingents, the pastoral chiefs from Shepherd's Bush, with their spears and fleeces, were seen advancing, and the rude clans from Paddington Green. They were advancing for a very good reason. Buck, of North Kensington, was signalling wildly; he was surrounded, and totally cut off. His regiments were a struggling mass of people, islanded in a red sea of Notting Hill.

The allies had been too careless and confident. They had allowed Barker's force to be broken to pieces by Turnbull, and the moment that was done, the astute old leader of Notting Hill swung his men round and attacked Buck behind and on both sides. At the same moment Wayne cried, "Charge!" and struck him in front like a thunderbolt.

Two-thirds of Buck's men were cut to pieces before their allies could reach them. Then the sea of cities came on with their banners like breakers, and swallowed Notting Hill for ever. The battle was not over, for not one of Wayne's men would surrender, and it lasted till sundown, and long after. But it was decided; the story of Notting Hill was ended.

When Turnbull saw it, he ceased a moment from fighting, and looked round him. The evening sunlight struck his face; it looked like a child's.

"I have had my youth," he said. Then, snatching an axe from a man, he dashed into the thick of the spears of Shepherd's Bush, and died somewhere far in the depths of their reeling ranks. Then the battle roared on; every man of Notting Hill was slain before night.

Wayne was standing by a tree alone after the battle. Several men approached him with axes. One struck at him. His foot seemed partly to slip; but he flung his hand out, and steadied himself against the tree.

Barker sprang after him, sword in hand, and shaking with excitement.

"How large now, my lord," he cried, "is the Empire of Notting Hill?"

Wayne smiled in the gathering dark.

"Always as large as this," he said, and swept his sword round in a semicircle of silver.

Barker dropped, wounded in the neck; and Wilson sprang over his body like a tiger-cat, rushing at Wayne. At the same moment there came behind the Lord of the Red Lion a cry and a flare of yellow, and a mass of the West Kensington halberdiers ploughed up the slope, knee-deep in grass, bearing the yellow banner of the city before them, and shouting aloud.

At the same second Wilson went down under Wayne's sword, seemingly smashed like a fly. The great sword rose again like a bird, but Wilson seemed to rise with it, and, his sword being broken, sprang at Wayne's throat like a dog. The foremost of the yellow halberdiers had reached the tree and swung his axe above the struggling Wayne. With a curse the King whirled up his own halberd, and dashed the blade in the man's face. He reeled and rolled down the slope, just as the furious Wilson was flung on his back again. And again he was on his feet, and again at Wayne's throat. Then he was flung again, but this time laughing triumphantly. Grasped in his hand was the red and yellow favour that Wayne wore as Provost of Notting Hill. He had torn it from the place where it had been carried for twenty-five years.

With a shout the West Kensington men closed round Wayne, the great yellow banner flapping over his head.

"Where is your favour now, Provost?" cried the West Kensington leader.

And a laugh went up.

Adam struck at the standard-bearer and brought him reeling forward. As the banner stooped, he grasped the yellow folds and tore off a shred. A halberdier struck him on the shoulder, wounding bloodily.

"Here is one colour!" he cried, pushing the yellow into his belt; "and here!" he cried, pointing to his own blood— "here is the other."

At the same instant the shock of a sudden and heavy halberd laid the King stunned or dead. In the wild visions of vanishing consciousness, he saw again something that belonged to an utterly forgotten time, something that he had seen somewhere long ago in a restaurant. He saw, with his swimming eyes, red and yellow, the colours of Nicaragua.

Quin did not see the end. Wilson, wild with joy, sprang again at Adam Wayne, and the great sword of Notting Hill was whirled above once more. Then men ducked instinctively at the rushing noise of the sword coming down out of the sky, and Wilson of Bayswater was smashed and wiped down upon the floor like a fly. Nothing was left of him but a wreck; but the blade that had broken him was broken. In dying he had snapped the great sword and the spell of it; the sword of Wayne was broken at the hilt. One rush of the enemy carried Wayne by force against the tree. They were too close to use halberd or even sword; they were breast to breast, even nostrils to nostrils. But Buck got his dagger free.

"Kill him!" he cried, in a strange stifled voice. "Kill him! Good or bad, he is none of us! Do not be blinded by the face!... God! have we not been blinded all along!" and he drew his arm back for a stab, and seemed to close his eyes.

Wayne did not drop the hand that hung on to the tree-branch. But a mighty heave went over his breast and his whole huge figure, like an earthquake over great hills. And with that convulsion of effort he rent the branch out of the tree, with tongues of torn wood; and, swaying it once only, he let the splintered club fall on Buck, breaking his neck. The planner of the Great Road fell face foremost dead, with his dagger in a grip of steel.

"For you and me, and for all brave men, my brother," said Wayne, in his strange chant, "there is good wine poured in the inn at the end of the world."

The packed men made another lurch or heave towards him; it was almost too dark to fight clearly. He caught hold of the oak again, this time getting his hand into a wide crevice and grasping, as it were, the bowels of the tree.

The whole crowd, numbering some thirty men, made a rush to tear him away from it; they hung on with all their weight and numbers, and nothing stirred. A solitude could not have been stiller than that group of straining men. Then there was a faint sound.

"His hand is slipping," cried two men in exultation.

"You don't know much of him," said another, grimly (a man of the old war). "More likely his bone cracks."

"It is neither—by God, it is neither!" said one of the first two.

"What is it, then?" asked the second.

"The tree is falling," he replied.

"As the tree falleth, so shall it lie," said Wayne's voice out of the darkness, and it had the same sweet and yet horrible air that it had had throughout, of coming from a great distance, from before or after the event. Even when he was struggling like an eel or battering like a madman, he spoke like a spectator. "As the tree falleth, so shall it lie," he said. "Men have called that a gloomy text. It is the essence of all exultation. I am doing now what I have done all my life, what is the only happiness, what is the only universality. I am clinging to something. Let it fall, and there let it lie. Fools, you go about and see the kingdoms of the earth, and are liberal and wise and cosmopolitan, which is all that the devil can give you—all that he could offer to Christ, only to be spurned away. I am doing what the truly wise do. When a child goes out into the garden and takes hold of a tree, saying, 'Let this tree be all I have,' that moment its roots take hold on hell and its branches on the stars. The joy I have is what the lover knows when a woman is everything. It is what a savage knows when his idol is everything. It is what I know when Notting Hill is everything. I have a city. Let it stand or fall."

As he spoke, the turf lifted itself like a living thing, and out of it rose slowly, like crested serpents, the roots of the oak. Then the great head of the tree, that seemed a green cloud among grey ones, swept the sky suddenly like a broom, and the whole tree heeled over like a ship, smashing every one in its fall.

III

Two Voices

In a place in which there was total darkness for hours, there was also for hours total silence. Then a voice spoke out of the darkness, no one could have told from where, and said aloud—

"So ends the Empire of Notting Hill. As it began in blood, so it ended in blood, and all things are always the same."

And there was silence again, and then again there was a voice, but it had not the same tone; it seemed that it was not the same voice.

"If all things are always the same, it is because they are always heroic. If all things are always the same, it is because they are always new. To each man one soul only is given; to each soul only is given a little power—the power at some moments to outgrow and swallow up the stars. If age after age that power comes upon men, whatever gives it to them is great. Whatever makes men feel old is mean—an empire or a skin-flint shop. Whatever makes men feel young is great—a great war or a love-story. And in the darkest of the books of God there is written a truth that is also a riddle. It is of the new things that men tire—of fashions and proposals and improvements and change. It is the old things that startle and intoxicate. It is the old things that are young. There is no sceptic who does not feel that many have doubted before. There is no rich and fickle man who does not feel that all his novelties are ancient. There is no worshipper of change who does not feel upon his neck the vast weight of the weariness of the universe. But we who do the old things are fed by nature with a perpetual infancy. No man who is in love thinks that any one has been in love before. No woman who has a child thinks that there have been such things as children. No people that fight for their own city are haunted with the burden of the

148

broken empires. Yes, O dark voice, the world is always the same, for it is always unexpected."

A little gust of wind blew through the night, and then the first voice answered—

"But in this world there are some, be they wise or foolish, whom nothing intoxicates. There are some who see all your disturbances like a cloud of flies. They know that while men will laugh at your Notting Hill, and will study and rehearse and sing of Athens and Jerusalem, Athens and Jerusalem were silly suburbs like your Notting Hill. They know that the earth itself is a suburb, and can feel only drearily and respectably amused as they move upon it."

"They are philosophers or they are fools," said the other voice. "They are not men. Men live, as I say, rejoicing from age to age in something fresher than progress—in the fact that with every baby a new sun and a new moon are made. If our ancient humanity were a single man, it might perhaps be that he would break down under the memory of so many loyalties, under the burden of so many diverse heroisms, under the load and terror of all the goodness of men. But it has pleased God so to isolate the individual soul that it can only learn of all other souls by hearsay, and to each one goodness and happiness come with the youth and violence of lightning, as momentary and as pure. And the doom of failure that lies on all human systems does not in real fact affect them any more than the worms of the inevitable grave affect a children's game in a meadow. Notting Hill has fallen; Notting Hill has died. But that is not the tremendous issue. Notting Hill has lived."

"But if," answered the other voice, "if what is achieved by all these efforts be only the common contentment of humanity, why do men so extravagantly toil and die in them? Has nothing been done by Notting Hill than any chance clump of farmers or clan of savages would not have done without it? What might have been done to Notting Hill if the world had been different may be a deep question; but there is a deeper. What could have happened to the world if Notting Hill had never been?"

The other voice replied—

"The same that would have happened to the world and all the starry systems if an apple-tree grew six apples instead of seven; something would have been eternally lost. There has never been anything in the world absolutely like Notting Hill. There will never be anything quite like it to the crack of doom. I cannot believe anything but that God loved it as He must surely love anything that is itself and unreplaceable. But even for that I do not care. If God, with all His thunders, hated it, I loved it."

And with the voice a tall, strange figure lifted itself out of the *débris* in the half-darkness.

The other voice came after a long pause, and as it were hoarsely.

"But suppose the whole matter were really a hocus-pocus. Suppose that whatever meaning you may choose in your fancy to give to it, the real meaning of the whole was mockery. Suppose it was all folly. Suppose—"

"I have been in it," answered the voice from the tall and strange figure, "and I know it was not."

A smaller figure seemed half to rise in the dark.

"Suppose I am God," said the voice, "and suppose I made the world in idleness. Suppose the stars, that you think eternal, are only the idiot fireworks of an everlasting schoolboy. Suppose the sun and the moon, to which you sing alternately, are only the two eyes of one vast and sneering giant, opened alternately in a never-ending wink. Suppose the trees, in my eyes, are as foolish as enormous toad-stools. Suppose Socrates and Charlemagne are to me only beasts, made funnier by walking on their hind legs. Suppose I am God, and having made things, laugh at them."

"And suppose I am man," answered the other. "And suppose that I give the answer that shatters even a laugh. Suppose I do not laugh back at you, do not blaspheme you, do not curse you. But suppose, standing up straight under the sky, with every power of my being, I thank you for the fools' paradise you have made. Suppose I praise you, with a literal pain of ecstasy, for the jest that has brought me so terrible a joy. If we have taken the child's games, and given them the seriousness of a Crusade, if we have drenched your grotesque Dutch garden with the blood of martyrs, we have turned a nursery into a temple. I ask you, in the name of Heaven, who wins?"

The sky close about the crests of the hills and trees was beginning to turn from black to grey, with a random suggestion of the morning. The slight figure seemed to crawl towards the larger one, and the voice was more human.

"But suppose, friend," it said, "suppose that, in a bitterer and more real sense, it was all a mockery. Suppose that there had been, from the beginning of these great wars, one who watched them with a sense that is beyond expression, a sense of detachment, of responsibility, of irony, of agony. Suppose that there were one who knew it was all a joke."

The tall figure answered—

"He could not know it. For it was not all a joke."

And a gust of wind blew away some clouds that sealed the sky-line, and showed a strip of silver behind his great dark legs. Then the other voice came, having crept nearer still.

"Adam Wayne," it said, "there are men who confess only in *articulo mortis*; there are people who blame themselves only when they can no longer help others. I am one of them. Here, upon the field of the bloody end of it all, I come to tell you plainly what you would never understand before. Do you know who I am?"

"I know you, Auberon Quin," answered the tall figure, "and I shall be glad to unburden your spirit of anything that lies upon it."

"Adam Wayne," said the other voice, "of what I have to say you cannot in common reason be glad to unburden me. Wayne, it was all a joke. When I made these cities, I cared no more for them than I care for a centaur, or a merman, or a fish with legs, or a pig with feathers, or any other absurdity. When I spoke to you solemnly and encouragingly about the flag of your freedom and the peace of your city, I was playing a vulgar practical joke on an honest gentleman, a vulgar practical joke that has lasted for twenty years. Though no one could believe it of me, perhaps, it is the truth that I am a man both timid and tender-hearted. I never dared in the early days of your hope, or the central days of your supremacy, to tell you this; I never dared to break the colossal calm of your face. God knows why I should do it now, when my farce has ended in tragedy and the ruin of all your people! But I say it now. Wayne, it was done as a joke."

There was silence, and the freshening breeze blew the sky clearer and clearer, leaving great spaces of the white dawn.

At last Wayne said, very slowly— "You did it all only as a joke?"

"Yes," said Quin, briefly.

"When you conceived the idea," went on Wayne, dreamily, "of an army for Bayswater and a flag for Notting Hill, there was no gleam, no suggestion in your mind that such things might be real and passionate?"

"No," answered Auberon, turning his round white face to the morning with a dull and splendid sincerity; "I had none at all."

Wayne sprang down from the height above him and held out his hand.

"I will not stop to thank you," he said, with a curious joy in his voice, "for the great good for the world you have actually wrought. All that I think of that I have said to you a moment ago, even when I thought that your voice was the voice of a derisive omnipotence, its laughter older than the winds of heaven. But let me say what is immediate and true. You and I, Auberon Quin, have both of us throughout our lives been again and again called mad. And we are mad. We are mad, because we are not two men, but one man. We are mad, because we are two lobes of the same brain, and that brain has been cloven in two. And if you ask for the proof of it, it is not hard to find. It is not merely that you, the humorist, have been in these dark days stripped of the joy of gravity. It is not merely that I, the fanatic, have had to grope without humour. It is that, though we seem to be opposite in everything, we have been opposite like man and woman, aiming at the same moment at the same practical thing. We are the father and the mother of the Charter of the Cities."

Quin looked down at the *débris* of leaves and timber, the relics of the battle and stampede, now glistening in the growing daylight, and finally said—

"Yet nothing can alter the antagonism—the fact that I laughed at these things and you adored them."

Wayne's wild face flamed with something god-like, as he turned it to be struck by the sunrise.

"I know of something that will alter that antagonism, something that is outside us, something that you and I have all our lives perhaps taken too little account of. The equal and eternal human being will alter that antagonism, for the human being sees no real antagonism between laughter and respect, the human being, the common man, whom mere geniuses like you and me can only worship like a god. When dark and dreary days come, you and I are necessary, the pure fanatic, the pure satirist. We have between us remedied a great wrong. We have lifted the modern cities into that poetry which every one who knows mankind knows to be immeasurably more common than the commonplace. But in healthy people there is no war between us. We are but the two lobes of the brain of a ploughman. Laughter and love are everywhere. The cathedrals, built in the ages that loved God, are full of blasphemous grotesques. The mother laughs continually at the child, the lover laughs continually at the lover, the wife at the husband, the friend at the friend. Auberon Quin, we have been too long separated; let us go out together. You have a halberd and I a sword, let us start our wanderings over the world. For we are its two essentials. Come, it is already day."

In the blank white light Auberon hesitated a moment. Then he made the formal salute with his halberd, and they went away together into the unknown world.

.

The Flying Inn

I

A Sermon on Inns

The sea was a pale elfin green and the afternoon had already felt the fairy touch of evening as a young woman with dark hair, dressed in a crinkly copper-coloured sort of dress of the artistic order, was walking rather listlessly along the parade of Pebblewick-on-Sea, trailing a parasol and looking out upon the sea's horizon. She had a reason for looking instinctively out at the sea-line; a reason that many young women have had in the history of the world. But there was no sail in sight.

On the beach below the parade were a succession of small crowds, surrounding the usual orators of the seaside; whether niggers or socialists, whether clowns or clergymen. Here would stand a man doing something or other with paper boxes; and the holiday makers would watch him for hours in the hope of some time knowing what it was that he was doing with them. Next to him would be a man in a top hat with a very big Bible and a very small wife, who stood silently beside him, while he fought with his clenched fist against the heresy of Milnian Sublapsarianism so wide-spread in fashionable watering-places. It was not easy to follow him, he was so very much excited; but every now and then the words "our Sublapsarian friends" would recur with a kind of wailing sneer. Next was a young man talking of nobody knew what (least of all himself), but apparently relying for public favour mainly on having a ring of carrots round his hat. He had more money lying in front of him than the others. Next were niggers. Next was a children's service conducted by a man with a long neck who beat time with a little wooden spade. Farther along there was an atheist, in a towering rage, who pointed every now and then at the children's service and spoke of Nature's fairest things being corrupted with the secrets of the Spanish

157

Inquisition—by the man with the little spade, of course. The atheist (who wore a red rosette) was very withering to his own audience as well. "Hypocrites!" he would say; and then they would throw him money. "Dupes and dastards!" and then they would throw him more money. But between the atheist and the children's service was a little owlish man in a red fez, weakly waving a green gamp umbrella. His face was brown and wrinkled like a walnut, his nose was of the sort we associate with Judaea, his beard was the sort of black wedge we associate rather with Persia. The young woman had never seen him before; he was a new exhibit in the now familiar museum of cranks and quacks. The young woman was one of those people in whom a real sense of humour is always at issue with a certain temperamental tendency to boredom or melancholia; and she lingered a moment, and leaned on the rail to listen.

It was fully four minutes before she could understand a word the man was saying; he spoke English with so extraordinary an accent that she supposed at first that he was talking in his own oriental tongue. All the noises of that articulation were odd; the most marked was an extreme prolongation of the short "u" into "oo"; as in "poo-oot" for "put." Gradually the girl got used to the dialect, and began to understand the words; though some time elapsed even then before she could form any conjecture of their subject matter. Eventually it appeared to her that he had some fad about English civilisation having been founded by the Turks; or, perhaps by the Saracens after their victory in the Crusades. He also seemed to think that Englishmen would soon return to this way of thinking; and seemed to be urging the spread of teetotalism as an evidence of it. The girl was the only person listening to him.

"Loo-ook," he said, wagging a curled brown finger, "loo-ook at your own inns" (which he pronounced as "ince"). "Your inns of which you write in your boo-ooks! Those inns were not poo-oot up in the beginning to sell ze alcoholic Christian drink. They were put up to sell ze non-alcoholic Islamic drinks. You can see this in the names of your inns. They are eastern names, Asiatic names. You have a famous public house to which your omnibuses go on the pilgrimage. It is called the Elephant and Castle. That is not an English name. It is an Asiatic name. You will say there are castles in England, and I will agree with you. There is the Windsor Castle. But where," he cried sternly, shaking his green umbrella at the girl in an angry oratorical triumph, "where is the Windsor Elephant? I have searched all Windsor Park. No elephants."

The girl with the dark hair smiled, and began to think that this man was better than any of the others. In accordance with the strange system of concurrent religious endowment which prevails at watering-places, she dropped a two shilling piece into the round copper tray beside him. With honourable and disinterested eagerness, the old gentleman in the red fez took no notice of this, but went on warmly, if obscurely, with his argument.

"Then you have a place of drink in this town which you call The Bool!"

"We generally call it The Bull," said the interested young lady, with a very melodious voice.

"You have a place of drink, which you call The Bool," he reiterated in a sort of abstract fury, "and surely you see that this is all vary ridiculous!"

"No, no!" said the girl, softly, and in deprecation.

"Why should there be a Bull?" he cried, prolonging the word in his own way. "Why should there be a Bull in connection with a festive locality? Who thinks about a Bull in gardens of delight? What need is there of a Bull when we watch the tulip-tinted maidens dance or pour the sparkling sherbert? You yourselves, my friends?" And he looked around radiantly, as if addressing an enormous mob. "You yourselves have a proverb, 'It is not calculated to promote prosperity to have a Bull in a china shop.' Equally, my friends, it would not be calculated to promote prosperity to have a Bull in a wine shop. All this is clear."

He stuck his umbrella upright in the sand and struck one finger against another, like a man getting to business at last.

"It iss as clear as the sun at noon," he said solemnly. "It iss as clear as the sun at noon that this word Bull, which is devoid of restful and pleasurable associations, is but the corruption of another word, which possesses restful and pleasurable associations. The word is not Bull; it is the Bul-Bul!" His voice rose suddenly like a trumpet and he spread abroad his hands like the fans of a tropic palm-tree.

After this great effect he was a little more subdued and leaned gravely on his umbrella. "You will find the same trace of Asiatic nomenclature in the names of all your English inns," he went on. "Nay, you will find it, I am almost certain, in all your terms in any way connected with your revelries and your reposes. Why, my good friends, the very name of that insidious spirit by which you make strong your drinks is an Arabic word: alcohol. It is obvious, is it not, that this is the Arabic article 'Al,' as in Alhambra, as in Algebra; and we need not pause here to pursue its many appearances in connection with your festive institutions, as in your Alsop's beer, your Ally Sloper, and your partly joyous institution of the Albert Memorial. Above all, in your greatest feasting day—your Christmas day—which you so erroneously suppose to be connected with your religion, what do you say then? Do you say the names of the Christian Nations? Do you say, 'I will have a little France. I will have a little Ireland. I will have a little Scotland. I will have a little Spain?' No-o." And the noise of the negative seemed to waggle as does the bleating of a sheep. "You say, 'I will have a little Turkey,' which is your name for the Country of the Servant of the Prophet!"

And once more he stretched out his arms sublimely to the east and west and appealed to earth and heaven. The young lady, looking at the sea-green horizon with a smile, clapped her grey gloved hands softly together as if at a peroration. But the little old man with the fez was far from exhausted yet.

"In reply to this you will object—" he began.

"O no, no," breathed the young lady in a sort of dreamy rapture. "I don't object. I don't object the littlest bit!"

"In reply to this you will object—" proceeded her preceptor, "that some inns are actually named after the symbols of your national superstitions. You will hasten to point out to me that the Golden Cross is situated opposite Charing Cross, and you will expatiate at length on King's Cross, Gerrard's Cross and the many crosses that are to be found in or near London. But you must not forget," and here he wagged his green umbrella roguishly at the girl, as if he was going to poke her with it, "none of you, my friends, must forget what a large number of Crescents there are in London! Denmark Crescent; Mornington Crescent! St. Mark's Crescent! St. George's Crescent! Grosvenor Crescent! Regent's Park Crescent! Nay, Royal Crescent! And why should we forget Pelham Crescent? Why, indeed? Everywhere, I say, homage paid to the holy symbol of the religion of the Prophet! Compare with this network and pattern of crescents, this city almost consisting of crescents, the meagre array of crosses, which remain to attest the ephemeral superstition to which you were, for one weak moment, inclined."

The crowds on the beach were rapidly thinning as tea-time drew nearer. The west grew clearer and clearer with the evening, till the sunshine seemed to have got behind the pale green sea and be shining through, as through a wall of thin green glass. The very transparency of sky and sea might have to this girl, for whom the sea was the romance and the tragedy, the hint of a sort of radiant hopelessness. The flood made of a million emeralds was ebbing as slowly as the sun was sinking: but the river of human nonsense flowed on for ever.

"I will not for one moment maintain," said the old gentleman, "that there are no difficulties in my case; or that all the examples are as obviously true as those that I have just demonstrated. No-o. It is obvious, let us say, that the 'Saracen's Head' is a corruption of the historic truth 'The Saracen is Ahead'—I am far from saying it is equally obvious that the 'Green Dragon' was originally 'the Agreeing Dragoman'; though I hope to prove in my book that it is so. I will only say here that it is su-urely more probable that one poo-ooting himself forward to attract the wayfarer in the desert, would compare himself to a friendly and persuadable guide or courier, rather than to a voracious monster. Sometimes the true origin is very hard to trace; as in the inn that commemorates our great Moslem Warrior, Amir Ali Ben Bhoze, whom you have so quaintly abbreviated into Admiral Benbow. Sometimes it is even more difficult for the seeker after truth. There is a place of drink near to here called 'The Old Ship'—"

The eyes of the girl remained on the ring of the horizon as rigid as the ring itself; but her whole face had coloured and altered. The sands were almost emptied by now: the atheist was as non-existent as his God; and those who had hoped to know what was being done to the paper boxes had gone away to their tea without knowing it. But the young woman still leaned on the railing. Her face was suddenly alive; and it looked as if her body could not move.

"It shood be admitted—" bleated the old man with the green umbrella, "that there is no literally self-evident trace of the Asiatic nomenclature in the words 'the old ship.' But even here the see-eeker after Truth can poot himself in touch with facts. I questioned the proprietor of 'The Old Ship' who is, according to such notes as I have kept, a Mr. Pumph."

The girl's lip trembled.

"Poor old Hump!" she said. "Why, I'd forgotten about him. He must be very nearly as worried as I am! I hope this man won't be too silly about this! I'd rather it weren't about this!"

"And Mr. Pumph to-old me the inn was named by a vary intimate friend of his, an Irishman who had been a Captain in the Britannic Royal Navy, but had resigned his po-ost in anger at the treatment of Ireland. Though quitting the service, he retained joost enough of the superstition of your western sailors, to wish his friend's inn to be named after his old ship. But as the name of the ship was 'The United Kingdom—'"

His female pupil, if she could not exactly be said to be sitting at his feet, was undoubtedly leaning out very eagerly above his head. Amid the solitude of the sands she called out in a loud and clear voice, "Can you tell me the Captain's name?"

The old gentleman jumped, blinked and stared like a startled owl. Having been talking for hours as if he had an audience of thousands, he seemed suddenly very much embarrassed to find that he had even an audience of one. By this time they seemed to be almost the only human creatures along the shore; almost the only living creatures, except the seagulls. The sun, in dropping finally, seemed to have broken as a blood orange might break; and lines of blood-red light were spilt along the split, low, level skies. This abrupt and belated brilliance took all the colour out of the man's red cap and green umbrella; but his dark figure, distinct against the sea and the sunset, remained the same, save that it was more agitated than before.

"The name," he said, "the Captain's name. I—I understood it was Dalroy. But what I wish to indicate, what I wish to expound, is that here again the seeker after truth can find the connection of his ideas. It was explained to me by Mr. Pumph that he was rearranging the place of festivity, in no inconsiderable proportion because of the anticipated return of the Captain in question, who had, as it appeared, taken service in some not very large Navy, but had left it and was coming home. Now, mark all of you, my friends," he said to the seagulls, "that even here the chain of logic holds."

He said it to the seagulls because the young lady, after staring at him with starry eyes for a moment and leaning heavily on the railing,

had turned her back and disappeared rapidly into the twilight. After her
hasty steps had fallen silent there was no other noise than the faint but
powerful purring of the now distant sea, the occasional shriek of a sea-
bird, and the continuous sound of a soliloquy.

"Mark, all of you," continued the man flourishing his green umbrella so furiously that it almost flew open like a green flag unfurled,
and then striking it deep in the sand, in the sand in which his fighting
fathers had so often struck their tents, "mark all of you this marvellous
fact! That when, being for a time, for a time, astonished—embarrassed—
brought up as you would say short—by the absence of any absolute
evidence of Eastern influence in the phrase 'the old ship,' I inquired
from what country the Captain was returning, Mr. Pumph said to me in
solemnity, 'From Turkey.' From Turkey! From the nearest country of
the Religion! I know men say it is not our country; that no man knows
where we come from, of what is our country. What does it matter where
we come from if we carry a message from Paradise? With a great gal-
loping of horses we carry it, and have no time to stop in places. But
what we bring is the only creed that has regarded what you will call in
your great words the virginity of a man's reason, that has put no man
higher than a prophet, and has respected the solitude of God."

And again he spread his arms out, as if addressing a mass meeting
of millions, all alone on the dark seashore.

II

THE END OF OLIVE ISLAND

The great sea-dragon of the changing colours that wriggles round the world like a chameleon, was pale green as it washed on Pebblewick, but strong blue where it broke on the Ionian Isles. One of the innumerable islets, hardly more than a flat white rock in the azure expanse, was celebrated as the Isle of Olives; not because it was rich in such vegetation, but because, by some freak of soil or climate, two or three little olives grew there to an unparalleled height. Even in the full heat of the South it is very unusual for an olive tree to grow any taller than a small pear tree; but the three olives that stood up as signals on this sterile place might well be mistaken, except for the shape, for moderate sized pines or larches of the north. It was also connected with some ancient Greek legend about Pallas the patroness of the olive; for all that sea was alive with the first fairyland of Hellas; and from the platform of marble under the olive trees could be seen the grey outline of Ithaca.

On the island and under the trees was a table set in the open air and covered with papers and inkstands. At the table were sitting four men, two in uniform and two in plain black clothes. Aides-de-camps, equerries and such persons stood in a group in the background; and behind them a string of two or three silent battle-ships lay along the sea. For peace was being given to Europe.

There had just come to an end the long agony of one of the many unsuccessful efforts to break the strength of Turkey and save the small Christian tribes. There had been many other such meetings in the later phases of the matter as, one after another, the smaller nations gave up the struggle, or the greater nations came in to coerce them. But the

interested parties had now dwindled to these four. For the Powers of
Europe being entirely agreed on the necessity for peace on a Turkish
basis, were content to leave the last negotiations to England and Germany, who could be trusted to enforce it; there was a representative of
the Sultan, of course; and there was a representative of the only enemy
of the Sultan who had not hitherto come to terms.

For one tiny power had alone carried on the war month after month,
and with a tenacity and temporary success that was a new nine-days
marvel every morning. An obscure and scarcely recognized prince calling himself the King of Ithaca had filled the Eastern Mediterranean
with exploits that were not unworthy of the audacious parallel that the
name of his island suggested. Poets could not help asking if it were
Odysseus come again; patriotic Greeks, even if they themselves had
been forced to lay down their arms, could not help feeling curious as to
what Greek race or name was boasted by the new and heroic royal house.
It was, therefore, with some amusement that the world at last discovered that the descendant of Ulysses was a cheeky Irish adventurer named
Patrick Dalroy; who had once been in the English Navy, had got into a
quarrel through his Fenian sympathies and resigned his commission.
Since then he had seen many adventures in many uniforms; and always
got himself or some one else into hot water with an extraordinary mixture of cynicism and quixotry. In his fantastic little kingdom, of course,
he had been his own General, his own Admiral, his own Foreign Secretary and his own Ambassador; but he was always careful to follow the
wishes of his people in the essentials of peace and war; and it was at
their direction that he had come to lay down his sword at last. Besides
his professional skill, he was chiefly famous for his enormous bodily
strength and stature. It is the custom in newspapers nowadays to say that
mere barbaric muscular power is valueless in modern military actions,
but this view may be as much exaggerated as its opposite. In such wars
as these of the Near East, where whole populations are slightly armed
and personal assault is common, a leader who can defend his head often
has a real advantage; and it is not true, even in a general way, that strength
is of no use. This was admitted by Lord Ivywood, the English Minister,
who was pointing out in detail to King Patrick the hopeless superiority
of the light pattern of Turkish field gun; and the King of Ithaca, remarking that he was quite convinced, said he would take it with him,

and ran away with it under his arm. It would be conceded by the greatest of the Turkish warriors, the terrifying Oman Pasha, equally famous for his courage in war and his cruelty in peace; but who carried on his brow a scar from Patrick's sword, taken after three hours mortal combat—and taken without spite or shame, be it said, for the Turk is always at his best in that game. Nor would the quality be doubted by Mr. Hart, a financial friend of the German Minister, whom Patrick Dalroy, after asking him which of his front windows he would prefer to be thrown into, threw into his bedroom window on the first floor with so considerate an exactitude that he alighted on the bed, where he was in a position to receive any medical attention. But, when all is said, one muscular Irish gentleman on an island cannot fight all Europe for ever, and he came, with a kind of gloomy good humour, to offer the terms now dictated to him by his adopted country. He could not even knock all the diplomatists down (for which he possessed both the power and the inclination), for he realised, with the juster part of his mind, that they were only obeying orders, as he was. So he sat heavily and sleepily at the little table, in the green and white uniform of the Navy of Ithaca (invented by himself); a big bull of a man, monstrously young for his size, with a bull neck and two blue bull's eyes for eyes, and red hair rising so steadily off his scalp that it looked as if his head had caught fire: as some said it had.

The most dominant person present was the great Oman Pasha himself, with his strong face starved by the asceticism of war, his hair and mustache seeming rather blasted with lightning than blanched with age; a red fez on his head, and between the red fez and mustache, a scar at which the King of Ithaca did not look. His eyes had an awful lack of expression.

Lord Ivywood, the English Minister, was probably the handsomest man in England, save that he was almost colourless both in hair and complexion. Against that blue marble sea he might almost have been one of its old marble statues that are faultless in line but show nothing but shades of grey or white. It seemed a mere matter of the luck of lighting whether his hair looked dull silver or pale brown; and his splendid mask never changed in colour or expression. He was one of the last of the old Parliamentary orators; and yet he was probably a comparatively young man; he could make anything he had to mention blossom into verbal beauty; yet his face remained dead while his lips were alive. He had little old-fashioned ways, as out of old Parliaments; for instance, he would always stand up, as in a Senate, to speak to those three other men, alone on a rock in the ocean.

In all this he perhaps appeared more personal in contrast to the man sitting next to him, who never spoke at all but whose face seemed to speak for him. He was Dr. Gluck, the German Minister, whose face had nothing German about it; neither the German vision nor the German sleep. His face was as vivid as a highly coloured photograph and altered like a cinema: but his scarlet lips never moved in speech. His almond eyes seemed to shine with all the shifting fires of the opal; his small, curled black mustache seemed sometimes almost to hoist itself afresh, like a live, black snake; but there came from him no sound. He put a paper in front of Lord Ivywood. Lord Ivywood took a pair of eyeglasses to read it, and looked ten years older by the act.

It was merely a statement of agenda; of the few last things to be settled at this last conference. The first item ran:

"The Ithacan Ambassador asks that the girls taken to harems after the capture of Pylos be restored to their families. This cannot be granted." Lord Ivywood rose. The mere beauty of his voice startled everyone who had not heard it before.

"Your Excellencies and gentlemen," he said, "a statement to whose policy I by no means assent, but to whose historic status I could not conceivably aspire, has familiarised you with a phrase about peace with honour. But when we have to celebrate a peace between such historic soldiers as Oman Pasha and His Majesty the King of Ithaca, I think we may say that it is peace with glory."

He paused for half an instant; yet even the silence of sea and rock seemed full of multitudinous applause, so perfectly had the words been spoken.

"I think there is but one thought among us, whatever our many just objections through these long and harassing months of negotiations— I think there is but one thought now. That the peace may be as full as the war—that the peace may be as fearless as the war."

Once more he paused an instant; and felt a phantom clapping, as it were, not from the hands but the heads of the men.

He went on.

"If we are to leave off fighting, we may surely leave off haggling. A statute of limitations or, if you will, an amnesty, is surely proper when so sublime a peace seals so sublime a struggle. And if there be anything in which an old diplomatist may advise you, I would most strongly say this: that there should be no new disturbance of whatever amicable or domestic ties have been formed during this disturbed time. I will admit I am sufficiently old-fashioned to think any interference with the interior life of the family a precedent of no little peril. Nor will I be so illiberal as not to extend to the ancient customs of Islam what I would extend to the ancient customs of Christianity. A suggestion has been brought before us that we should enter into a renewed war of recrimination as to whether certain women have left their homes with or without their own consent. I can conceive no controversy more perilous to begin or more impossible to conclude. I will venture to say that I express all your thoughts, when I say that, whatever wrongs may have been wrought on either side, the homes, the marriages, the family arrangements of this great Ottoman Empire, shall remain as they are today."

No one moved except Patrick Dalroy, who put his hand on his sword-hilt for a moment and looked at them all with bursting eyes; then his hand fell and he laughed out loud and sudden.

Lord Ivywood took no notice, but picked up the agenda paper again, and again fitted on the glasses that made him look older. He read the second item—needless to say, not aloud. The German Minister with the far from German face, had written this note for him:

"Both Coote and the Bernsteins insist there must be Chinese for the marble. Greeks cannot be trusted in the quarries just now."

"But while," continued Lord Ivywood, "we desire these fundamental institutions, such as the Moslem family, to remain as they are even at this moment, we do not assent to social stagnation. Nor do we say for one moment that the great tradition of Islam is capable alone of sustaining the necessities of the Near East. But I would seriously ask your Excellencies, why should we be so vain as to suppose that the only cure for the Near East is of necessity the Near West? If new ideas are needed, if new blood is needed, would it not be more natural to appeal to those most living, those most laborious civilisations which form the vast reserve of the Orient? Asia in Europe, if my friend Oman Pasha will allow me the criticism, has hitherto been Asia in arms. May we not yet

see Asia in Europe and yet Asia in peace? These at least are the reasons
which lead me to consent to a scheme of colonisation."

Patrick Dalroy sprang erect, pulling himself out of his seat by clutching at an olive-branch above his head. He steadied himself by putting
one hand on the trunk of the tree, and simply stared at them all. There
fell on him the huge helplessness of mere physical power. He could
throw them into the sea; but what good would that do? More men on
the wrong side would be accredited to the diplomatic campaign; and
the only man on the right side would be discredited for anything. He
shook the branching olive tree above him in his fury. But he did not for
one moment disturb Lord Ivywood, who had just read the third item
on his private agenda ("Oman Pasha insists on the destruction of the
vineyards") and was by this time engaged in a peroration which afterwards became famous and may be found in many rhetorical text books
and primers. He was well into the middle of it before Dalroy's rage and
wonder allowed him to follow the words.

"... do we indeed owe nothing," the diplomatist was saying "to that
gesture of high refusal in which so many centuries ago the great Arabian mystic put the wine-cup from his lips? Do we owe nothing to the
long vigil of a valiant race, the long fast by which they have testified
against the venomous beauty of the Vine? Ours is an age when men
come more and more to see that the creeds hold treasures for each
other, that each religion has a secret for its neighbour, that faith unto
faith uttereth speech, and church unto church showeth knowledge. If it
be true, and I claim again the indulgence of Oman Pasha when I say I
think it is true, that we of the West have brought some light to Islam in
the matter of the preciousness of peace and of civil order, may we not
say that Islam in answer shall give us peace in a thousand homes, and
encourage us to cut down that curse that has done so much to thwart
and madden the virtues of Western Christendom. Already in my own
country the orgies that made horrible the nights of the noblest families
are no more. Already the legislature takes more and more sweeping action to deliver the populace from the bondage of the all-destroying
drug. Surely the prophet of Mecca is reaping his harvest; the cession
of the disputed vineyards to the greatest of his champions is of all acts
the most appropriate to this day; to this happy day that may yet deliver
the East from the curse of war and the West from the curse of wine.

The gallant prince who meets us here at last, to offer an olive branch even more glorious than his sword, may well have our sympathy if he himself views the cession with some sentimental regret; but I have little doubt that he also will live to rejoice in it at last. And I would remind you that it is not the vine alone that has been the sign of the glory of the South. There is another sacred tree unstained by loose and violent memories, guiltless of the blood of Pentheus or of Orpheus and the broken lyre. We shall pass from this place in a little while as all things pass and perish:

> "Far called, our navies melt away.
>   On dune and headland sinks the fire,
> And all our pomp of yesterday
>   Is one with Nineveh and Tyre.

"But so long as sun can shine and soil can nourish, happier men and women after us shall look on this lovely islet and it shall tell its own story; for they shall see these three holy olive trees lifted in ever-lasting benediction, over the humble spot out of which came the peace of the world."

The other two men were staring at Patrick Dalroy; his hand had tightened on the tree, and a giant billow of effort went over his broad breast. A small stone jerked itself out of the ground at the foot of the tree as if it were a grasshopper jumping; and then the coiled roots of the olive tree rose very slowly out of the earth like the limbs of a dragon lifting itself from sleep.

"I offer an olive branch," said the King of Ithaca, totteringly lean-ing the loose tree so that its vast shadow, much larger than itself, fell across the whole council. "An olive branch," he gasped, "more glorious than my sword. Also heavier."

Then he made another effort and tossed it into the sea below.

The German, who was no German, had put up his arm in appre-hension when the shadow fell across him. Now he got up and edged away from the table; seeing that the wild Irishman was tearing up the second tree. This one came out more easily; and before he flung it after the first, he stood with it a moment, looking like a man juggling with a tower.

Lord Ivywood showed more firmness; but he rose in tremendous remonstrance. Only the Turkish Pasha still sat with blank eyes, immovable. Dalroy rent out the last tree and hurled it, leaving the island bare.

"There!" said Dalroy, when the third and last olive had splashed in the tide. "Now I will go. I have seen something today that is worse than death: and the name of it is Peace."

Oman Pasha rose and held out his hand.

"You are right," he said in French, "and I hope we meet again in the only life that is a good life. Where are you going now?"

"I am going," said Dalroy, dreamily, "to 'The Old Ship.'"

"Do you mean?" asked the Turk, "that you are going back to the warships of the English King?"

"No," answered the other, "I am going back to 'The Old Ship' that is behind the apple trees by Pebblewick; where the Ule flows among the trees. I fear I shall never see you there."

After an instant's hesitation he wrung the red hand of the great tyrant and walked to his boat without a glance at the diplomatists.

III
THE SIGN OF "THE OLD SHIP"

Upon few of the children of men has the surname of Pump fallen, and of these few have been maddened into naming a child Humphrey in addition to it. To such extremity, however, had the parents of the innkeeper at "The Old Ship" proceeded, that their son might come at last to be called "Hump" by his dearest friends, and "Pumph" by an aged Turk with a green umbrella. All this, or all he knew of it, he endured with a sour smile; for he was of a stoical temper.

Mr. Humphrey Pump stood outside his inn, which stood almost on the seashore, screened only by one line of apple trees, dwarfed, twisted and salted by the sea air; but in front of it was a highly banked bowling green, and behind it the land sank abruptly; so that one very steep sweeping road vanished into the depth and mystery of taller trees. Mr. Pump was standing immediately under his trim sign, which stood erect in the turf; a wooden pole painted white and suspending a square white board, also painted white but further decorated with a highly grotesque blue ship, such as a child might draw, but into which Mr. Pump's patriotism had insinuated a disproportionately large red St. George's cross.

Mr. Humphrey Pump was a man of middle size, with very broad shoulders, wearing a sort of shooting suit with gaiters. Indeed, he was engaged at the moment in cleaning and reloading a double-barrelled gun, a short but powerful weapon which he had invented, or at least improved, himself; and which, though eccentric enough as compared with latest scientific arms, was neither clumsy nor necessarily out of date. For Pump was one of those handy men who seem to have a hundred hands like Briareus; he made nearly everything for himself and everything in his house was slightly different from the same thing in

172

anyone else's house. He was also as cunning as Pan or a poacher in everything affecting every bird or dish, every leaf or berry in the woods. His mind was a rich soil of subconscious memories and traditions; and he had a curious kind of gossip so allusive as to almost amount to reticence; for he always took it for granted that everyone knew his county and its tales as intimately as he did; so he would mention the most mysterious and amazing things without relaxing a muscle on his face, which seemed to be made of knotted wood. His dark brown hair ended in two rudimentary side whiskers, giving him a slightly horsy look, but in the old-fashioned sportsman's style. His smile was rather wry and crabbed; but his brown eyes were kindly and soft. He was very English.

As a rule his movements, though quick, were cool; but on this occasion he put down the gun on the table outside the inn in a rather hurried manner and came forward dusting his hands in an unusual degree of animation and even defiance. Beyond the goblin green apple trees and against the sea had appeared the tall, slight figure of a girl, in a dress about the colour of copper and a large shady hat. Under the hat her face was grave and beautiful though rather swarthy. She shook hands with Mr. Pump; then he very ceremoniously put a chair for her and called her "Lady Joan."

"I thought I would like a look at the old place," she said. "We have had some happy times here when we were boys and girls. I suppose you hardly see any of your old friends now."

"Very little," answered Pump, rubbing his short whisker reflectively. "Lord Ivywood's become quite a Methody parson, you know, since he took the place; he's pulling down beer-shops right and left. And Mr. Charles was sent to Australia for lying down flat at the funeral. Pretty stiff I call it; but the old lady was a terror."

"Do you ever hear," asked Lady Joan Brett, carelessly, "of that Irishman, Captain Dalroy?"

"Yes, more often than from the rest," answered the innkeeper. "He seems to have done wonders in this Greek business. Ah! He was a sad loss to the Navy!"

"They insulted his country," said the girl, looking at the sea with a heightened colour. "After all, Ireland was his country; and he had a right to resent it being spoken of like that."

"And when they found he'd painted him green," went on Mr. Pump.

"Painted him what?" asked Lady Joan.

"Painted Captain Dawson green," continued Mr. Pump in colourless tones. "Captain Dawson said green was the colour of Irish traitors, so Dalroy painted him green. It was a great temptation, no doubt, with this fence being painted at the time and the pail of stuff there; but, of course, it had a very prejudicial effect on his professional career."

"What an extraordinary story!" said the staring Lady Joan, breaking into a rather joyless laugh. "It must go down among your county legends. I never heard that version before. Why, it might be the origin of the 'Green Man' over there by the town."

"Oh, no," said Pump, simply, "that's been there since before Waterloo times. Poor old Noyle had it until they put him away. You remember old Noyle, Lady Joan. Still alive, I hear, and still writing love-letters to Queen Victoria. Only of course they aren't posted now."

"Have you heard from your Irish friend lately?" asked the girl, keeping a steady eye on the sky-line.

"Yes, I had a letter last week," answered the innkeeper. "It seems not impossible that he may return to England. He's been acting for one of these Greek places, and the negotiations seem to be concluded. It's a queer thing that his lordship himself was the English minister in charge of them."

"You mean Lord Ivywood," said Lady Joan, rather coldly. "Yes, he has a great career before him, evidently."

"I wish he hadn't got his knife into us so much," chuckled Pump. "I don't believe there'll be an inn left in England. But the Ivywoods were always cranky. It's only fair to him to remember his grandfather."

"I think it's very ungallant on your part," said Lady Joan, with a mournful smile, "to ask a lady to remember his grandfather."

"You know what I mean, Lady Joan," said her host, good humouredly. "And I never was hard on the case myself; we all have our little ways. I shouldn't like it done to my pig; but I don't see why a man shouldn't have his own pig in his own pew with him if he likes it. It wasn't a free seat. It was the family pew."

Lady Joan broke out laughing again. "What horrible things you do seem to have heard of," she said. "Well, I must be going, Mr. Hump—I mean Mr. Pump—I used to call you Hump ... oh, Hump, do you think any of us will ever be happy again?"

"I suppose it rests with Providence," he said, looking at the sea.

"Oh, do say Providence again!" cried the girl. "It's as good as 'Masterman Ready.'"

With which inconsequent words she betook herself again to the path by the apple trees and walked back by the sea front to Pebblewick.

The inn of "The Old Ship" lay a little beyond the old fishing village of Pebblewick; and that again was separated by an empty half-mile or so from the new watering-place of Pebblewick-on-Sea. But the dark-haired lady walked steadily along the sea-front, on a sort of parade which had been stretched out to east and west in the insane optimism of watering-places, and, as she approached the more crowded part, looked more and more carefully at the groups on the beach. Most of them were much the same as she had seen them more than a month before. The seekers after truth (as the man in the fez would say) who assembled daily to find out what the man was doing with the paper-boxes, had not found out yet; neither had they wearied of their intellectual pilgrimage. Pennies were still thrown to the thundering atheist in acknowledgment of his incessant abuse; and this was all the more mysterious because the crowd was obviously indifferent, and the atheist was obviously sincere. The man with the long neck who led Low Church hymns with a little wooden spade had indeed disappeared; for children's services of this kind are generally a moving feast; but the man whose only claim consisted of carrots round his hat was still there; and seemed to have even more money than before. But Lady Joan could see no sign of the little old man in the fez. She could only suppose that he had failed entirely; and, being in a bitter mood, she told herself bitterly that he had sunk out of sight precisely because there was in his rubbish a touch of unearthly and insane clearheadedness of which all these vulgar idiots were incapable. She did not confess to herself consciously that what had made both the man in the fez and the man at the inn interesting was the subject of which they had spoken.

As she walked on rather wearily along the parade she caught sight of a girl in black with faint fair hair and a tremulous, intelligent face which she was sure she had seen before. Pulling together all her aristocratic training for the remembering of middle class people, she managed to remember that this was a Miss Browning who had done typewriting work for her a year or two before; and immediately went forward to greet her, partly out of genuine good nature and partly as a relief from her own rather dreary thoughts. Her tone was so seriously frank and friendly that the lady in black summoned the social courage to say:

"I've so often wanted to introduce you to my sister who's much cleverer than I am, though she does live at home; which I suppose is very old-fashioned. She knows all sorts of intellectual people. She is talking to one of them now; this Prophet of the Moon that everyone's talking about. Do let me introduce you."

Lady Joan Brett had met many prophets of the moon and of other things. But she had the spontaneous courtesy which redeems the vices of her class, and she followed Miss Browning to a seat on the parade. She greeted Miss Browning's sister with glowing politeness; and this may really be counted to her credit; for she had great difficulty in looking at Miss Browning's sister at all. For on the seat beside her, still in a red fez but in a brilliantly new black frock coat and every appearance of prosperity, sat the old gentleman who had lectured on the sands about the inns of England.

"He lectured at our Ethical Society," whispered Miss Browning, "on the word Alcohol. Just on the word Alcohol. He was perfectly thrilling. All about Arabia and Algebra, you know, and how everything comes from the East. You really would be interested."

"I am interested," said Lady Joan.

"Poot it to yourselfs," the man in the fez was saying to Miss Browning's sister, "joost what sort of meaning the names of your ince can have if they do not commemorate the unlimitable influence of Islam. There is a vary populous Inn in London, one of the most distinguished, one of the most of the Centre, and it is called the Horseshoe? Now, my friendss, why should anyone commemorate a horse-shoe? It iss but an appendage to a creature more interesting than itself. I have already demonstrated to you that the very fact that you have in your town a place of drink called the Bool—"

"I should like to ask—" began Lady Joan, suddenly.

"A place of drink called the Bool," went on the man in the fez, deaf to all distractions, "and I have urged that the Bool is a disturbing thought, while the Bul-Bul is a reassuring thought. But even you my friends, would not name a place after a ring in a Bool's nose and not after the Bool? Why then name an equivalent place after the shoo, the mere shoo, upon a horse's hoof, and not after the noble horse? Surely it is clear, surely it is evident that the term 'horse-shoe' is a cryptic term, an esoteric term, a term made during the days when the ancient Moslem faith of this English country was oppressed by the passing superstition of the Galileans. That bent shape, that duplex curving shape, which you call horse-shoe, is it not clearly the Crescent?" and he cast his arms wide as he had done on the sands, "the Crescent of the Prophet of the only God?"

"I should like to ask," began Lady Joan, again, "how you would explain the name of the inn called 'The Green Man,' just behind that row of houses."

"Exactly! exactly!" cried the Prophet of the Moon, in almost insane excitement. "The seeker after truth could not at all probably find a more perfect example of these principles. My friendss, how could there be a green man? You are acquainted with green grass, with green leaves, with green cheese, with green chartreuse. I ask if any one of you, however wide her social circle, has ever been acquainted with a green man. Surely, surely, it is evident, my friendss, that this is an imperfect version, an abbreviated version, of the original words. What can be clearer than that the original expression, was 'the green-turban'd man,' in allusion to the well-known uniform of the descendants of the Prophet? 'Turban'd' surely is just the sort of word, exactly the sort of foreign and unfamiliar word, that might easily be slurred over and ultimately suppressed."

"There is a legend in these parts," said Lady Joan, steadily, "that a great hero, hearing the colour that was sacred to his holy island insulted, really poured it over his enemy for a reply."

"A legend! a fable!" cried the man in the fez, with another radiant and rational expansion of the hands. "Is it not evident that no such thing can have really happened?"

"Oh, yes—it really happened," said the young lady, softly. "There is not much to comfort one in this world; but there are some things. Oh, it really happened."

And taking a graceful farewell of the group, she resumed her rather listless walk along the parade.

IV
THE INN FINDS WINGS

Mr. Humphrey Pump stood in front of his inn once more, the cleaned and loaded gun still lay on the table, and the white sign of The Ship still swung in the slight sea breeze over his head; but his leatherish features were knotted over a new problem. He held two letters in his hand, letters of a very different sort, but letters that pointed to the same difficult problem. The first ran:

"Dear Hump—

"I'm so bothered that I simply must call you by the old name again. You understand I've got to keep in with my people. Lord Ivywood is a sort of cousin of mine, and for that and some other reasons, my poor old mother would just die if I offended him. You know her heart is weak; you know everything there is to know in this county. Well, I only write to warn you that something is going to be done against your dear old inn. I don't know what this Country's coming to. Only a month or two ago I saw a shabby old pantaloon on the beach with a green gamp, talking the craziest stuff you ever heard in your life. Three weeks ago I heard he was lecturing at Ethical Societies—whatever they are—for a handsome salary. Well, when I was last at Ivywood—I must go because Mamma likes it—there was the living lunatic again, in evening dress, and talked about by people who really *know*. I mean who know better.

"Lord Ivywood is entirely under his influence and thinks him the greatest prophet the world has ever seen. And Lord Ivywood is not a fool; one can't help admiring him. Mamma, I

178

think, wants me to do more than admire him. I am telling you everything, Hump, because I think perhaps this is the last honest letter I shall ever write in the world. And I warn you seriously that Lord Ivywood is *sincere*, which is perfectly terrible. He will be the biggest English statesman, and he does really mean to ruin—the old ships. If ever you see me here again taking part in such work, I hope you may forgive me.

"Somebody we mentioned, whom I shall never see again, I leave to your friendship. It is the second best thing I can give, and I am not sure it may not be better than the first would have been. Goodbye.

J. B."

This letter seemed to distress Mr. Pump rather than puzzle him. It ran as follows:

"Sir—

"The Committee of the Imperial Commission of Liquor Control is directed to draw your attention to the fact you have disregarded the Committee's communications under section 5A of the Act for the Regulation of Places of Public Entertainment; and that you are now under Section 47C of the Act amending the Act for the Regulation of Places of Public Entertainment aforesaid. The charges on which prosecution will be founded are as follows:

"(1) Violation of sub-section 23f of the Act, which enacts that no pictorial signs shall be exhibited before premises of less than the ratable value of £2000 per annum.

"(2) Violation of sub-section 113d of the Act, which enacts that no liquor containing alcohol shall be sold in any inn, hotel, tavern or public-house, except when demanded under a medical certificate from one of the doctors licensed by the State Medical Council, or in the specially excepted cases of Claridge's Hotel and the Criterion Bar, where urgency has already been proved.

"As you have failed to acknowledge previous communications on this subject, this is to warn you that legal steps will be taken immediately,

"We are yours truly,
"Ivywood, *President*.
J. Leveson, *Secretary*."

Mr. Humphrey Pump sat down at the table outside his inn and whistled in a way which, combined with his little whiskers made him for the moment seem literally like an ostler. Then, the very real wit and learning he had returned slowly into his face and with his warm, brown eyes he considered the cold, grey sea. There was not much to be got out of the sea. Humphrey Pump might drown himself in the sea; which would be better for Humphrey Pump than being finally separated from "The Old Ship." England might be sunk under the sea; which would be better for England than never again having such places as "The Old Ship." But these were not serious remedies nor rationally attainable; and Pump could only feel that the sea had simply warped him as it had warped his apple trees. The sea was a dreary business altogether. There was only one figure walking on the sands. It was only when the figure drew nearer and nearer and grew to more than human size, that he sprang to his feet with a cry. Also the level light of morning lit the man's hair, and it was red.

The late King of Ithaca came casually and slowly up the slope of the beach that led to "The Old Ship." He had landed in a boat from a battleship that could still be seen near the horizon, and he still wore the astounding uniform of apple-green and silver which he had himself invented as that of a navy that had never existed very much, and which now did not exist at all. He had a straight naval sword at his side; for the terms of his capitulation had never required him to surrender it; and inside the uniform and beside the sword there was what there always had been, a big and rather bewildered man with rough red hair, whose misfortune was that he had good brains, but that his bodily strength and bodily passions were a little too strong for his brains.

He had flung his crashing weight on the chair outside the inn before the innkeeper could find words to express his astounded pleasure in seeing him. His first words were "have you got any rum?"

Then, as if feeling that his attitude needed explanation, he added, "I suppose I shall never be a sailor again after tonight. So I must have rum."

Humphrey Pump had a talent for friendship, and understood his old friend. He went into the inn without a word; and came back idly pushing or rolling with an alternate foot (as if he were playing football with two footballs at once) two objects that rolled very easily. One was a big keg or barrel of rum and the other a great solid drum of a cheese. Among his thousand other technical tricks he had a way of tapping a cask without a tap, or anything that could impair its revolutionary or revolving qualities. He was feeling in his pocket for the instrument with which he solved such questions, when his Irish friend suddenly sat bolt upright, as one startled out of sleep, and spoke with his strongest and most unusual brogue.

"Oh thank ye, Hump, a thousand times; and I don't think I really want something to drink at arl. Now I know I can have it, I don't seem to want it at arl. But hwhat I do want—" and he suddenly dashed his big fist on the little table so that one of its legs leapt and nearly snapped— "hwhat I do want is some sort of account of what's happening in this England of yours that shan't be just obviously rubbish."

"Ah," said Pump, fingering the two letters thoughtfully. "And what do you mean by rubbish?"

"I carl it rubbish" cried Patrick Dalroy, "when ye put the Koran into the Bible and not the Apocrypha; and I carl it rubbish when a mad parson's allowed to propose to put a crescent on St. Paul's Cathedral. I know the Turks are our allies now, but they often were before, and I never heard that Palmerston or Colin Campbell had any truck with such trash."

"Lord Ivywood is very enthusiastic, I know," said Pump, with a restrained amusement. "He was saying only the other day at the Flower Show here that the time had come for a full unity between Christianity and Islam."

"Something called Chrislam perhaps," said the Irishman, with a moody eye. He was gazing across the grey and purple woodlands that stretched below them at the back of the inn; and into which the steep, white road swept downwards and disappeared. The steep road looked like the beginning of an adventure; and he was an adventurer.

"But you exaggerate, you know," went on Pump, polishing his gun, "about the crescent on St. Paul's. It wasn't exactly that. What Dr. Moole suggested, I think, was some sort of double emblem, you know, combining cross and crescent."

"And carled the Crescent," muttered Dalroy.

"And you can't call Dr. Moole a parson either," went on Mr. Humphrey Pump, polishing industriously. "Why, they say he's a sort of atheist, or what they call an agnostic, like Squire Brunton who used to bite elm trees by Marley. The grand folks have these fashions, Captain, but they've never lasted long that I know of."

"I think it's serious this time," said his friend, shaking his big red head. "This is the last inn on this coast, and will soon be the last inn in England. Do you remember the 'Saracen's Head' in Plumsea, along the shore there?"

"I know," assented the innkeeper. "My aunt was there when he hanged his mother; but it's a charming place."

"I passed there just now; and it has been destroyed," said Dalroy.

"Destroyed by fire?" asked Pump, pausing in his gun-scrubbing.

"No," said Dalroy, "destroyed by lemonade. They've taken away its license or whatever you call it. I made a song about it, which I'll sing to you now!" And with an astounding air of suddenly revived spirits, he roared in a voice like thunder the following verses, to a simple but spirited tune of his own invention:

"The Saracen's Head looks down the lane,
    Where we shall never drink wine again;
For the wicked old Women who feel well-bred
    Have turned to a tea-shop the Saracen's Head.

"The Saracen's Head out of Araby came,
    King Richard riding in arms like flame,
And where he established his folk to be fed
    He set up his spear—and the Saracen's Head.

"But the Saracen's Head outlived the Kings,
    It thought and it thought of most horrible things;
Of Health and of Soap and of Standard Bread,
    And of Saracen drinks at the Saracen's Head."

"Hullo!" cried Pump, with another low whistle. "Why here comes his lordship. And I suppose that young man in the goggles is a Committee or something."

"Let him come," said Dalroy, and continued in a yet more earth-quake bellow:

> "So the Saracen's Head fulfils its name,
>   They drink no wine—a ridiculous game—
> And I shall wonder until I'm dead,
>   How it ever came into the Saracen's Head."

As the last echo of this lyrical roar rolled away among the apple-trees, and down the steep, white road into the woods, Captain Dalroy leaned back in his chair and nodded good humouredly to Lord Ivywood, who was standing on the lawn with his usual cold air, but with slightly compressed lips. Behind him was a dark young man with double eye-glasses and a number of printed papers in his hand; presumably J. Leveson, Secretary. In the road outside stood a group of three which struck Pump as strangely incongruous, like a group in a three act farce. The first was a police inspector in uniform; the second was a workman in a leather apron, more or less like a carpenter, and the third was an old man in a scarlet Turkish fez, but otherwise dressed in very fashion-able English clothes in which he did not seem very comfortable. He was explaining something about the inn to the policeman and the car-penter, who appeared to be restraining their amusement.

"Fine song that, my lord," said Dalroy, with cheerful egotism. "I'll sing you another," and he cleared his throat.

"Mr. Pump," said Lord Ivywood, in his bell-like and beautiful voice, "I thought I would come in person, if only to make it clear that every indulgence has been shown you. The mere date of this inn brings it within the statute of 1909; it was erected when my great grandfather was Lord of the Manor here, though I believe it then bore a different name, and—"

"Ah, my lord," broke in Pump with a sigh, "I'd rather deal with your great grandfather, I would, though he married a hundred negresses instead of one, than see a gentleman of your family taking away a poor man's livelihood."

"The act is specially designed in the interests of the relief of pov-erty," proceeded Lord Ivywood, in an unruffled manner, "and its final advantages will accrue to all citizens alike." He turned for an instant to the dark secretary, saying, "You have that second report?" and received a folded paper in answer.

"It is here fully explained," said Lord Ivywood, putting on his elderly eyeglasses, "that the purpose of the Act is largely to protect the savings of the more humble and necessitous classes. I find in paragraph three, 'we strongly advise that the deleterious element of alcohol be made illegal save in such few places as the Government may specially exempt for Parliamentary or other public reasons, and that the provocative and demoralising display on inn signs be strictly forbidden except in the cases thus specially exempted: the absence of such temptations will, in our opinion, do much to improve the precarious financial conditions of the working class.' That disposes, I think, of any such suggestion as Mr. Pump's, that our inevitable acts of social reform are in any sense oppressive. To Mr. Pump's prejudice it may appear for the moment to bear hardly upon him; but" (and here Lord Ivywood's voice took one of its moving oratorical turns), "what better proof could we desire of the insidiousness of the sleepy poison we denounce, what better evidence could we offer of the civic corruption that we seek to cure, than the very fact that good and worthy men of established repute in the county can, by living in such places as these, become so stagnant and sodden and unsocial, whether through the fumes of wine or through meditations as maudlin about the past, that they consider the case solely as their own case, and laugh at the long agony of the poor."

Captain Dalroy had been studying Ivywood with a very bright blue eye; and he spoke now much more quietly than he generally did.

"Excuse me one moment, my lord," he said. "But there was one point in your important explanation which I am not sure I have got right. Do I understand you to say that, though sign-boards are to be generally abolished, yet where, if anywhere, they are retained, the right to sell fermented liquor will be retained also? In other words, though an Englishman may at last find only one inn-sign left in England, yet if the place has an inn-sign, it will also have your gracious permission to be really an inn?"

Lord Ivywood had an admirable command of temper, which had helped him much in his career as a statesman. He did not waste time in wrangling about the Captain's *locus standi* in the matter. He replied quite simply,

"Yes, Your statement of the facts is correct."

"Whenever I find an inn-sign permitted by the police, I may go in and ask for a glass of beer—also permitted by the police."

"If you find any such, yes," answered Ivywood, quite temperately. "But we hope soon to have removed them altogether."

Captain Patrick Dalroy rose enormously from his seat with a sort of stretch and yawn.

"Well, Hump," he said to his friend, "the best thing, it seems to me, is to take the important things with us."

With two sight-staggering kicks he sent the keg of rum and the round cheese flying over the fence, in such a direction that they bounded on the descending road and rolled more and more rapidly down toward the dark woods into which the path disappeared. Then he gripped the pole of the inn-sign, shook it twice and plucked it out of the turf like a tuft of grass.

It had all happened before anyone could move, but as he strode out into the road the policeman ran forward. Dalroy smote him flat across face and chest with the wooden sign-board, so as to send him flying into the ditch on the other side of the road. Then turning on the man in the fez he poked him with the end of the pole so sharply in his new white waistcoat and watch-chain as to cause him to sit down suddenly in the road, looking very serious and thoughtful.

The dark secretary made a movement of rescue, but Humphrey Pump, with a cry, caught up his gun from the table and pointed it at him, which so alarmed J. Leveson, Secretary, as to cause him almost to double up with his emotions. The next moment Pump, with his gun under his arm, was scampering down the hill after the Captain, who was scampering after the barrel and the cheese.

Before the policeman had struggled out of the ditch, they had all disappeared into the darkness of the forest. Lord Ivywood who had remained firm through the scene, without a sign of fear or impatience (or, I will add, amusement), held up his hand and stopped the policeman in his pursuit.

"We should only make ourselves and the law ridiculous," he said, "by pursuing those ludicrous rowdies now. They can't escape or do any real harm in the state of modern communications. What is far more important, gentlemen, is to destroy their stores and their base. Under the Act of 1911 we have a right to confiscate and destroy any property in an inn where the law has been violated."

And he stood for hours on the lawn, watching the smashing of bottles and the breaking up of casks and feeding on fanatical pleasure: the pleasure his strange, cold, courageous nature could not get from food or wine or woman.

V

THE ASTONISHMENT OF THE AGENT

Lord Ivywood shared the mental weakness of most men who have fed on books; he ignored, not the value but the very existence of other forms of information. Thus Humphrey Pump was perfectly aware that Lord Ivywood considered him an ignorant man who carried a volume of Pickwick and could not be got to read any other book. But Lord Ivywood was quite unaware that Humphrey never looked at him without thinking that he could be most successfully hidden in a wood of small beeches, as his grey-brown hair and sallow, ashen face exactly reproduced the three predominant tints of such a sylvan twilight. Mr. Pump, I fear, had sometimes partaken of partridge or pheasant, in his early youth, under circumstances in which Lord Ivywood was not only unconscious of the hospitality he was dispensing, but would have sworn that it was physically impossible for anyone to elude the vigilance of his efficient system of game-keeping. But it is very unwise in one who counts himself superior to physical things to talk about physical impossibility.

Lord Ivywood was in error, therefore, when he said that the fugitives could not possibly escape in modern England. You can do a great many things in modern England if you have noticed; some things, in fact, which others know by pictures or current speech; if you know, for instance, that most roadside hedges are taller and denser than they look, and that even the largest man lying just behind them, takes up far less room than you would suppose; if you know that many natural sounds are much more like each other than the enlightened ear can believe, as in the case of wind in leaves and of the sea; if you know that it is easier to walk in socks than in boots, if you know how to take hold of the

187

ground; if you know that the proportion of dogs who will bite a man under any circumstances is rather less than the proportion of men who will murder you in a railway carriage; if you know that you need not be drowned even in a river, unless the tide is very strong, and unless you practise putting yourself into the special attitudes of a suicide; if you know that country stations have objectless, extra waiting rooms that nobody ever goes into; and if you know that county folk will forget you if you speak to them, but talk about you all day if you don't.

By the exercise of these and other arts and sciences Humphrey Pump was able to guide his friend across country, mostly in the character of trespasser and occasionally in that of something like housebreaker, and eventually, with sign, keg, cheese and all to step out of a black pinewood onto a white road in a part of the county where they would not be sought for the present.

Opposite them was a cornfield and on their right, in the shades of the pine trees, a cottage, a very tumbledown cottage that seemed to have collapsed under its own thatch. The red-haired Irishman's face wore a curious smile. He stuck the inn-sign erect in the road and went and hammered on the door.

It was opened tremulously by an old man with a face so wrinkled that the wrinkles seemed more distinctly graven than the features themselves, which seemed lost in the labyrinth of them. He might have crawled out of the hole in a gnarled tree and he might have been a thousand years old.

He did not seem to notice the sign-board, which stood rather to the left of the door; and what life remained in his eyes seemed to awake in wonder at Dalroy's stature and strange uniform and the sword at his side. "I beg your pardon," said the Captain, courteously. "I fear my uniform startles you. It is Lord Ivywood's livery. All his servants are to dress like this. In fact, I understand the tenants also and even yourself, perhaps... excuse my sword. Lord Ivywood is very particular that every man should have a sword. You know his beautiful, eloquent way of putting his views. 'How can we profess,' he was saying to me yesterday, while I was brushing his trousers. 'How can we profess that all men are brothers while we refuse to them the symbol of manhood; or with what assurance can we claim it as a movement of modern emancipation to deny the citizen that which has in all ages marked the difference between the free man and the slave. Nor need we anticipate any such barbaric abuses as my honourable friend who is cleaning the knives has prophesied, for this gift is a sublime act of confidence in your universal passion for the severe splendours of Peace; and he that has the right to strike is he who has learnt to spare.'"

Talking all this nonsense with extreme rapidity and vast oratorical flourishes of the hand, Captain Dalroy proceeded to trundle both the big cheese and the cask of rum into the house of the astonished cottager: Mr. Pump following with a grim placidity and his gun under his arm.

"Lord Ivywood," said Dalroy, setting the rum cask with a bump on the plain deal table, "wishes to take wine with you. Or, more strictly speaking, rum. Don't you run away, my friend, with any of these stories about Lord Ivywood being opposed to drink. Three-bottle Ivywood, we call him in the kitchen. But it must be rum; nothing but rum for the Ivywoods. 'Wine may be a mocker,' he was saying the other day (and I particularly noted the phrasing, which seemed to be very happy even for his lordship; he was standing at the top of the steps, and I stopped cleaning them to make a note of it), 'wine may be a mocker; strong drink may be raging, but nowhere in the sacred pages will you find one word of censure of the sweeter spirit sacred to them that go down to the sea in ships; no tongue of priest and prophet was ever lifted to break the sacred silence of Holy Writ about Rum.' He then explained to me," went on Dalroy, signing to Pump to tap the cask according to his own technical secret, "that the great tip for avoiding any bad results that a bottle or two of rum might have on young and inexperienced people was to eat cheese with it, particularly this kind of cheese that I have here. I've forgotten its name."

"Cheddar," said Pump, quite gravely.

"But mind you!" continued the Captain almost ferociously, shaking his big finger in warning at the aged man. "Mind you 'no *bread* with the cheese. All the devastating ruin wrought by cheese and the once happy homes of this country, has been due to the reckless and insane experiment of eating bread with it.' You'll get no bread from me, my friend. Indeed, Lord Ivywood has given directions that the allusion to this ignorant and depraved habit shall be eliminated from the Lord's Prayer. Have a drink."

He had already poured out a little of the spirit into two thick tumblers and a broken teacup, which he had induced the aged man to produce; and now solemnly pledged him.

"Thank ye kindly, sir," said the old man, using his cracked voice for the first time. Then he drank; and his old face changed as if it were an old horn lantern in which the flame began to rise.

"Ar," he said. "My son he be a sailor."

"I wish him a happy voyage," said the Captain. "And I'll sing you a song about the first sailor there ever was in the world; and who (as Lord Ivywood acutely observes) lived before the time of rum."

He sat down on a wooden chair and lifted his loud voice once more, beating on the table with the broken tea-cup.

"Old Noah, he had an ostrich farm, and fowls on the
    greatest scale;
He ate his egg with a ladle in an egg-cup big as a pail,
And the soup he took was Elephant Soup and the fish
    he took was Whale;
But they all were small to the cellar he took when he set
    out to sail;
And Noah, he often said to his wife when he sat down
    to dine,
'I don't care where the water goes if it doesn't get into
    the wine.'

"The cataract of the cliff of heaven fell blinding off
    the brink,
As if it would wash the stars away as suds go down a
    sink,
The seven heavens came roaring down for the throats
    of hell to drink,
And Noah, he cocked his eye and said, 'It looks like rain,
    I think,
The water has drowned the Matterhorn as deep as a
    Mendip mine,
But I don't care where the water goes if it doesn't get
    into the wine.'

"But Noah he sinned, and we have sinned; on tipsy feet
    we trod,
Till a great big black teetotaller was sent to us for a rod,
And you can't get wine at a P. S. A. or chapel or
    Eisteddfod;
For the Curse of Water has come again because of the
    wrath of God,
And water is on the Bishop's board and the Higher
    Thinker's shrine,
But I don't care where the water goes if it doesn't get
    into the wine."

"Lord Ivywood's favourite song," concluded Mr. Patrick Dalroy, drinking. "Sing us a song yourself."

Rather to the surprise of the two humourists, the old gentleman actually began in a quavering voice to chant,

"King George that lives in London Town,
    I hope they will defend his crown,
And Bonyparte be quite put down
    On Christmas Day in the morning.

"Old Squire is gone to the Meet today
    All in his—"

It is perhaps fortunate for the rapidity of this narrative that the old gentleman's favourite song, which consists of forty-seven verses, was interrupted by a curious incident. The door of the cottage opened and a sheepish-looking man in corduroys stood silently in the room for a few seconds and then said, without preface or further explanation,

"Four ale."

"I beg your pardon?" inquired the polite Captain.

"Four ale," said the man with solidity; then catching sight of Humphrey seemed to find a few more words in his vocabulary.

"Morning, Mr. Pump. Didn't know as how you'd moved 'The Old Ship.'"

Mr. Pump, with a twist of a smile, pointed to the old man whose song had been interrupted.

"Mr. Marne's seeing after it now, Mr. Gowl," said Pump with the strict etiquette of the country side. "But he's got nothing but this rum in stock as yet."

"Better'nowt," said the laconic Mr. Gowl; and put down some money in front of the aged Marne, who eyed it wonderingly. As he was turning with a farewell and wiping his mouth with the back of his hand, the door once more moved, letting in white sunlight and a man in a red neckerchief.

"Morning, Mr. Marne; Morning, Mr. Pump; Morning, Mr. Gowl," said the man in the red neckerchief.

"Morning, Mr. Coote," said the other three, one after another.

"Have some rum, Mr. Coote?" asked Humphrey Pump, genially. "That's all Mr. Marne's got just now."

Mr. Coote also had a little rum; and also laid a little money under the rather vague gaze of the venerable cottager. Mr. Coote was just proceeding to explain that these were bad times, but if you saw a sign you were all right still; a lawyer up at Grunton Abbot had told him so; when the company was increased and greatly excited by the arrival of a boisterous and popular tinker, who ordered glasses all round and said he had his donkey and cart outside. A prolonged, rich and confused conversation about the donkey and cart then ensued, in which the most varied views were taken of their merits; and it gradually began to dawn on Dalroy that the tinker was trying to sell them.

An idea, suited to the romantic opportunism of his present absurd career, suddenly swept over his mind, and he rushed out to look at the cart and donkey. The next moment he was back again, asking the tinker what his price was, and almost in the same breath offering a much bigger price than the tinker would have dreamed of asking. This was considered, however, as a lunacy specially allowed to gentlemen; the tinker had some more rum on the strength of the payment, and then Dalroy, offering his excuses, sealed up the cask and took it and the cheese to be stowed in the bottom of the cart. The money, however, he still left lying in shining silver and copper before the silver beard of old Marne.

No one acquainted with the quaint and often wordless camaraderie of the English poor will require to be told that they all went out and stared at him as he loaded the cart and saw to the harness of the donkey—all except the old cottager, who sat as if hypnotised by the sight of the money. While they were standing there they saw coming down the white, hot road, where it curled over the hill, a figure that gave them no pleasure, even when it was a mere marching black spot in the distance. It was a Mr. Bullrose, the agent of Lord Ivywood's estates.

Mr. Bullrose was a short, square man with a broad, square head with ridges of close, black curls on it, with a heavy, froglike face and starting, suspicious eyes; a man with a good silk hat but a square business jacket. Mr. Bullrose was not a nice man. The agent on that sort of estate hardly ever is a nice man. The landlord often is; and even Lord Ivywood had an arctic magnanimity of his own, which made most people want, if possible, to see him personally. But Mr. Bullrose was petty. Every really practical tyrant must be petty.

He evidently failed to understand the commotion in front of Mr. Marne's partly collapsed cottage, but he felt there must be something wrong about it. He wanted to get rid of the cottage altogether, and had not, of course, the faintest intention of giving the cottager any compensation for it. He hoped the old man would die; but in any case he could easily clear him out if it became suddenly necessary, for he could not possibly pay the rent for this week. The rent was not very much; but it was immeasurably too much for the old man who had no conceivable way of borrowing or earning it. That is where the chivalry of our aristocratic land system comes in.

"Good-bye, my friends," the enormous man in the fantastic uniform was saying, "all roads lead to rum, as Lord Ivywood said in one of his gayer moments, and we hope to be back soon, establishing a first class hotel here, of which prospectuses will soon be sent out."

The heavy froglike face of Mr. Bullrose, the agent, grew uglier with astonishment; and the eyes stood out more like a snail's than a frog's. The indefensible allusion to Lord Ivywood would in any case have caused a choleric intervention, if it had not been swallowed up in the earthquake suggestion of an unlicensed hotel on the estate. This again would have effected the explosion, if that and everything else had not been struck still and rigid by the sight of a solid, wooden sign-post already erected outside old Marne's miserable cottage.

"I've got him now," muttered Mr. Bullrose. "He can't possibly pay; and out he shall go." And he walked swiftly towards the door of the cottage, almost at the same moment that Dalroy went to the donkey's head, as if to lead it off along the road.

"Look here, my man," burst out Bullrose, the instant he was inside the cottage. "You've cooked yourself this time. His lordship has been a great deal too indulgent with you; but this is going to be the end of it. The insolence of what you've done outside, especially when you know his lordship's wishes in such things, has just put the lid on." He stopped a moment and sneered. "So unless you happen to have the exact rent down to a farthing or two about you, out you go. We're sick of your sort."

In a very awkward and fumbling manner, the old man pushed a heap of coins across the table. Mr. Bullrose sat down suddenly on the wooden chair with his silk hat on, and began counting them furiously. He counted them once; he counted them twice; and he counted them again. Then he stared at them more steadily than the cottager had done.

"Where did you get this money?" he asked in a thick, gross voice. "Did you steal it?"

"I ain't very spry for stealin'," said the old man in quavering comedy.

Bullrose looked at him and then at the money; and remembered with fury that Ivywood was a just though cold magistrate on the bench.

"Well, anyhow," he cried, in a hot, heady way, "we've got enough against you to turn you out of this. Haven't you broken the law, my man, to say nothing of the regulations for tenants, in sticking up that fancy sign of yours outside the cottage? Eh?"

The tenant was silent.

"Eh?" reiterated the agent.

"Ar," replied the tenant.

"Have you or have you not a sign-board outside this house?" shouted Bullrose, hammering the table.

The tenant looked at him for a long time with a patient and venerable face, and then said: "Mubbe, yes. Mubbe, no."

"I'll mubbe you," cried Mr. Bullrose, springing up and sticking his silk hat on the back of his head. "I don't know whether you people are too drunk to see anything, but I saw the thing with my own eyes out in the road. Come out, and deny it if you dare!"

"Ar," said Mr. Marne, dubiously.

He tottered after the agent, who flung open the door with a businesslike fury and stood outside on the threshold. He stood there quite a long time, and he did not speak. Deep in the hardened mud of his materialistic mind there had stirred two things that were its ancient enemies; the old fairy tale in which every thing can be believed; the new scepticism in which nothing can be believed—not even one's own eyes. There was no sign, nor sign of a sign, in the landscape.

On the withered face of the old man Marne there was a faint renewal of that laughter that has slept since the Middle Ages.

VI

The Hole in Heaven

That delicate ruby light which is one of the rarest but one of the most exquisite of evening effects warmed the land, sky and seas as if the whole world were washed in wine; and dyed almost scarlet the strong red head of Patrick Dalroy as he stood on the waste of furze and bracken, where he and his friends had halted. One of his friends was re-examining a short gun, rather like a double-barrelled carbine, the other was eating thistles.

Dalroy himself was idle and ruminant, with his hands in his pockets and his eye on the horizon. Land-wards the hills, plains and woods lay bathed in the rose-red light; but it changed somewhat to purple, to cloud and something like storm over the distant violet strip of sea. It was towards the sea that he was staring.

Suddenly he woke up; and seemed almost to rub his eyes, or at any rate, to rub his red eyebrow.

"Why, we're on the road back of Pebblewick," he said. "That's the damned little tin chapel by the beach."

"I know," answered his friend and guide. "We've done the old hare trick; doubled, you know. Nine times out of ten it's the best. Parson Whitelady used to do it when they were after him for dog-stealing. I've pretty much followed his trail; you can't do better than stick to the best examples. They tell you in London that Dick Turpin rode to York. Well, I know he didn't; for my old grandfather up at Cobble's End knew the Turpins intimately—threw one of them into the river on a Christmas day; but I think I can guess what he did do and how the tale got about. If Dick was wise, he went flying up the old North Road, shouting 'York! York!' or what not, before people recognised him; then if he did the thing properly, he might half an hour afterwards walk down the Strand with a pipe in his mouth. They say old Boney said, 'Go where you aren't expected,' and I suppose as a soldier he was right. But for a gentleman dodging the police like yourself, it isn't exactly the right way of putting it. I should say, 'Go where you ought to be expected'—and you'll generally find your fellow creatures don't do what they ought about expecting any more than about anything else."

"Well, this bit between here and the sea," said the Captain, in a brown study, "I know it so well—so well that—that I rather wish I'd never seen it again. Do you know," he asked, suddenly pointing to a patch and pit of sand that showed white in the dusky heath a hundred yards away, "do you know what makes that spot so famous in history?"

"Yes," answered Mr. Pump, "that's where old Mother Grouch shot the Methodist."

"You are in error," said the Captain. "Such an incident as you describe would in no case call for special comment or regret. No, that spot is famous because a very badly brought up girl once lost a ribbon off a plait of black hair and somebody helped her to find it."

"Has the other person been well brought up?" asked Pump, with a faint smile.

"No," said Dalroy, staring at the sea. "He has been brought down." Then, rousing himself again, he made a gesture toward a further part of the heath. "Do you know the remarkable history of that old wall, the one beyond the last gorge over there?"

"No," replied the other, "unless you mean Dead Man's Circus, and that happened further along."

"I do not mean Dead Man's Circus," said the Captain. "The remarkable history of that wall is that somebody's shadow once fell on it; and that shadow was more desirable than the substance of all other living things. It is *this*," he cried, almost violently, resuming his flippant tone, "it is this circumstance, Hump, and not the trivial and everyday incident of a dead man going to a circus to which you have presumed to compare it, it is *this* historical event which Lord Ivywood is about to commemorate by rebuilding the wall with solid gold and Greek marbles stolen by the Turks from the grave of Socrates, enclosing a column of solid gold four hundred feet high and surmounted by a colossal equestrian statue of a bankrupt Irishman riding backwards on a donkey."

He lifted one of his long legs over the animal, as if about to pose for the group; then swung back on both feet again, and again looked at the purple limit of the sea.

"Do you know, Hump," he said, "I think modern people have somehow got their minds all wrong about human life. They seem to expect what Nature has never promised; and then try to ruin all that Nature has really given. At all those atheist chapels of Ivywood's they're always talking of Peace, Perfect Peace, and Utter Peace, and Universal Joy and souls that beat as one. But they don't look any more cheerful than anyone else; and the next thing they do is to start smashing a thousand good jokes and good stories and good songs and good friendships by pulling down 'The Old Ship.'"

He gave a glance at the loose sign-post lying on the heath beside him, almost as if to reassure himself that it was not stolen. "Now it seems to me," he went on, "that this is asking for too much and getting too little. I don't know whether God means a man to have happiness in that All in All and Utterly Utter sense of happiness. But God does mean a man to have a little Fun; and I mean to go on having it. If I mustn't satisfy my heart, I can gratify my humour. The cynical fellows who think themselves so damned clever have a sort of saying, 'Be good and you will be happy; but you will not have a jolly time.' The cynical fellows are quite wrong, as they generally are. They have got hold of the exact opposite of the truth. God knows I don't set up to be good; but even a rascal sometimes has to fight the world in the same way as a saint. I think I have fought the world; *et militavi non sine*—what's the Latin for having a lark? I can't pretend to Peace and Joy, and all the rest of it, particularly in this original briar-patch. I haven't been happy, Hump, but I have had a jolly time."

The sunset stillness settled down again, save for the cropping of the donkey in the undergrowth; and Pump said nothing sympathetically; and it was Dalroy once more who took up his parable.

"So I think there's too much of this playing on our emotions, Hump; as this place is certainly playing the cat and banjo with mine. Damn it all, there are other things to do with the rest of one's life! I don't like all this fuss about feeling things—it only makes people miserable. In my present frame of mind I'm in favour of doing things. All of which, Hump," he said with a sudden lift of the voice that always went in him with a rushing, irrational return of merely animal spirits— "All of which I have put into a Song Against Songs, that I will now sing you."

"I shouldn't sing it here," said Humphrey Pump, picking up his gun and putting it under his arm. "You look large in this open place; and you sound large. But I'll take you to the Hole in Heaven you've been talking about so much, and hide you as I used to hide you from that tutor—I couldn't catch his name—man who could only get drunk on Greek wine at Squire Wimpole's."

"Hump!" cried the Captain, "I abdicate the throne of Ithaca. You are far wiser than Ulysses. Here I have had my heart torn with temptations to ten thousand things between suicide and abduction, and all by the mere sight of that hole in the heath, where we used to have picnics. And all that time I'd forgotten we used to call it the Hole in Heaven. And, by God, what a good name—in both senses."

"I thought you'd have remembered it, Captain," said the innkeeper, "from the joke young Mr. Matthews made."

"In the heat of some savage hand to hand struggle in Albania," said Mr. Dalroy, sadly, passing his palm across his brow, "I must have forgotten for one fatal instant the joke young Mr. Matthews made."

"It wasn't very good," said Mr. Pump, simply. "Ah, his aunt was the one for things like that. She went too far with old Gudgeon, though."

With these words he jumped and seemed to be swallowed up by the earth. But they had merely strolled the few yards needed to bring them to the edge of the sand-pit on the heath of which they had been speaking. And it is one of the truths concealed by Heaven from Lord Ivywood, and revealed by Heaven to Mr. Pump, that a hiding-place can be covered when you are close to it; and yet be open and visible from some spot of vantage far off. From the side by which they approached it, the sudden hollow of sand, a kind of collapsed chamber in the heath, seemed covered with a natural curve of fern and furze, and flashed out of sight like a fairy.

"It's all right," he called out from under a floor or roof of leaves. "You'll remember it all when you get here. This is the place to sing your song, Captain. Lord bless me, Captain, don't I remember your singing that Irish song you made up at college—bellowing it like a bull of Bashan—all about hearts and sleeves or some such things—and her ladyship and the tutor never heard a breath, because that bank of sand breaks everything. It's worth knowing all this, you know. It's a pity it's not part of a young gentleman's education. Now you shall sing me the song in favour of having no feelings, or whatever you call it."

Dalroy was staring about him at the cavern of his old picnics, so forgotten and so startlingly familiar. He seemed to have lost all thought of singing anything, and simply to be groping in the dark house of his own boyhood. There was a slight trickle from a natural spring in sand-stone just under the ferns, and he remembered they used to try to boil the water in a kettle. He remembered a quarrel about who had upset the kettle which, in the morbidity of first love, had given him for days the tortures of the damned. When the energetic Pump broke once more through the rather thorny roof, on an impulse to accumulate their other eccentric possessions, Patrick remembered about a thorn in a finger, that made his heart stop with something that was pain and perfect music. When Pump returned with the rum-keg and the cheese and rolled them with a kick down the shelving sandy side of the hole, he remembered, with almost wrathful laughter, that in the old days he had rolled down that slope himself, and thought it a rather fine thing to do. He felt then as if he were rolling down a smooth side of the Matterhorn. He observed now that the height was rather less than that of the second storey of one of the stunted cottages he had noted on his return. He suddenly understood he had grown bigger; bigger in a bodily sense. He had doubts about any other.

"The Hole in Heaven!" he said. "What a good name! What a good poet I was in those days! The Hole in Heaven. But does it let one in, or let one out?"

In the last level shafts of the fallen sun the fantastic shadow of the long-eared quadruped, whom Pump had now tethered to a new and nearer pasture, fell across the last sunlit scrap of sand. Dalroy looked at the long exaggerated shadow of the ass; and laughed that short explosive laugh he had uttered when the doors of the harems had been closed after the Turkish war. He was normally a man much too loquacious; but he never explained those laughs.

Humphrey Pump plunged down again into the sunken nest, and began to broach the cask of rum in his own secret style, saying— "We can get something else somehow tomorrow. For tonight we can eat cheese and drink rum, especially as there's water on tap, so to speak. And now, Captain, sing us the Song Against Songs."

Patrick Dalroy drank a little rum out of a small medicine glass which the generally unaccountable Mr. Pump unaccountably produced from his waistcoat pocket; but Patrick's colour had risen, his brow was almost as red as his hair; and he was evidently reluctant.

"I don't see why I should sing all the songs," he said. "Why the divil don't you sing a song yourself? And now I come to think of it," he cried, with an accumulating brogue, not, perhaps, wholly unaffected by the rum, which he had not, in fact, drunk for years, "and now I come to think of it, what about that song of yours? All me youth's coming back in this blest and cursed place; and I remember that song of yours, that never existed nor ever will. Don't ye remember now, Humphrey Pump, that night when I sang ye no less than seventeen songs of me own composition?"

"I remember it very well," answered the Englishman, with restraint.

"And don't ye remember," went on the exhilarated Irishman, with solemnity, "that unless ye could produce a poetic lyric of your own, written and sung by yourself, I threatened to ..."

"To sing again," said the impenetrable Pump. "Yes, I know."

He calmly proceeded to take out of his pockets, which were, alas, more like those of a poacher than an innkeeper, a folded and faded piece of paper.

"I wrote it when you asked me," he said simply. "I have never tried to sing it. But I'll sing it myself, when you've sung your song, against anybody singing at all."

"All right," cried the somewhat excited Captain, "to hear a song from you—why, I'll sing anything. This is the Song Against Songs, Hump."

And again he let his voice out like a bellow against the evening silence.

> "The song of the sorrow of Melisande is a weary song
>   and a dreary song,
> The glory of Mariana's grange had got into great decay,
> The song of the Raven Never More has never been called
>   a cheery song,
> And the brightest things in Baudelaire are anything else
>   but gay.

But who will write us a riding song,
Or a hunting song or a drinking song,
Fit for them that arose and rode,
When day and the wine were red?
But bring me a quart of claret out,
And I will write you a clinking song,
A song of war and a song of wine,
And a song to wake the dead.

"The song of the fury of Fragolette is a florid song and
   a torrid song,
The song of the sorrow of Tara is sung to a harp unstrung,
The song of the cheerful Shropshire Kid I consider a
   perfectly horrid song,
And the song of the happy Futurist is a song that can't
   be sung.
But who will write us a riding song,
Or a fighting song or a drinking song,
Fit for the fathers of you and me,
That knew how to think and thrive?
But the song of Beauty and Art and Love
Is simply an utterly stinking song,
To double you up and drag you down,
And damn your soul alive.

"Take some more rum," concluded the Irish officer, affably, "and let's hear your song at last."

With the gravity inseparable from the deep conventionality of country people, Mr. Pump unfolded the paper on which he had recorded the only antagonistic emotion that was strong enough in him to screw his infinite English tolerance to the pitch of song. He read out the title very carefully and in full.

"Song Against Grocers, by Humphrey Pump, sole proprietor of 'The Old Ship,' Pebblewick. Good Accommodation for Man and Beast. Celebrated as the House at which both Queen Charlotte and Jonathan Wilde put up on different occasions; and where the Ice-cream man was mistaken for Bonaparte. This song is written against Grocers."

"God made the wicked Grocer,
    For a mystery and a sign,
That men might shun the awful shops,
    And go to inns to dine;
Where the bacon's on the rafter
    And the wine is in the wood,
And God that made good laughter
    Has seen that they are good.

"The evil-hearted Grocer
    Would call his mother 'Ma'am,'
And bow at her and bob at her,
    Her aged soul to damn;
And rub his horrid hands and ask,
    What article was next;
Though *mortis in articulo,*
    Should be her proper text.

"His props are not his children
    But pert lads underpaid,
Who call out 'Cash!' and bang about,
    To work his wicked trade;
He keeps a lady in a cage,
    Most cruelly all day,
And makes her count and calls her 'Miss,'
    Until she fades away.

"The righteous minds of inn-keepers
    Induce them now and then
To crack a bottle with a friend,
    Or treat unmoneyed men;
But who hath seen the Grocer
    Treat housemaids to his teas,
Or crack a bottle of fish-sauce,
    Or stand a man a cheese?

"He sells us sands of Araby
     As sugar for cash down,
He sweeps his shop and sells the dust,
     The purest salt in town;
He crams with cans of poisoned meat
     Poor subjects of the King,
And when they die by thousands
     Why, he laughs like anything.

"The Wicked Grocer groces
     In spirits and in wine,
Not frankly and in fellowship,
     As men in inns do dine;
But packed with soap and sardines
     And carried off by grooms,
For to be snatched by Duchesses,
     And drunk in dressing-rooms.

"The hell-instructed Grocer
     Has a temple made of tin,
And the ruin of good inn-keepers
     Is loudly urged therein;
But now the sands are running out
     From sugar of a sort,
The Grocer trembles; for his time
     Just like his weight is short."

Captain Dalroy was getting considerably heated with his nautical liquor, and his appreciation of Pump's song was not merely noisy but active. He leapt to his feet and waved his glass. "Ye ought to be Poet Laureate, Hump—ye're right, ye're right; we'll stand all this no longer!"

He dashed wildly up the sand slope and pointed with the sign-post towards the darkening shore, where the low shed of corrugated iron stood almost isolated.

"There's your tin temple!" he said. "Let's burn it!"

They were some way along the coast from the large watering-place of Pebblewick and between the gathering twilight and the rolling country it could not be clearly seen. Nothing was now in sight but the corrugated iron hall by the beach and three half-built red brick villas.

Dalroy appeared to regard the hall and the empty houses with great malevolence.

"Look at it!" he said. "Babylon!"

He brandished the inn-sign in the air like a banner, and began to stride towards the place, showering curses.

"In forty days," he cried, "shall Pebblewick be destroyed. Dogs shall lap the blood of J. Leveson, Secretary, and Unicorns—"

"Come back Pat," cried Humphrey, "you've had too much rum."

"Lions shall howl in its high places," vociferated the Captain.

"Donkeys will howl, anyhow," said Pump. "But I suppose the other donkey must follow."

And loading and untethering the quadruped, he began to lead him along.

VII
THE SOCIETY OF SIMPLE SOULS

Under sunset, at once softer and more sombre, under which the leaden sea took on a Lenten purple, a tint appropriate to tragedy, Lady Joan Brett was once more drifting moodily along the sea-front. The evening had been rainy and lowering; the watering-place season was nearly over; and she was almost alone on the shore; but she had fallen into the habit of restlessly pacing the place, and it seemed to satisfy some subconscious hunger in her rather mixed psychology.

Through all her brooding her animal senses always remained abnormally active: she could *smell* the sea when it had ebbed almost to the horizon, and in the same way she heard, through every whisper of waves or wind, the swish or flutter of another woman's skirt behind her. There is, she felt, something unmistakable about the movements of a lady who is generally very dignified and rather slow, and who happens to be in a hurry.

She turned to look at the lady who was thus hastening to overtake her; lifted her eyebrows a little and held out her hand. The interruption was known to her as Lady Enid Wimpole, cousin of Lord Ivywood; a tall and graceful lady who unbalanced her own elegance by a fashionable costume that was at once funereal and fantastic; her fair hair was pale but plentiful; her face was not only handsome and fastidious in the aquiline style, but when considered seriously was sensitive, modest, and even pathetic, but her wan blue eyes seemed slightly prominent, with that expression of cold eagerness that is seen in the eyes of ladies who ask questions at public meetings.

Joan Brett was herself, as she had said, a connection of the Ivywood family; but Lady Enid was Ivywood's first cousin, and for all practical purposes his sister. For she kept house for him and his mother, who was now so incredibly old that she only survived to satisfy conventional opinion in the character of a speechless and useless *chaperon*. And Ivywood was not the sort who would be likely to call out any activity in an old lady exercising that office. Nor, for that matter, was Lady Enid Wimpole; there seemed to shine on her face the same kind of inhuman, absent-minded common sense that shone on her cousin's.

"Oh, I'm so glad I've caught you up," she said to Joan. "Lady Ivywood wants you *so* much to come to us for the week-end or so, while Philip is still there. He always admired your sonnet on Cyprus so much, and he wants to talk to you about this policy of his in Turkey. Of course he's awfully busy, but I shall be seeing him tonight after the meeting."

"No living creature," said Lady Joan, with a smile, "ever saw him except before or after a meeting."

"Are you a Simple Soul?" asked Lady Enid, carelessly.

"Am I a simple soul?" asked Joan, drawing her black brows together. "Merciful Heavens, no! What can you mean?"

"Their meeting's on tonight at the small Universal Hall, and Philip's taking the chair," explained the other lady. "He's very annoyed that he has to leave early to get up to the House, but Mr. Leveson can take the chair for the last bit. They've got Misysra Ammon."

"Got Mrs. Who?" asked Joan, in honest doubt.

"You make game of everything," said Lady Enid, in cheerless amiability. "It's the man everyone's talking about—*you* know as well as I do. It's really his influence that has *made* the Simple Souls."

"Oh!" said Lady Joan Brett.

Then after a long silence, she added: "Who are the Simple Souls? I should be interested in them, if I could meet any." And she turned her dark, brooding face on the darkening purple sea.

"Do you mean to say, my dear," asked Lady Enid Wimpole, "that you haven't met any of them yet?"

"No," said Joan, looking at the last dark line of sea. "I never met but one simple soul in my life."

"But you must come to the meeting!" cried Lady Enid, with frosty and sparkling gaiety. "You must come at once! Philip is certain to be eloquent on a subject like this, and of course Misysra Ammon is *always* so wonderful."

Without any very distinct idea of where she was going or why she was going there, Joan allowed herself to be piloted to a low lead or tin shed, beyond the last straggling hotels, out of the echoing shell of which she could prematurely hear a voice that she thought she recognised. When she came in Lord Ivywood was on his feet, in exquisite evening dress, but with a light overcoat thrown over the seat behind him. Beside him, in less tasteful but more obvious evening dress, was the little old man she had heard on the beach.

No one else was on the platform, but just under it, rather to Joan's surprise, sat Miss Browning, her old typewriting friend in her old black dress, industriously taking down Lord Ivywood's words in shorthand. A yard or two off, even more to her surprise, sat Miss Browning's more domestic sister, also taking down the same words in shorthand.

"That is Misysra Ammon," whispered Lady Enid, earnestly, pointing a delicate finger at the little old man beside the chairman.

"I know him," said Joan. "Where's the umbrella?"

"... at least evident," Lord Ivywood was saying, "that one of those ancestral impossibilities is no longer impossible. The East and the West are one. The East is no longer East nor the West West; for a small isthmus has been broken, and the Atlantic and Pacific are a single sea. No man assuredly has done more of this mighty work of unity than the brilliant and distinguished philosopher to whom you will have the pleasure of listening tonight; and I profoundly wish that affairs more practical, for I will not call them more important, did not prevent my remaining to enjoy his eloquence, as I have so often enjoyed it before. Mr. Leveson has kindly consented to take my place, and I can do no more than express my deep sympathy with the aims and ideals which will be developed before you tonight. I have long been increasingly convinced that underneath a certain mask of stiffness which the Mahommedan religion has worn through certain centuries, as a somewhat similar mask has been worn by the religion of the Jews, Islam has in it the potentialities of being the most progressive of all religions; so that a century or two to come we may see the cause of peace, of science and of reform everywhere supported by Islam as it is everywhere supported by Israel. Not in vain, I think, is the symbol of that faith the Crescent, the growing thing. While other creeds carry emblems implying more or less of finality, for this great creed of hope its very imperfection is its pride, and men shall walk fearlessly in new and wonderful paths, following the increasing curve which contains and holds up before them the eternal promises of the orb."

It was characteristic of Lord Ivywood that, though he was really in a hurry, he sat down slowly and gravely amid the outburst of applause. The quiet resumption of the speaker's seat, like the applause itself, was an artistic part of the peroration. When the last clap or stamp had subsided, he sprang up alertly, his light great-coat over his arm, shook hands with the lecturer, bowed to the audience and slid quickly out of the hall. Mr. Leveson, the swarthy young man with the drooping double-eyeglass rather bashfully to the front, took the empty seat on the platform, and in a few words presented the eminent Turkish mystic Misysra Ammon, sometimes called the Prophet of the Moon.

Lady Joan found the Prophet's English accent somewhat improved by good society, but he still elongated the letter "u" in the same bleating manner, and his remarks had exactly the same rabidly wrong-headed ingenuity as his lecture upon English inns. It appeared that he was speaking on the higher Polygamy; but he began with a sort of general defence of the Moslem civilisation, especially against the charge of sterility and worldly ineffectiveness.

"It iss joost in the practical tings," he was saying, "it iss joost in the practical tings, if you could come to consider them in a manner quite equal, that our methods are better than your methods. My ancestors invented the curved swords, because one cuts better with a curved sword. Your ancestors possessed the straight swords out of some romantic fancy of being what you call straight; or, I will take a more plain example, of which I have myself experience. When I first had the honour of meeting Lord Ivywood, I was unused to your various ceremonies and had a little difficulty, joost a little difficulty, in entering Mr. Claridge's hotel, where his lordship had invited me. A servant of the hotel was standing joost beside me on the doorstep. I stoo-ooped down to take off my boo-oots, and he asked me what I was dooing. I said to him: 'My friend, I am taking off my boo-oots.'"

A smothered sound came from Lady Joan Brett, but the lecturer did not notice it and went on with a beautiful simplicity.

"I told him that in my country, when showing respect for any spot, we do not take off our hats; we take off our boo-oots. And because I would keep on my hat and take off my boo-oots, he suggested to me that I had been afflicted by Allah, in the head. Now was not that foony?"

"Very," said Lady Joan, inside her handkerchief, for she was choking with laughter. Something like a faint smile passed over the earnest faces of the two or three most intelligent of the Simple Souls, but for the most part the Souls seemed very simple indeed, helpless looking people with limp hair and gowns like green curtains, and their dry faces were as dry as ever.

"But I explained to him. I explained to him for a long time, for a carefully occupied time, that it was more practical, more business-like, more altogether for utility, to take off the boo-oots than to remove the hat. 'Let us,' I said to him, 'consider what many complaints are made against the footwear, what few complaints against the headwear. You complain if in your drawing-rooms is the marching about of muddy boo-oots. Are any of your drawing-rooms marked thus with the marching about of muddy hats? How very many of your husbands kick you with the boo-oot! Yet how few of your husbands on any occasion butt you with the hat?'"

He looked round with a radiant seriousness, which made Lady Joan almost as speechless for sympathy as she was for amusement. With all that was most sound in his too complicated soul she realised the presence of a man really convinced.

"The man on the doorstep, he would not listen to me," went on Misysra Ammon, pathetically. "He said there would be a crowd if I stood on the doorstep, holding in my hand my boo-oots. Well, I do not know why, in your country you always send the young males to be the first of your crowds. They certainly were making a number of noises, the young males."

Lady Joan Brett stood up suddenly and displayed enormous interest in the rest of the audience in the back parts of the hall. She felt that if she looked for one moment more at the serious face with the Jewish nose and the Persian beard, she would publicly disgrace herself; or, what was quite as bad (for she was the generous sort of aristocrat) publicly insult the lecturer. She had a feeling that the sight of all the Simple Souls in bulk might have a soothing effect. It had. It had what might have been mistaken for a depressing effect. Lady Joan resumed her seat with a controlled countenance.

"Now, why," asked the Eastern philosopher, "do I tell so simple a little story of your London streets—a thing happening any day? The little mistake had no preju-udicial effect. Lord Ivywood came out, at the end. He made no attempt to explain the true view of so important matters to Mr. Claridge's servant, though Mr. Claridge's servant remained on the doorstep. But he commanded Mr. Claridge's servant to restore to me one of my boo-oots, which had fallen down the front steps, while I was explaining this harmlessness of the hat in the home. So all was, for me, very well. But why do I tell such little tales?"

He spread out his hands again, in his fanlike eastern style. Then he clapped them together, so suddenly that Joan jumped, and looked instinctively for the entrance of five hundred negro slaves, laden with jewels. But it was only his emphatic gesture of eloquence. He went on with an excited thickening of the accent.

"Because, my friends, this is the best example I could give of the wrong and slanderous character of the charge that we fail in our do-mesticities. That we fail especially in our treatment of the womankind. I appeal to any lady, to any Christian lady. Is not the boo-oot more devastating, more dreaded in the home than the hat? The boot jumps, he bound, he run about, he break things, he leave on the carpet the earths of the garden. The hat, he remain quiet on his hat-peg. Look at him on his hat-peg; how quiet and good he remain! Why not let him remain quiet also on his head?"

Lady Joan applauded warmly, as did several other ladies, and the sage went on, encouraged.

"Can you not therefore trust, dear ladies, this great religion to under-stand you concerning other things, as it understands you regarding boo-oots? What is the common objection our worthy enemies make against our polygamy? That it is disdainful of the womanhood. But how can this be so, my friends, when it allows the womanhood to be present in so large numbers? When in your House of Commons you put a hun-dred English members and joost one little Welsh member, you do not say 'The Welshman is on top; he is our Sultan; may he live for ever!' If your jury contained eleven great large ladies and one leetle man you would not say 'this is unfair to the great large ladies.' Why should you shrink, then, ladies, from this great polygamical experiment which Lord Ivywood himself—"

Joan's dark eyes were still fixed on the wrinkled, patient face of the
lecturer, but every word of the rest of the lecture was lost to her. Under
her glowing Spanish tint she had turned pale with extraordinary emotions, but she did not stir a hair.

The door of the hall stood open, and occasional sounds came even
from that deserted end of the town. Two men seemed to be passing
along the distant parade; one of them was singing. It was common
enough for workmen to sing going home at night, and the voice, though
a loud one, would have been too far off for Joan to hear the words.
Only Joan happened to know the words. She could almost see them
before her, written in a round swaggering hand on the pink page of an
old school-girl album at home. She knew the words and the voice.

> "I come from Castlepatrick and my heart is on my sleeve,
> And any sword or pistol boy can hit ut with me leave,
> It shines there for an epaulette, as golden as a flame,
> As naked as me ancestors, as noble as me name.
> For I come from Castlepatrick and my heart is on my sleeve,
> But a lady stole it from me on St. Gallowglass's Eve."

Startlingly and with strong pain there sprang up before Joan's eyes
a patch of broken heath with a very deep hollow of white sand, blinding in the sun. No words, no name, only the place.

> "The folks that live in Liverpool, their heart is in their
>   boots;
> They go to Hell like lambs, they do, because the hooter
>   hoots.
> Where men may not be dancin', though the wheels may
>   dance all day;
> And men may not be smokin', but only chimneys may.
> But I come from Castlepatrick and my heart is on my
>   sleeve,
> But a lady stole it from me on St. Poleyander's Eve.
>
> "The folks that live in black Belfast, their heart is in
>   their mouth;

They see us making murders in the meadows of the
    South;
They think a plough's a rack they do, and cattle-calls are
    creeds,
And they think we're burnin' witches when we're only
    burnin' weeds.
But I come from Castlepatrick, and me heart is on me
    sleeve;
But a lady stole it from me on St. Barnabas's Eve."

The voice had stopped suddenly, but the last lines were so much more distinct that it was certain the singer had come nearer, and was not marching away.

It was only after all this, and through a sort of cloud, that Lady Joan heard the indomitable Oriental bringing his whole eloquent address to a conclusion.

"... And if you do not refu-use the sun that returns and rises in the East with every morning, you will not refu-use either this great social experiment, this great polygamical method which also arose out of the East, and always returns. For this is that Higher Polygamy which always comes, like the sun itself, out of the orient, but is only at its noontide splendour when the sun is high in heaven."

She was but vaguely conscious of Mr. Leveson, the man with the dark face and the eyeglasses, acknowledging the entrancing lecture in suitable terms, and calling on any of the Simple Souls who might have questions to ask, to ask them. It was only when the Simple Souls had displayed their simplicity with the usual parade of well-bred reluctance and fussy self-effacement, that anyone addressed the chair. And it was only after somebody had been addressing the chair for some time that Joan gradually awoke to the fact that the address was somewhat unusual.

VIII

Vox Populi Vox Dei

"I am sure," Mr. Leveson, the Secretary, had said, with a somewhat constrained smile, "that after the eloquent and epoch-making speech to which we have listened there will be some questions asked, and we hope to have a debate afterwards. I am sure somebody will ask a question." Then he looked interrogatively at one weary looking gentleman in the fourth row and said, "Mr. Hinch?"

Mr. Hinch shook his head with a pallid passion of refusal, wonderful to watch, and said, "I couldn't! I really couldn't!"

"We should be very pleased," said Mr. Leveson, "if any lady would ask a question."

In the silence that followed it was somehow psychologically borne in on the whole audience that one particular great large lady (as the lecturer would say) sitting at the end of the second row was expected to ask a question. Her own wax-work immobility was witness both to the expectation and its disappointment. "Are there any other questions?" asked Mr. Leveson—as if there had been any yet. He seemed to speak with a slight air of relief.

There was a sort of stir at the back of the hall and half way down one side of it. Choked whispers could be heard of "Now then, Garge!"— "Go it Garge! Is there any questions! Gor!"

Mr. Leveson looked up with an alertness somewhat akin to alarm. He realised for the first time that a few quite common men in coarse, unclean clothes, had somehow strolled in through the open door. They were not true rustics, but the semi-rustic labourers that linger about the limits of the large watering-places. There was no "Mr." among them. There was a general tendency to call everybody George.

214

Mr. Leveson saw the situation and yielded to it. He modelled himself on Lord Ivywood and did much what he would have done in all
cases, but with a timidity Lord Ivywood would not have shown. And
the same social training that made him ashamed to be with such men,
made him ashamed to own his shame. The same modern spirit that
taught him to loathe such rags, also taught him to lie about his loathing.

"I am sure we should be very glad," he said, nervously, "if any friends
from outside care to join in our inquiry. Of course, we're all Demo-
crats," and he looked round at the grand ladies with a ghastly smile,
"and believe in the Voice of the People and so on. If our friend at the
back of the hall will put his question briefly, we need not insist, I think,
on his putting it in writing?"

There were renewed hoarse encouragements to George (that rightly
christened champion) and he wavered forward on legs tied in the middle
with string. He did not appear to have had any seat since his arrival,
and made his remarks standing half way down what we may call the
central aisle.

"Well, I want to ask the proprietor," he began.

"Questions," said Mr. Leveson, swiftly seizing a chance for that
construction of debate which is the main business of a modern chairman, "must be asked of the chair, if they are points of order. If they
concern the address, they should be asked of the lecturer."

"Well, I ask the lecturer," said the patient Garge, "whether it ain't
right that when you 'ave the thing outside you should 'ave the thing
inside." (Hoarse applause at the back.)

Mr. Leveson was evidently puzzled and already suspicious that something was quite wrong. But the enthusiasm of the Prophet of the Moon
sprang up instantly at any sort of question and swept the Chairman
along with it.

"But it iss the essence of our who-ole message," he cried, spreading out his arms to embrace the world, "that the outer manifestation
should be one with the inner manifestation. My friendss, it iss this very
tru-uth our friend has stated, that iss responsible for our apparent lack
of symbolism in Islam! We appear to neglect the symbol because we
insist on the satisfactory symbol. My friend in the middle will walk round
all our mosques and say loudly, 'Where is the statue of Allah?' But can

my friend in the middle really execute a complete and generally ap-
proved statue of Allah?”

Misysra Ammon sat down greatly satisfied with his answer, but it
was doubted by many whether, he had conveyed the satisfaction to his
friend in the middle. That seeker after truth wiped his mouth with the
back of his hand with an unsatisfied air and said:

“No offence, sir. But ain’t it the Law, sir, that if you ’ave that outside we’re all right? I came in ’ere as natural as could be. But Gorlumme,
I never see a place like this afore.” (Hoarse laughter behind.)

“No apology is needed, my friend,” cried the Eastern sage, eagerly,
“I can conceive you are not perhaps du-uly conversant with such schools
of truth. But the Law is All. The Law is Allah. The inmost u-unity of—”

“Well, ain’t it the Law?” repeated the dogged George, and every
time he mentioned the Law the poor men who are its chief victims
applauded loudly. “I’m not one to make a fuss. I never was one to make a
fuss. I’m a law-abidin’ man, I am. (More applause.) Ain’t it the Law that if
so be such is your sign and such is your profession, you ought to serve us?”

“I fear I not quite follow,” cried the eager Turk. “I ought?”

“To serve us,” shouted a throng of thick voices from the back of
the hall, which was already much more crowded than before.

“Serve you!” cried Misysra, leaping up like a spring released, “The
Holy Prophet came from Heaven to serve you! The virtue and valour
of a thousand years, my friends, has had no hunger but to serve you!
We are of all faiths, the most the faith of service. Our highest prophet
is no more than the servant of God, as I am, as you all are. Even for
our symbol we choose a satellite, and honour the Moon because it only
serves the Earth, and does not pretend to be the Sun.”

“I’m sure,” cried Mr. Leveson, jumping up with a tactful grin, “that
the lecturer has answered this last point in a most eloquent and effective way, and the motor cars are waiting for some of the ladies who
have come from some distance, and I really think the proceedings—”

All the artistic ladies were already getting on their wraps, with faces
varying from bewilderment to blank terror. Only Lady Joan lingered,
trembling with unexplained excitement. The hitherto speechless Hinch
had slid up to the Chairman’s seat and whispered to him:

“You must get all the ladies away. I can’t imagine what’s up, but
something’s up.”

"Well?" repeated the patient George. "So be it's the Law, where is it?"

"Ladies and Gentlemen," said Mr. Leveson, in his most ingratiating manner, "I think we have had a most delightful evening, and—"

"No, we ain't," cried a new and nastier voice from a corner of the room. "Where is it?"

"That's what we got a right to know," said the law-abiding George. "Where is it?"

"Where is what?" cried the nearly demented secretary in the chair. "What do you want?"

The law-abiding Mr. George made a half turn and a gesture towards the man in the corner and said:

"What's yours, Jim?"

"I'll 'ave a drop of Scotch," said the man in the corner.

Lady Enid Wimpole, who had lingered a little in loyalty to Joan, the only other lady still left, caught both her wrists and cried in a thrilling whisper,

"Oh, we must go to the car, dear! They're using the most awful language!"

Away on the wettest edge of the sands by the sea the prints of two wheels and four hoofs were being slowly washed away by a slowly rising tide; which was, indeed, the only motive of the man Humphrey Pump, leading the donkey cart, in leading it almost ankle deep in water.

"I hope you're sober again now," he said with some seriousness to his companion, a huge man walking heavily and even humbly with a straight sword swinging to and fro at his hip— "for honestly it was a mug's game to go and stick up the old sign before that tin place. I haven't often spoken to you like this, Captain, but I don't believe any other man in the county could get you out of the hole as I can. But to go down there and frighten the ladies—why there's been nothing so silly here since Bishop's Folly. You could hear the ladies screaming before we left."

"I heard worse than that long before we left," said the large man, without lifting his head. "I heard one of them laugh. ... Christ, do you think I shouldn't hear her laugh?"

There was a silence. "I didn't mean to speak sharp," said Humphrey Pump with that incorruptible kindliness which was the root of his

Englishry, and may yet save the soul of the English. "But it's the truth I was pretty well bothered about how to get out of this business. You're braver than I am, you see, and I own I was frightened about both of us. If I hadn't known my way to the lost tunnel, I should be fairly frightened still."

"Known your way to what?" asked the Captain, lifting his red head for the first time.

"Oh, you know all about No More Ivywood's lost tunnel," said Pump, carelessly. "Why, we all used to look for it when we were boys. Only I happened to find it."

"Have mercy on an exile," said Dalroy, humbly. "I don't know which hurt him most, the things he forgets or the things he remembers."

Mr. Pump was silent for a little while and then said, more seriously than usual, "Well, the people from London say you must put up placards and statues and subscriptions and epitaphs and the Lord knows what, to the people who've found some new trick and made it come off. But only a man that knows his own land for forty miles round, knows what a lot of people, and clever people too, there were who found new tricks, and had to hide them because they didn't come off. There was Dr. Boone, up by Gill-in-Hugby, who held out against Dr. Collison and the vaccination. His treatment saved sixty patients who had got small-pox; and Dr. Collison's killed ninety-two patients who hadn't got anything. But Boone had to keep it dark; naturally, because all his lady patients grew mustaches. It was a result of the treatment. But it wasn't a result he wishes to dwell on. Then there was old Dean Arthur, who discovered balloons if ever a man did. He discovered them long before they were discovered. But people were suspicious about such things just then—there was a revival of the witch business in spite of all the parsons—and he had to sign a paper saying where he'd got the notion. Well, it stands to reason, you wouldn't like to sign a paper saying you'd got it from the village idiot when you were both blowing soap-bubbles; and that's all he could have signed, for he was an honest gentleman, the poor old Dean. Then there was Jack Arlingham and the diving bell—but you remember all about that. Well, it was just the same with the man that made this tunnel—one of the mad Ivywoods. There's many a man, Captain, that has a statue in the great London squares for helping to make the railway trains. There's many a man has his name in

Westminster Abbey for doing something in discovering steamboats. Poor old Ivywood discovered both at once; and had to be put under control. He had a notion that a railway train might be made to rush right into the sea and turn into a steamboat; and it seemed all right, according as he worked it out. But his family were so ashamed of the thing, that they didn't like the tunnel even mentioned. I don't think anybody knows where it is but me and Bunchy Robinson. We shall be there in a minute or two. They've thrown the rocks about at this end; and let the thick plantation grow at the other, but I've got a race horse through before now, to save it from Colonel Chepstow's little games, and I think I can manage this donkey. Honestly, I think it's the only place we'll be safe in after what we've left behind us at Pebblewick. But it's the best place in the world, there's no doubt, for lying low and starting afresh. Here we are. You think you can't get behind that rock, but you can. In fact, you have."

Dalroy found himself, with some bewilderment, round the corner of a rock and in a long bore or barrel of blackness that ended in a very dim spot of green. Hearing the hoofs of the ass and the feet of his friend behind him, he turned his head, but could see nothing but the pitch darkness of a closed coal cellar. He turned again to the dim green speck, and marching forward was glad to see it grow larger and brighter, like a big emerald, till he came out on a throng of trees, mostly thin, but growing so thickly and so close to the cavernous entrance of the tunnel that it was quite clear the place was meant to be choked up by forests and forgotten. The light that came glimmering through the trees was so broken and tremulous that it was hard to tell whether it was daybreak or moonrise.

"I know there's water here," said Pump. "They couldn't keep it out of the stone-work when they made the tunnel, and old Ivywood hit the hydraulic engineer with a spirit level. With the bit of covert here and the sea behind us we ought to be able to get food of one kind or another, when the cheese has given out, and donkeys can eat anything. By the way," he added with some embarrassment, "you don't mind my saying it, Captain, but I think we'd better keep that rum for rare occasions. It's the best rum in England, and may be the last, if these mad games are going on. It'll do us good to feel it's there, so we can have it when we want it. The cask's still nearly full."

Dalroy put out his hand and shook the other's. "Hump," he said, seriously, "you're right. It's a sacred trust for Humanity; and we'll only drink it ourselves to celebrate great victories. In token of which I will take a glass now, to celebrate our glorious victory over Leveson and his tin tabernacle."

He drained one glass and then sat down on the cask, as if to put temptation behind him. His blue ruminant bull's eye seemed to plunge deeper and deeper into the emerald twilight of the trees in front of him, and it was long before he spoke again.

At last he observed, "I think you said, Hump, that a friend of yours—a gentleman named Bunchy Robinson, I think—was also a *habitué* here."

"Yes, he knew the way," answered Pump, leading the donkey to the most suitable patch of pasturage.

"May we, do you think, have the pleasure of a visit from Mr. Robinson?" inquired the Captain.

"Not unless they're jolly careless up in Blackstone Gaol," replied Pump. And he moved the cheese well into the arch of the tunnel. Dalroy still sat with his square chin on his hand, staring at the mystery of the little wood.

"You seem absent-minded, Captain," remarked Humphrey.

"The deepest thoughts are all commonplaces," said Dalroy. "That is why I believe in Democracy, which is more than you do, you foul blood-stained old British Tory. And the deepest commonplace of all is that Vanitas Vanitatem, which is not pessimism but is really the opposite of pessimism. It is man's futility that makes us feel he must be a god. And I think of this tunnel, and how the poor old lunatic walked about on this grass, watching it being built, the soul in him on fire with the future. And he saw the whole world changed and the seas thronged with his new shipping; and now," and Dalroy's voice changed and broke, "now there is good pasture for the donkey and it is very quiet here."

"Yes," said Pump, in some way that conveyed his knowledge that the Captain was thinking of other things also. The Captain went on dreamily:

"And I think about another Lord Ivywood recorded in history who also had a great vision. For it is a great vision after all, and though the man is a prig, he is brave. He also wants to drive a tunnel—between

East and West—to make the Indian Empire more British; to effect what he calls the orientation of England, and I call the ruin of Christendom. And I am wondering just now whether the clear intellect and courageous will of a madman will be strong enough to burst and drive that tunnel, as everything seems to show at this moment that it will. Or whether there be indeed enough life and growth in your England to leave it at last as this is left, buried in English forests and wasted by an English sea."

The silence fell between them again, and again there was only the slight sound the animal made in eating. As Dalroy had said, it was very quiet there.

But it was not quiet in Pebblewick that night; when the Riot Act was read, and all the people who had seen the sign-board outside fought all the people who hadn't seen the sign-board outside; or when babies and scientists next morning, seeking for shells and other common objects of the sea-shore, found that their study included fragments of the outer clothing of Leveson and scraps of corrugated iron.

IX
The Higher Criticism and Mr. Hibbs

Pebblewick boasted an enterprising evening paper of its own, called "The Pebblewick Globe," and it was the great vaunt of the editor's life that he had got out an edition announcing the mystery of the vanishing sign-board, almost simultaneously with its vanishing. In the rows that followed sandwich men found no little protection from the blows indiscriminately given them behind and before, in the large wooden boards they carried inscribed:

The Vanishing Pub
Pebblewick's Fairy Tale
Special

And the paper contained a categorical and mainly correct account of what had happened, or what seemed to have happened, to the eyes of the amazed Garge and his crowd of sympathisers. "George Burn, carpenter of this town, with Samuel Gripes, drayman in the service of Messrs. Jay and Gubbins, brewers, together with a number of other well-known residents, passed by the new building erected on the West Beach for various forms of entertainment and popularly called the small Universal Hall. Seeing outside it one of the old inn-signs now so rare, they drew the quite proper inference that the place retained the license to sell alcoholic liquors, which so many other places in this neighbourhood have recently lost. The persons inside, however, appear to have denied all knowledge of the fact, and when the party (after some regrettable scenes in which no life was lost) came out on the beach again, it was found that the inn-sign had been destroyed or stolen. All parties were quite sober, and had indeed obtained no opportunity to be anything else. The mystery is underlying inquiry."

But this comparatively realistic record was local and spontaneous, and owed not a little to the accidental honesty of the editor. Moreover, evening papers are often more honest than morning papers, because they are written by ill-paid and hardworked underlings in a great hurry, and there is no time for more timid people to correct them. By the time the morning papers came out next day a faint but perceptible change had passed over the story of the vanishing sign-board. In the daily paper which had the largest circulation and the most influence in that part of the world, the problem was committed to a gentleman known by what seemed to the non-journalistic world the singular name of Hibbs However. It had been affixed to him in jest in connection with the almost complicated caution with which all his public criticisms were qualified at every turn; so that everything came to depend upon the conjunctions; upon "but" and "yet" and "though" and similar words. As his salary grew larger (for editors and proprietors like that sort of thing) and his old friends fewer (for the most generous of friends cannot but feel faintly acid at a success which has in it nothing of the infectious flavour of glory) he grew more and more to value himself as a diplomatist; a man who always said the right thing. But he was not without his intellectual nemesis; for at last he became so very diplomatic as to be darkly and densely unintelligible. People who knew him had no difficulty in believing that what he had said was the right thing, the tactful thing, the thing that should save the situation; but they had great difficulty in discovering what it was. In his early days he had had a great talent for one of the worst tricks of modern journalism, the trick of dismissing the important part of a question as if it could wait, and appearing to get to business on the unimportant part of it. Thus, he would say, "Whatever we may think of the rights and wrongs of the vivisection of pauper children, we shall all agree that it should only be done, in any event, by fully qualified practitioners." But in the later and darker days of his diplomacy, he seemed rather to dismiss the important part of a subject, and get to grips with some totally different subject, following some timid and elusive train of associations of his own. In his late bad manner, as they say of painters, he was just as likely to say, "Whatever we may think of the rights and wrongs of the vivisection of pauper children, no progressive mind can doubt that the influence of the Vatican is on the decline." His nickname had stuck to him in honour of a paragraph he was alleged to have written when the American President was wounded by a bullet fired by a lunatic in New Orleans, and which was said to have run, "The President passed a good night and his condition is greatly improved. The assassin is not, however, a German, as was at first supposed." Men stared at that mysterious conjunction till they wanted to go mad and to shoot somebody themselves.

Hibbs However was a long, lank man, with straight, yellowish hair and a manner that was externally soft and mild but secretly supercilious. He had been, when at Cambridge, a friend of Leveson, and they had both prided themselves on being moderate politicians. But if you have had your hat smashed over your nose by one who has very recently described himself as a "law-abidin' man," and if you have had to run for your life with one coat-tail, and encouraged to further bodily activity by having irregular pieces of a corrugated iron roof thrown after you by men more energetic than yourself, you will find you emerge with emotions which are not solely those of a moderate politician. Hibbs However had already composed a leaderette on the Pebblewick incident, which rather pointed to the truth of the story, so far as his articles ever pointed to anything. His motives for veering vaguely in this direction were, as usual, complex. He knew the millionaire who owned the paper had a hobby of Spiritualism, and something might always come out of not suppressing a marvellous story. He knew that two at least of the prosperous artisans or small tradesmen who had attested the tale were staunch supporters of The Party. He knew that Lord Ivywood must be mildly but not effectually checked; for Lord Ivywood was of The Other Party. And there could be no milder or less effectual way of checking him than by allowing the paper to lend at least a temporary credit to a well-supported story that came from outside, and certainly had not been (like so many stories) created in the office. Amid all these considerations had Hibbs However steered his way to a more or less confirmatory article, when the sudden apparition of J. Leveson, Secretary, in the sub-editor's room with a burst collar and broken eyeglasses, led Mr. Hibbs into a long, private conversation with him and a comparative reversal of his plans. But of course he did not write a new article; he was not of that divine order who make all things new. He chopped and changed his original article in such a way that it was something quite beyond the most bewildering article he had written in the past; and is still prized by those highly cultured persons who collect the worst literature of the world.

It began, indeed, with the comparatively familiar formula, "Whether we take the more lax or the more advanced view of the old disputed problem of the morality or immorality of the wooden sign-board as such, we shall all agree that the scenes enacted at Pebblewick were very discreditable, to most, though not all, concerned." After that, tact degenerated into a riot of irrelevance. It was a wonderful article. The reader could get from it a faint glimpse of Mr. Hibbs's opinion on almost every other subject except the subject of the article. The first half of the next sentence made it quite clear that Mr. Hibbs (had he been present) would not have lent his active assistance to the Massacre of St. Bartholomew or the Massacres of September. But the second half of the sentence suggested with equal clearness that, since these two acts were no longer, as it were, in contemplation, and all attempts to prevent them would probably arrive a little late, he felt the warmest friendship for the French nation. He merely insisted that his friendship should never be mentioned except in the French language. It must be called an "entente" in the language taught to tourists by waiters. It must on no account be called an "understanding," in a language understanded of the people. From the first half of the sentence following it might safely be inferred that Mr. Hibbs had read Milton, or at least the passage about sons of Belial; from the second half that he knew nothing about bad wine, let alone good. The next sentence began with the corruption of the Roman Empire and contrived to end with Dr. Clifford. Then there was a weak plea for Eugenics; and a warm plea against Conscription, which was not True Eugenics. That was all; and it was headed "The Riot at Pebblewick."

Yet some injustice would be done to Hibbs However if we concealed the fact that this chaotic leader was followed by quite a considerable mass of public correspondence. The people who write to newspapers are, it may be supposed, a small, eccentric body, like most of those that sway a modern state. But at least, unlike the lawyers, or the financiers, or the members of Parliament, or the men of science, they are people of all kinds scattered all over the country, of all classes, counties, ages, sects, sexes, and stages of insanity. The letters that followed Hibbs's article are still worth looking up in the dusty old files of his paper.

A dear old lady in the densest part of the Midlands wrote to suggest that there might really have been an old ship wrecked on the shore, during the proceedings. "Mr. Leveson may have omitted to notice it, or, at that late hour of the evening, it may have been mistaken for a sign-board, especially by a person of defective sight. My own sight has been failing for some time; but I am still a diligent reader of your paper." If Mr. Hibbs's diplomacy had left one nerve in his soul undrugged, he would have laughed, or burst into tears, or got drunk, or gone into a monastery over a letter like that. As it was, he measured it with a pencil, and decided that it was just too long to get into the column.

Then there was a letter from a theorist, and a theorist of the worst sort. There is no great harm in the theorist who makes up a new theory to fit a new event. But the theorist who starts with a false theory and then sees everything as making it come true is the most dangerous enemy of human reason. The letter began like a bullet let loose by the trigger. "Is not the whole question met by Ex. iv. 3? I enclose pamphlets in which I have proved the point quite plainly, and which none of the Bishops or the so-called Free Church Ministers have attempted to answer. The connection between the rod or pole and the snake so clearly indicated in Scripture is no less clear in this case. It is well known that those who follow after strong drink often announce themselves as having seen a snake. Is it not clear that those unhappy revellers beheld it in its transformed state as a pole; see also Deut. xviii. 2. If our so-called religious leaders," etc. The letter went on for thirty-three pages and Hibbs was perhaps justified in this case in thinking the letter rather too long.

Then there was the scientific correspondent who said—Might it not be due to the acoustic qualities of the hall? He had never believed in the corrugated iron hall. The very word "hall" itself (he added playfully) was often so sharpened and shortened by the abrupt echoes of those repeated metallic curves, that it had every appearance of being the word "hell," and had caused many theological entanglements, and some police prosecutions. In the light of these facts, he wished to draw the editor's attention to some very curious details about this supposed presence or absence of an inn-sign. It would be noted that many of the witnesses, and especially the most respectable of them, constantly refer to something that is supposed to be outside. The word "outside" occurs at least five times in the depositions of the complaining persons. Surely by all scientific analogy we may infer that the unusual phrase "inn-sign" is an acoustic error for "inside." The word "inside" would so naturally occur in any discussion either about the building or the individual, when the debate was of a hygienic character. This letter was signed "Medical Student," and the less intelligent parts of it were selected for publication in the paper.

Then there was a really humorous man, who wrote and said there was nothing at all inexplicable or unusual about the case. He himself (he said) had often seen a sign-board outside a pub when he went into it, and been quite unable to see it when he came out. This letter (the only one that had any quality of literature) was sternly set aside by Mr. Hibbs.

Then came a cultured gentleman with a light touch, who merely made a suggestion. Had anyone read H. G. Wells's story about the kink in space? He contrived, indescribably, to suggest that no one had even heard of it except himself; or, perhaps, of Mr. Wells either. The story indicated that men's feet might be in one part of the world and their eyes in another. He offered the suggestion for what it was worth. The particular pile of letters on which Hibbs However threw it, showed only too clearly what it was worth.

Then there was a man, of course, who called it all a plot of frenzied foreigners against Britain's shore. But as he did not make it quite clear whether the chief wickedness of these aliens had lain in sticking the sign up or in pulling it down, his remarks (the remainder of which referred exclusively to the conversational misconduct of an Italian ice-cream man, whose side of the case seemed insufficiently represented) carried the less weight.

And then, last but the reverse of least, there plunged in all the people who think they can solve a problem they cannot understand by abolishing everything that has contributed to it. We all know these people. If a barber has cut his customer's throat because the girl has changed her partner for a dance or donkey ride on Hampstead Heath, there are always people to protest against the mere institutions that led up to it. This would not have happened if barbers were abolished, or if cutlery were abolished, or if the objection felt by girls to imperfectly grown beards were abolished, or if the girls were abolished, or if heaths and

open spaces were abolished, or if dancing were abolished, or if donkeys were abolished. But donkeys, I fear, will never be abolished.

There were plenty of such donkeys in the common land of this
particular controversy. Some made it an argument against democracy,
because poor Garge was a carpenter. Some made it an argument against
Alien Immigration, because Misysra Ammon was a Turk. Some proposed that ladies should no longer be admitted to any lectures anywhere, because they had constituted a slight and temporary difficulty at
this one, without the faintest fault of their own. Some urged that all
holiday resorts should be abolished; some urged that all holidays should
be abolished. Some vaguely denounced the sea-side; some, still more
vaguely, proposed to remove the sea. All said that if this or that, stones
or sea-weed or strange visitors or bad weather or bathing machines were
swept away with a strong hand, this which had happened would not
have happened. They only had one slight weakness, all of them; that
they did not seem to have the faintest notion of what *had* happened.
And in this they were not inexcusable. Nobody did know what had happened; nobody knows it to this day, of course, or it would be unnecessary to write this story. No one can suppose this story is written from
any motive save that of telling the plain, humdrum truth.

That queer confused cunning which was the only definable quality
possessed by Hibbs However had certainly scored a victory so far, for
the tone of the weekly papers followed him, with more intelligence and
less trepidation; but they followed him. It seemed more and more clear
that some kind of light and sceptical explanation was to be given of
the whole business, and that the whole business was to be dropped.

The story of the sign-board and the ethical chapel of corrugated
iron was discussed and somewhat disparaged in all the more serious
and especially in the religious weeklies, though the Low Church papers
seemed to reserve their distaste chiefly for the sign-board; and the High
Church papers chiefly for the Chapel. All agreed that the combination
was incongruous, and most treated it as fabulous. The only intellectual
organs which seemed to think it might have happened were the Spiritu-
alist papers, and their interpretation had not that solidity which would
have satisfied Mr. George.

It was not until almost a year after that it was felt in philosophical
circles that the last word had been said on the matter. An estimate of the

incident and of its bearing on natural and supernatural history occurred in Professor Widge's celebrated "Historicity of the Petro-Piscatorial Phenomena"; which so profoundly affected modern thought when it came out in parts in the *Hibbert Journal.* Everyone remembers Professor Widge's main contention, that the modern critic must apply to the thaumaturgics of the Lake of Tiberias the same principle of criticism which Dr. Bunk and others have so successfully applied to the thaumaturgics of the Cana narrative: "Authorities as final as Pink and Toscher," wrote the Professor, "have now shown with an emphasis that no emancipated mind is entitled to question, that the Aqua-Vinic thaumaturgy at Cana is wholly inconsistent with the psychology of the 'master of the feast,' as modern research has analysed it; and indeed with the whole Judaeo-Aramaic psychology at that stage of its development, as well as being painfully incongruous with the elevated ideals of the ethical teacher in question. But as we rise to higher levels of moral achievement, it will probably be found necessary to apply the Canaic principle to other and later events in the narrative. This principle has, of course, been mainly expounded by Huscher in the sense that the whole episode is unhistorical, while the alternative theory, that the wine was non-alcoholic and was naturally infused into the water, can claim on its side the impressive name of Minns. It is clear that if we apply the same alternative to the so-called Miraculous Draught of Fishes we must either hold with Gilp, that the fishes were stuffed representations of fishes artificially placed in the lake (see the Rev. Y. Wyse's "Christo-Vegetarianism as a World-System," where this position is forcibly set forth), or we must, on the Huscherian hypothesis, deprive the Piscatorial narrative of all claim to historicity whatever.

"The difficulty felt by the most daring critics (even Pooke) in adopting this entirely destructive attitude, is the alleged improbability of so detailed a narrative being founded on so slight a phrase as the anti-historical critics refer it to. It is urged by Pooke, with characteristic relentless reasoning, that according to Huscher's theory a metaphorical but at least noticeable remark, such as, 'I will make you fishers of men,' was expanded into a realistic chronicle of events which contains no mention, even in the passages evidently interpolated, of any men actually found in the nets when they were hauled up out of the sea; or, more properly, lagoon.

"It must appear presumptuous or even bad taste for anyone in the modern world to differ on any subject from Pooke; but I would venture to suggest that the very academic splendour and unique standing of the venerable professor (whose ninety-seventh birthday was so beautifully celebrated in Chicago last year), may have forbidden him all but intuitive knowledge of how errors arise among the vulgar. I crave pardon for mentioning a modern case known to myself (not indeed by personal presence, but by careful study of all the reports) which presents a curious parallel to such ancient expansions of a text into an incident, in accordance with Huscher's law.

"It occurred at Pebblewick, in the south of England. The town had long been in a state of dangerous religious excitement. The great religious genius who has since so much altered our whole attitude to the religions of the world, Misysra Ammon, had been lecturing on the sands to thousands of enthusiastic hearers. Their meetings were often interrupted, both by children's services run on the most ruthless lines of orthodoxy and by the League of the Red Rosette, the formidable atheist and anarchist organization. As if this were not enough to swell the whirlpool of fanaticism, the old popular controversy between the Milnian and the Complete Sublapsarians broke out again on the fated beach. It is natural to conjecture that in the thickening atmosphere of theology in Pebblewick, some controversialist quoted the text 'An evil and adulterous generation *seek for a sign*. But no sign shall be given it save the sign of the prophet Jonas.'

"A mind like that of Pooke will find it hard to credit, but it seems certain that the effect of this text on the ignorant peasantry of southern England was actually to make them go about looking for a sign, in the sense of those old tavern signs now so happily disappearing. The 'sign of the Prophet Jonas,' they somehow translated in their stunted minds into a sign-board of the ship out of which Jonah was thrown. They went about literally looking for 'The Sign of the Ship,' and there are some cases of their suffering Smail's Hallucination and actually seeing it. The whole incident is a curious parallel to the Gospel narrative and a triumphant vindication of Huscher's law."

Lord Ivywood paid a public compliment to Professor Widge, saying that he had rolled back from his country what might have been an ocean of superstitions. But, indeed, poor Hibbs had struck the first and stunning blow that scattered the brains of all men.

X
The Character of Quoodle

There lay about in Lord Ivywood's numerous gardens, terraces, out-houses, stable yards and similar places, a dog that came to be called by the name of Quoodle. Lord Ivywood did not call him Quoodle. Lord Ivywood was almost physically incapable of articulating such sounds. Lord Ivywood did not care for dogs. He cared for the Cause of dogs, of course; and he cared still more for his own intellectual self-respect and consistency. He would never have permitted a dog in his house to be physically ill-treated; nor, for that matter, a rat; nor, for that matter, even a man. But if Quoodle was not physically ill-treated, he was at least socially neglected, and Quoodle did not like it. For dogs care for companionship more than for kindness itself.

Lord Ivywood would probably have sold the dog, but he consulted experts (as he did on everything he didn't understand and many things that he did), and the impression he gathered from them was that the dog, technically considered, would fetch very little; mostly, it seemed, because of the mixture of qualities that it possessed. It was a sort of mongrel bull-terrier, but with rather too much of the bull-dog; and this fact seemed to weaken its price as much as it strengthened its jaw. His Lordship also gained a hazy impression that the dog might have been valuable as a watch dog if it had not been able to follow game like a pointer; and that even in the latter walk of life it would always be dis-credited by an unfortunate talent for swimming as well as a retriever. But Lord Ivywood's impressions may very well have been slightly con-fused, as he was probably thinking about the Black stone of Mecca, or some such subject at the moment. The victim of this entanglement of virtues, therefore, still lay about in the sunlight of Ivywood, exhibiting no general result of that entanglement except the most appalling ugliness.

Now Lady Joan Brett did appreciate dogs. It was the whole of her type and a great deal of her tragedy that all that was natural in her was still alive under all that was artificial; and she could smell hawthorn or the sea as far off as a dog can smell his dinner. Like most aristocrats she would carry cynicism almost to the suburbs of the city of Satan; she was quite as irreligious as Lord Ivywood, or rather more. She could be quite equally frigid or supercilious when she felt inclined. And in the great social talent of being tired, she could beat him any day of the week. But the difference remained in spite of her sophistries and ambitions; that her elemental communications were not cut, and his were. For her the sunrise was still the rising of a sun, and not the turning on of a light by a convenient cosmic servant. For her the Spring was really the Season in the country, and not merely the Season in town. For her cocks and hens were natural appendages to an English house; and not (as Lord Ivywood had proved to her from an encyclopaedia) animals of Indian origin, recently imported by Alexander the Great. And so for her a dog was a dog, and not one of the higher animals, nor one of the lower animals, nor something that had the sacredness of life, nor something that ought to be muzzled, nor something that ought not to be vivisected. She knew that in every practical sense proper provision would be made for the dog; as, indeed, provision was made for the yellow dogs in Constantinople by Abdul Hamid, whose life Lord Ivywood was writing for the *Progressive Potentates* series. Nor was she in the least sentimental about the dog or anxious to turn him into a pet. It simply came natural to her in passing to rub all his hair the wrong way and call him something which she instantly forgot.

The man who was mowing the garden lawn looked up for a moment, for he had never seen the dog behave in exactly that way before. Quoodle arose, shook himself, and trotted on in front of the lady, leading her up an iron side staircase, of which, as it happened, she had never made use before.

It was then, most probably, that she first took any special notice of him; and her pleasure, like that which she took in the sublime prophet from Turkey, was of a humorous character. For the complex quadruped had retained the bow legs of the bull-dog; and, seen from behind, reminded her ridiculously of a swaggering little Major waddling down to his Club.

The dog and the iron stairway between them led her into a series of long rooms, one opening into the other. They formed part of what she had known in earlier days as the disused Wing of Ivywood House, which had been neglected or shut up, probably because it bore some defacements from the fancies of the mad ancestor, the memory of whom the present Lord Ivywood did not think helpful to his own political career. But it seemed to Joan that there were indications of a recent attempt to rehabilitate the place. There was a pail of whitewash in one of the empty rooms, a step-ladder in another, here and there a curtain rod, and at last, in the fourth room a curtain. It hung all alone on the old woodwork, but it was a very gorgeous curtain, being a kind of orange-gold relieved with wavy bars of crimson, which somehow seemed to suggest the very spirit and presence of serpents, though they had neither eyes nor mouths among them.

In the next of the endless series of rooms she came upon a kind of ottoman, striped with green and silver standing alone on the bare floor. She sat down on it from a mixed motive of fatigue and of impudence, for she dimly remembered a story which she had always thought one of the funniest in the world, about a lady only partly initiated in Theosophy who had been in the habit of resting on a similar object, only to discover afterward that it was a Mahatma, covered with his eastern garment and prostrate and rigid in ecstasy. She had no hopes of sitting on a Mahatma herself, but the very thought of it made her laugh, because it would make Lord Ivywood look such a fool. She was not sure whether she liked or disliked Lord Ivywood, but she felt quite certain that it would gratify her to make him look a fool. The moment she had sat down on the ottoman, the dog, who had been trotting beside her, sat down also, and on the edge of her skirt.

After a minute or two she rose (and the dog rose), and she looked yet farther down that long perspective of large rooms, in which men like Philip Ivywood forget that they are only men. The next was more ornate and the next yet more so; it was plain that the scheme of decoration that was in progress had been started at the other end. She could now see that the long lane ended in rooms that from afar off looked like the end of a kaleidoscope, rooms like nests made only from humming

birds or palaces built of fixed fireworks. Out of this furnace of fragmentary colours she saw Ivywood advancing toward her, with his black
suit and his white face accented by the contrast. His lips were moving,
for he was talking to himself, as many orators do. He did not seem to
see her, and she had to strangle a subconscious and utterly senseless
cry, "He is blind!"

The next moment he was welcoming her intrusion with the well-
bred surprise and rather worldly simplicity suitable to such a case, and
Joan fancied she understood why his face had seemed a little bleaker
and blinder than usual. It was by contrast. He was carrying clutched to
his forefinger, as his ancestors might have carried a falcon clutched to
the wrist, a small bright coloured semi-tropical bird, the expression of
whose head, neck and eye was the very opposite of his own. Joan thought
she had never seen a living creature with a head so lively and insulting.
Its provocative eye and pointed crest seemed to be offering to fight
fifty game-cocks. It was no wonder (she told herself) that by the side of
this gaudy gutter-snipe with feathers Ivywood's faint-coloured hair and
frigid face looked like the hair and face of a corpse walking.

"You'll never know what this is," said Ivywood, in his most charming manner. "You've heard of him a hundred times and never had a
notion of what he was. This is the Bulbul."

"I never knew," replied Joan. "I am afraid I never cared. I always
thought it was something like a nightingale."

"Ah, yes," answered Ivywood, "but this is the real Bulbul peculiar
to the East, *Pycnonotus Haemorrhous*. You are thinking of *Daulias Golzii*."

"I suppose I am," replied Lady Joan with a faint smile. "It is an
obsession. When shall I not be thinking of Daulias Galsworthy? Was it
Galsworthy?" Then feeling quite touched by the soft austerity of her
companion's face, she caressed the gaudy and pugnacious bird with one
finger and said, "It's a dear little thing."

The quadruped intimately called Quoodle did not approve of all
this at all. Like most dogs, he liked to be with human beings when they
were silent, and he extended a magnificent toleration to them as long as
they were talking to each other. But conversational attention paid to
any other animal at all remote from a mongrel bull-terrier wounded Mr.
Quoodle in his most sensitive and gentlemanly feelings. He emitted a
faint growl. Joan, with all the instincts that were in her, bent down and

pulled his hair about once more, and felt the instant necessity of diverting the general admiration from *Pycnonotus Haemorrhous*. She turned it to
the decoration at the end of the refurnished wing; for they had already
come to the last of the long suite of rooms, which ended in some un-
finished but exquisite panelling in white and coloured woods, inlaid in
the oriental manner. At one corner the whole corridor ended by curving into a round turret chamber overlooking the landscape; and which
Joan, who had known the house in childhood, was sure was an innova-
tion. On the other hand a black gap, still left in the lower left-hand
corner of the oriental woodwork, suddenly reminded her of something
she had forgotten.

"Surely," she said (after much mere aesthetic ecstasy), "there used
to be a staircase there, leading to the old kitchen garden, or the old
chapel or something."

Ivywood nodded gravely. "Yes," he said, "it did lead to the ruins of
a Mediaeval Chapel, as you say. The truth is it led to several things that
I cannot altogether consider a credit to the family in these days. All
that scandal and joking about the unsuccessful tunnel (your mother may
have told you of it), well, it did us no good in the County, I'm afraid; so
as it's a mere scrap of land bordering on the sea, I've fenced it off and
let it grow wild. But I'm boarding up the end of the room here for
quite another reason. I want you to come and see it."

He led her into the round corner turret in which the new architecture ended, and Joan, with her thirst for the beautiful, could not stifle a
certain thrill of beatitude at the prospect. Five open windows of a light
and exquisite Saracenic outline looked out over the bronze and copper
and purple of the Autumn parks and forests to the peacock colours of
the sea. There was neither house nor living thing in sight, and, familiar
as she had been with that coast, she knew she was looking out from a
new angle of vision on a new landscape of Ivywood.

"You can write sonnets?" said Ivywood with something more like
emotion in his voice than she had ever heard in it. "What comes first
into your mind with these open windows?"

"I know what you mean," said Joan after a silence. "The same hath
oft ..."

"Yes," he said. "That is how I felt ... of perilous seas in fairy lands
forlorn."

There was another silence and the dog sniffed round and round the circular turret chamber.

"I want it to be like that," said Ivywood in a low and singularly moved intonation. "I want this to be the end of the house. I want this to be the end of the world. Don't you feel that is the real beauty of all this eastern art; that it is coloured like the edges of things, like the little clouds of morning and the islands of the blest? Do you know," and he lowered his voice yet more, "it has the power over me of making me feel as if I were myself absent and distant; some oriental traveller who was lost and for whom men were looking. When I see that greenish lemon yellow enamel there let into the white, I feel that I am standing thousands of leagues from where I stand."

"You are right," said Joan, looking at him with some wonder, "I have felt like that myself."

"This art," went on Ivywood as in a dream, "does indeed take the wings of the morning and abide in the uttermost parts of the sea. They say it contains no form of life, but surely we can read its alphabet as easily as the red hieroglyphics of sunrise and sunset which are on the fringes of the robe of God."

"I never heard you talk like that before," said the lady, and again stroked the vivid violet feathers of the small eastern bird.

Mr. Quoodle could stand it no longer. He had evidently formed a very low opinion of the turret chamber and of oriental art generally, but seeing Joan's attention once more transferred to his rival, he trotted out into the longer room, and finding the gap in the woodwork which was soon to be boarded up, but which still opened on an old dark stair-case, he went "galumphing" down the stairs.

Lord Ivywood gently placed the bird on the girl's own finger, and went to one of the open windows, leaning out a little.

"Look here," he said, "doesn't this express what we both feel? Isn't this the sort of fairy-tale house that ought to hang on the last wall of the world?"

And he motioned her to the window-sill, just outside which hung the bird's empty cage, beautifully wrought in brass or some of the yellow metals.

"Why that is the best of all!" cried Lady Joan. "It makes one feel as if it really were the Arabian Nights. As if this were a tower of the gigantic Genii with turrets up to the moon; and this were an enchanted Prince caged in a golden palace suspended by the evening star."

Something stirred in her dim but teeming subconsciousness, something like a chill or change like that by which we half know that weather has altered, or distant and unnoticed music suddenly ceased.

"Where is the dog?" she asked suddenly.

Ivywood turned with a mild, grey eye.

"Was there a dog here?" he asked.

"Yes," said Lady Joan Brett, and gave him back the bird, which he restored carefully to its cage.

The dog after whom she inquired had in truth trundled down a dark, winding staircase and turned into the daylight, into a part of the garden he had never seen before; nor, indeed, had anybody else for some time past. It was altogether tangled and overgrown with weeds, and the only trace of human handiwork, the wreck of an old Gothic Chapel, stood waist high in numberless nettles and soiled with crawling fungoids. Most of these merely discoloured the grey crumbling stone with shades of bronze or brown; but some of them, particularly on the side farthest from the house, were of orange or purple tints almost bright enough for Lord Ivywood's oriental decoration. Some fanciful eyes that fell on the place afterward found something like an allegory in those graven and broken saints or archangels feeding such fiery and ephemeral parasites as those toadstools like blood or gold. But Mr. Quoodle had never set himself up as an allegorist, and he merely trotted deeper and deeper into the grey-green English jungle. He grumbled very much at the thistles and nettles, much as a city man will grumble at the jostling of a crowd. But he continued to press forward, with his nose near the ground, as if he had already smelt something that interested him. And, indeed, he had smelt something in which a dog, except on special occasions, is much more interested than he is in dogs. Breaking through a last barrier of high and hoary purple thistles he came out on a semicircle of somewhat clearer ground, dotted with slender trees, and having, by way of back scene, the brown brick arch of an old tunnel. The tunnel was boarded up with a very irregular fence or mask made of motley wooden lathes, and looked, somehow, rather like a pantomime cottage. In front of this a sturdy man in very shabby shooting clothes was standing attending to a battered old frying-pan which he held over a rather irregular flame which, small as it was, smelt strongly of burnt rum. In the frying-pan, and also on the top of a cask or barrel that served for a table hard by, were a number of the grey, brown, and even orange fungi which were plastered over the stone angels and dragons of the fallen chapel.

"Hullo, old man," said the person in the shooting jacket with tranquillity and without looking up from his cooking. "Come to pay us a visit? Come along then." He flashed one glance at the dog and returned to the frying pan. "If your tail were two inches shorter, you'd be worth a hundred pounds. Had any breakfast?"

The dog trotted across to him and began nosing and sniffing round his dilapidated leather gaiters. The man did not interrupt his cookery, on which his eyes were fixed and both his hands were busy; but he crooked his knee and foot so as to caress the quadruped in a nerve under the angle of the jaw, the stimulation of which (as some men of science have held) is for a dog what a good cigar is for a man. At the same moment a huge voice like on ogre's came from within the masked tunnel, calling out, "And who are ye talking to?"

A very crooked kind of window in the upper part of the pantomime cottage burst open and an enormous head, with erect, startling, and almost scarlet hair and blue eyes as big as a bullfrog's, was thrust out above the scene.

"Hump," cried the ogre. "Me moral counsels have been thrown away. In the last week I've sung you fourteen and a half songs of me own composition; instead of which you go about stealing dogs. You're following in the path of Parson Whats-his-name in every way, I'm afraid."

"No," said the man with the frying pan, impartially, "Parson Whitelady struck a very good path for doubling on Pebblewick, that I was glad to follow. But I think he was quite silly to steal dogs. He was young and brought up pious. I know too much about dogs to steal one."

"Well," asked the large red-haired man, "and how do you get a dog like that?"

"I let him steal me," said the person stirring the pan. And indeed the dog was sitting erect and even arrogant at his feet, as if he was a watch-dog at a high salary, and had been there before the building of the tunnel.

XI

VEGETARIANISM IN THE DRAWING-ROOM

The Company that assembled to listen to the Prophet of the Moon, on the next occasion of his delivering any formal address, was much more select than the comparatively mixed and middle-class society of the Simple Souls. Miss Browning and her sister, Mrs. Mackintosh, were indeed present; for Lord Ivywood had practically engaged them both as private secretaries, and kept them pretty busy, too. There was also Mr. Leveson, because Lord Ivywood believed in his organizing power; and also Mr. Hibbs, because Mr. Leveson believed in his political judgment, whenever he could discover what it was. Mr. Leveson had straight, dark hair, and looked nervous. Mr. Hibbs had straight, fair hair, and also looked nervous. But the rest of the company were more of Ivywood's own world, or the world of high finance with which it mixes both here and on the continent. Lord Ivywood welcomed, with something approaching to warmth, a distinguished foreign diplomatist, who was, indeed, none other than that silent German representative who had sat beside him in that last conference on the Island of the Olives. Dr. Gluck was no longer in his quiet, black suit, but wore an ornate, diplomatic uniform with a sword and Prussian, Austrian or Turkish Orders; for he was going on from Ivywood to a function at Court. But his curl of red lips, his screw of black mustache, and his unanswering almond eyes had no more changed than the face of a wax figure in a barber's shop window.

The Prophet had also effected an improvement in his dress. When he had orated on the sands his costume, except for the fez, was the shabby but respectable costume of any rather unsuccessful English clerk. But now that he had come among aristocrats who petted their souls as they did their senses, there must be no such incongruity. He must be a proper, fresh-picked oriental tulip or lotus. So—he wore long, flowing robes of white, relieved here and there by flame-coloured threads of tracery, and round his head was a turban of a kind of pale golden green. He had to look as if he had come flying across Europe on the magic carpet, or fallen a moment before from his paradise in the moon.

The ladies of Lord Ivywood's world were much as we have already found them. Lady Enid Wimpole still overwhelmed her earnest and timid face with a tremendous costume, that was more like a procession than a dress. It looked rather like the funeral procession of Aubrey Beardsley. Lady Joan Brett still looked like a very beautiful Spaniard with no illusions left about her castle in Spain. The large and resolute lady who had refused to ask any questions at Misysra's earlier lecture, and who was known as Lady Crump, the distinguished Feminist, still had the air of being so full and bursting with questions fatal to Man as to have passed the speaking and reached the speechless stage of hostility. Throughout the proceedings she contributed nothing but bursting silence and a malevolent eye. And old Lady Ivywood, under the oldest and finest lace and the oldest and finest manners, had a look like death on her, which can often be seen in the parents of pure intellectuals. She had that face of a lost mother that is more pathetic than the face of a lost child.

"And what are you going to delight us with today?" Lady Enid was asking of the Prophet.

"My lecture," answered Misysra, gravely, "is on the Pig."

It was part of a simplicity really respectable in him that he never saw any incongruity in the arbitrary and isolated texts or symbols out of which he spun his thousand insane theories. Lady Enid endured the impact of this singular subject for debate without losing that expression of wistful sweetness which she wore on principle when talking to such people.

"The Pig, he is a large subject," continued the Prophet, making curves in the air, as if embracing some particularly prize specimen. "He includes many subjects. It is to me very strange that the Christians should so laugh and be surprised because we hold ourselves to be defiled by pork; we and also another of the Peoples of the Book. But, surely, you Christians yourselves consider the pig as a manner of pollution; since it is your most usual expression of your despising, of your very great dislike. You say 'swine,' my dear lady; you do not say animals far more unpopular, such as the alligator."

"I see," said the lady, "how wonderful!"

"If you are annoyed," went on the encouraged and excited gentleman, "if you are annoyed with anyone, with a—what you say?—a lady's maid, you do not say to her 'Horse.' You do not say to her 'Camel.'"

"Ah, no," said Lady Enid, earnestly.

"'Pig of a lady's maid,' you say in your colloquial English," continued the Prophet, triumphantly. "And yet this great and awful Pig, this monster whose very name, when whispered, you think will wither all your enemies, you allow, my dear lady, to approach yet closer to you. You incorporate this great Pig in the substance of your own person."

Lady Enid Wimpole was looking a little dazed at last, at this description of her habits, and Joan gave Lord Ivywood a hint that the lecturer had better be transferred to his legitimate sphere of lecturing. Ivywood led the way into a larger room that was full of ranked chairs, with a sort of lectern at the other end, and flanked on all four sides with tables laden with all kinds of refreshments. It was typical of the strange, half-fictitious enthusiasm and curiosity of that world, that one long table was set out entirely with vegetarian foods, especially of an eastern sort (like a table spread in the desert for a rather fastidious Indian hermit); but that tables covered with game patties, lobster and champagne were equally provided, and very much more frequented. Even Mr. Hibbs, who would honestly have thought entering a public-house more disgraceful than entering a brothel, could not connect any conception of disgrace with Lord Ivywood's champagne.

For the purpose of the lecture was not wholly devoted to the great and awful Pig, and the purpose of the meeting even less. Lord Ivywood, the white furnace of whose mind was always full of new fancies hardening into ambitions, wanted to have a debate on the diet of East and West, and felt that Misysra might very appropriately open with an account of the Moslem veto on pork or other coarse forms of flesh food. He reserved it to himself to speak second.

The Prophet began, indeed, with some of his dizziest flights. He informed the Company that they, the English, had always gone in hidden terror and loathing of the Pig, as a sacred symbol of evil. He proved it by the common English custom of drawing a pig with one's eyes shut. Lady Joan smiled, and yet she asked herself (in a doubt that had been darkening round her about many modern things lately) whether it was really much more fanciful than many things the scientists told her: as, the traces of Marriage by Capture which they found in that ornamental and even frivolous being, the Best Man.

He said that the dawn of greater enlightenment is shown in the use of the word "gammon," which still expresses disgust at "the porcine image," but no longer fear of it, but rather a rational disdain and disbelief. "Rowley," said the Prophet, solemnly, and then after a long pause, "Powley, *Gammon* and Spinach."

Lady Joan smiled again, but again asked herself if it was much more farfetched than a history book she had read, which proved the unpopularity of Catholicism in Tudor times from the word "hocus pocus."

He got into a most amazing labyrinth of philology between the red primeval sins of the first pages of Genesis and the Common English word "ham." But, again, Joan wondered whether it was much wilder than the other things she had heard said about Primitive Man by people who had never seen him.

He suggested that the Irish were set to keep pigs because they were a low and defiled caste, and the serfs of the pig-scorning Saxon; and Joan thought it was about as sensible as what the dear old Archdeacon had said about Ireland years ago; which had caused an Irishman of her acquaintance to play "the Shan Van Voght" and then smash the piano.

Joan Brett had been thoughtful for the last few days. It was partly due to the scene in the turret, where she had struck a sensitive and artistic side of Philip Ivywood she had never seen before, and partly to disturbing news of her mother's health, which, though not menacing, made her feel hypothetically how isolated she was in the world. On all previous occasions she had merely enjoyed the mad lecturer now at the reading-desk. Today she felt a strange desire to analyse him, and imagine how a man could be so connected and so convinced and yet so wildly wide of the mark. As she listened carefully, looking at the hands in her lap, she began to think she understood.

The lecturer did really try to prove that the "porcine image" had never been used in English history or literature, except in contempt. And the lecturer really did know a very great deal about English history and literature: much more than she did; much more than the aristocrats round her did. But she noted that in every case what he knew was a fragmentary fact. In every case what he did not know was the truth behind the fact. What he did not know was the atmosphere. What he did not know was the tradition. She found herself ticking off the cases like counts in an indictment.

Misysra Ammon knew, what next to none of the English present knew, that Richard III was called a "boar" by an eighteenth century poet and a "hog" by a fifteenth century poet. What he did not know was the habit of sport and of heraldry. He did not know (what Joan knew instantly, though she had never thought of it before in her life) that beasts courageous and hard to kill are noble beasts, by the law of chivalry. Therefore, the boar was a noble beast, and a common crest for great captains. Misysra tried to show that Richard had only been called a pig after he was cold pork at Bosworth.

Misysra Ammon knew, what next to none of the English present knew, that there never was such a person as Lord Bacon. The phrase is a falsification of what should be Lord Verulam or Lord St. Albans. What he did not know was exactly what Joan did know (though it had never crossed her mind till that moment) that when all is said and done, a title is a sort of joke, while a surname is a serious thing. Bacon was a gentleman, and his name was Bacon; whatever titles he took. But Misysra seriously tried to prove that "Bacon" was a term of abuse applied to him during his unpopularity or after his fall.

Misysra Ammon knew, what next to none of the English present knew, that the poet Shelley had a friend called Hogg, who treated him on one occasion with grave treachery. He instantly tried to prove that the man was only called "Hogg" because he had treated Shelley with grave treachery. And he actually adduced the fact that another poet, practically contemporary, was called "Hogg" as completing the connection with Shelley. What he did not know was just what Joan had always known without knowing it: the kind of people concerned, the traditions of aristocrats like the Shelleys or of Borderers like the Ettrick Shepherd.

The lecturer concluded with a passage of impenetrable darkness about pig-iron and pigs of lead, which Joan did not even venture to understand. She could only say that if it did not mean that some day our diet might become so refined that we ate lead and iron, she could form no fancy of what it did mean.

"Can Philip Ivywood believe this kind of thing?" she asked herself; and even as she did so, Philip Ivywood rose.

He had, as Pitt and Gladstone had, an impromptu classicism of diction, his words wheeling and deploying into their proper places like a well-disciplined army in its swiftest advance.

And it was not long before Joan perceived that the last phase of the picture, obscure and mon-strous as it seemed, gave Ivywood exactly the opening he wanted. Indeed, she felt, no doubt, that he had arranged for it beforehand.

"It is within my memory," said Lord Ivywood, "though it need in no case have encumbered yours, that when it was my duty to precede the admired lecturer whom I now feel it a privilege even to follow, I submitted a suggestion which, however simple, would appear to many paradoxical. I affirmed or implied the view that the religion of Mahomet was, in a peculiar sense, a religion of progress. This is so contrary, not only to historical convention but to common platitude, that I shall find no ground either of surprise or censure if it takes a perceptible time before it sinks into the mind of the English public. But I think, ladies and gentlemen, that this period is notably abbreviated by the remark-able exposition which we have heard today. For this question of the attitude of Islam toward food affords as excellent an example of its special mode of progressive purification as the more popular example of its attitude toward drink. For it illustrates that principle which I have ventured to call the principle of the Crescent: the principle of perpetual growth toward an implied and infinite perfection.

"The great religion of Islam does not of itself forbid the eating of flesh foods. But, in accordance with that principle of growth which is its life, it has pointed the way to a perfection not yet perhaps fully attainable by our nature; it has taken a plain and strong example of the dangers of meat-eating; and hung up the repellent carcass as a warning and a sign. In the gradual emergence of mankind from a gross and sanguinary mode of sustenance, the Semite has led the way. He has laid, as it were, a symbolic embargo upon the beast typical, the beast of beasts. With the instinct of the true mystic, he selected for exemption from such cannibal feasts the creature which appeals to both sides of the higher vegetarian ethic. The pig is at once the creature whose helpless-ness most moves our pity and whose ugliness most repels our taste.

"It would be foolish to affirm that no difficulty arises out of the different stages of moral evolution in which the different races find themselves. Thus it is constantly said, and such things are not said with-out some excuse in document or incident, that followers of the Prophet have specialised in the arts of war and have come into a contact, not invariably friendly, with those Hindoos of India who have specialised in the arts of Peace. In the same way the Hindoos, it must be con-fessed, have been almost as much in advance of Islam in the question of meat as Islam is in advance of Christianity in the matter of drink. It must be remembered again and again, ladies and gentlemen, that every allegation we have of any difference between Hindoo and Moslem comes through a Christian channel, and is therefore tainted evidence. But in this matter, even, can we not see the perils of disregarding such plain danger signals as the veto on pork? Did not an Empire nearly slip out of our hands because our hands were greased with cow-fat? And did not the well of Cawnpore brim with blood instead of water because we would not listen to the instinct of the Oriental about the shedding of sacred blood?

"But if it be proposed, with whatever graduation, to approach that repudiation of flesh food which Buddhism mainly and Islam partly rec-ommends, it will always be asked by those who hate the very vision of Progress— 'Where do you draw the line? May I eat oysters? May I eat eggs? May I drink milk?' You may. You may eat or drink anything es-sential to your stage of evolution, so long as you are evolving toward a clearer and cleaner ideal of bodily life. If," he said gravely, "I may em-ploy a phrase of flippancy, I would say that you may eat six dozen oys-ters today, but I should strongly advise five dozen oysters tomorrow. For how else has all progress in public or private manners been achieved? Would not the primitive cannibals be surprised at the strange distinc-tion we draw between men and beasts? All historians pay high honour to the Huguenots, and the great Huguenot Prince, Henri Quatre. None need deny that his aspiration that every Frenchman should have a chicken in his pot was, for his period, a high aspiration. It is no disrespect to him that we, mounting to higher levels, and looking down longer per-spectives, consider the chicken. And this august march of discovery passes figures higher than that of Henry of Navarre. I shall always give a high place, as Islam has always given a high place, to that figure, mythical or no, which we find presiding over the foundations of Christianity. I cannot doubt that the fable, incredible and revolting otherwise, which records the rush of swine into the sea, was an allegory of his early realisation that a spirit, evil indeed, does reside in all animals in so far as they tempt us to devour them. I cannot doubt that the Prodigal leaving his sins among the swine is another illustration of the great thesis of the Prophet of the Moon. But here, also, progress and relativity are relentless in their advance; and not a few of us may have risen today to the point of regretting that the joyful sounds around the return of the Prodigal should be marred by the moaning of a calf.

"For the rest, he who asks us whither we go knows not the meaning of Progress. If we come at last to live on light, as men said of the chameleon, if some cosmic magic closed to us now, as radium was but recently closed, allows us to transmute the very metals into flesh without breaking into the bloody house of life, we shall know these things when we have achieved them. It is enough for us now if we have reached a spiritual station, in which at least the living head we lop has not eyes to reproach us; and the herbs we gather cannot cry against our cruelty like the mandrake."

Lord Ivywood resumed his seat, his colourless lips still moving. By some previous arrangement, probably, Mr. Leveson rose to move a motion about Vegetarianism. Mr. Leveson was of opinion that the Jewish and Moslem veto on pork had been the origin of Vegetarianism. He thought it was a great step, and showed how progressive the creed could be. He thought the persecution of the Hindoos by Moslems had probably been much exaggerated; he thought our experience in the Indian Mutiny showed we considered the feeling of Easterners too little in such matters. He thought Vegetarianism in some ways an advance on orthodox Christianity. He thought we must be ready for yet further advances; and he sat down. And as he had said precisely, clause by clause, everything that Lord Ivywood had said, it is needless to say that that nobleman afterward congratulated him on the boldness and originality of his brilliant speech.

At a similar sort of preconcerted signal, Hibbs However rose rather vaguely to his feet to second the motion. He rather prided himself on being a man of few words, in the vocal sense; he was no orator, as Brutus was. It was only with pen in hand, in an office lined with works of reference, that he could feel that sense of confused responsibility that was the one pleasure of his life. But on this occasion he was brighter than usual; partly because he liked being in a lord's house; partly because he had never tasted champagne before, and he felt as if it agreed with him; partly because he saw in the subject of Progress an infinite opportunity of splitting hairs.

"Whatever," said Hibbs, with a solemn cough, "whatever we may think of the old belief that Moslems have differed from Buddhism in a regrettable way, there can be no doubt the responsibility lay with the Christian Churches. Had the Free Churches put their foot down and met Messrs. Opalstein's demand, we should have heard nothing of these old differences between one belief and another." As it was, it reminded him of Napoleon. He gave his own opinion for what it was worth, but he was not afraid to say at any cost, even there and in that company, that this business of Asiatic vegetation had occupied less of the time of the Wesleyan Conference than it should have done. He would be the last to say, of course, that anyone was in any sense to blame. They all knew Dr. Coon's qualifications. They all knew as well as he did, that a more strenuous social worker than Charles Chadder had never rallied the forces of progress. But that which was not really an indiscretion might be represented as an indiscretion, and perhaps we had had enough of that just lately. It was all very well to talk about Coffe but it should be remembered, with no disrespect to those in Canada to whom we owe so much, that all that happened before 1891. No one had less desire to offend our Ritualistic friends than he did, but he had no hesitation in saying that the question was a question that could be asked, and though no doubt, from one point of view the goat's—.

Lady Joan moved sharply in her chair, as if gripped by sudden pain. And, indeed, she had suddenly felt the chronic and recurrent pain of her life. She was brave about bodily pain, as are most women, even luxurious women: but the torment that from time to time returned and tore her was one to which many philosophical names have been given, but no name so philosophical as Boredom.

She felt she could not stand a minute more of Mr. Hibbs. She felt she would die if she heard about the goats—from one or any point of view. She slipped from her chair and somehow slid round the corner, in pretence of seeking one of the tables of refreshment in the new wing. She was soon among the new oriental apartments, now almost completed; but she took no refreshments, though attenuated tables could still be found here and there. She threw herself on an ottoman and stared toward the empty and elfin turret chambers in which Ivywood had made her understand that he, also, could thirst for beauty and desire to be at peace. He certainly had a poetry of his own, after all; a poetry that never touched earth; the poetry of Shelley rather than Shakespeare. His phrase about the fairy turret was true: it did look like the end of the world. It did seem to teach her that there is always some serene limit at last.

She started and half rose on her elbow with a small laugh. A dog of ludicrous but familiar appearance came shuffling toward her and she lifted herself in the act of lifting him. She also lifted her head, and saw something that seemed to her, in a sense more Christian and catastrophic, very like the end of the world.

XII

Vegetarianism in the Forest

Humphrey Pump's cooking of a fungus in an old frying-pan (which he had found on the beach) was extremely typical of him. He was, indeed, without any pretence of book-learning, a certain kind of scientific man that science has really been unfortunate in losing. He was the old-fashioned English Naturalist like Gilbert White or even Isaac Walton, who learned things not academically like an American Professor, but actually, like an American Indian. And every truth a man has found out as a man of science is always subtly different from any truth he has found out as a man, because a man's family, friends, habits and social type have always got well under way before he has thoroughly learned the theory of anything. For instance, any eminent botanist at a *Soirée* of the Royal Society could tell you, of course, that other edible fungi exist, as well as mushrooms and truffles. But long before he was a botanist, still less an eminent botanist, he had begun, so to speak, on a basis of mushrooms and truffles. He felt, in a vague way, that these were really edible, that mushrooms were a moderate luxury, proper to the middle classes, while truffles were a much more expensive luxury, more suitable to the Smart Set. But the old English Naturalists, of whom Isaac Walton was perhaps the first, and Humphrey Pump perhaps the last, had in many cases really begun at the other end, and found by experience (often most disastrous experience) that some fungi are wholesome and some are not; but the wholesome ones are, on a whole, the majority. So a man like Pump was no more afraid of a fungus as such than he was of an animal as such. He no more started with the supposition that a grey or purple growth on a stone must be a poisonous growth than he started with the supposition that the dog who came to

249

him out of the wood must be a mad dog. Most of them he knew; those he did not know he treated with rational caution, but to him, as a whole race, these weird-hued and one-legged goblins of the forests were creatures friendly to man.

"You see," he said to his friend the Captain, "eating vegetables isn't half bad, so long as you know what vegetables there are and eat all of them that you can. But there are two ways where it goes wrong among the gentry. First, they've never had to eat a carrot or a potato because it was all there was in the house; so they've never learnt how to be really hungry for carrots, as that donkey might be. They only know the vegetables that are meant to help the meat. They know you take duck and peas; and when they turn vegetarian they can only think of the peas without the duck. They know you take lobster in a salad; and when they turn vegetarian they can only think of the salad without the lobster. But the other reason is worse. There's plenty of good people even round here, and still more in the north, who get meat very seldom. But then, when they do get it, they gobble it up like good 'uns. But the trouble with the gentry is different. The trouble is, the same sort of gentry that don't want to eat meat don't really want to eat anything. The man called a Vegetarian who goes to Ivywood House is generally like a cow trying to live on a blade of grass a day. You and I, Captain, have pretty well been vegetarians for some time, so as not to break into the cheese, and we haven't found it so difficult, because we eat as much as we can."

"It's not so difficult as being teetotallers," answered Dalroy, "so as not to break into the cask. But I'll never deny that I feel the better for that, too, on the whole. But only because I could leave off being one whenever I chose. And, now I come to think of it," he cried, with one of his odd returns of animal energy, "if I'm to be a vegetarian why shouldn't I drink? Why shouldn't I have a purely vegetarian drink? Why shouldn't I take vegetables in their highest form, so to speak? The modest vegetarians ought obviously to stick to wine or beer, plain vegetarian drinks, instead of filling their goblets with the blood of bulls and elephants, as all conventional meat-eaters do, I suppose. What is the matter?"

"Nothing," answered Pump. "I was looking out for somebody who generally turns up about this time. But I think I'm fast."

"I should never have thought so from the look of you," answered the Captain, "but what I'm saying is that the drinking of decent fermented liquor is just simply the triumph of vegetarianism. Why, it's an inspiring idea! I could write a sort of song about it. As, for instance—

> "You will find me drinking rum
> Like a sailor in a slum,
>   You will find me drinking beer like a Bavarian;
> You will find me drinking gin
> In the lowest kind of inn,
>   Because I am a rigid Vegetarian."

Why, it's a vista of verbal felicity and spiritual edification! It has I don't know how many hundred aspects! Let's see; how could the second verse go? Something like—

> "So I cleared the inn of wine,
> And I tried to climb the Sign;
>   And I tried to hail the constable as 'Marion';
> But he said I couldn't speak,
> And he bowled me to the Beak,
>   Because I was a Happy Vegetarian."

"I really think something instructive to the human race may come out of all this ... Hullo! Is that what you were looking for?"

The quadruped Quoodle came in out of the woods a whole minute later than the usual time and took his seat beside Humphrey's left foot with a preoccupied air.

"Good old boy," said the Captain. "You seem to have taken quite a fancy to us. I doubt, Hump, if he's properly looked after up at the house. I particularly don't want to talk against Ivywood, Hump. I don't want his soul to be able in all eternity to accuse my soul of a mean detraction. I want to be fair to him, because I hate him like hell, and he has taken from me all for which I lived. But I don't think, with all this in my mind, I don't think I say anything beyond what he would own himself (for his brain is clear) when I say that he could never understand an animal. And so he could never understand the animal side of a man. He doesn't know to this day, Hump, that your sight and hearing are sixty times quicker than his. He doesn't know that I have a better circulation.

That explains the extraordinary people he picks up and acts with; he never looks at them as you and I look at that dog. There was a fellow calling himself Gluck who was (mainly by Ivywood's influence, I believe) his colleague on the Turkish Conferences, being supposed to represent Germany. My dear Hump, he was a man that a great gentleman like Ivywood ought not to have touched with a barge-pole. It's not the race he was—if it was one race—it's the Sort he was. A coarse, common, Levantine nark and eaves-dropper—but you mustn't lose your temper, Hump. I implore you, Hump, to control this tendency to lose your temper when talking at any length about such people. Have recourse, Hump, to that consoling system of versification which I have already explained to you.

"Oh I knew a Doctor Gluck,
And his nose it had a hook,
        And his attitudes were anything but Aryan;
So I gave him all the pork
That I had, upon a fork;
        Because I am myself a Vegetarian."

"If you are," said Humphrey Pump, "You'd better come and eat some vegetables. The White Hat can be eaten cold—or raw, for that matter. But Bloodspots wants some cooking."

"You are right, Hump," said Dalroy, seating himself with every appearance of speechless greed. "I will be silent. As the poet says—

"I am silent in the Club,
I am silent in the pub,
        I am silent on a bally peak in Darien;
For I stuff away for life,
Shoving peas in with a knife,
        Because I am at heart a Vegetarian."

He fell to his food with great gusto, dispatched a good deal of it in a very short time, threw a glance of gloomy envy at the cask, and then sprang to his feet again. He caught up the inn-sign from where it leant against the Pantomime Cottage, and planted it like a pike in the ground

beside him. Then he began to sing again, in an even louder voice than
before.

> "O, Lord Ivywood may lop,
>   And his privilege is sylvan and riparian;
> And is also free to top,
>   But—."

"Do you know," said Hump, also finishing his lunch, "that I'm rather
tired of that particular tune?"

"Tired, is it?" said the indignant Irishman, "then I'll sing you a longer
song, to an even worse tune, about more and more vegetarians, and you
shall see me dance as well; and I will dance till you burst into tears and
offer me the half of your kingdom; and I shall ask for Mr. Leveson's
head on the frying-pan. For this, let me tell you, is a song of oriental
origin, celebrating the caprices of an ancient Babylonian Sultan and
should be performed in palaces of ivory with palm trees and a bulbul
accompaniment."

And he began to bellow another and older lyric of his own on vegetarianism.

> "Nebuchadnezzar, the King of the Jews,
> Suffered from new and original views,
> He crawled on his hands and knees it's said,
> With grass in his mouth and a crown on his head,
>   With a wowtyiddly, etc.

> "Those in traditional paths that trod,
> Thought the thing was a curse from God;
> But a Pioneer men always abuse,
> Like Nebuchadnezzar the King of the Jews."

Dalroy, as he sang this, actually began to dance about like a ballet
girl, an enormous and ridiculous figure in the sunlight, waving the
wooden sign around his head. Quoodle opened his eyes and pricked up
his ears and seemed much interested in these extraordinary evolutions.
Suddenly, with one of those startling changes that will transfigure the

most sedentary dogs, Quoodle decided that the dance was a game, and
began to bark and bound round the performer, sometimes leaping so
far into the air as almost to threaten the man's throat. But, though the
sailor naturally knew less about dogs than the countryman, he knew
enough about them (as about many other things) not to be afraid, and
the voice he sang with might have drowned the baying of a pack.

> "Black Lord Foulon the Frenchmen slew,
> Thought it a Futurist thing to do;
> He offered them grass instead of bread,
> So they stuffed him with grass when they cut off his head.
>   With a wowtyiddly, etc.

> "For the pride of his soul he perished then,
> But of course it is always of Pride that men
> A Man in Advance of his Age accuse
> Like Nebuchadnezzar the King of the Jews.

> "Simeon Scudder of Styx, in Maine,
> Thought of the thing and was at it again;
> He gave good grass and water in pails
> To a thousand Irishmen hammering rails,
>   With a wowtyiddly, etc.

> "Appetites differ, and tied to a stake,
> He was tarred and feathered for Conscience Sake;
> But stoning the prophets is ancient news,
> Like Nebuchadnezzar the King of the Jews."

In an abandon, unusual even for him, he had danced his way down
through the thistles into the jungle of weeds risen round the sunken
Chapel. And the dog, now fully convinced that it was not only a game
but an expedition, perhaps a hunting expedition, ran barking in front
of him, along the path that his own dog's paws had already burst through
the tangle. Before Patrick Dalroy well knew what he was doing, or even
remembered that he still carried the ridiculous sign-board in his hand,
he found himself outside the open porch of a sort of narrow tower at

the angle of a building which, to the best of his recollection, he had never seen before. Quoodle instantly ran up four or five steps in the dark staircase inside, and then, lifting his ears again, looked back for his companion.

There is, perhaps, such a thing as asking too much of a man. If there is, it was asking too much of Patrick Dalroy to ask him not to accept so eccentric an invitation. Hurriedly plunging his unwieldy wooden ensign upright in the thick of thistles and grass, he bent his gigantic neck and shoulders to enter the porch, and proceeded to climb the stairs. It was quite dark, and it was only after at least two twists of the stone spiral that he saw light ahead of him, and then it was a sort of rent in the wall that seemed to him as ragged as the mouth of a Cornish cave. It was also so low that he had some difficulty in squeezing his bulk through it, but the dog had jumped through with an air of familiarity, and once more looked back to see him follow.

If he had found himself inside any ordinary domestic interior, he would instantly have repented his escapade and gone back. But he found himself in surroundings which he had never seen before, or even, in one sense, believed possible.

His first feeling was that he was walking in the most sealed and secret suite of apartments in the castle of a dream. All the chambers had that air of perpetually opening inwards which is the soul of the Arabian Nights. And the ornament was of the same tradition; gorgeous and flamboyant, yet featureless and stiff. A purple mansion seemed to be built inside a green mansion and a golden mansion inside that. And the quaintly cut doorways or fretted lattices all had wavy lines like a dancing sea, and for some reason (sea-sickness for all he knew) this gave him a feeling as if the place were beautiful but faintly evil: as if it were bored and twisted for the fallen palace of the Worm.

But he had also another sensation which he could not analyze; for it reminded him of being a fly on the ceiling or the wall. Was it the Hanging Gardens of Babylon coming back to his imagination; or the Castle East of the Sun and West of the Moon? Then he remembered that in some boyish illness he had stared at a rather Moorish sort of wall paper, which was like rows and rows of brightly coloured corridors, empty and going on forever. And he remembered that a fly was walking along one of the parallel lines; and it seemed to his childish fancy that the corridors were all dead in front of the fly, but all came to life as he passed.

"By George!" he cried, "I wonder whether that's the real truth about East and West! That the gorgeous East offers everything needed for adventures except the man to enjoy them. It would explain the tradition of the Crusades uncommonly well. Perhaps that's what God meant by Europe and Asia. We dress the characters and they paint the scenery. Well, anyhow, three of the least Asiatic things in the world are lost in this endless Asiatic palace—a good dog, a straight sword, and an Irishman."

But as he went down this telescope of tropical colours he really felt something of that hard fatalistic freedom of the heroes (or should we say villains?) in the Arabian Nights. He was prepared for any impossibility. He would hardly have been surprised if from under the lid of one of the porcelain pots standing in a corner had come a serpentine string of blue or yellow smoke, as if some wizard's oil were within. He would hardly have been surprised if from under the curtains or closed doors had crawled out a snaky track of blood, or if a dumb negro dressed in white had come out with a bow string, having done his work. He would not have been surprised if he had walked suddenly into the still chamber of some Sultan asleep, whom to wake was a death in torments. And yet he was very much more surprised by what he did see, and when he saw it, he was certain at last that he was only wandering in the labyrinth of his own brain. For what he saw was what was really in the core of all his dreams.

What he saw, indeed, was more appropriate to that inmost eastern chamber than anything he had imagined. On a divan of blood-red and orange cushions lay a startlingly beautiful woman, with a skin almost swarthy enough for an Arab's, and who might well have been the Princess proper to such an Arabian tale. But in truth it was not her appropriateness to the scene, but rather her inappropriateness, that made his heart bound. It was not her strangeness but her familiarity that made his big feet suddenly stop.

The dog ran on yet more rapidly, and the princess on the sofa welcomed him warmly, lifting him on his short hind legs. Then she looked up, and seemed turned to stone.

"Bismillah," said the oriental traveller, affably, "may your shadow never grow less—or more, as the ladies would say. The Commander of the Faithful has deputed his least competent slave to bring you back a dog. Owing to temporary delay in collecting the fifteen largest diamonds in the moon, he has been compelled to send the animal without any collar. Those responsible for the delay will instantly be beaten to death, with the tails of dragons—"

The frightful shock, which had not yet left the lady's face, brought him back to responsible speech.

"In short," he said, "in the name of the Prophet, dog. I say, Joan, I wish this wasn't a dream."

"It isn't," said the girl, speaking for the first time, "and I don't know yet whether I wish it was."

"Well," argued the dreamer, rationally, "what are you, anytime, if you're not a dream—or a vision? And what are all these rooms, if they aren't a dream—or rather a nightmare?"

"This is the new wing of Ivywood House," said the lady addressed as Joan, speaking with great difficulty. "Lord Ivywood has fitted them up in the eastern style; he is inside conducting a most interesting debate in defence of Eastern Vegetarianism. I only came out because the room was rather hot."

"Vegetarian!" cried Dalroy, with abrupt and rather unreasonable exasperation. "That table seems to fall a bit short of Vegetarianism." And he pointed to one of the long, narrow tables, laid somewhere in almost all the central rooms, and loaded with elaborate cold meats and expensive wines.

"He must be liberal-minded," cried Joan, who seemed to be on the verge of something, possibly temper. "He can't expect people suddenly to begin being Vegetarians when they've never been before."

"It has been done," said Dalroy, tranquilly, walking across to look at the table. "I say, your ascetical friends seem to have made a pretty good hole in the champagne. You may not believe it, Joan, but I haven't touched what you call alcohol for a month."

With which words he filled with champagne a large tumbler intended for claret cup and swallowed it at a draught.

Lady Joan Brett stood up straight but trembling.

"Now that's really wrong, Pat," she cried. "Oh, don't be silly—you know I don't care about the alcohol or all that. But you're in the man's house, uninvited, and he doesn't know. That wasn't like you."

"He shall know, all right," said the large man, quietly. "I know the exact price of a tumbler of that champagne."

And he scribbled some words in pencil on the back of a bill of fare on the table, and then carefully laid three shillings on top of it.

"And there you do Philip the worst wrong of all," cried Lady Joan, flaming white. "You know as well as I do, anyhow, that he would not take your money." Patrick Dalroy stood looking at her for some seconds with an expression on his broad and unusually open face which she found utterly puzzling.

"Curiously enough," he observed, at last, and with absolutely even temper, "curiously enough, it is you who are doing Philip Ivywood a wrong. I think him quite capable of breaking England or Creation. But I do honestly think he would never break his word. And what is more, I think the more arbitrary and literal his word had been, the more he would keep it. You will never understand a man like that, till you understand that he can have devotion to a definition; even a new definition. He can really feel about an amendment to an Act of Parliament, inserted at the last moment, as you feel about England or your mother."

"Oh, don't philosophise," cried Joan suddenly. "Can't you see this has been a shock?"

"I only want you to see the point," he replied. "Lord Ivywood clearly told me, with his own careful lips, that I might go in and pay for fermented liquor in any place displaying a public sign outside. And he won't go back on that definition or on any definition. If he finds me here, he may quite possibly put me in prison on some other charge, as a thief or a vagabond, or what not. But he will not grudge the champagne. And he will accept the three shillings. And I shall honour him for his glorious consistency."

"I don't understand," said Joan, "one word of what you are talking about. Which way did you come? How can I get you away? You don't seem to grasp that you're in Ivywood House."

"You see there's a new name outside the gate," observed Patrick, conversationally, and led the lady to the end of the corridor by which he had entered and into its ultimate turret chamber.

Following his indications, Lady Joan peered a little over the edge of the window where hung the brilliant purple bird in its brilliant golden cage. Almost immediately below, outside the entrance to the half-closed stairway, stood a wooden tavern sign, as solid and still as if it had been there for centuries.

"All back at the sign of 'The Old Ship,' you see," said the Captain. "Can I offer you anything in a lady-like way?"

There was a vast impudence in the slight, hospitable movement of his hand, that disturbed Lady Joan's features with an emotion other than any that she desired to show.

"Well!" cried Patrick, with a wild geniality, "I've made you laugh again, my dear."

He caught her to him as in a whirlwind, and then vanished from the fairy turret like a blast, leaving her standing with her hand up to her wild black hair.

XIII

The Battle of the Tunnel

What Joan Brett really felt, as she went back from the second tête-à-tête she had experienced in the turret, it is doubtful if anyone will ever know. But she was full of the pungent feminine instinct to "drive at practice," and what she did clearly realise was the pencil writing Dalroy had left on the back of Lord Ivywood's *menu*. Heaven alone knew what it was, and (as it pleased her profane temper to tell herself) she was not satisfied with Heaven alone knowing. She went swiftly back, with swishing skirts, to the table where it had been left. But her skirts fell more softly and her feet trailed slower and more in her usual manner as she came near the table. For standing at it was Lord Ivywood, reading the card with tranquil lowered eyelids, that set off perfectly the long and perfect oval of his face. He put down the card with a quite natural action; and, seeing Joan, smiled at her in his most sympathetic way.

"So you've come out too," he said. "So have I; it's really too hot for anything. Dr. Gluck is making an uncommonly good speech, but I couldn't stop even for that. Don't you think my eastern decorations are rather a success after all? A sort of Vegetarianism in design, isn't it?"

He led her up and down the corridors, pointing out lemon-coloured crescents or crimson pomegranates in the scheme of ornament, with such utter detachment that they twice passed the open mouth of the hall of debate, and Joan could distinctly hear the voice of the diplomatic Gluck saying:

"Indeed, we owe our knowledge of the pollution of the pork primarily to the Jewth and not the Mothlemth. I do not thare that prejudithe against the Jewth, which ith too common in my family and all the arithtocratic and military Prutthian familieth. I think we Prutthian

260

arithtocrats owe everything to the Jewth. The Jewth have given to our old Teutonic rugged virtueth, jutht that touch of refinement, jutht that intellectual thuperiority which—."

And then the voice would die away behind, as Lord Ivywood lectured luxuriantly, and very well, on the peacock tail in decoration, or some more extravagant eastern version of the Greek Key. But the third time they turned, they heard the noise of subdued applause and the breaking up the meeting; and people came pouring forth.

With stillness and swiftness, Ivywood pitched on the people he wanted and held them. He button-holed Leveson and was evidently asking him to do something which neither of the two liked doing.

"If your lordship insists," she heard Leveson whispering, "of course I will go myself; but there is a great deal to be done here with your lordship's immediate matters. And if there were anyone else—."

If Philip, Lord Ivywood, had ever looked at a human being in his life, he would have seen that J. Leveson, Secretary, was suffering from a very ancient human malady, excusable in all men and rather more excusable in one who has had his top-hat smashed over his eyes and has run for his life. As it was, he saw nothing, but merely said, "Oh, well, get someone else. What about your friend Hibbs?"

Leveson ran across to Hibbs, who was drinking another glass of champagne at one of the innumerable buffets.

"Hibbs," said Leveson, rather nervously, "will you do Lord Ivywood a favour? He says you have so much tact. It seems possible that a man may be hanging about the grounds just below that turret there. He is a man it would certainly be Lord Ivywood's public duty to put into the hands of the police, if he is there. But then, again, he is quite capable of not being there at all—I mean of having sent his message from somewhere else and in some other way. Naturally, Lord Ivywood doesn't want to alarm the ladies and perhaps turn the laugh against himself, by getting up a sort of police raid about nothing. He wants some sensible, tactful friend of his to go down and look round the place—it's a sort of disused garden—and report if there's anyone about. I'd go myself, but I'm wanted here."

Hibbs nodded, and filled another glass.

"But there's a further difficulty," went on Leveson. "He's a clever brute, it seems, a 'remarkable and a dangerous man,' were his lordship's words; and it looks as if he'd spotted a very good hiding-place, a disused tunnel leading to the sands, just beyond the disused garden and chapel. It's a smart choice, you see, for he can bolt into the woods if anyone comes from the shore, or on to the shore if anyone comes from the woods. But it would take a good time even to get the police here, and it would take ten times longer to get 'em round to the sea end of the tunnel, especially as the sea comes up to the cliffs once or twice between here and Pebblewick. So we mustn't frighten him away, or he'll get a start. If you meet anyone down there talk to him quite naturally, and come back with the news. We won't send for the police till you come. Talk as if you were just wandering like himself. His lordship wishes your presence to appear quite accidental."

"Wishes my presence to appear quite accidental," repeated Hibbs, gravely.

When the feverish Leveson had flashed off satisfied, Hibbs took a glass or two more of wine; feeling that he was going on a great diplomatic mission to please a lord. Then he went through the opening, picked his way down the stair, and somehow found his way out into the neglected garden and shrubbery.

It was already evening, and an early moon was brightening over the sunken chapel with its dragon-coloured scales of fungus. The night breeze was very fresh and had a marked effect on Mr. Hibbs. He found himself taking a meaningless pleasure in the scene; especially in one fungus that was white with brown spots. He laughed shortly, to think that it should be white with brown spots. Then he said, with carefully accurate articulation, "His lordship wishes my presence to appear quite accidental." Then he tried to remember something else that Leveson had said.

He began to wade through the waves of weed and thorn past the Chapel, but he found the soil much more uneven and obstructive than he had supposed.

He slipped, and sought to save himself by throwing one arm round a broken stone angel at a corner of the heap of Gothic fragments; but it was loose and rocked in its socket.

Mr. Hibbs presented for a moment the appearance of waltzing with the Angel in the moonlight, in a very amorous and irreverent manner. Then the statue rolled over one way and he rolled over the other, and lay on his face in the grass, making inaudible remarks. He might have lain there for some time, or at least found some difficulty in rising, but for another circumstance. The dog Quoodle, with characteristic officiousness, had followed him down the dark stairs and out of the doorway, and, finding him in this unusual posture, began to bark as if the house were on fire.

This brought a heavy human footstep from the more hidden parts of the copse; and in a minute or two the large man with the red hair was looking down at him in undisguised wonder. Hibbs said, in a muffled voice which came obscurely from under his hidden face, "Wish my presence to appear quite accidental."

"It does," said the Captain, "can I help you up? Are you hurt?"

He gently set the prostrate gentleman on his feet, and looked genuinely concerned. The fall had somewhat sobered Lord Ivywood's representative; and he really had a red graze on the left cheek that looked more ugly than it was.

"I am so sorry," said Patrick Dalroy, cordially, "come and sit down in our camp. My friend Pump will be back presently, and he's a capital doctor."

His friend Pump may or may not have been a capital doctor, but the Captain himself was certainly a most inefficient one. So small was his talent for diagnosing the nature of a disease at sight, that having given Mr. Hibbs a seat on a fallen tree by the tunnel, he proceeded to give him (in mere automatic hospitality) a glass of rum.

Mr. Hibbs's eyes awoke again, when he had sipped it, but they awoke to a new world.

"Wherever may be our invidual pinions," he said, and looked into space with an expression of humorous sagacity.

He then put his hand hazily in his pocket, as if to find some letter he had to deliver. He found nothing but his old journalistic note book, which he often carried when there was a chance of interviewing anybody. The feel of it under his fingers changed the whole attitude of his mind. He took it out and said:

"And wha' would you say of Vegetarianism, Colonel Pump?"

"I think it palls," replied the recipient of this complex title, staring.

"Sha' we say," asked Hibbs brightly, turning a leaf in his note book, "sha' we say long been strong vegetarian by conviction?"

"No; I have only once been convicted," answered Dalroy, with restraint, "and I hope to lead a better life when I come out."

"Hopes lead better life," murmured Hibbs, writing eagerly, with the wrong end of his pencil. "And wha' would you shay was best vegable food for really strong vegetarian by conviction?"

"Thistles," said the Captain, wearily. "But I don't know much about it, you know."

"Lord Ivywoo' strong veg'tarian by conviction," said Mr. Hibbs, shaking his head with unction. "Lord Ivywoo' says tact. Talk to him naturally. And so I do. That's what I do. Talk to him naturally."

Humphrey Pump came through the clearer part of the wood, leading the donkey, who had just partaken of the diet recommended to a vegetarian by conviction; the dog sprang up and ran to them. Pump was, perhaps, the most naturally polite man in the world, and said nothing. But his eyes had accepted, with one snap of surprise, the other fact, also not unconnected with diet, which had escaped Dalroy's notice when he administered rum as a restorative.

"Lord Ivywoo' says," murmured the journalistic diplomatist. "Lord Ivywoo' says, 'talk as if you were just wandering.' That's it. That's tact. That's what I've got to do—talk as if I was just wandering. Long way round to other end tunnel; sea and cliffs. Don' sphose they can swim." He seized his note book again and looked in vain for his pencil. "Good subjec' correspondence. Can policem'n swim?"

"Policemen?" said Dalroy, in a dead silence. The dog looked up, and the innkeeper did not.

"Get to Ivywoo' one thing," reasoned the diplomatist. "Get policemen beach other end other thing. No good do one thing no' do other thing, 'no goo' do other thing no' do other thing. Wish my presence appear quite accidental. Haw!"

"I'll harness the donkey," said Pump.

"Will he go through that door?" asked Dalroy, with a gesture toward the entrance of the rough boarding with which they had faced the tunnel, "or shall I smash it all at once?"

"He'll go through all right," answered Pump. "I saw to that when I made it. And I think I'll get him to the safe end of the tunnel before I load him up. The best thing you can do is to pull up one of those saplings to bar the door with. That'll delay them a minute or two; though I think we've got warning in pretty easy time." He led his donkey to the cart, and carefully harnessed the donkey; like all men cunning in the old healthy sense he knew that the last chance of leisure ought to be leisurely, in order that it may be lucid. Then he led the whole equipment through the temporary wooden door of the tunnel, the inquisitive Quoodle, of course, following at his heels.

"Excuse me if I take a tree," said Dalroy, politely, to his guest, like a man reaching across another man for a match. And with that he rent up a young tree by its roots, as he had done in the Island of the Olives, and carried it on his shoulder, like the club of Hercules.

Up in Ivywood House Lord Ivywood had telephoned twice to Pebblewick. It was a delay he seldom suffered; and, though he never expressed impatience in unnecessary words he expressed it in unnecessary walking. He would not yet send for the police without news from his Ambassador, but he thought a preliminary conversation with some police authorities he knew well, might advance matters. Seeing Leveson rather shrunk in a corner, he wheeled round in his walk and said abruptly:

"You must go and see what has happened to Hibbs. If you have any other duties here, I authorize you to neglect them. Otherwise, I can only say—"

At this moment the telephone rang, and the impatient nobleman rushed for his delayed call with a rapidity he seldom showed. There was simply nothing for Leveson to do except to do as he was told, or be sacked. He walked swiftly toward the staircase, and only stopped once at the table where Hibbs had stood and gulped down two goblets of the same wine.

But let no man attribute to Mr. Leveson the loose and luxurious social motives of Mr. Hibbs. Mr. Leveson did not drink for pleasure; in fact, he hardly knew what he was drinking. His motive was something far more simple and sincere; a sentiment forcibly described in legal phraseology as going in bodily fear.

He was partly nerved, but by no means reconciled to his adventure, when he crept carefully down the stairs and peered about the thicket for any signs of his diplomatic friend. He could find neither sight nor sound to guide him, except a sort of distant singing, which greatly increased in volume of sound as he pursued it. The first words he heard seemed to run something like—

"No more the milk of cows
Shall pollute my private house,
      Than the milk of the wild mares of the Barbarian;
I will stick to port and sherry,
For they are so very, very,
      So very, very, very Vegetarian."

Leveson did not know the huge and horrible voice in which these words were shouted, but he had a most strange and even sickening suspicion that he did know the voice, however altered, the quavering and rather refined voice that joined in the chorus and sang,

"Because they are so vegy,
      So vegy, vegy, vegy Vegetarian."

Terror lit up his wits, and he made a wild guess at what had happened. With a gasp of relief he realised that he had now good excuse for returning to the house with the warning. He ran there like a hare, still hearing the great voice from the woods like the roaring of a lion in his ear.

He found Lord Ivywood in consultation with Dr. Gluck, and also with Mr. Bullrose the Agent, whose froglike eyes hardly seemed to have recovered yet from the fairy-tale of the flying sign-board in the English lane; but who, to do him justice, was more plucky and practical than most of Lord Ivywood's present advisers.

"I'm afraid Mr. Hibbs has inadvertently," stammered Leveson. "I'm afraid he has—I'm afraid the man is making his escape, my lord. You had better send for the police."

Ivywood turned to the agent. "You go and see what's happening," he said simply. "I will come myself when I've rung them up. And get some of the servants up with sticks and things. Fortunately the ladies have gone to bed. Hullo! Is that the Police Station?"

Bullrose went down into the shrubbery and had, for many reasons, less difficulty in crossing it than the hilarious Hibbs. The moon had increased to an almost unnatural brilliancy, so that the whole scene was like a rather silver daylight; and in this clear medium he beheld a very tall man with erect, red hair and a colossal cylinder of cheese carried under one arm, while he employed the other to wag a big forefinger at a dog with whom he was conversing.

It was the Agent's duty and desire to hold the man, whom he recognised from the sign-board mystery, in play and conversation, and prevent his final escape. But there are some people who really cannot be courteous, even when they want to be, and Mr. Bullrose was one of them.

"Lord Ivywood," he said abruptly, "wants to know what you want."

"Do not, however, fall into the common error, Quoodle," Dalroy was saying to the dog, whose unfathomable eyes were fixed on his face, "of supposing that the phrase 'good dog' is used in its absolute sense. A dog is good or bad negatively to a limited scheme of duties created by human civilization—"

"What are you doing here?" asked Mr. Bullrose.

"A dog, my dear Quoodle," continued the Captain, "cannot be either so good or bad as a man. Nay, I should go farther. I would almost say a dog cannot be so stupid as a man. He cannot be utterly wanting as a dog—as some men are as men."

"Answer me, you there!" roared the Agent.

"It is all the more pathetic," continued the Captain, to whose monologue Quoodle seemed to listen with magnetized attention. "It is all the more pathetic because this mental insufficiency is sometimes found in the good; though there are, I should imagine, at least an equal number of opposite examples. The person standing a few feet off us, for example, is both stupid and wicked. But be very careful, Quoodle, to remember that any disadvantage under which we place him should be based on the *moral* and not his *mental* defects. Should I say to you at any time, 'Go for him, Quoodle,' or 'Hold him, Quoodle,' be certain in your own mind, please, that it is solely because he is *wicked* and not because he is *stupid*, that I am entitled to do so. The fact that he is *stupid* would not justify me in saying 'hold him, Quoodle,' with the realistic intonation I now employ—"

"Curse you, call him off!" cried Mr. Bullrose, retreating, for Quoodle was coming toward him with the bulldog part of his pedigree very prominently displayed, like a pennon. "Should Mr. Bullrose find it expedient to climb a tree, or even a sign-post," proceeded Dalroy, for indeed the Agent had already clasped the pole of "The Old Ship," which was stouter than the slender trees standing just around it, "you will keep an eye on him, Quoodle, and, I doubt not, constantly remind him that it is his *wickedness*, and not, as he might hastily be inclined to suppose, *stupidity* that has placed him on so conspicuous an elevation—"

"Some of you'll wish yourself dead for this," said the Agent; who was by this time clinging to the wooden sign like a monkey on a stick, while Quoodle watched him from below with an unsated interest. "Some of you'll see something. Here comes his lordship and the police, I reckon."

"Good morning, my lord," said Dalroy, as Ivywood, paler than ever in the strong moonshine, came through the thicket toward them. It seemed to be his fate that his faultless and hueless face should always be contrasted with richer colours; and even now it was thrown up by the gorgeous diplomatic uniform of Dr. Gluck, who walked just behind him.

"I am glad to see you, my lord," said Dalroy, in a stately manner, "it is always so awkward doing business with an Agent. Especially for the Agent."

"Captain Dalroy," said Lord Ivywood, with a more serious dignity, "I am sorry we meet again like this, and such things are not of my seeking. It is only right to tell you that the police will be here in a moment."

"Quite time, too!" said Dalroy, shaking his head. "I never saw anything so disgraceful in my life. Of course, I am sorry it's a friend of yours; and I hope the police will keep Ivywood House out of the papers. But I won't be a party to one law for the rich and another for the poor, and it would be a great shame if a man in that state got off altogether merely because he had got the stuff at your house."

"I do not understand you," said Ivywood. "What are you talking of?"

"Why of him," replied the Captain, with a genial gesture toward a fallen tree trunk that lay a yard or two from the tunnel wall, "the poor chap the police are coming for."

Lord Ivywood looked at the forest log by the tunnel which he had not glanced at before, and in his pale eyes, perhaps for the first time, stood a simple astonishment.

Above the log appeared two duplicate objects, which, after a prolonged stare, he identified as the soles of a pair of patent leather shoes, offered to his gaze, as if demanding his opinion in the matter of resoling. They were all that was visible of Mr. Hibbs who had fallen backward off his woodland seat and seemed contented with his new situation.

His lordship put up the pince-nez that made him look ten years older, and said with a sharp, steely accent, "What is all this?"

The only effect of his voice upon the faithful Hibbs was to cause him to feebly wave his legs in the air in recognition of a feudal superior. He clearly considered it hopeless to attempt to get up, so Dalroy, striding across to him, lugged him up by his shirt collar and exhibited him, limp and wild-eyed to the company.

"You won't want many policemen to take him to the station," said the Captain. "I'm sorry, Lord Ivywood, I'm afraid it's no use your asking me to overlook it again. We can't afford it," and he shook his head implacably. "We've always kept a respectable house, Mr. Pump and I. 'The Old Ship' has a reputation all over the country—in quite a lot of different parts, in fact. People in the oddest places have found it a quiet, family house. Nothing gadabout in 'The Old Ship.' And if you think you can send all your staggering revellers—"

"Captain Dalroy," said Ivywood, simply, "you seem to be under a misapprehension, which I think it would be hardly honourable to leave undisturbed. Whatever these extraordinary events may mean and whatever be fitting in the case of this gentleman, when I spoke of the police coming, I meant they were coming for you and your confederate."

"For me!" cried the Captain, with a stupendous air of surprise. "Why, I have never done anything naughty in my life."

"You have been selling alcohol contrary to Clause V. of the Act of—"

"But I've got a sign," cried Dalroy, excitedly, "you told me yourself it was all right if I'd got a sign. Oh, do look at our new sign! The 'Sign of the Agile Agent.'"

Mr. Bullrose had remained silent, feeling his position none of the most dignified, and hoping his employer would go away. But Lord Ivywood looked up at him, and thought he had wandered into a planet of monsters.

As he slowly recovered himself Patrick Dalroy said briskly, "All quite correct and conventional, you see. You can't run us in for not having a sign; we've rather an extra life-like one. And you can't run us in as rogues and vagabonds either. Visible means of subsistence," and he slapped the huge cheese under his arm with his great flat hand, so that it reverberated like a drum. "Quite visible. Perceptible," he added, holding it out suddenly almost under Lord Ivywood's nose. "Perceptible to the naked eye through your lordship's eyeglasses."

He turned abruptly, burst open the pantomime door behind him and bowled the big cheese down the tunnel with a noise like thunder, which ended in a cry of acceptation in the distant voice of Mr. Humphrey Pump. It was the last of their belongings left at this end of the tunnel, and Dalroy turned again, a man totally transfigured.

"And now, Ivywood," he said, "what can I be charged with? Well, I have a suggestion to make. I will surrender to the police quite quietly when they come, if you will do me one favour. Let me choose my crime."

"I don't understand you," answered the other coolly, "what crime? What favour?"

Captain Dalroy unsheathed the straight sword that still hung on his now shabby uniform. The slender blade sparkled splendidly in the moonlight as he pointed it straight at Dr. Gluck.

"Take away his sword from the little pawnbroker," he said. "It's about the length of mine; or we'll change if you like. Give me ten minutes on that strip of turf. And then it may be, Ivywood, that I shall be removed from your public path in a way a little worthier of enemies who have once been friends, than if you tripped me up with Bow Street runners, of whose help every ancestor you have would have been ashamed. Or, on the other hand, it may be—that when the police come there will be something to arrest me for."

There was a long silence, and the elf of irresponsibility peeped out again for an instant in Dalroy's mind.

"Mr. Bullrose will see fair play for you, from a throne above the lists," he said. "I have already put my honour in the hands of Mr. Hibbs."

"I must decline Captain Dalroy's invitation," said Ivywood at last, in a curious tone. "Not so much because—"

Before he could proceed, Leveson came racing across the copse, hallooing, "The police are here!"

Dalroy, who loved leaving everything to the last instant, tore up the sign, with Bullrose literally hanging to it, shook him off like a ripe fruit, and then plunged into the tunnel, the clamorous Quoodle at his heels. Before even Ivywood (the promptest of his party) could reach the spot, he had clashed to the wood door and bolted it across with his wooden staple. He had not had time even to sheath his sword.

"Break down this door," said Lord Ivywood, calmly. "I noticed they haven't finished loading their cart."

Under his directions, and vastly against their will, Bullrose and Leveson lifted the tree-trunk vacated by Hibbs, and swinging it thrice as a battering-ram, burst in the door. Lord Ivywood instantly sprang into the entrance.

A voice called out to him quietly from the other end of the tunnel. There was something touching and yet terrible about a voice so human coming out of that inhuman darkness. If Philip Ivywood had been really a poet, and not rather its opposite, an aesthete, he would have known that all the past and people of England were uttering their oracle out of the cavern. As it was, he only heard a publican wanted by the police.— Yet even he paused, and indeed seemed spellbound.

"My lord, I would like a word. I learned my catechism and never was with the Radicals. I want you to look at what you've done to me. You've stolen a house that was mine as that one's yours. You've made me a dirty tramp, that was a man respected in church and market. Now you send me where I might have cells or the Cat. If I might make so bold, what do you suppose I think of you? Do you think because you go up to London and settle it with lords in Parliament and bring back a lot of papers and long words, that makes any difference to the man you do it to? By what I can see, you're just a bad and cruel master, like those God punished in the old days; like Squire Varney the weasels killed in Holy Wood. Well, parson always said one might shoot at robbers, and I want to tell your lordship," he ended respectfully, "that I have a gun."

Ivywood instantly stepped into the darkness, and spoke in a voice shaken with some emotion, the nature of which was never certainly known.

"The police are here," he said, "but I'll arrest you myself."

A shot shrieked and rattled through the thousand echoes of the tunnel. Lord Ivywood's legs doubled and twisted under him, and he collapsed on the earth with a bullet above his knee.

Almost at the same instant a shout and a bark announced that the cart had started as a complete equipage. It was even more than complete, for the instant before it moved Mr. Quoodle had sprung into it, and, as it was driven off, sat erect in it, looking solemn.

XIV

The Creature That Man Forgets

Despite the natural hubbub round the wound of Lord Ivywood and the difficulties of the police in finding their way to the shore, the fugitives of the Flying Inn must almost certainly have been captured but for a curious accident, which also flowed, as it happened, from the great Ivywood debate on Vegetarianism.

The comparatively late hour at which Lord Ivywood had made his discovery had been largely due to a very long speech which Joan had not heard, and which was delivered immediately before the few concluding observations she had heard from Dr. Gluck. The speech was made by an eccentric, of course. Most of those who attended, and nearly all of those who talked, were eccentric in one way or another. But he was an eccentric of great wealth and good family, an M.P., a J.P., a relation of Lady Enid, a man well known in art and letters; in short, a personality who could not be prevented from being anything he chose, from a revolutionist to a bore. Dorian Wimpole had first become famous outside his own class under the fanciful title of the Poet of the Birds. A volume of verse, expanding the several notes or cries of separate song-birds into fantastic soliloquies of these feathered philosophers, had really contained a great deal of ingenuity and elegance. Unfortunately, he was one of those who always tend to take their own fancies seriously, and in whose otherwise legitimate extravagance there is too little of the juice of jest. Hence, in his later works, when he explained "The Fable of the Angel," by trying to prove that the fowls of the air were creatures higher than man or the anthropoids, his manner was felt to be too austere; and when he moved an amendment to Lord Ivywood's scheme for the model village called Peaceways, urging that its houses should all follow the more hygienic architecture of nests hung in trees, many regretted that he had lost his light touch. But, when he went beyond birds and filled his poems with conjectural psychology about all the Zoological Gardens, his meaning became obscure; and Lady Susan had even described it as his bad period. It was all the more uncomfortable reading because he poured forth the imaginary hymns, love-songs and war-songs of the lower animals, without a word of previous explanation. Thus, if someone seeking for an ordinary drawing-room song came on lines that were headed "A Desert Love Song," and which began—

> "Her head is high against the stars,
> Her hump is heaved in pride,"

the compliment to the lady would at first seem startling, until the reader realised that all the characters in the idyll were camels. Or, if he began a poem simply entitled, "The March of Democracy," and found in the first lines—

> "Comrades, marching evermore,
> Fix your teeth in floor and door,"

he might be doubtful about such a policy for the masses; until he discovered that it was supposed to be addressed by an eloquent and aspiring rat to the social solidarity of his race. Lord Ivywood had nearly quarrelled with his poetic relative over the uproarious realism of the verses called "A Drinking Song," until it was carefully explained to him that the drink was water, and that the festive company consisted of bisons. His vision of the perfect husband, as it exists in the feelings of the young female walrus, is thoughtful and suggestive; but would doubtless receive many emendations from anyone who had experienced those feelings. And in his sonnet called "Motherhood" he has made the young scorpion consistent and convincing, yet somehow not wholly lovable. In justice to him, however, it should be remembered that he attacked the most difficult cases on principle, declaring that there was no earthly creature that a poet should forget.

He was of the blond type of his cousin, with flowing fair hair and mustache, and a bright blue, absent-minded eye; he was very well dressed in the carefully careless manner, with a brown velvet jacket and the image on his ring of one of those beasts men worshipped in Egypt.

His speech was graceful and well worded and enormously long, and it was all about an oyster. He passionately protested against the suggestion of some humanitarians who were vegetarians in other respects, but maintained that organisms so simple might fairly be counted as exceptions. Man, he said, even at his miserable best, was always trying to excommunicate some one citizen of the cosmos, to forget some one creature that he should remember. Now, it seemed that creature was the oyster. He gave a long account of the tragedy of the oyster, a really imaginative and picturesque account; full of fantastic fishes, and coral crags crawling and climbing, and bearded creatures streaking the sea-shore and the green darkness in the cellars of the sea.

"What a horrid irony it is," he cried, "that this is the only one of the lower creatures whom we call a Native! We speak of him, and of him alone as if he were a native of the country. Whereas, indeed, he is an exile in the universe. What can be conceived more pitiful than the eternal frenzy of the impotent amphibian? What is more terrible than the tear of an oyster? Nature herself has sealed it with the hard seal of eternity. The creature man forgets bears against him a testimony that cannot be forgotten. For the tears of widows and of captives are wiped away at last like the tears of children. They vanish like the mists of morning or the small pools after a flood. But the tear of the oyster is a pearl."

The Poet of the Birds was so excited with his own speech that, after the meeting, he walked out with a wild eye to the motor car, which had been long awaiting him, the chauffeur giving some faint signs of relief.

"Toward home, for the present," said the poet, and stared at the moon with an inspired face.

He was very fond of motoring, finding it fed him with inspirations; and he had been doing it from an early hour that morning, having enjoyed a slightly lessened sleep. He had scarcely spoken to anybody until he spoke to the cultured crowd at Ivywood. He did not wish to speak to anyone for many hours yet. His ideas were racing. He had thrown on a fur coat over his velvet jacket, but he let it fly open, having long forgotten the coldness in the splendour of the moonstruck night. He realised only two things: the swiftness of his car and the swiftness of his thoughts. He felt, as it were, a fury of omniscience; he seemed flying with every bird that sped or spun above the woods, with every squirrel that had leapt and tumbled within them, with every tree that had swung under and sustained the blast.

Yet in a few moments he leaned forward and tapped the glass frontage of the car, and the chauffeur suddenly squaring his shoulders, jarringly stopped the wheels. Dorian Wimpole had just seen something in the clear moonlight by the roadside, which appealed both to this and to the other side of his tradition; something that appealed to Wimpole as well as to Dorian.

Two shabby looking men, one in tattered gaiters and the other in what looked like the remains of fancy dress with the addition of hair, of so wild a red that it looked like a wig, were halted under the hedge, apparently loading a donkey cart. At least two rounded, rudely cylindrical objects, looking more or less like tubs, stood out in the road beside the wheels, along with a sort of loose wooden post that lay along the road beside them. As a matter of fact, the man in the old gaiters had just been feeding and watering the donkey, and was now adjusting its harness more easily. But Dorian Wimpole naturally did not expect that sort of thing from that sort of man. There swelled up in him the sense that his omnipotence went beyond the poetical; that he was a gentleman, a magistrate, an M.P. and J.P., and so on. This callousness or ignorance about animals should not go on while he was a J.P.; especially since Ivywood's last Act. He simply strode across to the stationary cart and said:

"You are overloading that animal, and it is forfeited. And you must come with me to the police station."

Humphrey Pump, who was very considerate to animals, and had always tried to be considerate to gentlemen, in spite of having put a bullet into one of their legs, was simply too astounded and distressed to make any answer at all. He moved a step or two backward and stared with brown, blinking eyes at the poet, the donkey, the cask, the cheese, and the sign-board lying in the road.

But Captain Dalroy, with the quicker recovery of his national temperament, swept the poet and magistrate a vast fantastic bow and said with agreeable impudence, "interested in donkeys, no doubt?"

"I am interested in all things men forget," answered the poet, with a fine touch of pride, "but mostly in those like this, that are most easily forgotten."

Somehow from those two first sentences Pump realised that these two eccentric aristocrats had unconsciously recognised each other. The fact that it was unconscious seemed, somehow, to exclude him all the more. He stirred a little the moonlit dust of the road with his rather dilapidated boots and eventually strolled across to speak to the chauffeur.

"Is the next police station far from here?" he asked.

The chauffeur answered with one syllable of which the nearest literal rendering is "dno." Other spellings have been attempted, but the sentiment expressed is that of agnosticism.

But something of special brutality of abbreviation made the shrewd, and therefore sensitive, Mr. Pump look at the man's face. And he saw it was not only the moonlight that made it white.

With that dumb delicacy that was so English in him, Pump looked at the man again, and saw he was leaning heavily on the car with one arm, and saw that the arm was shaking. He understood his countrymen enough to know that whatever he said he must say in a careless manner.

"I hope it's nearer to your place. You must be a bit done up."

"Oh hell!" said the driver and spat on the road.

Pump was sympathetically silent, and Mr. Wimpole's chauffeur broke out incoherently, as if in another place.

"Blarsted beauties o' dibrike and no breakfast. Blarsted lunch Hivywood and no lunch. Blarsted black everlastin' hours artside while 'e 'as 'is cike an' champine. And then it's a dornkey."

"You don't mean to say," said Pump in a very serious voice, "that you've had no food today?"

"Ow no!" replied the cockney, with the irony of the deathbed. "Ow, of course not."

Pump strolled back into the road again, picked up the cheese in his left hand, and landed it on the seat beside the driver. Then his right hand went to one of his large loose equivocal pockets, and the blade of a big jack-knife caught and recaught the steady splendours of the moon.

The driver stared for several instants at the cheese, with the knife shaking in his hand. Then he began to hack it, and in that white witchlike light the happiness of his face was almost horrible.

Pump was wise in all such things, and knew that just as a little food will sometimes prevent sheer intoxication, so a little stimulant will sometimes prevent sudden and dangerous indigestion. It was practically impossible to make the man stop eating cheese. It was far better to give him a very little of the rum, especially as it was very good rum, and better than anything he could find in any of the public-houses that were still permitted.

He walked across the road again and picked up the small cask, which he put on the other side of the cheese and from which he filled, in his own manner, the little cup he carried in his pocket.

But at the sight of this the cockney's eyes lit at once with terror and desire.

"But yer cawnt do it," he whispered hoarsely, "its the pleece. It's gile for that, with no doctor's letter nor sign-board nor nothink."

Mr. Humphrey Pump made yet another march back into the road. When he got there he hesitated for the first time, but it was quite clear from the attitude of the two insane aristocrats who were arguing and posturing in the road that they would notice nothing except each other. He picked the loose post off the road and brought it to the car, humorously propping it erect in the aperture between keg and cheese.

The little glass of rum was wavering in the poor chauffeur's hand exactly as the big knife had done, but when he looked up and actually saw the wooden sign above him, he seemed not so much to pluck up his courage, but rather to drag up some forgotten courage from the foundations of some unfathomable sea. It was indeed the forgotten courage of the people.

He looked once at the bleak, black pinewoods around him and took the mouthful of golden liquid at a gulp, as if it were a fairy potion. He sat silent; and then, very slowly, a sort of stony glitter began to come into his eyes. The brown and vigilant eyes of Humphrey Pump were studying him with some anxiety or even fear. He did look rather like a man enchanted or turned to stone. But he spoke very suddenly.

"The blighter!" he said. "I'll give 'im 'ell. I'll give 'im bleeding 'ell. I'll give 'im somethink wot 'e don't expect."

"What do you mean?" asked the inn-keeper.

"Why," answered the chauffeur, with abrupt composure, "I'll give 'im a little dornkey."

Mr. Pump looked troubled. "Do you think," he observed, affecting to speak lightly, "that he's fit to be trusted even with a little donkey?"

"Ow, yes," said the man. "He's very amiable with donkeys, and donkeys we is to be amiable with 'im."

Pump still looked at him doubtfully, appearing or affecting not to follow his meaning. Then he looked equally anxiously across at the other two men; but they were still talking. Different as they were in every other way, they were of the sort who forget everything, class, quarrel, time, place and physical facts in front of them, in the lust of lucid explanation and equal argument.

Thus, when the Captain began by lightly alluding to the fact that after all it was his donkey, since he had bought it from a tinker for a just price, the police station practically vanished from Wimpole's mind—and I fear the donkey-cart also. Nothing remained but the necessity of dissipating the superstition of personal property.

"I own nothing," said the poet, waving his hands outward, "I own nothing save in the sense that I own everything. All depends whether wealth or power be used for or against the higher purposes of the cosmos."

"Indeed," replied Dalroy, "and how does your motor car serve the higher purposes of the cosmos?"

"It helps me," said Mr. Wimpole, with honourable simplicity, "to produce my poems."

"And if it could be used for some higher purpose (if such a thing could be), if some new purpose had come into the cosmos's head by accident," inquired the other, "I suppose it would cease to be your property."

"Certainly," replied the dignified Dorian. "I should not complain. Nor have you any title to complain when the donkey ceases to be yours when you depress it in the cosmic scale."

"What makes you think," asked Dalroy, "that I wanted to depress it?"

"It is my firm belief," replied Dorian Wimpole, sternly, "that you wanted to ride on it" (for indeed the Captain had once repeated his playful gesture of putting his large leg across). "Is not that so?"

"No," answered the Captain, innocently, "I never ride on a donkey. I'm afraid of it."

"Afraid of a donkey!" cried Wimpole, incredulously.

"Afraid of an historical comparison," said Dalroy.

There was a short pause, and Wimpole said coolly enough, "Oh, well, we've outlived those comparisons."

"Easily," answered the Irish Captain. "It is wonderful how easily one outlives someone else's crucifixion."

"In this case," said the other grimly, "I think it is the donkey's crucifixion."

"Why, you must have drawn that old Roman caricature of the crucified donkey," said Patrick Dalroy, with an air of some wonder. "How well you have worn; why, you look quite young! Well, of course, if this donkey is crucified, he must be uncrucified. But are you quite sure," he added, very gravely, "that you know how to uncrucify a donkey? I assure you it's one of the rarest of human arts. All a matter of knack. It's like the doctors with the rare diseases, you know; the necessity so seldom arises. Granted that, by the higher purposes of the cosmos, I am unfit to look after this donkey, I must still feel a faint shiver of responsibility in passing him on to you. Will you understand this donkey? He is a delicate-minded donkey. He is a complex donkey. How can I be certain that, on so short an acquaintance, you will understand every shade of his little likes and dislikes?"

The dog Quoodle, who had been sitting as still as the sphinx under the shadow of the pine trees, waddled out for an instant into the middle of the road and then returned. He ran out when a slight noise as of rotatory grinding was heard; and ran back when it had ceased. But Dorian Wimpole was much too keen on his philosophical discovery to notice either dog or wheel.

"I shall not sit on its back, anyhow," he said proudly, "but if that were all it would be a small matter. It is enough for you that you have left it in the hands of the only person who could really understand it; one who searches the skies and seas so as not to neglect the smallest creature."

"This is a very curious creature," said the Captain, anxiously, "he has all sorts of odd antipathies. He can't stand a motor car, for instance, especially one that throbs like that while it's standing still. He doesn't mind a fur coat so much, but if you wear a brown velvet jacket under it, he bites you. And you must keep him out of the way of a certain kind of people. I don't suppose you've met them; but they always think that anybody with less than two hundred a year is drunk and very cruel, and that anybody with more than two thousand a year is conducting the Day of Judgment. If you will keep our dear donkey from the society of such persons—Hullo! Hullo! Hullo!"

He turned in genuine disturbance, and dashed after the dog, who had dashed after the motor car and jumped inside. The Captain jumped in after the dog, to pull him out again. But before he could do so, he found the car was flying along too fast for any such leap. He looked up and saw the sign of "The Old Ship" erect in the front like a rigid banner; and Pump, with his cask and cheese, sitting solidly beside the driver.

The thing was more of an earthquake and transformation to him even than to any of the others; but he rose waveringly to his feet and shouted out to Wimpole.

"You've left it in the right hands. I've never been cruel to a motor."

In the moonlight of the magic pine-wood far behind, Dorian and the donkey were left looking at each other.

To the mystical mind, when it is a mind at all (which is by no means always the case), there are no two things more impressive and symbolical than a poet and a donkey. And the donkey was a very genuine donkey, and the poet was a very genuine poet; however lawfully he might be mistaken for the other animal at times. The interest of the donkey in the poet will never be known. The interest of the poet in the donkey was perfectly genuine; and survived even that appalling private interview in the owlish secrecy of the woods.

But I think even the poet would have been enlightened if he had seen the white, set, frantic face of the man on the driver's seat of his vanishing motor. If he had seen it he might have remembered the name, or, perhaps, even begun to understand the nature of a certain animal which is neither the donkey nor the oyster; but the creature whom man has always found it easiest to forget, since the hour he forgot God in a Garden.

XV

THE SONGS OF THE CAR CLUB

More than once as the car flew through black and silver fairylands of fir wood and pine wood, Dalroy put his head out of the side window and remonstrated with the chauffeur without effect. He was reduced at last to asking him where he was going.

"I'm goin' 'ome," said the driver in an undecipherable voice. "I'm a goin' 'ome to my mar."

"And where does she live?" asked Dalroy, with something more like diffidence than he had ever shown before in his life.

"Wiles," said the man, "but I ain't seen 'er since I was born. But she'll do."

"You must realise," said Dalroy, with difficulty, "that you may be arrested—it's the man's own car; and he's left behind with nothing to eat, so to speak."

"'E's got 'is dornkey," grunted the man. "Let the stinker eat 'is dornkey, with thistle sauce. 'E would if 'e was as 'ollow as I was."

Humphrey Pump opened the glass window that separated him from the rear part of the car, and turned to speak to his friend over his square elbow and shoulder.

"I'm afraid," he said, "he won't stop for anything just yet. He's as mad as Moody's aunt, as they say."

"Do they say it?" asked the Captain, with a sort of anxiety. "They never said it in Ithaca."

"Honestly, I think you'd better leave him alone," answered Pump, with his sagacious face. "He'd just run us into a Scotch Express like Dandy Mutton did, when they said he was driving carelessly. We can send the car back to Ivywood somehow later on, and really, I don't

281

think it'll do the gentleman any harm to spend a night with a donkey. The donkey might teach him something, I tell you."

"It's true he denied the Principle of Private Property," said Dalroy, reflectively, "but I fancy he was thinking of a plain house fixed on the ground. A house on wheels, such as this, he might perhaps think a more permanent possession. But I never understand it;" and again he passed a weary palm across his open forehead. "Have you ever noticed, Hump, what is really odd about those people?"

The car shot on amid the comfortable silence of Pump, and then the Irishman said again:

"That poet in the pussy-cat clothes wasn't half bad. Lord Ivywood isn't cruel; but he's inhuman. But that man wasn't inhuman. He was ignorant, like most cultured fellows. But what's odd about them is that they try to be simple and never clear away a single thing that's complicated. If they have to choose between beef and pickles, they always abolish the beef. If they have to choose between a meadow and a motor, they forbid the meadow. Shall I tell you the secret? These men only surrender the things that bind them to other men. Go and dine with a temperance millionaire and you won't find he's abolished the *hors d'oeuvres* or the five courses or even the coffee. What he's abolished is the port and sherry, because poor men like that as well as rich. Go a step farther, and you won't find he's abolished the fine silver forks and spoons, but he's abolished the meat, because poor men like meat—when they can get it. Go a step farther, and you won't find he goes without gardens or gorgeous rooms, which poor men can't enjoy at all. But you will find he boasts of early rising, because sleep is a thing poor men can still enjoy. About the only thing they can still enjoy. Nobody ever heard of a modern philanthropist giving up petrol or typewriting or troops of servants. No, no! What he gives up must be some simple and universal thing. He will give up beef or beer or sleep—because these pleasures remind him that he is only a man."

Humphrey Pump nodded, but still answered nothing; and the voice of the sprawling Dalroy took one of its upward turns of a sort of soaring flippancy; which commonly embodied itself in remembering some song he had composed.

"Such," he said, "was the case of the late Mr. Mandragon, so long popular in English aristocratic society as a bluff and simple democrat from the West, until he was unfortunately sand-bagged by six men whose wives he had had shot by private detectives, on his incautiously landing on American soil.

"Mr. Mandragon the Millionaire, he wouldn't have wine
   or wife,
He couldn't endure complexity; he lived the simple life;
He ordered his lunch by megaphone in manly, simple
   tones,
And used all his motors for canvassing voters, and twenty
   telephones;
      Besides a dandy little machine,
      Cunning and neat as ever was seen,
      With a hundred pulleys and cranks between,
      Made of iron and kept quite clean,
To hoist him out of his healthful bed on every day of
   his life,
And wash him and brush him and shave him and dress
   him to live the Simple Life.

"Mr. Mandragon was most refined and quietly, neatly
   dressed,
Say all the American newspapers that know refinement
   best;
Quiet and neat the hair and hat, and the coat quiet and
   neat,
A trouser worn upon either leg, while boots adorned
   the feet;
      And not, as anyone might expect,
      A Tiger Skin, all striped and specked,
      And a Peacock Hat with the tail erect,
      A scarlet tunic with sunflowers decked— That
         might have had a more marked effect,
And pleased the pride of a weaker man that yearned for
   wine or wife;
But fame and the flagon for Mr. Mandragon obscured
   the Simple Life.

"Mr. Mandragon the Millionaire, I am happy to say, is
    dead.
He enjoyed a quiet funeral in a crematorium shed,
And he lies there fluffy and soft and grey and certainly
    quite refined,
When he might have rotted to flowers and fruit with
    Adam and all mankind.
        Or been eaten by bears that fancy blood,
        Or burnt on a big tall tower of wood,
        In a towering flame as a heathen should,
        Or even sat with us here at food,
Merrily taking twopenny rum and cheese with a pocket
    knife,
But these were luxuries lost for him that lived for the
    Simple Life."

Mr. Pump had made many attempts to arrest this song, but they
were as vain as all attempts to arrest the car. The angry chauffeur seemed,
indeed, rather inspired to further energy by the violent vocal noises
behind; and Pump again found it best to fall back on conversation.

"Well, Captain," he said, amicably. "I can't quite agree with you about
those things. Of course, you can trust foreigners too much as poor
Thompson did; but then you can go too far the other way. Aunt Sarah
lost a thousand pounds that way. I told her again and again he wasn't a
nigger, but she wouldn't believe me. And, of course, that was just the kind
of thing to offend an ambassador if he was an Austrian. It seems to me,
Captain, you aren't quite fair to these foreign chaps. Take these Americans,
now! There were many Americans went by Pebblewick, you may suppose.
But in all the lot there was never a bad lot; never a nasty American, nor a
stupid American—nor, well, never an American that I didn't rather like."

"I know," said Dalroy, "you mean there was never an American who
did not appreciate 'The Old Ship.'"

"I suppose I do mean that," answered the inn-keeper, "and somehow, I feel 'The Old Ship' might appreciate the American too."

"You English are an extraordinary lot," said the Irishman, with a
sudden and sombre quietude. "I sometimes feel you may pull through
after all."

After another silence he said, "You're always right, Hump, and one oughtn't to think of Yankees like that. The rich are the scum of the earth in every country. And a vast proportion of the real Americans are among the most courteous, intelligent, self-respecting people in the world. Some attribute this to the fact that a vast proportion of the real Americans are Irishmen."

Pump was still silent, and the Captain resumed in a moment.

"All the same," he said, "it's very hard for a man, especially a man of a small country like me, to understand how it must feel to be an American; especially in the matter of nationality. I shouldn't like to have to write the American National Anthem, but fortunately there is no great probability of the commission being given. The shameful secret of my inability to write an American patriotic song is one that will die with me."

"Well, what about an English one," said Pump, sturdily. "You might do worse, Captain."

"English, you bloody tyrant," said Patrick, indignantly. "I could no more fancy a song by an Englishman than you could one by that dog."

Mr. Humphrey Pump gravely took the paper from his pocket, on which he had previously inscribed the sin and desolation of grocers, and felt in another of his innumerable pockets for a pencil.

"Hullo," cried Dalroy. "Are you going to have a shy at the Ballad of Quoodle?"

Quoodle lifted his ears at his name. Mr. Pump smiled a slight and embarrassed smile. He was secretly proud of Dalroy's admiration for his previous literary attempts and he had some natural knack for verse as a game, as he had for all games; and his reading, though desultory, had not been merely rustic or low.

"On condition," he said, deprecatingly, "that you write a song for the English."

"Oh, very well," said Patrick, with a huge sigh that really indicated the very opposite of reluctance. "We must do something till the thing stops, I suppose, and this seems a blameless parlour game. 'Songs of the Car Club.' Sounds quite aristocratic."

And he began to make marks with a pencil on the fly-leaf of a little book he had in his pocket—Wilson's *Noctes Ambrosianae*. Every now and then, however, he looked up and delayed his own composition by watching Pump and the dog, whose proceedings amused him very much. For the owner of "The Old Ship" sat sucking his pencil and looking at Mr. Quoodle with eyes of fathomless attention. Every now and then he slightly scratched his brown hair with the pencil, and wrote down a word. And the dog Quoodle, with that curious canine power of either understanding or most brazenly pretending to understand what is going on, sat erect with his head at an angle, as if he were sitting for his portrait.

Hence it happened that though Pump's poem was a little long, as are often the poems of inexperienced poets, and though Dalroy's poem was very short (being much hurried toward the end) the long poem was finished some time before the short one.

Therefore it was that there was first produced for the world the song more familiarly known as "No Noses," or more correctly called "The Song of Quoodle." Part of it ran eventually thus:—

"They haven't got no noses
    The fallen sons of Eve,
Even the smell of roses
Is not what they supposes,
But more than mind discloses,
    And more than men believe.
"They haven't got no noses,
    They cannot even tell
When door and darkness closes
The park a Jew encloses,
Where even the Law of Moses
    Will let you steal a smell;

"The brilliant smell of water,
    The brave smell of a stone,
The smell of dew and thunder
And old bones buried under,
Are things in which they blunder
    And err, if left alone.
"The wind from winter forests,
    The scent of scentless flowers,

The breath of bride's adorning,
The smell of snare and warning,
The smell of Sunday morning,
    God gave to us for ours."

*   *   *   *   *   *

"And Quoodle here discloses
    All things that Quoodle can;
They haven't got no noses,
They haven't got no noses,
And goodness only knowses
    The Noselessness of Man."

This poem also shows traces of haste in its termination, and the present editor (who has no aim save truth) is bound to confess that parts of it were supplied in the criticisms of the Captain, and even enriched (in later and livelier circumstances) by the Poet of the Birds himself. At the actual moment the chief features of this realistic song about dogs was a crashing chorus of "Bow-wow, wow," begun by Mr. Patrick Dalroy; but immediately imitated (much more successfully) by Mr. Quoodle. In the face of all this Dalroy suffered some real difficulty in fulfilling the bargain by reading out his much shorter poem about what he imagined an Englishman might feel. Indeed there was something very rough and vague in his very voice as he read it out; as of one who had not found the key to his problem. The present compiler (who has no aim save truth) must confess that the verses ran as follows:—

"St. George he was for England,
    And before he killed the dragon
He drank a pint of English ale
    Out of an English flagon.
For though he fast right readily
    In hair-shirt or in mail,
It isn't safe to give him cakes
    Unless you give him ale.

"St. George he was for England,
  And right gallantly set free
The lady left for dragon's meat
  And tied up to a tree;
But since he stood for England
  And knew what England means,
Unless you give him bacon,
  You mustn't give him beans.

"St. George he was for England,
  And shall wear the shield he wore
When we go out in armour,
  With the battle-cross before;
But though he is jolly company
  And very pleased to dine,
It isn't safe to give him nuts
  Unless you give him wine.

"Very philosophical song that," said Dalroy, shaking his head solemnly, "full of deep thought. I really think that is about the truth of the matter, in the case of the Englishman. Your enemies say you're stupid, and you boast of being illogical—which is about the only thing you do that really is stupid. As if anybody ever made an Empire or anything else by saying that two and two make five. Or as if anyone was ever the stronger for *not* understanding anything—if it were only tipcat or chemistry. But this *is* true about you Hump. You English are supremely an artistic people, and therefore you go by associations, as I said in my song. You won't have one thing without the other thing that goes with it. And as you can't imagine a village without a squire and parson, or a college without port and old oak, you get the reputation of a Conservative people. But it's because you're sensitive, Hump, not because you're stupid, that you won't part with things. It's lies, lies and flattery they tell you, Hump, when they tell you you're fond of compromise. I tell ye, Hump, every real revolution is a compromise. D'ye think Wolfe Tone or Charles Stuart Parnell never compromised? But it's just because you're afraid of a compromise that you won't have a revolution. If you really overhauled 'The Old Ship'—or Oxford—you'd have to make up your mind what to take and what to leave, and it would break your heart, Humphrey Pump."

He stared in front of him with a red and ruminant face, and at length added, somewhat more gloomily,

"This aesthetic way we have, Hump, has only two little disadvantages which I will now explain to you. The first is exactly what has sent us flying in this contraption. When the beautiful, smooth, harmonious thing you've made is worked by a new type, in a new spirit, then I tell you it would be better for you a thousand times to be living under the thousand paper constitutions of Condorcet and Sieyès. When the English oligarchy is run by an Englishman who hasn't got an English mind—then you have Lord Ivywood and all this nightmare, of which God could only guess the end."

The car had beaten some roods of dust behind it, and he ended still more darkly:

"And the other disadvantage, my amiable aesthete, is this. If ever, in blundering about the planet, you come on an island in the Atlantic—Atlantis, let us say—which won't accept *all* your pretty picture—to which you can't give everything—*why* you will probably decide to give nothing. You will say in your hearts: 'Perhaps they will starve soon'; and you will become, for that island, the deafest and the most evil of all the princes of the earth."

It was already daybreak, and Pump, who knew the English boundaries almost by intuition, could tell even through the twilight that the tail of the little town they were leaving behind was of a new sort, the sort to be seen in the western border. The chauffeur's phrase about his mother might merely have been a music-hall joke; but certainly he had driven darkly in that direction.

White morning lay about the grey stony streets like spilt milk. A few proletarian early risers, wearier at morning than most men at night, seemed merely of opinion that it was no use crying over it. The two or three last houses, which looked almost too tired to stand upright, seemed to have moved the Captain into another sleepy explosion.

"There are two kinds of idealists, as everybody knows—or must have thought of. There are those who idealize the real and those who (precious seldom) realise the ideal. Artistic and poetical people like the English generally idealize the real. This I have expressed in a song, which—"

"No, really," protested the innkeeper, "really now, Captain—"

"This I have expressed in a song," repeated Dalroy, in an adamantine manner, "which I will now sing with every circumstance of leisure, loudness, or any other—"

He stopped because the flying universe seemed to stop. Charging hedgerows came to a halt, as if challenged by the bugle. The racing forests stood rigid. The last few tottering houses stood suddenly at attention. For a noise like a pistol-shot from the car itself had stopped all that race, as a pistol-shot might start any other.

The driver clambered out very slowly, and stood about in various tragic attitudes round the car. He opened an unsuspected number of doors and windows in the car, and touched things and twisted things and felt things.

"I must back as best I can to that there garrige, sir," he said, in a heavy and husky tone they had not heard from him before.

Then he looked round on the long woods and the last houses, and seemed to gnaw his lip, like a great general who has made a great mistake. His brow seemed as black as ever, yet his voice, when he spoke again, had fallen many further degrees toward its dull and daily tone.

"Yer see, this is a bit bad," he said. "It'll be a beastly job even at the best plices, if I'm gettin' back at all."

"Getting back," repeated Dalroy, opening the blue eyes of a bull. "Back where?"

"Well, yer see," said the chauffeur, reasonably, "I was bloody keen to show 'im it was me drove the car and not 'im. By a bit o' bad luck, I done damage to 'is car. Well—if *you* can stick in 'is car—"

Captain Patrick Dalroy sprang out of the car so rapidly that he almost reeled and slipped upon the road. The dog sprang after him, barking furiously.

"Hump," said Patrick, quietly. "I've found out everything about you. I know what always bothered me about the Englishman."

Then, after an instant's silence, he said, "That Frenchman was right who said (I forget how he put it) that you march to Trafalgar Square to rid yourself of your temper; not to rid yourself of your tyrant. Our friend was quite ready to rebel, rushing away. To rebel sitting still was too much for him. Do you read *Punch*? I am sure you do. Pump and *Punch* must be almost the only survivors of the Victorian Age. Do you remember an old joke in an excellent picture, representing two ragged Irishmen with guns, waiting behind a stone wall to shoot a landlord? One of the Irishmen says the landlord is late, and adds, 'I hope no accident's happened to the poor gentleman.' Well, it's all perfectly true; I knew that Irishman intimately, but I want to tell you a secret about him. He was an Englishman."

The chauffeur had backed with breathless care to the entrance of the garage, which was next door to a milkman's or merely separated from it by a black and lean lane, looking no larger than the crack of a door. It must, however, have been larger than it looked, because Captain Dalroy disappeared down it.

He seemed to have beckoned the driver after him; at any rate that functionary instantly followed. The functionary came out again in an almost guilty haste, touching his cap and stuffing loose papers into his pocket. Then the functionary returned yet again from what he called the "garrige," carrying larger and looser things over his arm.

All this did Mr. Humphrey Pump observe, not without interest. The place, remote as it was, was evidently a *rendez-vous* for motorists. Otherwise a very tall motorist, throttled and masked in the most impenetrable degree, would hardly have strolled up to speak to him. Still less would the tall motorist have handed him a similar horrid disguise of wraps and goggles, in a bundle over his arm. Least of all would any motorist, however tall, have said to him from behind the cap and goggles, "Put on these things, Hump, and then we'll go into the milk shop. I'm waiting for the car. Which car, my seeker after truth? Why the car I'm going to buy for you to drive."

The remorseful chauffeur, after many adventures, did actually find his way back to the little moonlit wood where he had left his master and the donkey. But his master and the donkey had vanished.

XVI

The Seven Moods of Dorian

That timeless clock of all lunatics, which was so bright in the sky that night, may really have had some elfin luck about it, like a silver penny. Not only had it initiated Mr. Hibbs into the mysteries of Dionysius, and Mr. Bullrose into the arboreal habits of his ancestors, but one night of it made a very considerable and rather valuable change in Mr. Dorian Wimpole, the Poet of the Birds. He was a man neither foolish nor evil, any more than Shelley; only a man made sterile by living in a world of indirectness and insincerity, with words rather than with things. He had not had the smallest intention of starving his chauffeur; he did not realise that there was worse spiritual murder in merely forgetting him. But as hour after hour passed over him, alone with the donkey and the moon, he went through a raging and shifting series of frames of mind, such as his cultured friends would have described as moods.

The First Mood, I regret to say, was one of black and grinding hatred. He had no notion of the chauffeur's grievance, and could only suppose he had been bribed or intimidated by the demonic donkey-torturers. But Mr. Wimpole was much more capable at that moment of torturing a chauffeur than Mr. Pump had ever been of torturing a donkey; for no sane man can hate an animal. He kicked the stones in the road, sending them flying into the forest, and wished that each one of them was a chauffeur. The bracken by the roadside he tore up by the roots, as representing the hair of the chauffeur, to which it bore no resemblance. He hit with his fist such trees, as, I suppose, seemed in form and expression most reminiscent of the chauffeur; but desisted from this, finding that in this apparently one-sided contest the tree had rather the

292

best of it. But the whole wood and the whole world had become a kind of omnipresent and pantheistic chauffeur, and he hit at him everywhere.

The thoughtful reader will realise that Mr. Wimpole had already taken a considerable upward stride in what he would have called the cosmic scale. The next best thing to really loving a fellow creature is really hating him: especially when he is a poorer man separated from you otherwise by mere social stiffness. The desire to murder him is at least an acknowledgment that he is alive. Many a man has owed the first white gleams of the dawn of Democracy in his soul to a desire to find a stick and beat the butler. And we have it on the unimpeachable local authority of Mr. Humphrey Pump that Squire Merriman chased his librarian through three villages with a horse-pistol; and was a Radical ever after.

His rage also did him good merely as a relief, and he soon passed into a second and more positive mood of meditation.

"The damnable monkeys go on like this," he muttered, "and then they call a donkey one of the Lower Animals. Ride on a donkey would he? I'd like to see the donkey riding on him for a bit. Good old man."

The patient ass turned mild eyes on him when he patted it, and Dorian Wimpole discovered, with a sort of subconscious surprise, that he really was fond of the donkey. Deeper still in his subliminal self he knew that he had never been fond of an animal before. His poems about fantastic creatures had been quite sincere, and quite cold. When he said he loved a shark, he meant he saw no reason for hating a shark, which was right enough. There is no reason for hating a shark, however much reason there may be for avoiding one. There is no harm in a craken if you keep it in a tank—or in a sonnet.

But he also realised that his love of creatures had been turned round and was working from the other end. The donkey was a companion, and not a monstrosity. It was dear because it was near, not because it was distant. The oyster had attracted him because it was utterly unlike a man; unless it be counted a touch of masculine vanity to grow a beard. The fancy is no idler than that he had himself used, in suggesting a sort of feminine vanity in the permanence of a pearl. But in that maddening vigil among the mystic pines, he found himself more and more drawn toward the donkey, because it was more like a man than anything else around him; because it had eyes to see, and ears to hear—and the latter even unduly developed.

"He that hath ears to hear, let him hear," he said, scratching those grey hairy flappers with affection. "Haven't you lifted your ears toward Heaven? And will you be the first to hear the Last Trumpet?"

The ass rubbed his nose against him with what seemed almost like a human caress. And Dorian caught himself wondering how a caress from an oyster could be managed. Everything else around him was beautiful, but inhuman. Only in the first glory of anger could he really trace in a tall pine-tree the features of an ex-taxi-cabman from Kennington. Trees and ferns had no living ears that they could wag nor mild eyes that they could move. He patted the donkey again.

But the donkey had reconciled him to the landscape, and in his third mood he began to realise how beautiful it was. On a second study, he was not sure it was so inhuman. Rather he felt that its beauty at least was half human; that the aureole of the sinking moon behind the woods was chiefly lovely because it was like the tender-coloured aureole of an early saint; and that the young trees were, after all, noble because they held up their heads like virgins. Cloudily there crowded into his mind ideas with which it was imperfectly familiar, especially an idea which he had heard called "The Image of God." It seemed to him more and more that all these things, from the donkey to the very docks and ferns by the roadside, were dignified and sanctified by their partial resemblance to something else. It was as if they were baby drawings: the wild, crude sketches of Nature in her first sketch-books of stone.

He had flung himself on a pile of pine-needles to enjoy the gathering darkness of the pinewoods as the moon sank behind them. There is nothing more deep and wonderful than really impenetrable pinewoods where the nearer trees show against the more shadowy; a tracery of silver upon grey and of grey upon black.

It was by this time, in pure pleasure and idleness that he picked up a pine-needle to philosophise about it.

"Think of sitting on needles!" he said. "Yet, I suppose this is the sort of needle that Eve, in the old legend, used in Eden. Aye, and the old legend was right, too! Think of sitting on all the needles in London! Think of sitting on all the needles in Sheffield! Think of sitting on any needles, except on all the needles of Paradise! Oh, yes, the old legend was right enough. The very needles of God are softer than the carpets of men."

He took a pleasure in watching the weird little forest animals creeping out from under the green curtains of the wood. He reminded himself that in the old legend they had been as tame as the ass, as well as being as comic. He thought of Adam naming the animals, and said to a beetle, "I should call *you* Budger."

The slugs gave him great entertainment, and so did the worms. He felt a new and realistic interest in them which he had not known before; it was, indeed, the interest that a man feels in a mouse in a dungeon; the interest of any man tied by the leg and forced to see the fascination of small things. Creatures of the wormy kind, especially, crept out at very long intervals; yet he found himself waiting patiently for hours for the pleasure of their acquaintance. One of them rather specially arrested his eye, because it was a little longer than most worms and seemed to be turning its head in the direction of the donkey's left foreleg. Also, it had a head to turn, which most worms have not.

Dorian Wimpole did not know much about exact Natural History, except what he had once got up very thoroughly from an encyclopaedia for the purposes of a sympathetic *vilanelle*. But as this information was entirely concerned with the conjectural causes of laughter in the Hyena, it was not directly helpful in this case. But though he did not know much Natural History, he knew some. He knew enough to know that a worm ought not to have a head, and especially not a squared and flattened head, shaped like a spade or a chisel. He knew enough to know that a creeping thing with a head of that pattern survives in the English country sides, though it is not common. In short, he knew enough to step across the road and set a sharp and savage boot-heel on the neck and spine of the creature, breaking it into three black bits that writhed once more before they stiffened.

Then he gave out a great explosive sigh. The donkey, whose leg had been in such danger, looked at the dead adder with eyes that had never lost their moony mildness. Even Dorian, himself, looked at it for a long time, and with feelings he could neither arrest nor understand, before he remembered that he had been comparing the little wood to Eden.

"And even in Eden," he said at last; and then the words of Fitzgerald failed upon his lips.

And while he was warring with such words and thoughts, something happened about him and behind him; something he had written about a hundred times and read about a thousand; something he had never seen in his life. It flung faintly across the broad foliage a wan and pearly light far more mysterious than the lost moonshine. It seemed to enter through all the doors and windows of the woodland, pale and silent but confident, like men that keep a tryst; soon its white robes had threads of gold and scarlet: and the name of it was morning.

For some time past, loud and in vain, all the birds had been singing to the Poet of the Birds. But when that minstrel actually saw broad daylight breaking over wood and road, the effect on him was somewhat curious. He stood staring at it in gaping astonishment, until it had fulfilled the fulness of its shining fate; and the pine-cones and the curling ferns and the live donkey and the dead viper were almost as distinct as they could be at noon, or in a Preraphaelite picture. And then the Fourth Mood fell upon him like a bolt from the blue, and he strode across and took the donkey's bridle, as if to lead it along.

"Damn it all," he cried, in a voice as cheerful as the cockcrow that rang recently from the remote village, "it's not everybody who's killed a snake." Then he added, reflectively, "I bet Dr. Gluck never did. Come along, donkey, let's have some adventures."

The finding and fighting of positive evil is the beginning of all fun—and even of all farce. All the wild woodland looked jolly now the snake was killed. It was one of the fallacies of his literary clique to refer all natural emotions to literary names, but it might not untruly be said that he had passed out of the mood of Maeterlinck into the mood of Whitman, and out of the mood of Whitman into the mood of Stevenson. He had not been a hypocrite when he asked for gilded birds of Asia or purple polypi out of the Southern Seas; he was not a hypocrite now, when he asked for mere comic adventures along a common English road. It was his misfortune and not his fault if his first adventure was his last; and was much too comic to laugh at.

Already the wan morning had warmed into a pale blue and was spotted with those little plump pink clouds which must surely have been the origin of the story that pigs might fly. The insects of the grass chattered so cheerfully that every green tongue seemed to be talking. The skyline on every side was broken only by objects that encouraged such swashbucklering comedy. There was a windmill that Chaucer's Miller might have inhabited or Cervantes's champion charged. There was an old leaden church spire that might have been climbed by Robert Clive. Away toward Pebblewick and the sea, there were the two broken stumps of wood which Humphrey Pump declares to this day to have been the stands for an unsuccessful children's swing; but which tourists always accept as the remains of the antique gallows. In the gaiety of such surroundings, it is small wonder if Dorian and the donkey stepped briskly along the road. The very donkey reminded him of Sancho Panza.

He did not wake out of this boisterous reverie of the white road and the wind till a motor horn had first hooted and then howled, till the ground had shaken with the shock of a stoppage, and till a human hand fell heavily and tightly on his shoulder. He looked up and saw the complete costume of a Police Inspector. He did not worry about the face. And there fell on him the Fifth, or Unexpected Mood, which is called by the vulgar Astonishment.

In despair he looked at the motor car itself that had anchored so abruptly under the opposite hedge. The man at the steering wheel was so erect and unresponsive that Dorian felt sure he was feasting his eyes on yet another policeman. But on the seat behind was a very different figure, a figure that baffled him all the more because he felt certain he had seen it somewhere. The figure was long and slim, with sloping shoulders, and the costume, which was untidy, yet contrived to give the impression that it was tidy on other occasions. The individual had bright yellow hair, one lock of which stuck straight up and was exalted, like the little horn in his favourite scriptures. Another tuft of it, in a bright but blinding manner, fell across and obscured the left optic, as in literal fulfilment of the parable of a beam in the eye. The eyes, with or without beams in them, looked a little bewildered, and the individual was always nervously resettling his necktie. For the individual went by the name of Hibbs, and had only recently recovered from experiences wholly new to him.

"What on earth do you want?" asked Wimpole of the policeman.

His innocent and startled face, and perhaps other things about his appearance, evidently caused the Inspector to waver.

"Well, it's about this 'ere donkey, sir," he said.

"Do you think I stole it?" cried the indignant aristocrat. "Well, of all the mad worlds! A pack of thieves steal my Limousine, I save their damned donkey's life at the risk of my own—and *I'm* run in for stealing."

The clothes of the indignant aristocrat probably spoke louder than his tongue; the officer dropped his hand, and after consulting some papers in his hand, walked across to consult with the unkempt gentleman in the car.

"That seems to be a similar cart and donkey," Dorian heard him saying, "but the clothes don't seem to fit your description of the men you saw."

Now, Mr. Hibbs had extremely vague and wild recollections of the men he saw; he could not even tell what he had done and what he had merely dreamed. If he had spoken sincerely, he would have described a sort of green nightmare of forests, in which he found himself in the power of an ogre about twelve feet high, with scarlet flames for hair and dressed rather like Robin Hood. But a long course of what is known as "keeping the party together" had made it as unnatural to him to tell anyone (even himself) what he really thought about anything, as it would have been to spit—or to sing. He had at present only three motives and strong resolves: (1) not to admit that he had been drunk; (2) not to let anyone escape whom Lord Ivywood might possibly want to question; and (3) not to lose his reputation for sagacity and tact.

"This party has a brown velvet suit, you see, and a fur overcoat," the Inspector continued, "and in the notes I have from you, you say the man wore a uniform."

"When we say uniform," said Mr. Hibbs, frowning intellectually, "when we say *uniform*, of course—we must distinguish some of our friends who don't quite see eye to eye with us, you know," and he smiled with tender leniency, "some of our friends wouldn't like it called a *uniform* perhaps. But—of course—well, it wasn't a police uniform, for instance. Ha! Ha!"

"I should hope not," said the official, shortly.

"So—in a way—however," said Hibbs, clutching his verbal talisman at last, "it might be brown velvet in the dark."

The Inspector replied to this helpful suggestion with some wonder. "But it was a moon, like limelight," he protested.

"Yars, yars," cried Hibbs, in a high tone that can only be described as a hasty drawl. "Yars—discolours everything of course. The flowers and things—"

"But look here," said the Inspector, "you said the principal man's hair was red."

"A blond type! A blond type!" said Hibbs, waving his hand with a solemn lightness. "Reddish, yellowish, brownish sort of hair, you know." Then he shook his head and said with the heaviest solemnity the word was capable of carrying, "Teutonic, purely Teutonic."

The Inspector began to feel some wonder that, even in the confusion following on Lord Ivywood's fall, he had been put under the guidance of this particular guide. The truth was that Leveson, once more masking his own fears under his usual parade of hurry, had found Hibbs at a table by an open window, with wild hair and sleepy eyes, picking himself up with some sort of medicine. Finding him already fairly clear-headed in a dreary way, he had not scrupled to use the remains of his bewilderment to despatch him with the police in the first pursuit. Even the mind of a semi-recovered drunkard, he thought, could be trusted to recognise anyone so unmistakable as the Captain.

But, though the diplomatist's debauch was barely over, his strange, soft fear and cunning were awake. He felt fairly certain the man in the fur coat had something to do with the mystery, as men with fur coats do not commonly wander about with donkeys. He was afraid of offending Lord Ivywood, and at the same time, afraid of exposing himself to a policeman.

"You have large discretion," he said, gravely. "Very right you should have large discretion in the interests of the public. I think you would be quite authorised, for the present, in preventing the man's escape."

"And the other man?" inquired the officer, with knitted brow. "Do you suppose he has escaped?"

"The *other* man," repeated Hibbs However, regarding the distant windmill through half-closed lids, as if this were a new fine shade introduced into an already delicate question.

"Well, hang it all," said the police officer, "you must know whether there were two men or one."

Gradually it dawned, in a grey dawn of horror, over the brain of Hibbs that this was what he specially couldn't know. He had always heard, and read in comic papers, that a drunken man "sees double" and beholds two lamp-posts, one of which is (as the Higher Critic would have said) purely subjective. For all he knew (being a mere novice) inebriation might produce the impression of the two men of his dream-like adventure, when in truth there had only been one.

"Two men, you know—one man," he said with a sort of moody carelessness. "Well we can go into their numbers later; they can't have a very large following." Here he shook his head very firmly. "Quite impossible. And as the late Lord Goschen used to say, 'You can prove anything by statistics.'"

And here came an interruption from the other side of the road.

"And how long am I to wait here for you and your Goschens, you silly goat," were the intemperate wood-notes issuing from the Poet of the Birds. "I'm shot if I'll stand this! Come along, donkey, and let's pray for a better adventure next time. These are very inferior specimens of your own race." And seizing the bridle of the ass again, he strode past them swiftly, and almost as if urging the animal to a gallop.

Unfortunately this disdainful dash for liberty was precisely what was wanting to weigh down the rocking intelligence of the Inspector on the wrong side. If Wimpole had stood still a minute or two longer, the official, who was no fool, might have ended in disbelieving Hibbs's story altogether. As it was, there was a scuffle, not without blows on both sides, and eventually the Honourable Dorian Wimpole, donkey and all, was marched off to the village, in which there was a Police Station; in which was a temporary cell; in which a Sixth Mood was experienced.

His complaints, however, were at once so clamorous and so convincing, and his coat was so unquestionably covered with fur, that after some questioning and cross purposes they agreed to take him in the afternoon to Ivywood House, where there was a magistrate incapacitated by a shot only recently extracted from his leg.

They found Lord Ivywood lying on a purple ottoman, in the midst of his Chinese puzzle of oriental apartments. He continued to look away as they entered, as if expecting, with Roman calm, the entrance of a recognised enemy. But Lady Enid Wimpole, who was attending to the wants of the invalid, gave a sharp cry of astonishment; and the next moment the three cousins were looking at each other. One could almost have guessed they were cousins, all being (as Mr. Hibbs subtly put it) a blond type. But two of the blond types expressed amazement, and one blond type merely rage.

"I am sorry, Dorian," said Ivywood, when he had heard the whole story. "These fanatics are capable of anything, I fear, and you very rightly resent their stealing your car—"

"You are wrong, Philip," answered the poet, emphatically. "I do not even faintly resent their stealing my car. What I do resent is the continued existence on God's earth of this Fool" (pointing to the serious Hibbs) "and of that Fool" (pointing to the Inspector) "and—yes, by thunder, of *that* Fool, too" (and he pointed straight at Lord Ivywood). "And I tell you frankly, Philip, if there really are, as you say, two men who are bent on smashing your schemes and making your life a hell—I am very happy to put my car at their disposal. And now I'm off."

"You'll stop to dinner?" inquired Ivywood, with frigid forgiveness.

"No, thanks," said the disappearing bard, "I'm going up to town."

The Seventh Mood of Dorian Wimpole had a grand finale at the Café Royal, and consisted largely of oysters.

XVII
THE POET IN PARLIAMENT

During the singular entrance and exit of Dorian Wimpole, M.P., J.P., etc., Lady Joan was looking out of the magic casements of that turret room which was now literally, and not only poetically, the last limit of Ivywood House. The old broken hole and black staircase up which the lost dog Quoodle used to come and go, had long ago been sealed up and cemented with a wall of exquisite Eastern workmanship. All through the patterns Lord Ivywood had preserved and repeated the principle that no animal shape must appear. But, like all lucid dogmatists, he perceived all the liberties his dogma allowed him. And he had irradiated this remote end of Ivywood with sun and moon and solar and starry systems, with the Milky Way for a dado and a few comets for comic relief. The thing was well done of its kind (as were all the things that Philip Ivywood got done for him); and if all the windows of the turret were closed with their peacock curtains, a poet with anything like a Hibbsian appreciation of the family champagne might almost fancy he was looking out across the sea on a night crowded with stars. And (what was yet more important) even Misysra (that exact thinker) could not call the moon a live animal without falling into idolatry.

But Joan, looking out of real windows on a real sky and sea, thought no more about the astronomical wall-paper than about any other wallpaper. She was asking herself in sullen emotionalism, and for the thousandth time, a question she had never been able to decide. It was the final choice between an ambition and a memory. And there was this heavy weight in the scale: that the ambition would probably materialise, and the memory probably wouldn't. It has been the same weight in the same scale a million times since Satan became the prince of this world.

302

But the evening stars were strengthening over the old sea-shore, and they also wanted weighing like diamonds.

As once before at the same stage of brooding, she heard behind her the swish of Lady Enid's skirts, that never came so fast save for serious cause.

"Joan! Please do come! Nobody but you, I do believe, could move him." Joan looked at Lady Enid and realised that the lady was close on crying. She turned a trifle pale and asked quietly for the question. "Philip says he's going to London now, with that leg and all," cried Enid, "and he won't let us say a word."

"But how did it all happen?" asked Joan.

Lady Enid Wimpole was quite incapable of explaining how it all happened, so the task must for the moment devolve on the author. The simple fact was that Ivywood in the course of turning over magazines on his sofa, happened to look at a paper from the Midlands.

"The Turkish news," said Mr. Leveson, rather nervously, "is on the other side of the page."

But Lord Ivywood continued to look at the side of the paper that did not contain the Turkish news, with the same dignity of lowered eyelids and unconscious brow with which he had looked at the Captain's message when Joan found him by the turret.

On the page covered merely with casual, provincial happenings was a paragraph, "Echo of Pebblewick Mystery. Reported Reappearance of the Vanishing Inn." Underneath was printed, in smaller letters:

"An almost incredible report from Wyddington announces that the mysterious 'Sign of the Old Ship' has once more been seen in this country; though it has long been relegated by scientific investigators to the limbo of old rustic superstitions. According to the local version, Mr. Simmons, a dairyman of Wyddington, was serving in his shop when two motorists entered, one of them asking for a glass of milk. They were in the most impenetrable motoring panoply, with darkened goggles and waterproof collars turned up, so that nothing can be recalled of them personally, except that one was a person of unusual stature. In a few moments, this latter individual went out of the shop again and returned with a miserable specimen out of the street, one of the tattered loafers that linger about our most prosperous towns, tramping the streets all night and even begging in defiance of the police. The

filth and disease of the creature were so squalid that Mr. Simmons at
first refused to serve him with the glass of milk which the taller motorist wished to provide for him. At length, however, Mr. Simmons consented, and was immediately astonished by an incident against which
he certainly had a more assured right to protest.

"The taller motorist, saying to the loafer, 'but, man, you're blue in
the face,' made a species of signs to the smaller motorist, who there-
upon appears to have pierced a sort of cylindrical trunk or chest that
seemed to be his only luggage, and drawn from it a few drops of a
yellow liquid which he deliberately dropped into the ragged creature's
milk. It was afterward discovered to be rum, and the protests of Mr.
Simmons may be imagined. The tall motorist, however, warmly defended
his action, having apparently some wild idea that he was doing an act
of kindness. 'Why, I found the man nearly fainting,' he said. 'If you'd
picked him off a raft, he couldn't be more collapsed with cold and sickness; and if you'd picked him off a raft you'd have given him rum—yes,
by St. Patrick, if you were a bloody pirate and made him walk the plank
afterward.' Mr. Simmons replied with dignity, that he did not know how
it was with rafts, and could not permit such language in his shop. He
added that he would lay himself open to a police prosecution if he
permitted the consumption of alcohol in his shop; since he did not
display a sign. The motorist then made the amazing reply, 'But you *do*
display a sign, you jolly old man. Did you think I couldn't find my way
to the sign of The Old Ship, you sly boots?' Mr. Simmons was now
fully convinced of the intoxication of his visitors, and refusing a glass
of rum rather boisterously offered him, went outside his shop to look
round for a policeman. To his surprise he found the officer engaged in
dispersing a considerable crowd, which was staring up at some object
behind him. On looking round (he states in his deposition) he 'saw
what was undoubtedly one of the low tavern signs at one time common
in England.' He was wholly unable to explain its presence outside his
premises, and as it undoubtedly legalised the motorist's action, the police
declined to move in the matter.

"*Later.* The two motorists have apparently left the town, unmolested,
in a small second-hand two-seater. There is no clue to their destination,
except it be indicated by a single incident. It appears that when they were
waiting for the second glass of milk, one of them drew attention to a milk

can of a shape seemingly unfamiliar to him, which was, of course, the Mountain Milk now so much recommended by doctors. The taller motorist (who seemed in every way strangely ignorant of modern science and social life) asked his companion where it came from, receiving, of course, the reply that it is manufactured in the model village of Peaceways, under the personal superintendence of its distinguished and philanthropic inventor, Dr. Meadows. Upon this the taller person, who appeared highly irresponsible, actually bought the whole can; observing, as he tucked it under his arm, that it would help him to remember the address.

"*Later.* Our readers will be glad to hear that the legend of 'The Old Ship' sign has once more yielded to the wholesome scepticism of science. Our representative reached Wyddington after the practical jokers, or whatever they were, had left; but he searched the whole frontage of Mr. Simmons's shop, and we are in a position to assure the public that there is no trace of the alleged sign."

Lord Ivywood laid down the newspaper and looked at the rich and serpentine embroideries on the wall with the expression that a great general might have if he saw a chance of really ruining his enemy, if he would also ruin all his previous plan of campaign. His pallid and classic profile was as immovable as a cameo; but anyone who had known him at all would have known that his brain was going like a motor car that has broken the speed limit long ago.

Then he turned his head and said, "Please tell Hicks to bring round the long blue car in half an hour; it can be fitted up for a sofa. And ask the gardener to cut a pole of about four feet nine inches, and put a cross-piece for a crutch. I'm going up to London to-night."

Mr. Leveson's lower jaw literally fell with astonishment.

"The Doctor said three weeks," he said. "If I may ask it, where are you going?"

"St. Stephens, Westminster," answered Ivywood.

"Surely," said Mr. Leveson, "I could take a message."

"You could take a message," assented Ivywood, "I'm afraid they would not allow you to make a speech."

It was a moment or two afterward that Enid Wimpole had come into the room, and striven in vain to shake his decision. Then it was that Joan had been brought out of the turret and saw Philip standing,

sustained upon a crutch of garden timber; and admired him as she had
never admired him before. While he was being helped downstairs, while
he was being propped in the car with such limited comfort as was possible, she did really feel in him something worthy of his ancient roots,
worthy of such hills and of such a sea. For she felt God's wind from
nowhere which is called the Will; and is man's only excuse upon this
earth. In the small toot of the starting motor she could hear a hundred
trumpets, such as might have called her ancestors and his to the glories
of the Third Crusade.

Such imaginary military honours were not, at least in the strategic
sense, undeserved. Lord Ivywood really had seen the whole map of the
situation in front of him, and swiftly formed a plan to meet it, in a
manner not unworthy of Napoleon. The realities of the situation unrolled themselves before him, and his mind was marking them one by
one as with a pencil.

First, he knew that Dalroy would probably go to the Model Village.
It was just the sort of place he would go to. He knew Dalroy was almost constitutionally incapable of not kicking up some kind of row in
a place of that kind.

Second, he knew that if he missed Dalroy at this address, it was
very likely to be his last address; he and Mr. Pump were quite clever
enough to leave no more hints behind.

Third, he guessed, by careful consideration of map and clock, that
they could not get to so remote a region in so cheap a car under something like two days, nor do anything very conclusive in less than three.
Thus, he had just time to turn round in.

Fourth, he realised that ever since that day when Dalroy swung round
the sign-board and smote the policeman into the ditch, Dalroy had
swung round the Ivywood Act on Lord Ivywood. He (Lord Ivywood)
had thought, and might well have thought rightly, that by restricting
the old sign-posts to a few places so select that they can afford to be
eccentric, and forbidding such artistic symbols to all other places, he
could sweep fermented liquor for all practical purposes out of the land.
The arrangement was exactly that at which all such legislation is consciously or unconsciously aiming. A sign-board could be a favour granted
by the governing class to itself. If a gentleman wished to claim the
liberties of a Bohemian, the path would be open. If a Bohemian wished

to claim the liberties of a gentleman, the path would be shut. So, gradually, Lord Ivywood had thought, the old signs which can alone sell alcohol, will dwindle down to mere curiosities, like Audit Ale or the Mead that may still be found in the New Forest. The calculation was by no means unstatesmanlike. But, like many other statesmanlike calculations, it did not take into account the idea of dead wood walking about. So long as his flying foes might set up their sign anywhere, it mattered little whether the result was enjoyment or disappointment for the populace. In either case it must mean constant scandal or riot. If there was one thing worse than the appearance of "The Old Ship" it was its disappearance.

He realised that his own law was letting them loose every time; for the local authorities hesitated to act on the spot, in defiance of a symbol now so exclusive and therefore impressive. He realised that the law must be altered. Must be altered at once. Must be altered, if possible, before the fugitives broke away from the Model Village of Peaceways.

He realised that it was Thursday. This was the day on which any private member of Parliament could introduce any private bill of the kind called "non-contentious," and pass it without a division, so long as no particular member made any particular fuss. He realised that it was improbable that any particular member would make any particular fuss about Lord Ivywood's own improvement on Lord Ivywood's own Act.

Finally, he realised that the whole case could be met by so slight an improvement as this. Change the words of the Act (which he knew by heart, as happier men might know a song): "If such sign be present liquids containing alcohol can be sold on the premises," to these other words: "Liquids containing alcohol can be sold, if previously preserved for three days on the premises"; it was mate in a few moves. Parliament could never reject or even examine so slight an emendation. And the revolution of "The Old Ship" and the late King of Ithaca would be crushed for ever.

It does undoubtedly show, as we have said, something Napoleonic in the man's mind that the whole of this excellent and even successful plan was complete long before he saw the great glowing clock on the towers of Westminster; and knew he was in time.

It was unfortunate, perhaps, that about the same time, or not long after, another gentleman of the same rank, and indirectly of the same family, having left the restaurant in Regent Street and the tangle of Piccadilly, had drifted serenely down Whitehall, and had seen the same great golden goblin's eye on the tall tower of St. Stephen.

The Poet of the Birds, like most aesthetes, had known as little of the real town as he had of the real country. But he had remembered a good place for supper; and as he passed certain great cold clubs, built of stone and looking like Assyrian Sarcophagi, he remembered that he belonged to many of them. And so when he saw afar off, sitting above the river, what has been very erroneously described as the best club in London, he suddenly remembered that he belonged to that too. He could not at the moment recall what constituency in South England it was that he sat for; but he knew he could walk into the place if he wanted to. He might not so have expressed the matter, but he knew that in an oligarchy things go by respect for persons and not for claims; by visiting cards and not by voting cards. He had not been near the place for years, being permanently paired against a famous Patriot who had accepted an important government appointment in a private madhouse. Even in his silliest days, he had never pretended to feel any respect for modern politics, and made all haste to put his "leaders" and the mad patriot's "leaders" on the well selected list of the creatures whom man forgets. He had made one really eloquent speech in the House (on the subject of gorillas), and then found he was speaking against his party. It was an indescribable sort of place, anyhow. Even Lord Ivywood did not go to it except to do some business that could be done nowhere else; as was the case that night.

Ivywood was what is called a peer by courtesy; his place was in the Commons, and for the time being on the Opposition side. But, though he visited the House but seldom, he knew far too much about it to go into the Chamber itself. He limped into the Smoking Room (though he did not smoke), procured a needless cigarette and a much-needed sheet of note-paper, and composed a curt but careful note to the one member of the government whom he knew must be in the House. Having sent it up to him, he waited.

Outside, Mr. Dorian Wimpole also waited, leaning on the parapet of Westminster Bridge and looking down the river. He was becoming one with the oysters in a more solemn and solid sense than he had hitherto conceived possible, and also with a strictly Vegetarian beverage

which bears the noble and starry name of Nuits. He felt at peace with
all things, even in a manner with politics. It was one of those magic
hours of evening when the red and golden lights of men are already lit
along the river, and look like the lights of goblins, but daylight still
lingers in a cold and delicate green. He felt about the river something
of that smiling and glorious sadness which two Englishmen have expressed under the figure of the white wood of an old ship fading like a
phantom; Turner, in painting, and Henry Newbolt, in poetry. He had
come back to earth like a man fallen from the moon; he was at bottom
not only a poet but a patriot, and a patriot is always a little sad. Yet his
melancholy was mixed up with that immutable yet meaningless faith
which few Englishmen, even in modern times, fail to feel at the unexpected sight either of Westminster or of that height on which stands
the temple of St. Paul.

> "While flows the sacred river,
> While stands the sacred hill,"

he murmured in some schoolboy echo of the ballad of Lake Regillus,

> "While flows the sacred river,
> While stands the sacred hill,
> The proud old pantaloons and nincompoops,
> Who yawn at the very length of their own lies
> in that accursed sanhedrim where
> people put each other's hats on in a poisonous
> room with no more windows than hell
> Shall have such honour still."

Relieved by this rendering of Macaulay in the style known among
his cultured friends as *vers libre*, or poesy set free from the shackles of
formal metre, he strolled toward the members' entrance and went in.

Lacking Lord Ivywood's experience, he strolled into the Common's
Chamber itself and sat down on a green bench, under the impression
that the House was not sitting. He was, however, gradually able to distinguish some six or eight drowsy human forms from the seats on which
they sat; and to hear a senile voice with an Essex accent, saying, all on

one note, and without beginning or end, in a manner which it is quite impossible to punctuate,

"... no wish at all that this proposal should be regarded except in the right way and have tried to put it in the right way and cannot think the honourable member was altogether adding to his reputation in putting it in what those who think with me must of course consider the wrong way and I for one am free to say that if in his desire to settle this great question he takes this hasty course and this revolutionary course about slate pencils he may not be able to prevent the extremists behind him from applying it to lead pencils and while I should be the last to increase the heat and the excitement and the personalities of this debate if I could possibly help it I must confess that in my opinion the honourable gentleman has himself encouraged that heat and personality in a manner that he now doubtless regrets I have no desire to use abusive terms indeed you Mr. Speaker would not allow me of course to use abusive terms but I must tell the honourable member face to face that the perambulators with which he has twitted me cannot be germane to this discussion I should be the last person. ...."

Dorian Wimpole had softly risen to go, when he was arrested by the sight of someone sliding into the House and handing a note to the solitary young man with heavy eyelids who was at that moment governing all England from the Treasury Bench. Seeing him go out, Dorian had a sickening sweetness of hope (as he might have said in his earlier poems), that something intelligible might happen after all, and followed him out almost with alacrity.

The solitary and sleepy governor of Great Britain went down into the lower crypts of its temple of freedom and turned into an apartment where Wimpole was astonished to see his cousin Ivywood sitting at a little table with a large crutch leaning beside him, as serene as Long John Silver. The young man with the heavy eyelids sat down opposite him and they had a conversation which Wimpole, of course, did not hear. He withdrew into an adjoining room where he managed to procure coffee and a liqueur; an excellent liqueur which he had forgotten and of which he had more than one glass.

But he had so posted himself that Ivywood could not come out without passing him, and he waited for what might happen with exquisite patience. The only thing that seemed to him queer was that every now and then a bell rang in several rooms at once. And whenever the bell rang, Lord Ivywood nodded, as if he were part of the electrical machinery. And whenever Lord Ivywood nodded the young man turned and sped upstairs like a mountaineer, returning in a short time to resume the conversation. On the third occasion the poet began to observe that many others from the other rooms could be heard running upstairs at the sound of this bell, and returning with the slightly less rapid step which expresses relief after a duty done. Yet did he not know that this duty was Representative Government; and that it is thus that the cry of Cumberland or Cornwall can come to the ears of an English King.

Suddenly the sleepy young man sprang erect, uninspired by any bell, and strode out once more. The poet could not help hearing him say as he left the table, jotting down something with a pencil: "Alcohol can be sold if previously preserved for three days on the premises. I think we can do it, but you can't come on for half an hour."

Saying this, he darted upstairs again, and when Dorian saw Ivywood come out laboriously, afterward, on his large country crutch, he had exactly the same revulsion in his favour that Joan had had. Jumping up from his table, which was in one of the private dining-rooms, he touched the other on the elbow and said:

"I want to apologise to you, Philip, for my rudeness this afternoon. Honestly, I am sorry. Pinewoods and prison-cells try a man's temper, but I had no rag of excuse for not seeing that for neither of them were you to blame. I'd no notion you were coming up to town tonight; with your leg and all. You mustn't knock yourself up like this. Do sit down a minute."

It seemed to him that the bleak face of Philip softened a little; how far he really softened will never be known until such men as he are understood by their fellows. It is certain that he carefully unhooked himself from his crutch and sat down opposite his cousin. Whereupon his cousin struck the table so that it rang like a dinner-bell and called out, "Waiter!" as if he were in a crowded restaurant. Then, before Lord Ivywood could protest, he said:

"It's awfully jolly that we've met. I suppose you've come up to make a speech. I *should* like to hear it. We haven't always agreed; but, by God, if there's anything good left in literature it's your speeches reported in a newspaper. That thing of yours that ended, 'death and the last shutting of the iron doors of defeat'—Why you must go back to Strafford's last speech for such English. Do let me hear your speech! I've got a seat upstairs, you know."

"If you wish it," said Ivywood hurriedly, "but I shan't make much of a speech to-night." And he looked at the wall behind Wimpole's head with thunderous wrinkles thickening on his brow. It was essential to his brilliant and rapid scheme, of course, that the Commons should make no comment at all on his little alteration in the law.

An attendant hovered near in response to the demand for a waiter, and was much impressed by the presence and condition of Lord Ivywood. But as that exalted cripple resolutely refused anything in the way of liquor, his cousin was so kind as to have a little more himself, and resumed his remarks.

"It's about this public-house affair of yours, I suppose. I'd like to hear you speak on that. P'raps I'll speak myself. I've been thinking about it a good deal all day, and a good deal of last night, too. Now, here's what I should say to the House, if I were you. To begin with, can you abolish the public-house? Are you *important* enough now to abolish the public-house? Whether it's right or wrong, can you in the long run prevent haymakers having ale any more than you can prevent me having this glass of Chartreuse?"

The attendant, hearing the word, once more drew near; but heard no further order; or, rather, the orders he heard were such as he was less able to cope with.

"Remember the curate!" said Dorian, abstractedly shaking his head at the functionary, "remember the sensible little High-Church curate, who when asked for a Temperance Sermon preached on the text 'Suffer us not to be overwhelmed in the water-floods.' Indeed, indeed, Philip, you are in deeper waters than you know. *You* will abolish ale! *You* will make Kent forget hop-poles, and Devonshire forget cider! The fate of the Inn is to be settled in that hot little room upstairs! Take care its fate and yours are not settled in the Inn. Take care Englishmen don't sit in judgment on you as they do on many another corpse at an inquest—at a common public-house! Take care that the one tavern that is really neglected and shut up and passed like a house of pestilence is not the tavern in which I drink to-night, and that merely because it is the worst tavern on the King's highway. Take care this place where we sit does not get a name like any pub where sailors are hocussed or girls debauched.

That is what I shall say to them," said he, rising cheerfully, "that's what I shall say. See you to it," he cried with sudden passion and apparently to the waiter, "see you to it if the sign that is destroyed is not the sign of 'The Old Ship' but the sign of the Mace and Bauble, and, in the words of a highly historical brewer, if we see a dog bark at your going."

Lord Ivywood was observing him with a deathly quietude; another idea had come into his fertile mind. He knew his cousin, though excited, was not in the least intoxicated; he knew he was quite capable of making a speech and even a good one. He knew that any speech, good or bad, would wreck his whole plan and send the wild inn flying again. But the orator had resumed his seat and drained his glass, passing a hand across his brow. And he remembered that a man who keeps a vigil in a wood all night and drinks wine on the following evening is liable to an accident that is not drunkenness, but something much healthier.

"I suppose your speech will come on pretty soon," said Dorian, looking at the table. "You'll let me know when it does, of course. Really and truly, I don't want to miss it. And I've forgotten all the ways here, and feel pretty tired. You'll let me know?"

"Yes," said Lord Ivywood.

Stillness fell along all the rooms until Lord Ivywood broke it by saying:

"Debate is a most necessary thing; but there are times when it rather impedes than assists parliamentary government."

He received no reply. Dorian still sat as if looking at the table, but his eyelids had lightly fallen; he was asleep. Almost at the same moment the Member of Government, who was nearly asleep, appeared at the entrance of the long room and made some sort of weary signal.

Philip Ivywood raised himself on his crutch and stood for a moment looking at the sleeping man. Then he and his crutch trailed out of the long room, leaving the sleeping man behind. Nor was that the only thing that he left behind. He also left behind an unlighted cigarette and his honour and all the England of his father's; everything that could really distinguish that high house beside the river from any tavern for the hocussing of sailors. He went upstairs and did his business in twenty minutes in the only speech he had ever delivered without any trace of eloquence. And from that hour forth he was the naked fanatic; and could feed on nothing but the future.

XVIII
The Republic of Peaceways

In a hamlet round about Windermere, let us say, or somewhere in Wordsworth's country, there could be found a cottage, in which could be found a cottager. So far all is as it should be; and the visitor would first be conscious of a hearty and even noisy elderly man, with an apple face and a short white beard. This person would then loudly proffer to the visitor the opportunity of seeing his father, a somewhat more elderly man, with a somewhat longer white beard, but still "up and about." And these two together would then initiate the neophyte into the joys of the society of a grandfather, who was more than a hundred years old, and still very proud of the fact.

This miracle, it seemed, had been worked entirely on milk. The subject of this diet the oldest of the three men continued to discuss in enormous detail. For the rest, it might be said that his pleasures were purely arithmetical. Some men count their years with dismay, and he counted his with a juvenile vanity. Some men collect stamps or coins, and he collected days. Newspaper men interviewed him about the historic times through which he had lived, without eliciting anything whatever; except that he had apparently taken to an exclusive milk diet at about the age when most of us leave it off. Asked if he was alive in 1815, he said that was the very year he found it wasn't any milk, but must be Mountain Milk, like Dr. Meadows says. Nor would his calculating creed of life have allowed him to understand you if you had said that in a meadowland oversea that lies before the city of Brussels, boys of his old school in that year gained the love of the gods and died young.

It was the philanthropic Dr. Meadows, of course, who discovered this deathless tribe, and erected on it the whole of his great dietetic

314

philosophy, to say nothing of the houses and dairies of Peaceways. He
attracted many pupils and backers among the wealthy and influential;
young men who were, so to speak, training for extreme old age, infant
old men, embryo nonagenarians. It would be an exaggeration to say
that they watched joyfully for the first white hair as Fascination Fledgeby
watched for his first whisker; but it is quite true to say that they seemed
to have scorned the beauty of woman and the feasting of friends and,
above all, the old idea of death with glory; in comparison with this
vision of the sports of second childhood.

Peaceways was in its essential plan much like what we call a Garden
City; a ring of buildings where the work people did their work, with a
pretty ornamental town in the centre, where they lived in the open country outside. This was no doubt much healthier than the factory system
in the great towns and may have partly accounted for the serene expression of Dr. Meadows and his friends, if any part of the credit can be
spared from the splendours of Mountain Milk. The place lay far from
the common highways of England, and its inhabitants were enabled to
enjoy their quiet skies and level woods almost undisturbed, and fully
absorb whatever may be valuable in the Meadows method and view;
until one day a small and very dirty motor drove into the middle of
their town. It stopped beside one of those triangular islets of grass
that are common at forked roads, and two men in goggles, one tall and
the other short, got out and stood on the central space of grass, as if
they were buffoons about to do tricks. As, indeed, they were.

Before entering the town they had stopped by a splendid mountain
stream quickening and thickening rapidly into a river; unhelmed and
otherwise eased themselves, eaten a little bread bought at Wyddington
and drank the water of the widening current which opened on the valley
of Peaceways.

"I'm beginning quite to like water," said the taller of the two knights.
"I used to think it a most dangerous drink. In theory, of course, it
ought only to be given to people who are fainting. It's really good for
them, much better than brandy. Besides, think of wasting good brandy
on people who are fainting! But I don't go so far as I did; I shouldn't
insist on a doctor's prescription before I allow people water. That was
the too severe morality of youth; that was my innocence and goodness.
I thought that if I fell once, water-drinking might become a habit. But

I do see the good side of water now. How good it is when you're really
thirsty, how it glitters and gurgles! How alive it is! After all, it's the best
of drinks, after the other. As it says in the song:

"Feast on wine or fast on water,
    And your honour shall stand sure;
God Almighty's son and daughter,
    He the valiant, she the pure.
If an angel out of heaven
    Brings you other things to drink,
Thank him for his kind intentions,
    Go and pour them down the sink.

"Tea is like the East he grows in,
    A great yellow Mandarin,
With urbanity of manner,
    And unconsciousness of sin;
All the women, like a harem,
    At his pig-tail troop along,
And, like all the East he grows in,
    He is Poison when he's strong.

"Tea, although an Oriental,
    Is a gentleman at least;
Cocoa is a cad and coward,
    Cocoa is a vulgar beast;
Cocoa is a dull, disloyal,
    Lying, crawling cad and clown,
And may very well be grateful
    To the fool that takes him down.

"As for all the windy waters,
    They were rained like trumpets down,
When good drink had been dishonoured
    By the tipplers of the town.
When red wine had brought red ruin,
    And the death-dance of our times,

Heaven sent us Soda Water
    As a torment for our crimes."

"Upon my soul, this water tastes quite nice. I wonder what vintage now?" and he smacked his lips with solemnity. "It tastes just like the year 1881 tasted."

"You can fancy anything in the tasting way," returned his shorter companion. "Mr. Jack, who was always up to his tricks, did serve plain water in those little glasses they drink liqueurs out of, and everyone swore it was a delicious liqueur, and wanted to know where they could get it—all except old Admiral Guffin, who said it tasted too strong of olives. But water's much the best for our game, certainly."

Patrick nodded, and then said:

"I doubt if I could do it, if it weren't for the comfort of looking at that," and he kicked the rum-keg, "and feeling we shall have a good swig at it some day. It feels like a fairy-tale, carrying that about—as if rum were a pirate's treasure, as if it were molten gold. Besides, we can have such fun with it with other people—what was that joke I thought of this morning? Oh, I remember! Where's that milk can of mine?"

For the next twenty minutes he was industriously occupied with his milk can and the cask; Pump watching him with an interest amounting to anxiety.

Lifting his head, however, at the end of that time, he knotted his red brows and said, "What's that?"

"What's what?" asked the other traveller.

"That!" said Captain Patrick Dalroy, and pointed to a figure approaching on the road parallel to the river, "I mean, what's it for?"

The figure had a longish beard and very long hair falling far below its shoulders. It had a serious and steadfast expression. It was dressed in what the inexperienced Mr. Pump at first took to be its nightgown; but afterward learned to be its complete goats' hair tunic, unmixed even with a thread of the destructive and deadly wool of the sheep. It had no boots on its feet. It walked very swiftly to a particular turn of the stream and then turned very sharply (since it had accomplished its constitutional), and walked back toward the perfect town of Peaceways.

"I suppose it's somebody from that milk place," said Humphrey Pump, indulgently. "They seem to be pretty mad."

"I don't mind that so much," said Dalroy, "I'm mad myself some-times. But a madman has only one merit and last link with God. A mad-man is always logical. Now what is the logical connection between liv-ing on milk and wearing your hair long? Most of us lived on milk when we had no hair at all. How do they connect it up? Are there any heads even for a synopsis? Is it, say, 'milk—water—shaving-water—shaving—hair?' Is it 'milk—kindness—unkindness—convicts—hair?' What is the logical connection between having too much hair and having far too few boots? What *can* it be? Is it 'hair—hair-trunk—leather-trunk—leather-boots?' Is it 'hair—beard—oysters—seaside—paddling—no boots?' Man is liable to err—especially when every mistake he makes is called a movement—but why should all the lunacies live together?"

"Because all the lunatics should live together," said, Humphrey, "and if you'd seen what happened up at Crampton, with the farming-out idea, you'd know. It's all very well, Captain; but if people can prevent a guest of great importance being buried up to the neck in farm manure, they will. They will, really." He coughed almost apologetically. He was about to attempt a resumption of the conversation, when he saw his companion slap the milk can and keg back into the car, and get into it himself. "You drive," he said, "drive me where those things live; you know, Hump."

They did not, however, arrive in the civic centre of such things without yet another delay. They left the river and followed the man with the long hair and the goatskin frock; and he stopped as it hap-pened at a house on the outskirts of the village. The adventurers stopped also, out of curiosity, and were at first relieved to see the man almost instantly reappear, having transacted his business with a quickness that seemed incredible. A second glance showed them it was not the man, but another man dressed exactly like him. A few minutes more of in-quisitive delay, showed them many of the kilty and goatish sect going in and out of this particular place, each clad in his innocent uniform.

"This must be the temple and chapel," muttered Patrick, "it must be here they sacrifice a glass of milk to a cow, or whatever it is they do. Well, the joke is pretty obvious, but we must wait for a lull in the crowd-ing of the congregation."

When the last long-haired phantom had faded up the road, Dalroy sprang from the car and drove the sign-board deep into the earth with savage violence, and then very quietly knocked at the door.

The apparent owner of the place, of whom the two last of the long-haired and bare-footed idealists were taking a rather hurried farewell, was a man curiously ill-fitted for the part he seemed cast for in the only possible plot.

Both Pump and Dalroy thought they had never seen a man look so sullen. His face was of the rubicund sort that does not suggest jollity, but merely a stagnant indigestion in the head. His mustache hung heavy and dark, his brows yet heavier and darker. Dalroy had seen something of the sort on the faces of defeated people disgracefully forced into submission, but he could not make head or tail of it in connection with the priggish perfections of Peaceways. It was all the odder because he was manifestly prosperous; his clothes were smartly cut in something of the sporting manner, and the inside of his house was at least four times grander than the outside.

But what mystified them most was this, that he did not so much exhibit the natural curiosity of a gentleman whose private house is entered by strangers, but rather an embarrassed and restless expectation. During Dalroy's eager apologies and courteous inquiries about the direction and accommodations of Peaceways, his eye (which was of the boiled gooseberry order) perpetually wandered from them to the cupboard and then again to the window, and at last he got up and went to look out into the road.

"Oh, yes, sir; very healthy place, Peaceways," he said, peering through the lattice. "Very ... dash it, what do they mean? ... Very healthy place. Of course they have their little ways."

"Only drink pure milk, don't they?" asked Dalroy.

The householder looked at him with a rather wild eye and grunted.

"Yes; so they say," and he went again to the window.

"I've bought some of it," said Patrick, patting his pet milk can, which he carried under his arm, as if unable to be separated from Dr. Meadows's discovery. "Have a glass of milk, sir."

The man's boiled eye began to bulge in anger—or some other emotion.

"What do you want?" he muttered, "are you 'tecs or what?"

"Agents and Distributors of the Meadows's Mountain Milk," said the Captain, with simple pride, "taste it?"

The dazed householder took a glass of the blameless liquid and sipped it; and the change on his face was extraordinary.

"Well, I'm jiggered," he said, with a broad and rather coarse grin. "That's a queer dodge. You're in the joke, I see." Then he went again restlessly to the window; and added, "but if we're all friends, why the blazes don't the others come in? I've never known trade so slow before."

"Who are the others?" asked Mr. Pump.

"Oh, the usual Peaceways people," said the other. "They generally come here before work. Dr. Meadows don't work them for very long hours, that wouldn't be healthy or whatever he calls it; but he's particular about their being punctual. I've seen 'em running, with all their pure-minded togs on, when the hooter gave the last call."

Then he abruptly opened the front door and called out impatiently, but not loudly:

"Come along in if you're coming. You'll give the show away if you play the fool out there."

Patrick looked out also and the view of the road outside was certainly rather singular. He was used to crowds, large and small, collecting outside houses which he had honoured with the sign of "The Old Ship," but they generally stared up at it in unaffected wonder and amusement. But outside this open door, some twenty or thirty persons in what Pump had called their night-gowns were moving to and fro like somnambulists, apparently blind to the presence of the sign; looking at the other side of the road, looking at the horizon, looking at the clouds of morning; and only occasionally stopping to whisper to each other. But when the owner of the house called to one of these ostentatiously abstracted beings and asked him hoarsely what the devil was the matter, it was natural for the milk-fed one to turn his feeble eye toward the sign. The gooseberry eyes followed his, and the face to which they belonged was a study in apoplectic astonishment.

"What the hell have you done to my house?" he demanded. "Of course they can't come in if this thing's here."

"I'll take it down, if you like," said Dalroy, stepping out and picking it up like a flower from the front garden (to the amazement of the men in the road, who thought they had strayed into a nursery fairy-tale), "but I wish, in return, you'd give me some idea of what the blazes all this means."

"Wait till I've served these men," replied his host.

The goat-garbed persons went very sheepishly (or goatishly) into the now signless building, and were rapidly served with raw spirits, which Mr. Pump suspected to be of no very superior quality. When the last goat was gone, Captain Dalroy said:

"I mean that all this seems to me topsy-turvy. I understood that as the law stands now, if there's a sign they are allowed to drink and if there isn't they aren't."

"The Law!" said the man, in a voice thick with scorn. "Do you think these poor brutes are afraid of the Law as they are of the Doctor?"

"Why should they be afraid of the Doctor?" asked Dalroy, innocently. "I always heard that Peaceways was a self-governing republic."

"Self-governing be damned," was the illiberal reply. "Don't he own all the houses and could turn 'em out in a snow storm? Don't 'e pay all the wages and could starve 'em stiff in a month? The Law!" And he snorted. A moment after he squared his elbows on the table and began to explain more fully.

"I was a brewer about here and had the biggest brewery in these parts. There were only two houses which didn't belong to me, and the magistrates took away their licenses after a time. Ten years ago you could see Hugby's Ales written beside every sign in the county. Then came these cursed Radicals, and our leader, Lord Ivywood, must go over to their side about it, and let this Doctor buy all the land under some new law that there shan't be any pubs at all. And so my business is ruined so that he can sell his milk. Luckily I'd done pretty well before and had some compensation, of course; and I still do a fair trade on the Q.T., as you see. But of course that don't amount to half the old one, for they're afraid of old Meadows finding out. Snuffling old blighter!"

And the gentleman with the good clothes spat on the carpet.

"I am a Radical myself," said the Irishman, rather coldly, "for all information on the Conservative party I must refer you to my friend, Mr. Pump, who is, of course, in the inmost secrets of his leaders. But it seems to me very rum sort of Radicalism to eat and drink at the orders of a master who is a madman, merely because he's also a millionaire. O Liberty, what very complicated and even unsatisfactory social developments are committed in thy name! Why don't they kick the old ass round the town a bit? No boots? Is that why they're allowed no boots? Oh, roll him down hill in a milk can: he can't object to that."

"I don't know," said Pump, in his ruminant way, "Master Christian's aunt did, but ladies are more particular, of course."

"Look here!" cried Dalroy, in some excitement, "if I stick up that sign outside, and stay here to help, will you defy them? You'd be strictly within the law, and any private coercion I can promise you they shall repent. Plant the sign and sell the stuff openly like a man, and you may stand in English history like a deliverer."

Mr. Hugby, of Hugby's Ales, only looked gloomily at the table. His was not the sort of drinking nor the sort of drink-selling on which the revolutionary sentiment flourishes.

"Well," said the Captain, "will you come with me and say 'Hear, hear!' and 'How true!'— 'What matchless eloquence!' if I make a speech in the market-place? Come along! There's room in our car."

"Well, I'll come with you, if you like," replied Mr. Hugby, heavily. "It's true if yours is allowed we might get our trade back, too." And putting on a silk hat he followed the Captain and the innkeeper out to their little car. The model village was not an appropriate background for Mr. Hugby's silk hat. Indeed, the hat somehow seemed to bring out by contrast all that was fantastic in the place.

It was a superb morning, some hours after sunrise. The edges of the sky touching the ring of dim woods and distant hills were still jewelled with the tiny transparent clouds of daybreak, delicate red and green or yellow. But above the vault of Heaven rose through turquoise into a torrid and solid blue in which the other clouds, the colossal cumuli, tumbled about like a celestial pillow-fight. The bulk of the houses were as white as the clouds, so that it looked (to use another simile) as if some of the whitewashed cottages were flying and falling about the sky. But most of the white houses were picked out here and there with bright colours, here an ornament in orange or there a stripe of lemon yellow, as if by the brush of a baby giant. The houses had no thatching (thatching is not hygienic) but were mostly covered with a sort of peacock green tiles bought cheap at a Preraphaelite Bazaar; or, less frequently, by some still more esoteric sort of terra cotta bricks. The houses were not English, nor homelike, nor suited to the landscape; for the houses had not been built by free men for themselves, but at the fancy of a whimsical lord. But considered as a sort of elfin city in a pantomime it was a really picturesque background for pantomimic proceedings.

I fear Mr. Dalroy's proceedings from the first rather deserved that name. To begin with, he left the sign, the cask, and the keg all wrapped and concealed in the car, but removed all the wraps of his own disguise, and stood on the central patch of grass in that green uniform that looked all the more insolent for being as ragged as the grass. Even that was less ragged than his red hair, which no red jungle of the East could imitate. Then he took out, almost tenderly, the large milk can, and deposited it, almost reverently, on the island of turf. Then he stood beside it, like Napoleon beside a gun, with an expression of tremendous seriousness and even severity. Then he drew his sword, and with that flashing weapon, as with a flail, lashed and thrashed the echoing metal can till the din was deafening, and Mr. Hugby hastily got out of the car and withdrew to a slight distance, stopping his ears. Mr. Pump sat solidly at the steering wheel, well knowing it might be necessary to start in some haste.

"Gather, gather, gather, Peaceways," shouted Patrick, still banging on the can and lamenting the difficulties of adapting "Macgregor's Gathering" to the name and occasion, "We're landless, *landless*, landless, Peaceways!"

Two or three of the goat-clad, recognising Mr. Hugby with a guilty look, drew near with great caution, and the Captain shouted at them as if they were an army covering Salisbury Plain.

"Citizens," he roared, saying anything that came into his head, "try the only original unadulterated Mountain Milk, for which alone Mahomet came to the mountain. The original milk of the land flowing with milk and honey; the high quality of which could alone have popularised so unappetising a combination. Try our milk! None others are genuine! Who can do without milk. Even whales can't do without milk. If any lady or gentleman keeps a favourite whale at home, now's their chance! The early whale catches the milk. Just look at our milk! If you say you can't look at the milk, because it's in the can—well, look at the can! You must look at the can! You simply must! When Duty whispers low 'Thou Must!'" he bellowed at the top of his voice in a highly impromptu peroration, "When Duty whispers low 'Thou Must,' the Youth replies, 'I can!'" And with the word "Can" he hit the can with a shocking and shattering noise, like a peal of demoniac bells of steel.

This introductory speech is open to criticism from those who regard it as intended for the study rather than the stage. The present chronicler

(who has no aim save truth) is bound to record that for its own unscrupulous purpose it was extremely successful: a great mass of the citizens
of Peaceways having been attracted by the noise of one man shouting
like a crowd. There are crowds who do not care to revolt; but there are
no crowds who do not like someone else to do it for them; a fact which
the safest oligarchs may be wise to learn.

But Dalroy's ultimate triumph (I regret to say) consisted in actually
handing to a few of the foremost of his audience some samples of his
blameless beverage. The fact was certainly striking. Some were paraly-
sed with surprise. Some were abruptly broken double with laughter.
Many chuckled. Some cheered. All looked radiantly toward the eccentric
orator.

And yet the radiance died quietly and suddenly from their faces.
And only because one little old man had joined the group; a little old
man in white linen with a white pointed beard and a white powder-puff
of hair like thistledown: a man whom almost every man present could
have killed with the left arm.

XIX

THE HOSPITALITY OF THE CAPTAIN

Dr. Moses Meadows, whether that was his name or an Anglicised version of it, had certainly come in the first instance from a little town in Germany and his first two books were written in German. His first two books were his best, for he began with a genuine enthusiasm for physical science, and this was adulterated with nothing worse than a hatred of what he thought was superstition, and what many of us think is the soul of the state. The first enthusiasm was most notable in the first book, which was concerned to show that "in the female not upsprouting of the whiskers was from the therewith increasing arrested mentality derived." In his second book he came more to grips with delusions, and for some time he was held to have proved (to everyone who agreed with him already) that the Time Ghost had been walking particularly "rapidly, lately; and that the Christus Mythus was by the alcoholic mind's trouble explained." Then, unfortunately, he came across the institution called Death, and began to argue with it. Not seeing any rational explanation of this custom of dying, so prevalent among his fellow-citizens, he concluded that it was merely traditional (which he thought meant "effete"), and began to think of nothing but ways of evading or delaying it. This had a rather narrowing effect on him, and he lost much of that acrid ardour which had humanised the atheism of his youth, when he would almost have committed suicide for the pleasure of taunting God with not being there. His later idealism grew more and more into materialism and consisted of his changing hypotheses and discoveries about the healthiest foods. There is no need to detain the reader over what has been called his Oil Period; his Sea-weed Period has been authoritatively expounded in Professor Nym's valuable little work; and on the events of his Glue Period it is, perhaps, not very generous to dwell. It was during his prolonged stay in England that he chanced on the instance of the longevity of milk consumers, and built on it a theory which was, at the beginning at least, sincere. Unfortunately it was also successful: wealth flowed in to the inventor and proprietor of Mountain Milk, and he began to feel a fourth and last enthusiasm, which, also, can come late in life and have a narrowing effect on the mind.

In the altercation which naturally followed on his discovery of the antics of Mr. Patrick Dalroy, he was very dignified, but naturally not very tolerant; for he was quite unused to anything happening in spite of him, or anything important even happening without him, in the land that lay around. At first he hinted severely that the Captain had stolen the milk can from the milk-producing premises, and sent several workmen to count the cans in each shed; but Dalroy soon put him right about that.

"I bought it in a shop at Wyddington," he said, "and since then I have used no other. You'll hardly believe me" he said, with some truth, "but when I went into that shop I was quite a little man. I had one glass of your Mountain Milk; and look at me now."

"You have no right to sell the milk here," said Dr. Meadows, with the faintest trace of a German accent. "You are not in my employment; I am not responsible for your methods. You are not a representative of the business."

"I'm an Advertisement," said the Captain. "We advertise you all over England. You see that lean, skimpy, little man over there," pointing to the indignant Mr. Pump, "He's Before Taking Meadows's Mountain Milk. I'm After," added Mr. Dalroy, with satisfaction.

"You shall laugh at the magistrate," said the other, with a thickening accent.

"I shall," agreed Patrick. "Well, I'll make a clean breast of it, sir. The truth is it isn't your milk at all. It has quite a different taste. These gentlemen will tell you so."

A smothered giggle sent all the blood to the eminent capitalist's face.

"Then, either you have stolen my can and are a thief," he said, stamping, "or you have introduced inferior substances into my discovery and are an adulterer—er—"

"Try adulteratist," said Dalroy, kindly. "Prince Albert always said 'adulteratarian.' Dear old Albert! It seems like yesterday! But it is, of course, today. And it's as true as daylight that this stuff tastes different. I can't tell you what the taste is" (subdued guffaws from the outskirts of the crowd). "It's something between the taste of your first sugar-stick and the fag-end of your father's cigar. It's as innocent as Heaven and as hot as hell. It tastes like a paradox. It tastes like a prehistoric inconsistency—I trust I make myself clear. The men who taste it most are the simplest men that God has made, and it always reminds them of the salt, because it is made out of sugar. Have some!"

And with a gesture of staggering hospitality, he shot out his long arm with the little glass at the end of it. The despotic curiosity in the Prussian overcame even his despotic dignity. He took a sip of the liquid, and his eyes stood out from his face.

"You've been mixing something with the milk," were the first words that came to him.

"Yes," answered Dalroy, "and so have you, unless you're a swindler. Why is your milk advertised as different from everyone else's milk, if you haven't made the difference? Why does a glass of your milk cost threepence, and a glass of ordinary milk, a penny, if you haven't put twopennorth of something into it? Now, look here, Dr. Meadows. The Public Analyst who would judge this, happens to be an honest man. I have a list of the twenty-one and a half honest men still employed in such posts. I make you a fair offer. He shall decide what it is I add to the milk, if you let him decide what it is you add to the milk. You must add something to the milk, or what can all these wheels and pumps and pulleys be for? Will you tell me, here and now, what you add to the milk which makes it so exceedingly Mountain?"

There was a long silence, full of the same sense of submerged mirth in the mob.

But the philanthropist had fallen into a naked frenzy in the sunlight, and shaking his fists aloft in a way unknown to all the English around him, he cried out:

"Ach! but I know what you add! I know what you add! It is the Alcohol! And you have no sign and you shall laugh at a magistrate."

Dalroy, with a bow, retired to the car, removed a number of wrappings and produced the prodigious wooden sign-post of "The Old Ship," with its blue three-decker and red St. George's cross conspicuously displayed. This he planted on his narrow territory of turf and looked round serenely.

"In this old oak-panelled inn of mine," he said, "I will laugh at a million magistrates. Not that there's anything unhygienic about this inn. No low ceilings or stuffiness here. Windows open everywhere, except in the floor. And as I hear some are saying there ought always to be food sold with fermented liquor, why, my dear Dr. Meadows, I've got a cheese here that will make another man of you. At least, we'll hope so. We can but try."

But Dr. Meadows was long past being merely angry. The exhibition of the sign had put him into a serious difficulty. Like most sceptics, like even the most genuine sceptics such as Bradlaugh, he was as legal as he was sceptical. He had a profound fear, which also had in it something better than fear, of being ultimately found in the wrong in a police court or a public inquiry. And he also suffered the tragedy of all such men living in modern England; that he must always be certain to respect the law, while never being certain of what it was. He could only remember generally that Lord Ivywood, when introducing or defending the great Ivywood Act on this matter, had dwelt very strongly on the unique and significant nature of the sign. And he could not be certain that if he disregarded it altogether, he might not eventually be cast in heavy damages—or even go to prison, in spite of his success in business. Of course he knew quite well that he had a thousand answers to such nonsense: that a patch of grass in the road couldn't be an inn; that the sign wasn't even produced when the Captain began to hand round the rum. But he also knew quite well that in the black peril we call British law that is not the point. He had heard points quite as obvious urged to a judge and urged in vain. At the bottom of his mind he found this fact: rich as he was, Lord Ivywood had made him—and on which side would Lord Ivywood be?

"Captain," said Humphrey Pump, speaking for the first time, "we'd better be getting away. I feel it in my bones."

"Inhospitable innkeeper!" cried the Captain, indignantly. "And after I have gone out of the way to license your premises! Why, this is the dawn of peace in the great city of Peaceways. I don't despair of Dr. Meadows tossing off another bumper before we've done. For the moment, Brother Hugby will engage."

As he spoke, he served out milk and rum at random; and still the Doctor had too much terror of our legal technicalities to make a final interference. But when Mr. Hugby, of Hugby's Ales, heard his name called, he first of all jumped so as almost to dislodge the silk hat, then he stood quite still. Then he accepted a glass of the new Mountain Milk; and then his very face became full of speech, before he had spoken a word.

"There's a motor coming along the road from the far hills," said Humphrey, quietly. "It'll be across the last bridge down stream in ten minutes and come up on this side."

"Well," said the Captain, impatiently, "I suppose you've seen a motor before."

"Not in this valley all this morning," answered Pump.

"Mr. Chairman," said Mr. Hugby, feeling a dim disposition to say "Mr. Vice," in memory of old commercial banquets, "I'm sure we're all law-abiding people here, and wish to remain friends, especially with our good friend the Doctor; may he never want a friend or a bottle— that is in short, anything he wants, as we go up the hill of prosperity, and so on. But, as our friend here with the sign-board seems to be within his rights, well, I think the time's come when we can look at these things more broadly, so to speak. Now I know it's quite true those dirty little pubs do a lot of harm to a property, and you get a lot of ignorant people there who are just like pigs; and I don't say our friend the Doctor hasn't done good by clearing 'em away. But a big, well-man-aged business with plenty of capital behind it is quite another thing. Well, friends, you all know that I was originally in the Trade; though I have, of course, left off selling under the new regulations." Here the goats looked rather guiltily at their cloven hoofs. "But I've got my little bit and I wouldn't mind putting it into this 'Old Ship' here, if our friend would allow it to be run on business lines. And especially if he'd en-large the premises a bit. Ha! ha! And if our good friend, the Doctor— "

"You rascal fellow!" spluttered Meadows, "your goot friend the doctor will make you dance before a magistrate."

"Now, don't be unbusinesslike," reasoned the brewer. "It won't hurt your sales. It's quite a different public, don't you see? Do talk like a business man."

"I am not a business man," said the scientist, with fiery eyes, "I am a servant of humanity."

"Then," said Dalroy, "why do you never do what your master tells you?"

"The motor has crossed the river," said Humphrey Pump.

"You would undo all my works," cried the Doctor, with sincere passion. "When I have built this town myself, when I have made it sober and healthful myself, when I am awake and about before anyone in the town myself, watching over its interests—you would ruin all to sell your barbaric and fundamentally beastly beer. And then you call me a goot friend. I am not a goot friend!"

"That I can't say," growled Hugby, "but if it comes to that—aren't you trying to sell—"

A motor car drove up with a white explosion of dust, and about six very dusty people got out of it. Even through the densest disguise of the swift motorist, Pump perceived in many of them the peculiar style and bodily carriage of the police. The most evident exception was a long and more slender figure, which, on removing its cap and goggles, disclosed the dark and drooping features of J. Leveson, Secretary. He walked across to the little, old millionaire, who instantly recognized him and shook hands. They confabulated for some little time, turning over some official documents. Dr. Meadows cleared his throat and said to the whole crowd.

"I am very glad to be able to announce to you all that this extraordinary outrage has been too late attempted. Lord Ivywood, with the promptitude he so invariably shows, has immediately communicated to places of importance such as this a most just and right alteration of the law, which exactly meets the present case.

"We shall sleep in jail tonight," said Humphrey, Pump. "I know it in my bones."

"It is enough to say," proceeded the millionaire, "that by the law as it now stands, any innkeeper, even if he display a sign, is subject to imprisonment if he sells alcohol on premises where it has not been previously kept for three days."

"I thought it would be something like that," muttered Pump. "Shall we give up, Captain, or shall we try a bolt for it?"

Even the impudence of Dalroy appeared for the instant dazed and stilled. He was staring forlornly up into the abyss of sky above him, as if, like Shelley, he could get inspiration from the last and purest clouds and the perfect hues of the ends of Heaven.

At last he said, in a soft and meditative voice, the single syllable, "Sells!"

Pump looked at him sharply with a remarkable expression growing on his grim face. But the Doctor was far too rabidly rejoicing in his triumph to understand the Captain's meaning.

"Sells alcohol, are the exact words," he insisted, brandishing the blue oblong of the new Act of Parliament.

"So far as I am concerned they are inexact words," said Captain Dalroy, with polite indifference. "I have not been selling alcohol, I have been giving it away. Has anybody here paid me money? Has anybody here seen anybody else pay me money? I'm a philanthropist just like Dr. Meadows. I'm his living image!"

Mr. Leveson and Dr. Meadows looked across at each other, and on the face of the first was consternation, and on the second a full return of all his terrors of the complicated law.

"I shall remain here for several weeks," continued the Captain, leaning elegantly on the can, "and shall give away, gratis, such supplies of this excellent drink as may be demanded by the citizens. It appears that there is no such supply at present in this district, and I feel sure that no person present can object to so strictly legal and highly charitable an arrangement."

In this he was apparently in error; for several persons present seemed to object to it. But curiously enough it was not the withered and fanatical face of the philanthropist Meadows, nor the dark and equine face of the official Leveson, which stood out most vividly as a picture of protest. The face most strangely unsympathetic with this form of charity was that of the ex-proprietor of Hugby's Ales. His gooseberry eyes were almost dropping from his head and his words sprang from his lips before he could stop them.

"And you blooming well think you can come here like a big buffoon, you beast, and take away all my trade—"

Old Meadows turned on him with the swiftness of an adder.

"And what is your trade, Mr. Hugby?" he asked.

The brewer bubbled with a sort of bursting anger. The goats all looked at the ground as is, according to a Roman poet, the habit of the lower animals. Man (in the character of Mr. Patrick Dalroy) taking advantage of a free but fine translation of the Latin passage, "looked aloft, and with uplifted eyes beheld his own hereditary skies."

"Well, all I can say is," roared Mr. Hugby, "if the police come all this way and can't lock up a dirty loafer whose coat's all in rags, there's an end of me paying these fat infernal taxes and—"

"Yes," said Dalroy, in a voice that fell like an axe, "there is an end of you, please God. It's brewers like you that have made the inns stink with poison, till even good men asked for no inns at all. And you are worse than the teetotallers, for you prevented what they never knew. And as for you, eminent man of science, great philanthropist, idealist and destroyer of inns, let me give one cold fact for your information. You are not respected. You are obeyed. Why should I or anyone respect you particularly? You say you built this town and get up at daybreak to watch this town. You built it for money and you watch it for more money. Why should I respect you because you are fastidious about food, that your poor old digestion may outlive the hearts of better men? Why should you be the god of this valley, whose god is your belly, merely because you do not even love your god, but only fear him? Go home to your prayers, old man; for all men shall die. Read the Bible, if you like, as they do in your German home; and I suppose you once read it to pick texts as you now read it to pick holes. I don't read it myself, I'm afraid, but I remember some words in old Mulligan's translation; and I leave them with you. 'Unless God,'" and he made a movement with his arm, so natural and yet so vast that for an instant the town really looked like a toy of bright coloured cardboard at the feet of the giant; "'unless God build the city, their labour is but lost that build it; unless God keep the city, the watchman watcheth in vain. It is lost labour that you rise up early in the morning and eat the bread of carefulness; while He giveth His beloved sleep.' Try and understand what that means, and never mind whether it's Elohistic. And now, Hump, we'll away and away. I'm tired of the green tiles over there. Come, fill up my cup," and he banged down the cask in the car, "come saddle my horses and call out my men. And tremble, gay goats, in the midst of your glee; for you've no' seen the last of my milk can and me."

This song was joyously borne away with Mr. Dalroy in the disappearing car; and the motorists were miles beyond pursuit from Peaceways before they thought of halting again. But they were still beside the bank of that noble and enlarging river; and in a place of deep fern and fairy-ribboned birches with the glowing and gleaming water behind them, Patrick asked his friend to stop the car.

"By the way," said Humphrey, suddenly, "there was one thing I didn't understand. Why was he so afraid of the Public Analyst? What poison and chemicals does he put in the milk?"

"H_2O," answered the Captain, "I take it without milk myself."

And he bent over as if to drink of the stream, as he had done at daybreak.

XX

The Turk and the Futurists

Mr. Adrian Crooke was a successful chemist whose shop was in the neighbourhood of Victoria, but his face expressed more than is generally required in a successful chemist. It was a curious face, prematurely old and like parchment, but acute and decisive, with real headwork in every line of it. Nor was his conversation, when he did converse, out of keeping with this: he had lived in many countries, and had a rich store of anecdote about the more quaint and sometimes the more sinister side of his work, visions of the vapour of eastern drugs or guesses at the ingredients of Renascence poisons. He himself, it need hardly be said, was a most respectable and reliable apothecary, or he would not have had the custom of families, especially among the upper classes; but he enjoyed as a hobby, the study of the dark days and lands where his science had lain sometimes on the borders of magic and sometimes upon the borders of murder. Hence it often happened that persons, who in their serious senses were well aware of his harmless and useful habits, would leave his shop on some murky and foggy night, with their heads so full of wild tales of the eating of hemp or the poisoning of roses, they could hardly help fancying that the shop, with its glowing moon of crimson or saffron, like bowls of blood and sulphur, was really a house of the Black Art.

It was doubtless for such conversational pleasures, in part, that Hibbs However entered the shop; as well as for a small glass of the same restorative medicine which he had been taking when Leveson found him by the open window. But this did not prevent Hibbs from expressing considerable surprise and some embarrassment when Leveson entered the same chemist's and asked for the same chemical. Indeed, Leveson looked harassed and weary enough to want it.

"You've been out of town, haven't you?" said Leveson. "No luck. They got away again on some quibble. The police wouldn't make the arrest; and even old Meadows thought it might be illegal. I'm sick of it. Where are you going?"

"I thought," said Mr. Hibbs, "of dropping in at this Post-Futurist exhibition. I believe Lord Ivywood will be there; he is showing it to the Prophet. I don't pretend to know much about art, but I hear it's very fine."

There was a long silence and Mr. Leveson said, "People always prejudiced against new ideas."

Then there was another long silence and Mr. Hibbs said, "After all, they said the same of Whistler."

Refreshed by this ritual, Mr. Leveson became conscious of the existence of Crooke, and said to him, cheerfully, "That's so in your department, too, isn't it? I suppose the greatest pioneers in chemistry were unpopular in their own time."

"Look at the Borgias," said Mr. Crooke. "They got themselves quite disliked."

"You're very flippant, you know," said Leveson, in a fatigued way. "Well, so long. Are you coming, Hibbs?"

And the two gentlemen, who were both attired in high hats and afternoon callers' coats, betook themselves down the street. It was a fine, sunny day, the twin of the day before that had shone so brightly on the white town of Peaceways; and their walk was a pleasant one, along a handsome street with high houses and small trees that overlooked the river all the way. For the pictures were exhibited in a small but famous gallery, a rather rococo building of which the entrance steps almost descended upon the Thames. The building was girt on both sides and behind with gaudy flower-beds, and on the top of the steps, in front of the Byzantine doorway, stood their old friend, Misysra Ammon, smiling broadly, and in an unusually sumptuous costume. But even the sight of that fragrant eastern flower did not seem to revive altogether the spirits of the drooping Secretary.

"You have coome," said the beaming Prophet, "to see the decoration? It is approo-ooved. I haf approo-ooved it."

"We came to see the Post-Futurist pictures," began Hibbs; but Leveson was silent.

"There are no pictures," said the Turk, simply, "if there had been I could not haf approo-ooved. For those of our Religion pictures are not goo-ood; they are Idols, my friendss. Loo-ook in there," and he turned and darted a solemn forefinger just under his nose toward the gates of the gallery; "Loo-ook in there and you will find no Idols. No Idols at all. I have most carefully loo-ooked into every one of the frames. Every one I have approo-ooved. No trace of ze Man form. No trace of ze Animal form. All decoration as goo-ood as the goo-oodest of carpets; it harms not. Lord Ivywood smile of happiness; for I tell him Islam indeed progresses. Ze old Moslems allow to draw the picture of the vegetable. Here I hunt even for the vegetable. And there is no vegetable."

Hibbs, whose trade was tact, naturally did not think it wise that the eminent Misysra should go on lecturing from a tall flight of steps to the whole street and river, so he had slipped past with a general proposal to go in and see. The Prophet and the Secretary followed; and all entered the outer hall where Lord Ivywood stood with the white face of a statue. He was the only statue the New Moslems were allowed to worship.

On a sofa like a purple island in the middle of the sea of floor sat Enid Wimpole, talking eagerly to her cousin, Dorian; doing, in fact, her best to prevent the family quarrel, which threatened to follow hard on the incident at Westminster. In the deeper perspective of the rooms Lady Joan Brett was floating about. And if her attitude before the Post-Futurist pictures could not be called humble, or even inquiring, it is but just to that school to say that she seemed to be quite as bored with the floor that she walked on, and the parasol she held. Bit by bit other figures or groups of that world drifted through the Exhibition of the Post-Futurists. It is a very small world, but it is just big enough and just small enough to govern a country—that is, a country with no religion. And it has all the vanity of a mob; and all the reticence of a secret society.

Leveson instantly went up to Lord Ivywood, pulled papers from his pocket and was plainly telling him of the escape from Peaceways. Ivywood's face hardly changed; he was, or felt, above some things; and one of them was blaming a servant before the servant's social superiors. But no one could say he looked less like cold marble than before.

"I made all possible inquiries about their subsequent route," the Secretary was heard saying, "and the most serious feature is that they seem to have taken the road for London."

"Quite so," replied the statue, "they will be easier to capture here."

Lady Enid, by a series of assurances (most of which were, I regret to say, lies) had succeeded in preventing the scandal of her cousin, Dorian, actually cutting her cousin, Philip. But she knew very little of the masculine temper if she really thought she had prevented the profound intellectual revolt of the poet against the politician. Ever since he heard Mr. Hibbs say, "Yars! Yars!", and order his arrest by a common policeman, the feelings of Dorian Wimpole had flowed for some four days and nights in a direction highly contrary to the ideals of Mr. Hibbs, and the sudden appearance of that blameless diplomatist quickened the mental current to a cataract. But as he could not insult Hibbs, whom socially he did not even know; and could not insult Ivywood, with whom he had just had a formal reconciliation, it was absolutely necessary that he should insult something else instead. All watchers for the Dawn will be deeply distressed to know that the Post-Futurist School of Painting received the full effects of this perverted wrath. In vain did Mr. Leveson affirm from time to time, "People always prejudiced against new ideas." Vainly did Mr. Hibbs say at the proper intervals, "After all, they said the same of Whistler." Not by such decent formalities was the frenzy of Dorian to be appeased.

"That little Turk has more sense than you have," he said, "he passes it as a good wall-paper. I should say it was a bad wall-paper; the sort of wall-paper that gives a sick man fever when he hasn't got it. But to call it pictures—you might as well call it seats for the Lord Mayor's Show. A seat isn't a seat if you can't see the Lord Mayor's Show. A picture isn't a picture if you can't see any picture. You can sit down at home more comfortably than you can at a procession. And you can walk about at home more comfortably than you can at a picture gallery. There's only one thing to be said for a street show or a picture show—and that is whether there is anything to be shown. Now, then! Show me something!"

"Well," said Lord Ivywood, good humouredly, motioning toward the wall in front of him, "let me show you the 'Portrait of an Old Lady.'"

"Well," said Dorian, stolidly, "which is it?"

Mr. Hibbs made a hasty gesture of identification, but was so unfortunate as to point to the picture of "Rain in the Apennines," instead of the "Portrait of an Old Lady," and his intervention increased the irritation of Dorian Wimpole. Most probably, as Mr. Hibbs afterward explained, it was because a vivacious movement of the elbow of Mr. Wimpole interfered with the exact pointing of the forefinger of Mr. Hibbs. In any case, Mr. Hibbs was sharply and horridly fixed by embarrassment; so that he had to go away to the refreshment bar and eat three lobster-patties, and even drink a glass of that champagne that had once been his ruin. But on this occasion he stopped at one glass, and returned with a full diplomatic responsibility.

He returned to find that Dorian Wimpole had forgotten all the facts of time, place, and personal pride, in an argument with Lord Ivywood, exactly as he had forgotten such facts in an argument with Patrick Dalroy, in a dark wood with a donkey-cart. And Philip Ivywood was interested also; his cold eyes even shone; for though his pleasure was almost purely intellectual, it was utterly sincere.

"And I do trust the untried; I do follow the inexperienced," he was saying quietly, with his fine inflections of voice. "You say this is changing the very nature of Art. I want to change the very nature of Art. Everything lives by turning into something else. Exaggeration is growth."

"But exaggeration of what?" demanded Dorian. "I cannot see a trace of exaggeration in these pictures; because I cannot find a hint of what it is they want to exaggerate. You can't exaggerate the feathers of a cow or the legs of a whale. You can draw a cow with feathers or a whale with legs for a joke—though I hardly think such jokes are in your line. But don't you see, my good Philip, that even then the joke depends on its looking like a cow and not only like a thing with feathers. Even then the joke depends on the whale as well as the legs. You can combine up to a certain point; you can distort up to a certain point; after that you lose the identity; and with that you lose everything. A Centaur is so much of a man with so much of a horse. The Centaur must not be hastily identified with the Horsy Man. And the Mermaid must be maidenly; even if there is something fishy about her social conduct."

"No," said Lord Ivywood, in the same quiet way, "I understand what you mean, and I don't agree. I should like the Centaur to turn into something else, that is neither man nor horse."

"But not something that has nothing of either?" asked the poet.

"Yes," answered Ivywood, with the same queer, quiet gleam in his colourless eyes, "something that has nothing of either."

"But what's the good?" argued Dorian. "A thing that has changed entirely has not changed at all. It has no bridge of crisis. It can remember no change. If you wake up tomorrow and you simply *are* Mrs. Dope, an old woman who lets lodgings at Broadstairs—well, I don't doubt Mrs. Dope is a saner and happier person than you are. But in what way have *you* progressed? What part of *you* is better? Don't you see this prime fact of identity is the limit set on all living things?"

"No," said Philip, with suppressed but sudden violence, "I deny that any limit is set upon living things."

"Why, then I understand," said Dorian, "why, though you make such good speeches, you have never written any poetry."

Lady Joan, who was looking with tedium at a rich pattern of purple and green in which Misysra attempted to interest her (imploring her to disregard the mere title, which idolatrously stated it as "First Communion in the Snow"), abruptly turned her full face to Dorian. It was a face to which few men could feel indifferent, especially when thus suddenly shown them.

"Why can't he write poetry?" she asked. "Do you mean he would resent the limits of metre and rhyme and so on?"

The poet reflected for a moment and then said, "Well, partly; but I mean more than that too. As one can be candid in the family, I may say that what everyone says about him is that he has no humour. But that's not my complaint at all. I think my complaint is that he has no pathos. That is, he does not feel human limitations. That is, he will not write poetry."

Lord Ivywood was looking with his cold, unconscious profile into a little black and yellow picture called "Enthusiasm"; but Joan Brett leaned across to him with swarthy eagerness and cried quite provocatively,

"Dorian says you've no pathos. Have you any pathos? He says it's a sense of human limitations."

Ivywood did not remove his gaze from the picture of "Enthusiasm," but simply said "No; I have no sense of human limitations." Then he put up his elderly eyeglass to examine the picture better. Then he dropped it again and confronted Joan with a face paler than usual.

"Joan," he said, "I would walk where no man has walked; and find something beyond tears and laughter. My road shall be my road indeed; for I will make it, like the Romans. And my adventures shall not be in the hedges and the gutters, but in the borders of the ever advancing brain. I will think what was unthinkable until I thought it; I will love what never lived until I loved it—I will be as lonely as the First Man."

"They say," she said, after a silence, "that the first man fell."

"You mean the priests?" he answered. "Yes, but even they admit that he discovered good and evil. So are these artists trying to discover some distinction that is still dark to us."

"Oh," said Joan, looking at him with a real and unusual interest, "then you don't *see* anything in the pictures, yourself?"

"I see the breaking of the barriers," he answered, "beyond that I see nothing."

She looked at the floor for a little time and traced patterns with her parasol, like one who has really received food for thought. Then she said, suddenly, "But perhaps the breaking of barriers might be the breaking of everything." The clear and colourless eyes looked at her quite steadily.

"Perhaps," said Lord Ivywood.

Dorian Wimpole made a sudden movement a few yards off, where he was looking at a picture, and said, "Hullo! What's this?" Mr. Hibbs was literally gaping in the direction of the entrance.

Framed in that fine Byzantine archway stood a great big, bony man in threadbare but careful clothes, with a harsh, high-featured, intelligent face, to which a dark beard under the chin gave something of the Puritanic cast. Somehow his whole personality seemed to be pulled together and explained when he spoke with a North Country accent.

"Weel, lards," he said, genially, "t'hoose be main great on t'pictures. But I coom for suthin' in a moog. Haw! Haw!"

Leveson and Hibbs looked at each other. Then Leveson rushed from the room. Lord Ivywood did not move a finger; but Mr. Wimpole, with a sort of poetic curiosity, drew nearer to the stranger, and studied him.

"It's perfectly awful," cried Enid Wimpole, in a loud whisper, "the man must be drunk."

"Na, lass," said the man with gallantry, "a've not been droonk, nobbut at Hurley Fair, these years and all; a'm a decent lad and workin' ma way back t'Wharfdale. No harm in a moog of ale, lass."

"Are you quite sure," asked Dorian Wimpole, with a singular sort of delicate curiosity, "are you quite *sure* you're not drunk."

"A'm not droonk," said the man, jovially.

"Even if these were licensed premises," began Dorian, in the same diplomatic manner.

"There's t'sign on t'hoose," said the stranger.

The black, bewildered look on the face of Joan Brett suddenly altered. She took four steps toward the doorway, and then went back and sat on the purple ottoman. But Dorian seemed fascinated with his inquiry into the alleged decency of the lad who was working his way to Wharfdale.

"Even if these were licensed premises," he repeated, "drink could be refused you if you were drunk. Now, are you *really* sure you're not drunk. Would you know if it was raining, say?"

"Aye," said the man, with conviction.

"Would you know any common object of your countryside," inquired Dorian, scientifically, "a woman—let us say an old woman."

"Aye," said the man, with good humour.

"What on earth are you doing with the creature?" whispered Enid, feverishly.

"I am trying," answered the poet, "to prevent a very sensible man from smashing a very silly shop. I beg your pardon, sir. As I was saying, would you know these things in a picture, now? Do you know what a landscape is and what a portrait is? Forgive my asking; you see we are responsible while we keep the place going."

There soared up into the sky like a cloud of rooks the eager vanity of the North.

"We collier lads are none so badly educated, lad," he said. "In the town a' was born in there was a gallery of pictures as fine as Lunnon. Aye, and a' knew 'em, too."

"Thank you," said Wimpole, pointing suddenly at the wall. "Would you be so kind, for instance, as to look at those two pictures. One represents an old woman and the other rain in the hills. It's a mere formality. You shall have your drink when you've said which is which."

The northerner bowed his huge body before the two frames and peered into them patiently. The long stillness that followed seemed to be something of a strain on Joan, who rose in a restless manner, first went to look out of a window and then went out of the front door.

At length the art-critic lifted a large, puzzled but still philosophical face.

"Soomehow or other," he said, "a' mun be droonk after all."

"You have testified," cried Dorian with animation. "You have all but saved civilization. And by God, you shall have your drink."

And he brought from the refreshment table a huge bumper of the Hibbsian champagne, and declined payment by the rapid method of running out of the gallery on to the steps outside.

Joan was already standing there. Out the little side window she had seen the incredible thing she expected to see; which explained the ludicrous scene inside. She saw the red and blue wooden flag of Mr. Pump standing up in the flower-beds in the sun, as serenely as if it were a tall and tropical flower; and yet, in the brief interval between the window and the door it had vanished, as if to remind her it was a flying dream. But two men were in a little motor outside, which was in the very act of starting. They were in motoring disguise, but she knew who they were. All that was deep in her, all that was sceptical, all that was stoical, all that was noble, made her stand as still as one of the pillars of the porch; but a dog, bearing the name of Quoodle, sprang up in the moving car, and barked with joy at the mere sight of her, and though she had borne all else, something in that bestial innocence of an animal suddenly blinded her with tears.

It could not, however, blind her to the extraordinary fact that followed. Mr. Dorian Wimpole, attired in anything but motoring costume, dressed in that compromise between fashion and art which seems proper to the visiting of picture-galleries, did not by any means stand as still as one of the pillars of the porch. He rushed down the steps, ran after the car and actually sprang into it, without disarranging his Whistlerian silk hat.

"Good afternoon," he said to Dalroy, pleasantly. "You owe me a motor-ride, you know."

XXI

The Road to Roundabout

Patrick Dalroy looked at the invader with a heavy and yet humorous expression, and merely said, "I didn't steal your car; really, I didn't."

"Oh, no," answered Dorian, "I've heard all about it since, and as you're rather the persecuted party, so to speak, it wouldn't be fair not to tell you that I don't agree much with Ivywood about all this. I disagree with him; or rather, to speak medically, he disagrees with me. He has, ever since I woke up after an oyster supper and found myself in the House of Commons with policemen calling out, 'Who goes home?'"

"Indeed," inquired Dalroy, drawing his red bushy eyebrows together. "Do the officials in Parliament say, 'Who goes home?'"

"Yes," answered Wimpole, indifferently, "it's a part of some old custom in the days when Members of Parliament might be attacked in the street."

"Well," inquired Patrick, in a rational tone, "why aren't they attacked in the street?"

There was a silence. "It is a holy mystery," said the Captain at last. "But, 'Who goes home?'—that is uncommonly good."

The Captain had received the poet into the car with all possible expressions of affability and satisfaction, but the poet, who was keen-sighted enough about people of his own sort, could not help thinking that the Captain was a little absent-minded. As they flew thundering through the mazes of South London (for Pump had crossed Westminster Bridge and was making for the Surrey hills), the big blue eyes of the big red-haired man rolled perpetually up and down the streets; and, after longer and longer silences, he found expression for his thoughts.

"Doesn't it strike you that there are a very large number of chemists in London nowadays?"

"Are there?" asked Wimpole, carelessly. "Well, there certainly are two very close to each other just over there."

"Yes, and both the same name," replied Dalroy, "Crooke. And I saw the same Mr. Crooke chemicalizing round the corner. He seems to be a highly omnipresent deity."

"A large business, I suppose," observed Dorian Wimpole.

"Too large for its profits, I should say," said Dalroy. "What can people want with two chemists of the same sort within a few yards of each other? Do they put one leg into one shop and one into the other and have their corns done in both at once? Or, do they take an acid in one shop and an alkali in the next, and wait for the fizz? Or, do they take the poison in the first shop and the emetic in the second shop? It seems like carrying delicacy too far. It almost amounts to living a double life."

"But, perhaps," said Dorian, "he is an uproariously popular chemist, this Mr. Crooke. Perhaps there's a rush on some specialty of his."

"It seems to me," said the Captain, "that there are certain limitations to such popularity in the case of a chemist. If a man sells very good tobacco, people may smoke more and more of it from sheer self-indulgence. But I never heard of anybody exceeding in cod-liver oil. Even castor-oil, I should say, is regarded with respect rather than true affection."

After a few minutes of silence, he said, "Is it safe to stop here for an instant, Pump?"

"I think so," replied Humphrey, "if you'll promise me not to have any adventures in the shop."

The motor car stopped before yet a fourth arsenal of Mr. Crooke and his pharmacy, and Dalroy went in. Before Pump and his companion could exchange a word, the Captain came out again, with a curious expression on his countenance, especially round the mouth.

"Mr. Wimpole," said Dalroy, "will you give us the pleasure of dining with us this evening? Many would consider it an unceremonious invitation to an unconventional meal; and it may be necessary to eat it under a hedge or even up a tree; but you are a man of taste, and one does not apologise for Hump's rum or Hump's cheese to persons of taste. We will eat and drink of our best tonight. It is a banquet. I am not very certain whether you and I are friends or enemies, but at least there shall be peace tonight."

"Friends, I hope," said the poet, smiling, "but why peace especially tonight?"

"Because there will be war tomorrow," answered Patrick Dalroy, "whichever side of it you may be on. I have just made a singular discovery."

And he relapsed into his silence as they flew out of the fringe of London into the woods and hills beyond Croydon. Dalroy remained in the same mood of brooding, Dorian was brushed by the butterfly wing of that fleeting slumber that will come on a man hurried, through the air, after long lounging in hot drawing rooms; even the dog Quoodle was asleep at the bottom of the car. As for Humphrey Pump, he very seldom talked when he had anything else to do. Thus it happened that long landscapes and perspectives were shot past them like suddenly shifted slides, and long stretches of time elapsed before any of them spoke again. The sky was changing from the pale golds and greens of evening to the burning blue of a strong summer night, a night of strong stars. The walls of woodland that flew past them like long assegais, were mostly, at first, of the fenced and park-like sort; endless oblong blocks of black pinewood shut in by boxes of thin grey wood. But soon fences began to sink, and pinewoods to straggle, and roads to split and even to sprawl. Half an hour later Dalroy had begun to realise something romantic and even faintly reminiscent in the roll of the country, and Humphrey Pump had long known he was on the marches of his native land.

So far as the difference could be defined by a detail, it seemed to consist not so much in the road rising as in the road perpetually winding. It was more like a path; and even where it was abrupt or aimless, it seemed the more alive. They appeared to be ascending a big, dim hill that was built of a crowd of little hills with rounded tops; it was like a cluster of domes. Among these domes the road climbed and curled in multitudinous curves and angles. It was almost impossible to believe that it could turn itself and round on itself so often without tying itself in a knot and choking.

"I say," said Dalroy, breaking the silence suddenly, "this car will get giddy and fall down."

"Perhaps," said Dorian, beaming at him, "my car, as you may have noticed, was much steadier."

Patrick laughed, but not without a shade of confusion. "I hope you got back your car all right," he said. "This is really nothing for speed; but it's an uncommonly good little climber, and it seems to have some climbing to do just now. And even more wandering."

"The roads certainly seem to be very irregular," said Dorian, reflectively.

"Well," cried Patrick, with a queer kind of impatience, "you're English and I'm not. You ought to know why the road winds about like this. Why, the Saints deliver us!" he cried, "it's one of the wrongs of Ireland that she can't understand England. England won't understand herself, England won't tell us why these roads go wriggling about. Englishmen won't tell us! You won't tell us!"

"Don't be too sure," said Dorian, with a quiet irony.

Dalroy, with an irony far from quiet emitted a loud yell of victory.

"Right," he shouted. "More songs of the car club! We're all poets here, I hope. Each shall write something about why the road jerks about so much. So much as this, for example," he added, as the whole vehicle nearly rolled over in a ditch.

For, indeed, Pump appeared to be attacking such inclines as are more suitable for a goat than a small motor car. This may have been exaggerated in the emotions of his companions, who had both, for different reasons, seen much of mere flat country lately. The sensation was like a combination of trying to get into the middle of the maze at Hampton Court, and climbing the spiral staircase to the Belfry at Bruges.

"This is the right way to Roundabout," said Dalroy, cheerfully, "charming place; salubrious spot. You can't miss it. First to the left and right and straight on round the corner and back again. That'll do for my poem. Get on, you slackers; why aren't you writing your poems?"

"I'll try one if you like," said Dorian, treating his flattered egotism lightly. "But it's too dark to write; and getting darker."

Indeed they had come under a shadow between them and the stars, like the brim of a giant's hat; only through the holes and rents in which the summer stars could now look down on them. The hill, like a cluster of domes, though smooth and even bare in its lower contours was topped with a tangle of spanning trees that sat above them like a bird brooding over its nest. The wood was larger and vaguer than the clump that is the crown of the hill at Chanctonbury, but was rather like it and held much the same high and romantic position. The next moment they were in the wood itself, and winding in and out among the trees by a ribbon of paths. The emerald twilight between the stems, combined with the dragon-like contortions of the great grey roots of the beeches, had a suggestion of monsters and the deep sea; especially as a long litter of crimson and copper-coloured fungi, which might well have been the more gorgeous types of anemone or jelly-fish, reddened the ground like a sunset dropped from the sky. And yet, contradictorily enough, they had also a strong sense of being high up; and even near to heaven; and the brilliant summer stars that stared through the chinks of the leafy roof might almost have been white starry blossoms on the trees of the wood.

But though they had entered the wood as if it were a house, their strongest sensation still was the rotatory; it seemed as if that high green house went round and round like a revolving lighthouse or the whizgig temple in the old pantomimes. The stars seemed, to circle over their heads; and Dorian felt almost certain he had seen the same beech-tree twice.

At length they came to a central place where the hill rose in a sort of cone in the thick of its trees, lifting its trees with it. Here Pump stopped the car, and clambering up the slope, came to the crawling colossal roots of a very large but very low beech-tree. It spread out to the four quarters of heaven more in the manner of an octopus than a tree, and within its low crown of branches there was a kind of hollow, like a cup, into which Mr. Humphrey Pump, of "The Old Ship," Pebblewick, suddenly and entirely disappeared.

When he appeared it was with a kind of rope ladder, which he politely hung over the side for his companions to ascend by, but the Captain preferred to swing himself onto one of the octopine branches with a whirl of large wild legs worthy of a chimpanzee. When they were established there, each propped in the hollow against a branch, almost as comfortably as in an arm chair, Humphrey himself descended once more and began to take out their simple stores. The dog was still asleep in the car.

"An old haunt of yours, Hump, I suppose," said the Captain. "You seem quite at home."

"I am at home," answered Pump, with gravity, "at the sign of 'The Old Ship.'" And he stuck the old blue and red sign-board erect among the toadstools, as if inviting the passer-by to climb the trees for a drink.

The tree just topped the mound or clump of trees, and from it they could see the whole champaign of the country they had passed, with the silver roads roaming about in it like rivers. They were so exalted they could almost fancy the stars would burn them.

"Those roads remind me of the songs you've all promised," said Dalroy at last. "Let's have some supper, Hump, and then recite."

Humphrey had hung one of the motor lanterns onto a branch above him, and proceeded by the light of it to tap the keg of rum and hand round the cheese. "What an extraordinary thing," exclaimed Dorian Wimpole, suddenly. "Why, I'm quite comfortable! Such a thing has never happened before, I should imagine. And how holy this cheese tastes."

"It has gone on a pilgrimage," answered Dalroy, "or rather a Crusade. It's a heroic, a fighting cheese. 'Cheese of all Cheeses, Cheeses of all the world,' as my compatriot, Mr. Yeats, says to the Something-or-other of Battle. It's almost impossible that this cheese can have come out of such a coward as a cow. I suppose," he added, wistfully, "I suppose it wouldn't do to explain that in this case Hump had milked the bull. That would be classed by scientists among Irish legends—those that have the Celtic glamour and all that. No, I think this cheese must have come from that Dun Cow of Dunsmore Heath, who had horns bigger than elephant's tusks, and who was so ferocious that one of the greatest of the old heroes of chivalry was required to do battle with it. The rum's good, too. I've earned this glass of rum—earned it by Christian humility. For nearly a month I've lowered myself to the beasts of the field, and gone about on all fours like a teetotaller. Hump, circulate the bottle—I mean the cask—and let us have some of this poetry you're so keen about. Each poem must have the same title, you know; it's a rattling good title. It's called 'An Inquiry into the Causes geological, historical, agricultural, psychological, psychical, moral, spiritual and theological of the alleged cases of double, treble, quadruple and other curvature in the English Road, conducted by a specially appointed secret commission in a hole in a tree, by admittedly judicious and academic authorities specially appointed by themselves to report to the Dog Quoodle, having power to add to their number and also to take away the number they first thought of; God save the King." Having delivered this formula with blinding rapidity, he added rather breathlessly, "that's the note to strike, the lyric note."

For all his rather formless hilarity, Dalroy still impressed the poet as being more *distrait* than the others, as if his mind were labouring with some bigger thing in the background. He was in a sort of creative trance; and Humphrey Pump, who knew him like his own soul, knew well that it was not mere literary creation. Rather it was a kind of creation which many modern moralists would call destruction. For Patrick Dalroy was, not a little to his misfortune, what is called a man of action; as Captain Dawson realised when he found his entire person a bright pea-green. Fond as he was of jokes and rhymes, nothing he could write or even sing ever satisfied him like something he could do.

Thus it happened that his contribution to the metrical inquiry into the crooked roads was avowedly hasty and flippant. While Dorian who was of the opposite temper, the temper that receives impressions instead of pushing out to make them, found his artist's love of beauty fulfilled as it had never been before in that noble nest; and was far more serious and human than usual. Patrick's verses ran:

> "Some say that Guy of Warwick,
>   The man that killed the Cow,
> And brake the mighty Boar alive,
>   Beyond the Bridge at Slough,
> Went up against a Loathly Worm
>   That wasted all the Downs,
> And so the roads they twist and squirm
>   (If I may be allowed the term)
> From the writhing of the stricken Worm
>   That died in seven towns.
>   I see no scientific proof
>   That this idea is sound,
>   And I should say they wound about
>   To find the town of Roundabout,
>   The merry town of Roundabout
>   That makes the world go round.
>
> "Some say that Robin Goodfellow,
>   Whose lantern lights the meads,
> (To steal a phrase Sir Walter Scott

In heaven no longer needs)
Such dance around the trysting-place
The moonstruck lover leads;
Which superstition I should scout;
There is more faith in honest doubt,
(As Tennyson has pointed out)
Than in those nasty creeds.
But peace and righteousness (St. John)
In Roundabout can kiss,
And since that's all that's found about
The pleasant town of Roundabout,
The roads they simply bound about
To find out where it is.

"Some say that when Sir Lancelot
Went forth to find the Grail,
Grey Merlin wrinkled up the roads
For hope that he should fail;
All roads led back to Lyonesse
And Camelot in the Vale;
I cannot yield assent to this
Extravagant hypothesis,
The plain, shrewd Briton will dismiss
Such rumours (Daily Mail).
But in the streets of Roundabout
Are no such factions found,
Or theories to expound about
Or roll upon the ground about,
In the happy town of Roundabout
That makes the world go round."

Patrick Dalroy relieved his feelings by finishing with a shout, draining a stiff glass of his sailor's wine, turning restlessly on his elbow and looking across the landscape toward London.

Dorian Wimpole had been drinking golden rum and strong starlight and the fragrance of forests; and, though his verses, too, were burlesque, he read them more emotionally than was his wont.

"Before the Roman came to Rye or out to Severn strode,
The rolling English drunkard made the rolling English
　road.
A reeling road, a rolling road, that rambles round the shire,
And after him the parson ran, the sexton and the squire.
A merry road, a mazy road, and such as we did tread
That night we went to Birmingham by way of Beachy
　Head.

"I knew no harm of Bonaparte and plenty of the Squire,
And for to fight the Frenchmen I did not much desire;
But I did bash their baggonets because they came arrayed
To straighten out the crooked road an English drunkard
　made,
Where you and I went down the lane with ale-mugs in
　our hands
The night we went to Glastonbury by way of Goodwin
　Sands.

"His sins they were forgiven him; or why do flowers run
Behind him; and the hedges all strengthening in the sun?
The wild thing went from left to right and knew not
　which was which,
But the wild rose was above him when they found him
　in the ditch.
God pardon us, nor harden us; we did not see so clear
The night we went to Bannockburn by way of Brighton
　Pier.

"My friends, we will not go again or ape an ancient rage,
Or stretch the folly of our youth to be the shame of age,
But walk with clearer eyes and ears this path that
　wandereth,
And see undrugged in evening light the decent inn of death;
For there is good news yet to hear and fine things to be
　seen
Before we go to Paradise by way of Kensal Green."

"Have you written one, Hump?" asked Dalroy. Humphrey, who had been scribbling hard under the lamp, looked up with a dismal face.

"Yes," he said. "But I write under a great disadvantage. You see, I know why the road curves about." And he read very rapidly, all on one note:

> "The road turned first toward the left
> Where Pinker's quarry made the cleft;
> The path turned next toward the right
> Because the mastiff used to bite;
> Then left, because of Slippery Height,
> And then again toward the right.
> We could not take the left because
> It would have been against the laws;
> Squire closed it in King William's day
> Because it was a Right of Way.
> Still right; to dodge the ridge of chalk
> Where Parson's Ghost it used to walk,
> Till someone Parson used to know
> Met him blind drunk in Callao.
> Then left, a long way round, to skirt
> The good land where old Doggy Burt
> Was owner of the Crown and Cup,
> And would not give his freehold up;
> Right, missing the old river-bed,
> They tried to make him take instead
> Right, since they say Sir Gregory
> Went mad and let the Gypsies be,
> And so they have their camp secure.
> And, though not honest, they are poor,
> And that is something; then along
> And first to right—no, I am wrong!
> Second to right, of course; the first
> Is what the holy sisters cursed,
> And none defy their awful oaths
> Since the policeman lost his clothes
> Because of fairies; right again,
> What used to be High Toby Lane,

Left by the double larch and right
Until the milestone is in sight,
Because the road is firm and good
From past the milestone to the wood;
And I was told by Dr. Lowe
Whom Mr. Wimpole's aunt would know,
Who lives at Oxford writing books,
And ain't so silly as he looks;
The Romans did that little bit
And we've done all the rest of it;
By which we hardly seem to score;
Left, and then forward as before
To where they nearly hanged Miss Browne,
Who told them not to cut her down,
But loose the rope or let her swing,
Because it was a waste of string;
Left once again by Hunker's Cleft,
And right beyond the elm, and left,
By Pill's right by Nineteen Nicks
And left—"

"No! No! No! Hump! Hump! Hump!" cried Dalroy in a sort of terror. "Don't be exhaustive! Don't be a scientist, Hump, and lay waste fairyland! How long does it go on? Is there a lot more of it?"

"Yes," said Pump, in a stony manner. "There is a lot more of it."

"And it's all true?" inquired Dorian Wimpole, with interest.

"Yes," replied Pump with a smile, "it's all true."

"My complaint, exactly," said the Captain. "What you want is legends. What you want is lies, especially at this time of night, and on rum like this, and on our first and our last holiday. What do you think about rum?" he asked Wimpole.

"About this particular rum, in this particular tree, at this particular moment," answered Wimpole, "I think it is the nectar of the younger gods. If you ask me in a general, synthetic sense what I think of rum—well, I think it's rather rum."

"You find it a trifle sweet, I suppose," said Dalroy, with some bitterness. "Sybarite! By the way," he said abruptly, "what a silly word that word 'Hedonist' is! The really self-indulgent people generally like sour things and not sweet; bitter things like caviar and curries or what not. It's the Saints who like the sweets. At least I've known at least five women who were practically saints, and they all preferred sweet champagne. Look here, Wimpole! Shall I tell you the ancient oral legend about the origin of rum? I told you what you wanted was legends. Be careful to preserve this one, and hand it on to your children; for, unfortunately, my parents carelessly neglected the duty of handing it on to me. After the words 'A Farmer had three sons...' all that I owe to tradition ceases. But when the three boys last met in the village market-place, they were all sucking sugar-sticks. Nevertheless, they were all discontented, and, on that day parted for ever. One remained on his father's farm, hungering for his inheritance. One went up to London to seek his fortune, as fortunes are found today in that town forgotten of God. The third ran away to sea. And the first two flung away their sugar-sticks in shame; and he on the farm was always drinking smaller and sourer beer for the love of money; and he that was in town was always drinking richer and richer wines, that men might see that he was rich. But he who ran away to sea actually ran on board with the sugar-stick in his mouth; and St. Peter or St. Andrew, or whoever is the patron of men in boats, touched it and turned it into a fountain for the comfort of men upon the sea. That is the sailor's theory of the origin of rum. Inquiry addressed to any busy Captain with a new crew in the act of shipping an unprecedented cargo, will elicit a sympathetic agreement."

"Your rum at least," said Dorian, good-humouredly, "may well produce a fairy-tale. But, indeed, I think all this would have been a fairy-tale without it."

Patrick raised himself from his arboreal throne, and leaned against his branch with a curious and sincere sense of being rebuked.

"Yours was a good poem," he said, with seeming irrelevance, "and mine was a bad one. Mine was bad, partly because I'm not a poet as you are; but almost as much because I was trying to make up another song at the same time. And it went to another tune, you see."

He looked out over the rolling roads and said almost to himself:

> "In the city set upon slime and loam
> They cry in their parliament 'Who goes home?'

And there is no answer in arch or dome,
For none in the city of graves goes home.
Yet these shall perish and understand,
For God has pity on this great land.
Men that are men again; who goes home?
Tocsin and trumpeter! Who goes home?
For there's blood on the field and blood on the foam,
And blood on the body when man goes home.
And a voice valedictory—Who is for Victory?
Who is for Liberty? Who goes home?"

Softly and idly as he had said this second rhyme, there were circumstances about his attitude that must have troubled or interested anyone who did not know him well.

"May I ask," asked Dorian, laughing, "why it is necessary to draw your sword at this stage of the affair?"

"Because we have left the place called Roundabout," answered Patrick, "and we have come to a place called Rightabout."

And he lifted his sword toward London, and the grey glint upon it came from a low, grey light in the east.

XXII

The Chemistry of Mr. Crooke

When the celebrated Hibbs next visited the shop of Crooke, that mystic and criminologist chemist, he found the premises were impressively and even amazingly enlarged with decorations in the eastern style. Indeed, it would not have been too much to say that Mr. Crooke's shop occupied the whole of one side of a showy street in the West End; the other side being a blank façade of public buildings. It would be no exaggeration to say that Mr. Crooke was the only shopkeeper for some distance round. Mr. Crooke still served in his shop, however; and politely hastened to serve his customer with the medicine that was customary. Unfortunately, for some reason or other, history was, in connection with this shop, only too prone to repeat itself. And after a vague but soothing conversation with the chemist (on the subject of vitriol and its effects on human happiness), Mr. Hibbs experienced the acute annoyance of once more beholding his most intimate friend, Mr. Joseph Leveson, enter the same fashionable emporium. But, indeed, Leveson's own annoyance was much too acute for him to notice any on the part of Hibbs.

"Well," he said, stopping dead in the middle of the shop, "here is a fine confounded kettle of fish!"

It is one of the tragedies of the diplomatic that they are not allowed to admit either knowledge or ignorance; so Hibbs looked gloomily wise; and said, pursing his lips, "you mean the *general* situation."

"I mean the situation about this everlasting business of the inn-signs," said Leveson, impatiently. "Lord Ivywood went up specially, when his leg was really bad, to get it settled in the House in a small non-contentious bill, providing that the sign shouldn't be enough if the liquor hadn't been on the spot three days."

"Oh, but," said Hibbs, sinking his voice to a soft solemnity, as being one of the initiate, "a thing like *that* can be managed, don't you know."

"Of course it can," said the other, still with the same slightly irritable air. "It was. But it doesn't seem to occur to you, any more than it did to his lordship, that there is rather a weak point after all in this business of passing acts quietly because they're unpopular. Has it ever occurred to you that if a law is really kept too quiet to be opposed, it may also be kept too quiet to be obeyed. It's not so easy to hush it up from a big politician without running the risk of hushing it up even from a common policeman."

"But surely that can't happen, by the nature of things?"

"Can't it, by God," said J. Leveson, appealing to a less pantheistic authority. He unfolded a number of papers from his pocket, chiefly cheap local newspapers, but some of them letters and telegrams.

"Listen to this!" he said. "A curious incident occurred in the village of Poltwell in Surrey yesterday morning. The baker's shop of Mr. Whiteman was suddenly besieged by a knot of the looser types of the locality, who appear to have demanded beer instead of bread; basing their claim on some ornamental object erected outside the shop; which object they asserted to be a sign-board within the meaning of the act. There, you see, they haven't even heard of the new act! What do you think of this, from the *Clapton Conservator*. 'The contempt of Socialists for the law was well illustrated yesterday, when a crowd, collected round some wooden ensign of Socialism set up before Mr. Dugdale's Drapery Stores, refused to disperse, though told that their action was contrary to the law. Eventually the malcontents joined the procession following the wooden emblem.' And what do you say to this? 'Stop-press news. A chemist in Pimlico has been invaded by a huge crowd, demanding beer; and asserting the provision of it to be among his duties. The chemist is, of course, well acquainted with his immunities in the matter, especially under the new act; but the old notion of the importance of the sign seems still to possess the populace and even, to a certain extent, to paralyze the police.' What do you say to that? Isn't it as plain as Monday morning that this Flying Inn has flown a day in front of us, as all such lies do?" There was a diplomatic silence.

"Well," asked the still angry Leveson of the still dubious Hibbs, "what do you make of all that?"

One ill-acquainted with that relativity essential to all modern minds, might possibly have fancied that Mr. Hibbs could not make much of it. However that may be, his explanations or incapacity for explanations, were soon tested with a fairly positive test. For Lord Ivywood actually walked into the shop of Mr. Crooke.

"Good day, gentlemen," he said, looking at them with an expression which they both thought baffling and even a little disconcerting. "Good morning, Mr. Crooke. I have a celebrated visitor for you." And he introduced the smiling Misysra. The Prophet had fallen back on a comparatively quiet costume this morning, a mere matter of purple and orange or what not; but his aged face was now perennially festive.

"The Cause progresses," he said. "Everywhere the Cause progresses. You heard his lordship's beau-uti-ful speech?"

"I have heard many," said Hibbs, gracefully, "that can be so described."

"The Prophet means what I was saying about the Ballot Paper Amendment Act," said Ivywood, casually. "It seems to be the alphabet of statesmanship to recognise now that the great oriental British Empire has become one corporate whole with the occidental one. Look at our universities, with their Mohammedan students; soon they may be a majority. Now are we," he went on, still more quietly, "are we to rule this country under the forms of representative government? I do not pretend to believe in democracy, as you know, but I think it would be extremely unsettling and incalculable to destroy representative government. If we are to give Moslem Britain representative government, we must not make the mistake we made about the Hindoos and military organization—which led to the Mutiny. We must not ask them to make a cross on their ballot papers; for though it seems a small thing, it may offend them. So I brought in a little bill to make it optional between the old-fashioned cross and an upward curved mark that might stand for a crescent—and as it's rather easier to make, I believe it will be generally adopted."

"And so," said the radiant old Turk, "the little, light, easily made, curly mark is substituted for the hard, difficult, double-made, cutting both ways mark. It is the more good for hygi-e-ene. For you must know, and indeed our good and wise Chemist will tell you, that the Saracenic and the Arabian and the Turkish physicians were the first of all physicians; and taught all medicals to the barbarians of the Frankish territories.

And many of the moost modern, the moost fashionable remedies, are thus of the oriental origin."

"Yes, that is quite true," said Crooke, in his rather cryptic and un-sympathetic way, "the powder called Arenine, lately popularised by Mr. Boze, now Lord Helvellyn, who tried it first on birds, is made of plain desert sand. And what you see in prescriptions as *Cannabis Indiensis* is what our lively neighbours of Asia describe more energetically as bhang."

"And so-o—in the sa-ame way," said Misysra, making soothing passes with his brown hand like a mesmerist, "in the sa-ame way the making of the crescent is hy-gienic; the making of the cross is non-hy-gienic. The crescent was a little wave, as a leaf, as a little curling feather," and he waved his hand with real artistic enthusiasm toward the capering curves of the new Turkish decoration which Ivywood had made fash-ionable in many of the fashionable shops. "But when you make the cross you must make the one line *so-o*," and he swept the horizon with the brown hand, "and then you must go back and make the other line so-o," and he made an upward gesture suggestive of one constrained to lift a pine-tree. "And then you become very ill."

"As a matter of fact, Mr. Crooke," said Ivywood, in his polite manner, "I brought the Prophet here to consult you as the best authority on the very point you have just mentioned—the use of hashish or the hemp-plant. I have it on my conscience to decide whether these oriental stimu-lants or sedatives shall come under the general veto we are attempting to impose on the vulgar intoxicants. Of course one has heard of the horrible and voluptuous visions, and a kind of insanity attributed to the Assassins and the Old Man of the Mountain. But, on the one hand, we must clearly discount much for the illimitable pro-Christian bias with which the history of these eastern tribes is told in this country. Would you say the effect of hashish was extremely bad?" And he turned first to the Prophet.

"You will see mosques," said that seer with candour, "many mosques—more mosques—taller and taller mosques till they reach the moon and you bear a dreadful voice in the very high mosque calling the muezzin; and you will think it is Allah. Then you will see wives—many, many wives—more wives than you yet have. Then you will be rolled over and over in a great pink and purple sea—which is still wives. Then you will go to sleep. I have only done it once," he concluded mildly.

"And what do you think about hashish, Mr. Crooke?" asked Ivywood, thoughtfully.

"I think it's hemp at both ends," said the Chemist.

"I fear," said Lord Ivywood, "I don't quite understand you."

"A hempen drink, a murder, and a hempen rope. That's my experience in India," said Mr. Crooke.

"It is true," said Ivywood, yet more reflectively, "that the thing is not Moslem in any sense in its origin. There is that against the Assassins always. And, of course," he added, with a simplicity that had something noble about it, "their connection with St. Louis discredits them rather."

After a space of silence, he said suddenly, looking at Crooke, "So it isn't the sort of thing you chiefly sell?"

"No, my lord, it isn't what I chiefly sell," said the Chemist. He also looked steadily, and the wrinkles of his young-old face were like hieroglyphics.

"The Cause progress! Everywhere it progress!" cried Misysra, spreading his arms and relieving a momentary tension of which he was totally unaware. "The hygienic curve of the crescent will soon superimpose himself for your plus sign. You already use him for the short syllables in your dactyl; which is doubtless of oriental origin. You see the new game?"

He said this so suddenly that everyone turned round, to see him produce from his purple clothing a brightly coloured and highly polished apparatus from one of the grand toy-shops; which, on examination, seemed to consist of a kind of blue slate in a red and yellow frame; a number of divisions being already marked on the slate, about seventeen slate pencils with covers of different colours, and a vast number of printed instructions, stating that it was but recently introduced from the remote East, and was called Naughts and Crescents.

Strangely enough, Lord Ivywood, with all his enthusiasm, seemed almost annoyed at the emergence of this Asiatic discovery; more especially as he really wanted to look at Mr. Crooke, as hard as Mr. Crooke was looking at him.

Hibbs coughed considerately and said, "Of course all our things came from the East, and"—and he paused, being suddenly unable to remember anything but curry; to which he was very rightly attached.

He then remembered Christianity, and mentioned that too. "Everything from the East is good, of course," he ended, with an air of light omni-science.

Those who in later ages and other fashions failed to understand how Misysra had ever got a mental hold on men like Lord Ivywood, left out two elements in the man, which are very attractive, especially to other men. One was that there was *no* subject on which the little Turk could not instantly produce a theory. The other was that though the theories were crowded, they were consistent. He was never known to accept an illogical compliment.

"You are in error," he said, solemnly, to Hibbs, "because you say all things from the East are good. There is the east wind. I do not like him. He is not good. And I think very much that all the warmth and all the wealthiness and the colours and the poems and the religiousness that the East was meant to give you have been much poisoned by this accident, this east wind. When you see the green flag of the Prophet, you do not think of a green field in Summer, you think of a green wave in your seas of Winter; for you think it blown by the east wind. When you read of the moon-faced houris you think not of our moons like oranges but of your moons like snowballs—"

Here a new voice contributed to the conversation. Its contribution, though imperfectly understood, appeared to be "Nar! Why sh'd I wite for a little Jew in 'is dressin' gown? Little Jews in their dressin' gowns 'as their drinks, and we 'as our drinks. Bitter, miss."

The speaker, who appeared to be a powerful person of the plaster-ing occupation, looked round for the unmarried female he had ceremo-nially addressed; and seemed honestly abashed that she was not present.

Ivywood looked at the man with that expression of one turned to stone, which his physique made so effective in him. But J. Leveson, Secretary, could summon no such powers of self petrification. Upon his soul the slaughter red of that unhallowed eve arose when first the Ship and he were foes; when he discovered that the poor are human beings, and therefore are polite and brutal within a comparatively short space of time. He saw that two other men were standing behind the plastering person, one of them apparently urging him to counsels of moderation; which was an ominous sign. And then he lifted his eyes and saw something worse than any omen.

All the glass frontage of the shop was a cloud of crowding faces. They could not be clearly seen, since night was closing in on the street; and the dazzling fires of ruby and amethyst which the lighted shop gave to its great globes of liquid, rather veiled than revealed them. But the foremost actually flattened and whitened their noses on the glass, and the most distant were nearer than Mr. Leveson wanted them. Also he saw a shape erect outside the shop; the shape of an upright staff and a square board. He could not see what was on the board. He did not need to see.

Those who saw Lord Ivywood at such moments understood why he stood out so strongly in the history of his time, in spite of his frozen face and his fanciful dogmas. He had all the negative nobility that is possible to man. Unlike Nelson and most of the great heroes, he knew not fear. Thus he was never conquered by a surprise, but was cold and collected when other men had lost their heads even if they had not lost their nerve.

"I will not conceal from you, gentlemen," said Lord Ivywood, "that I have been expecting this. I will not even conceal from you that I have been occupying Mr. Crooke's time until it occurred. So far from excluding the crowd, I suggest it would be an excellent thing if Mr. Crooke could accommodate them all in this shop. I want to tell, as soon as possible, as large a crowd as possible that the law is altered and this folly about the Flying Inn has ceased. Come in, all of you! Come in and listen!"

"Thank yer," said a man connected in some way with motor buses, who lurched in behind the plasterer.

"Thanky, sir," said a bright little clock-mender from Croydon, who immediately followed him.

"Thanks," said a rather bewildered clerk from Camberwell, who came next in the rather bewildered procession.

"Thank you," said Mr. Dorian Wimpole, who entered, carrying a large round cheese.

"Thank you," said Captain Dalroy, who entered carrying a large cask of rum.

"Thank you very much," said Mr. Humphrey Pump, who entered the shop carrying the sign of "The Old Ship."

I fear it must be recorded that the crowd which followed them dispensed with all expressions of gratitude. But though the crowd filled the shop so that there was no standing room to spare, Leveson still lifted his gloomy eyes and beheld his gloomy omen. For, though there were very many more people standing in the shop, there seemed to be no less people looking in at the window.

"Gentlemen," said Ivywood, "all jokes come to an end. This one has gone so far as to be serious; and it might have become impossible to correct public opinion, and expound to law-abiding citizens the true state of the law, had I not been able to meet so representative an assembly in so central a place. It is not pertinent to my purpose to indicate what I think of the jest which Captain Dalroy and his friends have been play-ing upon you for the last few weeks. But I think Captain Dalroy will himself concede that I am not jesting."

"With all my heart," said Dalroy, in a manner that was unusually serious and even sad. Then he added with a sigh, "And as you truly say, my jest has come to an end."

"That wooden sign," said Ivywood, pointing at the queer blue ship, "can be cut up for firewood. It shall lead decent citizens a devil's dance no more. Understand it once and for all, before you learn it from police-men or prison warders. You are under a new law. That sign is the sign of nothing. You can no more buy and sell alcohol by having that out-side your house, than if it were a lamp-post."

"D'you meanter say, guv'ner," said the plasterer, with a dawn of intelligence on his large face which was almost awful to watch, "that I ain't to 'ave a glass o' bitter?"

"Try a glass of rum," said Patrick.

"Captain Dalroy," said Lord Ivywood, "if you give one drop from that cask to that man, you are breaking the law and you shall sleep in jail."

"Are you quite sure?" asked Dalroy, with a strange sort of anxiety. "I might escape."

"I am quite sure," said Ivywood. "I have posted the police with full powers for the purpose, as you will find. I mean that this business shall end here tonight."

"If I find that pleeceman what told me I could 'ave a drink just now, I'll knock 'is 'elmet into a fancy necktie, I will," said the plasterer. "Why ain't people allowed to know the law?"

"They ain't got no right to alter the law in the dark like that," said the clock-mender. "Damn the new law."

"What is the new law?" asked the clerk.

"The words inserted by the recent Act," said Lord Ivywood, with the cold courtesy of the Conqueror, "are to the effect that alcohol cannot be sold, even under a lawful sign, unless alcoholic liquors have been kept for three days on the premises. Captain Dalroy, that cask of yours has not, I think, been three days on these premises. I command you to seal it up and take it away."

"Surely," said Patrick, with an innocent air, "the best remedy would be to wait till it *has been three days* on the premises. We might all get to know each other better." And he looked round at the ever-increasing multitude with hazy benevolence.

"You shall do nothing of the kind," said his lordship, with sudden fierceness.

"Well," answered Patrick, wearily, "now I come to think of it, perhaps I won't. I'll have one drink here and go home to bed like a good little boy."

"And the constables shall arrest you," thundered Ivywood.

"Why, nothing seems to suit you," said the surprised Dalroy. "Thank you, however, for explaining the new law so clearly— 'unless alcoholic liquors have been three days on the premises' I shall remember it now. You always explain such things so clearly. You only made one legal slip. The constables will not arrest me."

"And why not?" demanded the nobleman, white with passion.

"Because," cried Patrick Dalroy; and his voice lifted itself like a lonely trumpet before the charge, "because I shall not have broken the law. Because alcoholic liquors *have* been three days on these premises. Three months more likely. Because this is a common grog-shop, Philip Ivywood. Because that man behind the counter lives by selling spirits to all the cowards and hypocrites who are rich enough to bribe a bad doctor."

And he pointed suddenly at the small medicine glass on the counter by Hibbs and Leveson.

"What is that man drinking?" he demanded.

Hibbs put out his hand hastily for his glass, but the indignant clock-mender had snatched it first and drained it at a gulp.

"Scortch," he said, and dashed the glass to atoms on the floor. "Right you are too," roared the plasterer, seizing a big medicine bottle in each hand. "We're goin' to 'ave a little of the fun now, we are. What's in that big red bowl up there—I reckon it's port. Fetch it down, Bill."

Ivywood turned to Crooke and said, scarcely moving his lips of marble, "This is a lie."

"It is the truth," answered Crooke, looking back at him with equal steadiness. "Do you think you made the world, that you should make it over again so easily?"

"The world was made badly," said Philip, with a terrible note in his voice, "and *I will make it over again*."

Almost as he spoke the glass front of the shop fell inward, shattered, and there was wreckage among the moonlike, coloured bowls; almost as if spheres of celestial crystal cracked at his blasphemy. Through the broken windows came the roar of that confused tongue that is more terrible than the elements; the cry that the deaf kings have heard at last; the terrible voice of mankind. All the way down the long, fashionable street, lined with the Crooke plate-glass, that glass was crashing amid the cries of a crowd. Rivers of gold and purple wines sprawled about the pavement.

"Out in the open!" shouted Dalroy, rushing out of the shop, signboard in hand, the dog Quoodle barking furiously at his heels, while Dorian with the cheese and Humphrey with the keg followed as rapidly as they could. "Goodnight, my lord.

> "Perhaps our meeting next may fall,
> At Tomworth in your castle hall.

"Come along, friends, and form up. Don't waste time destroying property. We're all to start now."

"Where are we all going to?" asked the plasterer.

"We're all going into Parliament," answered the Captain, as he went to the head of the crowd.

The marching crowd turned two or three corners, and at the end of the next long street, Dorian Wimpole, who was toward the tail of the procession, saw again the grey Cyclops tower of St. Stephens, with its one great golden eye, as he had seen it against that pale green sunset that was at once quiet and volcanic on the night he was betrayed by sleep and by a friend. Almost as far off, at the head of the procession,

he could see the sign with the ship and the cross going before them like
an ensign, and hear a great voice singing—

> "Men that are men again, Who goes home?
> Tocsin and trumpeter! Who goes home?
> The voice valedictory—who is for Victory?
> Who is for Liberty? Who goes home?"

XXIII

The March on Ivywood

That storm-spirit, or eagle of liberty, which is the sudden soul in a crowd, had descended upon London after a foreign tour of some centuries in which it had commonly alighted upon other capitals. It is always impossible to define the instant and the turn of mood which makes the whole difference between danger being worse than endurance and endurance being worse than danger. The actual outbreak generally has a symbolic or artistic, or, what some would call whimsical cause. Somebody fires off a pistol or appears in an unpopular uniform, or refers in a loud voice to a scandal that is never mentioned in the newspapers; somebody takes off his hat, or somebody doesn't take off his hat; and a city is sacked before midnight. When the ever-swelling army of revolt smashed a whole street full of the shops of Mr. Crooke, the chemist, and then went on to Parliament, the Tower of London and the road to the sea, the sociologists hiding in their coal-cellars could think (in that clarifying darkness) of many material and spiritual explanations of such a storm in human souls; but of none that explained it quite enough. Doubtless there was a great deal of sheer drunkenness when the urns and goblets of Aesculapius were reclaimed as belonging to Bacchus: and many who went roaring down that road were merely stored with rich wines and liqueurs which are more comfortably and quietly digested at a City banquet or a West End restaurant. But many of these had been blind drunk twenty times without a thought of rebellion; you could not stretch the material explanation to cover a corner of the case. Much more general was a savage sense of the meanness of Crooke's wealthy patrons, in keeping a door open for themselves which they had wantonly shut on less happy people. But no explanation can explain it; and no man can say when it will come.

367

Dorian Wimpole was at the tail of the procession, which grew more
and more crowded every moment. For one space of the march he even
had the misfortune to lose it altogether; owing to the startling activity
which the rotund cheese when it escaped from his hands showed, in
descending a somewhat steep road toward the river. But in recent days
he had gained a pleasure in practical events which was like a second
youth. He managed to find a stray taxi-cab; and had little difficulty in
picking up again the trail of the extraordinary cortège. Inquiries addressed to a policeman with a black eye outside the House of Commons informed him sufficiently of the rebels' line of retreat or advance, or whatever it was; and in a very short time he beheld the unmistakable legion once more. It was unmistakable, because in front of it
there walked a red-headed giant, apparently carrying with him a wooden
portion of some public building; and also because so big a crowd had
never followed any man in England for a long time past. But except for
such things the unmistakable crowd might well have been mistaken for
another one. Its aspect had been altered almost as much as if it had
grown horns or tusks; for many of the company walked with outlandish weapons like iron teeth or horns, bills and pole axes, and spears
with strangely shaped heads. What was stranger still, whole rows and
rows of them had rifles, and even marched with a certain discipline;
and yet again, others seemed to have snatched up household or work-
shop tools, meat axes, pick axes, hammers and even carving knives. Such
things need be none the less deadly because they are domestic. They
have figured in millions of private murders before they appeared in any
public war.

Dorian was so fortunate as to meet the flame-haired Captain almost
face to face, and easily fell into step with him at the head of the march.
Humphrey Pump walked on the other side, with the celebrated cask
suspended round his neck by something resembling braces, as if it were
a drum. Mr. Wimpole had himself taken the opportunity of his brief
estrangement to carry the cheese somewhat more easily in a very large,
loose, waterproof knapsack on his shoulders. The effect in both cases
was to suggest dreadful deformities in two persons who happened to
be exceptionally cleanly built. The Captain, who seemed to be in tearing and towering spirits, gained great pleasure from this. But Dorian
had his sources of amusement too.

"What have you been doing with yourselves since you lost my judicious guidance?" he asked, laughing, "and why are parts of you a dull review and parts of you a fancy dress ball? What have you been up to?"

"We've been shopping," said Mr. Patrick Dalroy, with some pride. "We are country cousins. I know all about shopping; let us see, what are the phrases about it? Look at those rifles now! We got them quite at a bargain. We went to all the best gunsmiths in London, and we didn't pay much. In fact, we didn't pay anything. That's what is called a bargain, isn't it? Surely, I've seen in those things they send to ladies something about 'giving them away.' Then we went to a remnant sale. At least, it was a remnant sale when we left. And we bought that piece of stuff we've tied round the sign. Surely, it must be what ladies called chiffon?"

Dorian lifted his eyes and perceived that a very coarse strip of red rag, possibly collected from a dust bin, had been tied round the wooden sign-post by way of a red flag of revolution.

"Not what ladies call chiffon?" inquired the Captain with anxiety. "Well, anyhow, it is what *chiffoniers* call it. But as I'm going to call on a lady shortly, I'll try to remember the distinction."

"Is your shopping over, may I ask?" asked Mr. Wimpole.

"All but one thing," answered the other. "I must find a music shop—you know what I mean. Place where they sell pianos and things of that sort."

"Look here," said Dorian, "this cheese is pretty heavy as it is. Have I got to carry a piano, too?"

"You misunderstand me," said the Captain, calmly. And as he had never thought of music shops until his eye had caught one an instant before, he darted into the doorway. Returning almost immediately with a long parcel under his arm, he resumed the conversation.

"Did you go anywhere else," asked Dorian, "except to shops?"

"Anywhere else!" cried Patrick, indignantly, "haven't you got any country cousins? Of course we went to all the right places. We went to the Houses of Parliament. But Parliament isn't sitting; so there are no eggs of the quality suitable for elections. We went to the Tower of London—you can't tire country cousins like us. We took away some curiosities of steel and iron. We even took away the halberds from the Beef-eaters. We pointed out that for the purpose of eating beef (their only avowed public object) knives and forks had always been found more convenient. To tell the truth, they seemed rather relieved to be relieved of them."

"And may I ask," said the other with a smile, "where you are off to now?"

"Another beauty spot!" cried the Captain, boisterously, "no tiring the country cousin! I am going to show my young friends from the provinces what is perhaps the finest old country house in England. We are going to Ivywood, not far from that big watering place they call Pebblewick."

"I see," said Dorian; and for the first time looked back with intelligent trouble on his face, on the marching ranks behind him.

"Captain Dalroy," said Dorian Wimpole, in a slightly altered tone, "there is one thing that puzzles me. Ivywood talked about having set the police to catch us; and though this is a pretty big crowd, I simply cannot believe that the police, as I knew them in my youth, could not catch us. But where are the police? You seem to have marched through half London with much (if you'll excuse me) of the appearance of carrying murderous weapons. Lord Ivywood threatened that the police would stop us. Well, why didn't they stop us?"

"Your subject," said Patrick, cheerfully, "divides itself into three heads."

"I hope not," said Dorian.

"There really are three reasons why the police should not be prominent in this business; as their worst enemy cannot say that they were."

He began ticking off the three on his own huge fingers; and seemed to be quite serious about it.

"First," he said, "you have been a long time away from town. Probably you do not know a policeman when you see him. They do not wear helmets, as our line regiments did after the Prussians had won. They wear fezzes, because the Turks have won. Shortly, I have little doubt, they will wear pigtails, because the Chinese have won. It is a very interesting branch of moral science. It is called Efficiency.

"Second," explained the Captain, "you have, perhaps, omitted to notice that a very considerable number of those wearing such fezzes are walking just behind us. Oh, yes, it's quite true. Don't you remember that the whole French Revolution really began because a sort of City

Militia refused to fire on their own fathers and wives; and even showed some slight traces of a taste for firing on the other side? You'll see lots of them behind; and you can tell them by their revolver belts and their walking in step; but don't look back on them too much. It makes them nervous."

"And the third reason?" asked Dorian.

"For the real reason," answered Patrick, "I am not fighting a hopeless fight. People who have fought in real fights don't, as a rule. But I noticed something singular about the very point you mention. Why are there no more police? Why are there no more soldiers? I will tell you. There really are very few policemen or soldiers left in England today."

"Surely, that," said Wimpole, "is an unusual complaint."

"But very clear," said the Captain, gravely, "to anyone who has ever seen sailors or soldiers. I will tell you the truth. Our rulers have come to count on the bare bodily cowardice of a mass of Englishmen, as a sheep dog counts on the cowardice of a flock of sheep. Now, look here, Mr. Wimpole, wouldn't a shepherd be wise to limit the number of his dogs if he could make his sheep pay by it? At the end you might find millions of sheep managed by a solitary dog. But that is because they are sheep. Suppose the sheep were turned by a miracle into wolves. There are very few dogs they could not tear in pieces. But, what is my practical point, there are really very few dogs to tear."

"You don't mean," said Dorian, "that the British Army is practically disbanded?"

"There are the sentinels outside Whitehall," replied Patrick, in a low voice. "But, indeed, your question puts me in a difficulty. No; the army is not entirely disbanded, of course. But the *British* army—. Did you ever hear, Wimpole, of the great destiny of the Empire?"

"I seem to have heard the phrase," replied his companion.

"It is in four acts," said Dalroy. "Victory over barbarians. Employment of barbarians. Alliance with barbarians. Conquest by barbarians. That is the great destiny of Empire."

"I think I begin to see what you mean," returned Dorian Wimpole. "Of course Ivywood and the authorities do seem very prone to rely on the sepoy troops."

"And other troops as well," said Patrick. "I think you will be surprised when you see them."

He tramped on for a while in silence and then said, with some air of abruptness, which yet did not seem to be entirely a changing of the subject,

"Do you know the man who lives now on the estate next to Ivywood?"

"No," replied Dorian, "I am told he keeps himself very much to himself."

"And his estate, too," said Patrick, rather gloomily. "If you would climb his garden-wall, Wimpole, I think you would find an answer to a good many of your questions. Oh, yes, the right honourable gentlemen are making full provision for public order and national defence—in a way."

He fell into an almost sullen silence again; and several villages had been passed before he spoke again.

They tramped through the darkness; and dawn surprised them somewhere in the wilder and more wooded parts where the roads began to rise and roam. Dalroy gave an exclamation of pleasure and pointed ahead, drawing the attention of Dorian to the distance. Against the silver and scarlet bars of the daybreak could be seen afar a dark purple dome, with a crown of dark green leaves; the place they had called Roundabout.

Dalroy's spirit seemed to revive at the sight, with the customary accompaniment of the threat of vocalism.

"Been making any poems lately?" he asked of Wimpole.

"Nothing particular," replied the poet.

"Then," said the Captain, portentously, clearing his throat, "you shall listen to one of mine, whether you like it or not—nay, the more you dislike it the longer and longer it will be. I begin to understand why soldiers want to sing when on the march; and also why they put up with such rotten songs.

> "The Druids waved their golden knives
> And danced around the Oak,
> When they had sacrificed a man;
> But though the learnèd search and scan
> No single modern person can
> Entirely see the joke;
> But though they cut the throats of men

They cut not down the tree,
And from the blood the saplings sprang
Of oak-woods yet to be.
    But Ivywood, Lord Ivywood,
    He rots the tree as ivy would,
    He clings and crawls as ivy would
    About the sacred tree.

"King Charles he fled from Worcester fight
And hid him in an Oak;
In convent schools no man of tact
Would trace and praise his every act,
Or argue that he was in fact
A strict and sainted bloke;
But not by him the sacred woods
Have lost their fancies free,
And though he was extremely big,
He did not break the tree.
    But Ivywood, Lord Ivywood,
    He breaks the tree as ivy would
    And eats the woods as ivy would
    Between us and the sea.

"Great Collingwood walked down the glade
And flung the acorns free,
That oaks might still be in the grove
As oaken as the beams above
When the great Lover sailors love
Was kissed by Death at sea.
But though for him the oak-trees fell
To build the oaken ships,
The woodman worshipped what he smote
And honoured even the chips.
    But Ivywood, Lord Ivywood,
    He hates the tree as ivy would,
    As the dragon of the ivy would,
    That has us in his grips."

374

They were ascending a sloping road, walled in on both sides by solemn woods, which somehow seemed as watchful as owls awake. Though daybreak was going over them with banners, scrolls of scarlet and gold, and with a wind like trumpets of triumph, the dark woods seemed to hold their secret like dark, cool cellars; nor was the strong sunlight seen in them, save in one or two brilliant shafts, that looked like splintered emeralds.

"I should not wonder," said Dorian, "if the ivy does not find the tree knows a thing or two also."

"The tree does," assented the Captain. "The trouble was that until a little while ago the tree did not know that it knew."

There was a silence; and as they went up the incline grew steeper and steeper, and the tall trees seemed more and more to be guarding something from sight, as with the grey shields of giants.

"Do you remember this road, Hump?" asked Dalroy of the inn-keeper.

"Yes," answered Humphrey Pump, and said no more; but few have ever heard such fulness in an affirmative.

They marched on in silence and about two hours afterward, toward eleven o'clock, Dalroy called a halt in the forest, and said that everybody had better have a few hours' sleep. The impenetrable quality in the woods and the comparative softness of the carpet of beech-mast, made the spot as appropriate as the time was inappropriate. And if anyone thinks that common people, casually picked up in a street, could not follow a random leader on such a journey or sleep at his command in such a spot, given the state of the soul, then someone knows no history.

"I'm afraid," said Dalroy, "you'll have to have your supper for breakfast. I know an excellent place for having breakfast, but it's too exposed for sleep. And sleep you must have; so we won't unpack the stores just now. We'll lie down like Babes in the Wood, and any bird of an industrious disposition is free to start covering me with leaves. Really, there are things coming, before which you will want sleep."

When they resumed the march it was nearly the middle of the afternoon; and the meal which Dalroy insisted buoyantly on describing as breakfast was taken about that mysterious hour when ladies die without tea. The steep road had consistently grown steeper and steeper; and steeper; and at last, Dalroy said to Dorian Wimpole,

"Don't drop that cheese again just here, or it will roll right away down into the woods. I know it will. No scientific calculations of grades and angles are necessary; because I have seen it do so myself. In fact, I have run after it."

Wimpole realised they were mounting to the sharp edge of a ridge, and in a few moments he knew by the oddness in the shape of the trees what it had been that the trees were hiding. They had been walking along a swelling, woodland path beside the sea. On a particular high plateau, projecting above the shore, stood some dwarfed and crippled apple-trees, of whose apples no man alive would have eaten, so sour and salt they must be. All the rest of the plateau was bald and feature-less, but Pump looked at every inch of it, as if at an inhabited place.

"This is where we'll have breakfast," he said, pointing to the naked grassy waste. "It's the best inn in England."

Some of his audience began to laugh, but somehow suddenly ceased doing so, as Dalroy strode forward and planted the sign of "The Old Ship" on the desolate sea-shore.

"And now," he said, "you have charge of the stores we brought, Hump, and we will picnic. As it said in a song I once sang,

> "The Saracen's Head out of Araby came,
> King Richard riding in arms like flame,
> And where he established his folk to be fed
> He set up his spear, and the Saracen's Head."

It was nearly dusk before the mob, much swelled by the many dis-contented on the Ivywood estates, reached the gates of Ivywood House. Strategically, and for the purposes of a night surprise, this might have done credit to the Captain's military capacity. But the use to which he put it actually was what some might call eccentric. When he had dis-posed his forces, with strict injunctions of silence for the first few min-utes, he turned to Pump, and said, "And now, before we do anything else, I'm going to make a noise." And he produced from under brown paper what appeared to be a musical instrument.

"A summons to parley?" inquired Dorian, with interest, "a trumpet of defiance, or something of that kind?"

"No," said Patrick, "a serenade."

XXIV

THE ENIGMAS OF LADY JOAN

On an evening when the sky was clear and only its fringes embroi-dered with the purple arabesques of the sunset, Joan Brett was walking on the upper lawn of the terraced garden at Ivywood, where the pea-cocks trail themselves about. She was not unlike one of the peacocks herself in beauty, and some might have said, in inutility; she had the proud head and the sweeping train; nor was she, in these days, devoid of the occasional disposition to scream. For, indeed, for some time past she had felt her existence closing round her with an incomprehen-sible quietude; and that is harder for the patience than an incompre-hensible noise. Whenever she looked at the old yew hedges of the garden they seemed to be higher than when she saw them last; as if those living walls could still grow to shut her in. Whenever from the turret win-dows she had a sight of the sea, it seemed to be farther away. Indeed, the whole closing of the end of the turret wing with the new wall of eastern woodwork seemed to symbolise all her shapeless sensations. In her childhood the wing had ended with a broken-down door and a dis-used staircase. They led to an uncultivated copse and an abandoned railway tunnel, to which neither she nor anyone else ever wanted to go. Still, she knew what they led to. Now it seemed that this scrap of land had been sold and added to the adjoining estate; and about the adjoin-ing estate nobody seemed to know anything in particular. The sense of things closing in increased upon her. All sorts of silly little details mag-nified the sensation. She could discover nothing about this new land-lord next door, so to speak, since he was, it seemed, an elderly man who preferred to live in the greatest privacy. Miss Browning, Lord Ivywood's secretary, could give her no further information than that he was a gentleman from the Mediterranean coast; which singular form of words seemed to have been put into her mouth. As a Mediterranean gentleman might mean anything from an American gentleman living in Venice to a black African on the edge of the Atlas, the description did not illuminate; and probably was not intended to do so. She occasionally saw his liveried servants going about; and their liveries were not like English liveries. She was also, in her somewhat morbid state, annoyed by the fact that the uniforms of the old Pebblewick militia had been changed, under the influence of the Turkish *prestige* in the recent war. They wore fezzes like the French Zouaves, which were certainly much more practical than the heavy helmets they used to wear. It was a small matter, but it annoyed Lady Joan, who was, like so many clever women, at once subtle and conservative. It made her feel as if the whole world was being altered outside, and she was not allowed to know about it.

But she had deeper spiritual troubles also, while, under the pathetic entreaties of old, Lady Ivywood and her own sick mother, she stayed on week after week at Ivywood House. If the matter be stated cynically (as she herself was quite capable of stating it) she was engaged in the established feminine occupation of trying to like a man. But the cynicism would have been false; as cynicism nearly always is; for during the most crucial days of that period, she had really liked the man.

She had liked him when he was brought in with Pump's bullet in his leg; and was still the strongest and calmest man in the room. She had liked him when the hurt took a dangerous turn, and when he bore pain to admiration. She had liked him when he showed no malice against the angry Dorian; she had liked him with something like enthusiasm on the night he rose rigid on his rude crutch, and, crushing all remonstrance, made his rash and swift rush to London. But, despite the queer closing-in-sensations of which we have spoken, she never liked him better than that evening when he lifted himself laboriously on his crutch up the terraces of the old garden and came to speak to her as she stood among the peacocks. He even tried to pat a peacock in a hazy way, as if it were a dog. He told her that these beautiful birds were, of course, imported from the East—by the semi-eastern empire of Macedonia. But, all the same, Joan had a dim suspicion that he had never noticed before that there were any peacocks at Ivywood. His greatest fault was a pride in the faultlessness of his mental and moral strength; but, if he had only known, something faintly comic in the unconscious side of him did him more good with the woman than all the rest.

"They were said to be the birds of Juno," he said, "but I have little doubt that Juno, like so much else of the Homeric mythology, has also an Asiatic origin."

"I always thought," said Joan, "that Juno was rather too stately for the seraglio."

"You ought to know," replied Ivywood, with a courteous gesture, "for I *never* saw anyone who looked so like Juno as you do. But, indeed, there is a great deal of misunderstanding about the Arabian or Indian view of women. It is, somehow, too simple and solid for our paradoxical Christendom to comprehend. Even the vulgar joke against the Turks, that they like their brides fat, has in it a sort of distorted shadow of what I mean. They do not look so much at the individual, as at Womanhood and the power of Nature."

"I sometimes think," said Joan, "that these fascinating theories are a little strained. Your friend Misysra told me the other day that women had the highest freedom in Turkey; as they were allowed to wear trousers."

Ivywood smiled his rare and dry smile. "The Prophet has something of a simplicity often found with genius," he answered. "I will not deny that some of the arguments he has employed have seemed to me crude and even fanciful. But he is right at the root. There is a kind of freedom that consists in never rebelling against Nature; and I think they understand it in the Orient better than we do in the West. You see, Joan, it is all very well to talk about love in our narrow, personal, romantic way; but there is something higher than the love of a lover or the love of love."

"What is that?" asked Joan, looking down.

"The love of Fate," said Lord Ivywood, with something like spiritual passion in his eyes. "Doesn't Nietzsche say somewhere that the delight in destiny is the mark of the hero? We are mistaken if we think that the heroes and saints of Islam say 'Kismet' with bowed heads and in sorrow. They say 'Kismet' with a shout of joy. That which is fitting—that is what they really mean. In the Arabian tales, the most perfect prince is wedded to the most perfect princess—because it is fitting. The spiritual giants, the Genii, achieve it—that is, the purposes of Nature. In the selfish, sentimental European novels, the loveliest princess on earth might have run away with her middle-aged drawing-master. These things are not in the Path. The Turk rides out to wed the fairest queen of the earth; he conquers empires to do it; and he is not ashamed of his laurels."

The crumpled violet clouds around the edge of the silver evening looked to Lady Joan more and more like vivid violet embroideries hemming some silver curtain in the closed corridor at Ivywood. The peacocks looked more lustrous and beautiful than they ever had before; but for the first time she really felt they came out of the land of the Arabian Nights.

"Joan," said Philip Ivywood, very softly, in the twilight, "I am not ashamed of my laurels, I see no meaning in what these Christians call humility. I will be the greatest man in the world if I can; and I think I can. Therefore, something that is higher than love itself, Fate and what is fitting, make it right that I should wed the most beautiful woman in the world. And she stands among the peacocks and is more beautiful and more proud than they."

Joan's troubled eyes were on the violet horizon and her troubled lips could utter nothing but something like "don't."

"Joan," said Philip, again, "I have told you, you are the woman one of the great heroes could have desired. Let me now tell you something I could have told no one to whom I had not thus spoken of love and betrothal. When I was twenty years old in a town in Germany, pursuing my education, I did what the West calls falling in love. She was a fisher-girl from the coast; for this town was near the sea. My story might have ended there. I could not have entered diplomacy with such a wife, but I should not have minded then. But a little while after, I wandered into the edges of Flanders, and found myself standing above some of the last grand reaches of the Rhine. And things came over me but for which I might be crying stinking fish to this day. I thought how many holy or lovely nooks that river had left behind, and gone on. It might anywhere in Switzerland have spent its weak youth in a spirit over a high crag, or anywhere in the Rhinelands lost itself in a marsh covered with flowers. But it went on to the perfect sea, which is the fulfilment of a river."

Again, Joan could not speak; and again it was Philip who went on.

"Here is yet another thing that could not be said, till the hand of the prince had been offered to the princess. It may be that in the East they carry too far this matter of infant marriages. But look round on the mad young marriages that go to pieces everywhere! And ask yourself whether you don't wish they had been infant marriages! People talk in the newspapers of the heartlessness of royal marriages. But you and I do not believe the newspapers, I suppose. We know there is no King in England; nor has been since his head fell before Whitehall. You know that you and I and the families are the Kings of England; and our marriages are royal marriages. Let the suburbs call them heartless. Let us say they need the brave heart that is the only badge of aristocracy. Joan," he said, very gently, "perhaps you have been near a crag in Switzerland, or a marsh covered with flowers. Perhaps you have known—a fisher-girl. But there is something greater and simpler than all that; something you find in the great epics of the East—the beautiful woman, and the great man, and Fate."

"My lord," said Joan, using the formal phrase by an unfathomable instinct, "will you allow me a little more time to think of this? And let there be no notion of disloyalty, if my decision is one way or the other?"

"Why, of course," said Ivywood, bowing over his crutch; and he limped off, picking his way among the peacocks.

For days afterward Joan tried to build the foundations of her earthly destiny. She was still quite young, but she felt as if she had lived thousands of years, worrying over the same question. She told herself again and again, and truly, that many a better woman than she had taken a second-best which was not so first-class a second-best. But there was something complicated in the very atmosphere. She liked listening to Philip Ivywood at his best, as anyone likes listening to a man who can really play the violin; but the great trouble always is that at certain awful moments you cannot be certain whether it is the violin or the man.

Moreover, there was a curious tone and spirit in the Ivywood household, especially after the wound and convalescence of Ivywood, about which she could say nothing except that it annoyed her somehow. There was something in it glorious—but also languorous. By an impulse by no means uncommon among intelligent, fashionable people, she felt a desire to talk to a sensible woman of the middle or lower classes; and almost threw herself on the bosom of Miss Browning for sympathy.

But Miss Browning, with her curling, reddish hair and white, very clever face, struck the same indescribable note. Lord Ivywood was assumed as a first principle; as if he were Father Time, or the Clerk of the Weather. He was called "He." The fifth time he was called "He," Joan could not understand why she seemed to smell the plants in the hot conservatory.

"You see," said Miss Browning, "we mustn't interfere with his career; that is the important thing. And, really, I think the quieter we keep about everything the better. I am sure he is maturing very big plans. You heard what the Prophet said the other night?"

"The last thing the Prophet said to me," said the darker lady, in a dogged manner, "was that when we English see the English youth, we cry out 'He is crescent!' But when we see the English aged man, we cry out 'He is cross!'"

A lady with so clever a face could not but laugh faintly; but she continued on a determined theme, "The Prophet said, you know, that all real love had in it an element of fate. And I am sure that is his view, too. People cluster round a centre as little stars do round a star; because a star is a magnet. You are never wrong when destiny blows behind you like a great big wind; and I think many things have been judged unfairly that way. It's all very well to talk about the infant marriages in India."

"Miss Browning," said Joan, "are you interested in the infant marriages in India?"

"Well—" said Miss Browning.

"Is your sister interested in them? I'll run and ask her," cried Joan, plunging across the room to where Mrs. Mackintosh was sitting at a table scribbling secretarial notes.

"Well," said Mrs. Mackintosh, turning up a rich-haired, resolute head, more handsome than her sister's, "I believe the Indian way is the best. When people are left to themselves in early youth, any of them might marry anything. We might have married a nigger or a fish-wife or—a criminal."

"Now, Mrs. Mackintosh," said Joan, with black-browed severity, "you well know you would never have married a fish-wife. Where is Enid?" she ended suddenly.

"Lady Enid," said Miss Browning, "is looking out music in the music room, I think."

Joan walked swiftly through several long salons, and found her fair-haired and pallid relative actually at the piano.

"Enid," cried Joan, "you know I've always been fond of you. For God's sake tell me what is the matter with this house? I admire Philip as everybody does. But what is the matter with the house? Why do all these rooms and gardens seem to be shutting me in and in and in? Why does everything look more and more the same? Why does everybody say the same thing? Oh, I don't often talk metaphysics; but there is a purpose in this. That's the only way of putting it; there is a purpose. And I don't know what it is."

Lady Enid Wimpole played a preliminary bar or two on the piano. Then she said,

"Nor do I, Joan. I don't indeed. I know exactly what you mean. But it's just because there is a purpose that I have faith in him and trust him." She began softly to play a ballad tune of the Rhineland; and perhaps the music suggested her next remark. "Suppose you were looking at some of the last reaches of the Rhine, where it flows—"

"Enid!" cried Joan, "if you say 'into the North Sea,' I shall scream. Scream, do you hear, louder than all the peacocks together."

"Well," expostulated Lady Enid, looking up rather wildly, "The Rhine *does* flow into the North Sea, doesn't it?"

"I dare say," said Joan, recklessly, "but the Rhine might have flowed into the Round Pond, before you would have known or cared, until—"

"Until what?" asked Enid; and her music suddenly ceased.

"Until something happened that I cannot understand," said Joan, moving away.

"*You* are something I cannot understand," said Enid Wimpole. "But I will play something else, if this annoys you." And she fingered the music again with an eye to choice.

Joan walked back through the corridor of the music room, and restlessly resumed her seat in the room with the two lady secretaries.

"Well," asked the red-haired and good-humoured Mrs. Mackintosh, without looking up from her work of scribbling, "have you discovered anything?"

For some moments Joan appeared to be in a blacker state of brooding than usual; then she said, in a candid and friendly tone, which somehow contrasted with her knit and swarthy brows— "No, really. At least I think I've only found out two things; and they are only things about myself. I've discovered that I do like heroism, but I don't like hero worship."

"Surely," said Miss Browning, in the Girton manner, "the one always flows from the other."

"I hope not," said Joan.

"But what else can you do with the hero?" asked Mrs. Mackintosh, still without looking up from her writing, "except worship him?"

"You might crucify him," said Joan, with a sudden return of savage restlessness, as she rose from her chair. "Things seem to happen then."

"Aren't you tired?" asked the Miss Browning who had the clever face.

"Yes," said Joan, "and the worst sort of tiredness; when you don't even know what you're tired of. To tell the honest truth, I think I'm tired of this house."

"It's very old, of course, and parts of it are still dismal," said Miss Browning, "but he has enormously improved it. The decoration, with the moon and stars, down in the wing with the turret is really—"

Away in the distant music room, Lady Enid, having found the music she preferred, was fingering its prelude on the piano. At the first few notes of it, Joan Brett stood up, like a tigress.

"Thanks—" she said, with a hoarse softness, "that's it, of course! and that's just what we all are! She's found the right tune now."

"What tune is it?" asked the wondering secretary.

"The tune of harp, sackbut, psaltery, dulcimer and all kinds of music," said Joan, softly and fiercely, "when we shall bow down and worship the Golden Image that Nebuchadnezzar the King has set up. Girls! Women! Do you know what this place is? Do you know why it is all doors within doors and lattice behind lattice; and everything is curtained and cushioned; and why the flowers that are so fragrant here are not the flowers of our hills?"

From the distant and slowly darkening music room, Enid Wimpole's song came thin and clear:

"Less than the dust beneath thy chariot wheel,
    Less than the rust that never stained thy sword—"

"Do you know what we are?" demanded Joan Brett, again. "We are a Harem."

"Why, what can you mean?" cried the younger girl, in great agitation. "Why, Lord Ivywood has never—"

"I know he has never. I am not sure," said Joan, "even whether he would ever. I shall never understand that man, nor will anybody else.

But I tell you that is the spirit. That is what we *are*. And this room stinks of polygamy as certainly as it smells of tube-roses."

"Why, Joan," cried Lady Enid, entering the room like a well-bred ghost, "what on earth is the matter with you. You all look as white as sheets."

Joan took no heed of her but went on with her own obstinate argument.

"And, besides," she said, "if there's one thing we do know about him it is that he believes on principle in doing things slowly. He calls it evolution and relativity and the expanding of an idea into larger ideas. How do we know he isn't doing that slowly; getting us accustomed to living like this, so that it may be the less shock when he goes further— steeping us in the atmosphere before he actually introduces," and she shuddered, "the institution. Is it any more calmly outrageous a scheme than any other of Ivywood's schemes; than a sepoy commander-in-chief, or Misysra preaching in Westminster Abbey, or the destruction of all the inns in England? I will not wait and expand. I will not be evolved. I will not develop into something that is not me. My feet shall be outside these walls if I walk the roads for it afterward; or I will scream as I would scream trapped in any den by the Docks."

She swept down the rooms toward the turret, with a sudden passion for solitude; but as she passed the astronomical wood-carving that had closed up the end of the old wing, Enid saw her strike it with her clinched hand.

It was in the turret that she had a strange experience. She was again, later on, using its isolation to worry out the best way of having it out with Philip, when he should return from his visit to London; for to tell old Lady Ivywood what was on her mind would be about as kind and useful as describing Chinese tortures to a baby. The evening was very quiet, of the pale grey sort, and all that side of Ivywood lay before her eyes, undisturbed. She was the more surprised when her dreaming took note of a sort of stirring in the grey-purple dusk of the bushes; of whisperings; and of many footsteps. Then the silence settled down again; and then it was startlingly broken by a big voice singing in the dark distance. It was accompanied by faint sounds that might have been from the fingering of some lute or viol:

> "Lady, the light is dying in the skies,
> Lady, and let us die when honour dies,
> Your dear, dropped glove was like a gauntlet flung,
>> When you and I were young.
> For something more than splendour stood; and ease was
>> not the only good
> About the woods in Ivywood when you and I were young.

> "Lady, the stars are falling pale and small,
> Lady, we will not live if life be all
> Forgetting those good stars in heaven hung
>> When all the world was young,
> For more than gold was in a ring, and love was not a
>> little thing
> Between the trees in Ivywood when all the world was
>> young."

The singing ceased; and the bustle in the bushes could hardly be called more than a whisper. But sounds of the same sort and somewhat louder seemed wafted round corners from other sides of the house; and the whole night seemed full of something that was alive, but was more than a single man.

She heard a cry behind her, and Enid rushed into the room as white as one of the lilies.

"What awful thing is happening?" she cried. "The courtyard is full of men shouting, and there are torches everywhere and—"

Joan heard a tramp of men marching and heard, afar off, another song, sung on a more derisive note, something like—

> "But Ivywood, Lord Ivywood,
> He rots the tree as ivy would."

"I think," said Joan, thoughtfully, "it is the End of the World."

"But where are the police?" wailed her cousin. "They don't seem to be anywhere about since they wore those fezzes. We shall be murdered or—"

Three thundering and measured blows shook the decorative wood panelling at the end of the wing; as if admittance were demanded with the club of a giant. Enid remembered that she had thought Joan's little blow energetic, and shuddered. Both the girls stared at the stars and moons and suns blazoned on that sacred wall that leapt and shuddered under the strokes of the doom.

Then the sun fell from Heaven, and the moon and stars dropped down and were scattered about the Persian carpet; and by the opening of the end of the world, Patrick Dalroy came in, carrying a mandolin.

XXV

The Finding of the Superman

"I've brought you a little dog," said Mr. Dalroy, introducing the rampant Quoodle. "I had him brought down here in a large hamper labelled 'Explosives,' a title which appears to have been well selected."

He had bowed to Lady Enid on entering and taken Joan's hand with the least suggestion that he wanted to do something else with it; but he resolutely resumed his conversation, which was on the subject of dogs.

"People who bring back dogs," he said, "are always under a cloud of suspicion. Sometimes it is hideously hinted that the citizen who brings the dog back with him is identical with the citizen who took the dog away with him. In my case, of course, such conduct is inconceivable. But the returners of dogs, that prosperous and increasing class, are also accused," he went on, looking straight at Joan, with blank blue eyes, "of coming back for a Reward. There is more truth in this charge."

Then, with a change of manner more extraordinary than any revolution, even the revolution that was roaring round the house, he took her hand again and kissed it, saying, with a confounding seriousness,

"I know at least that you will pray for my soul."

"You had better pray for mine, if I have one," answered Joan, "but why now?"

"Because," said Patrick, "you will hear from outside, you may even see from that turret window something which in brute fact has never been seen in England since Poor Monmouth's army went down. In spirit and in truth it has not happened since Saladin and Coeur de Lion crashed together.

"I only add one thing, and that you know already. I have lived loving you and I shall die loving you. It is the only dimension of the Universe

387

in which I have not wandered and gone astray. I leave the dog to guard you;" and he disappeared down the old broken staircase.

Lady Enid was much mystified that no popular pursuit assailed this stair or invaded the house. But Lady Joan knew better. She had gone, on the suggestion she most cared about, into the turret room and looked out of its many windows on to the abandoned copse and tunnel, which were now fenced off with high walls, the boundary of the mysterious property next door. Across that high barrier she could not even see the tunnel, and barely the tops of the tallest trees which hid its entrance from sight. But in an instant she knew that Dalroy was not hurling his forces on Ivywood at all, but on the house and estate beyond it.

And then followed a sight that was not an experience but rather a revolving vision. She could never describe it afterward, nor could any of those involved in so violent and mystical a wheel. She had seen a huge wall of a breaker wash all over the parade at Pebblewick; and wondered that so huge a hammer could be made merely of water. She had never had a notion of what it is like when it is made of men.

The palisade, put up by the new landlord in front of the old tangled ground by the tunnel, she had long regarded as something as settled and ordinary as one of the walls of the drawing room. It swung and split and sprang into a thousand pieces under the mere blow of human bodies bursting with rage; and the great wave crested the obstacle more clearly than she had ever seen any great wave crest the parade. Only, when the fence was broken, she saw behind it something that robbed her of reason; so that she seemed to be living in all ages and all lands at once. She never could describe the vision afterward; but she always denied it was a dream. She said it was worse; it was something more real than reality. It was a line of real soldiers, which is always a magnificent sight. But they might have been the soldiers of Hannibal or of Attila, they might have been dug up from the cemeteries of Sidon and Babylon, for all Joan had to do with them. There, encamped in English meadows, with a hawthorn-tree in front of them and three beeches behind, was something that has never been in camp nearer than some leagues south of Paris, since that Carolus called The Hammer broke it backward at Tours.

There flew the green standard of that great faith and strong civilization which has so often almost entered the great cities of the West;

which long encircled Vienna, which was barely barred from Paris; but
which had never before been seen in arms on the soil of England. At
one end of the line stood Philip Ivywood, in a uniform of his own
special creation, a compromise between the Sepoy and the Turkish uniform. The compromise worked more and more wildly in Joan's mind.
If any impression remained it was merely that England had conquered
India and Turkey had conquered England. Then she saw that Ivywood,
for all his uniform, was not the Commander of these forces, for an old
man, with a great scar on his face, which was not a European face, set
himself in the front of the battle, as if it had been a battle in the old
epics, and crossed swords with Patrick Dalroy. He had come to return
the scar upon his forehead; and he returned it with many wounds, though
at last it was he who sank under the sword thrust. He fell on his face;
and Dalroy looked at him with something that is much more great than
pity. Blood was flowing from Patrick's wrist and forehead, but he made
a salute with his sword. As he was doing so, the corpse, as it appeared,
laboriously lifted a face, with feeble eyelids. And, seeming to understand the quarters of the sky by instinct, Oman Pasha dragged himself
a foot or so to the left; and fell with his face toward Mecca.

After that the turret turned round and round about Joan and she
knew not whether the things she saw were history or prophecy. Something in that last fact of being crushed by the weapons of brown men and
yellow, secretly entrenched in English meadows, had made the English
what they had not been for centuries. The hawthorn-tree was twisted
and broken, as it was at the Battle of Ashdown, when Alfred led his
first charge against the Danes. The beech-trees were splashed up to
their lowest branches with the mingling of brave heathen and brave
Christian blood. She knew no more than that when a column of the
Christian rebels, led by Humphrey of the Sign of the Ship, burst through
the choked and forgotten tunnel and took the Turkish regiment in the
rear, it was the end.

That violent and revolving vision became something beyond the
human voice or human ear. She could not intelligently hear even the
shots and shouts round the last magnificent rally of the Turks. It was
natural, therefore, that she should not hear the words Lord Ivywood
addressed to his next-door neighbour, a Turkish officer, or rather to
himself. But his words were:

"I have gone where God has never dared to go. I am above the silly supermen as they are above mere men. Where I walk in the Heavens, no man has walked before me; and I am alone in a garden. All this passing about me is like the lonely plucking of garden flowers. I will have this blossom, I will have that."

The sentence ended so suddenly that the officer looked at him, as if expecting him to speak. But he did not speak.

But Patrick and Joan, wandering together in a world made warm and fresh again, as it can be for few in a world that calls courage frenzy and love superstition, feeling every branching tree as a friend with arms open for the man, or every sweeping slope as a great train trailing behind the woman, did one day climb up to the little white cottage that was now the home of the Superman.

He sat playing with a pale, reposeful face, with scraps of flower and weed put before him on a wooden table. He did not notice them, nor anything else around him; scarcely even Enid Wimpole, who attended to all his wants.

"He is perfectly happy," she said quietly.

Joan, with the glow on her dark face, could not prevent herself from replying, "And we are so happy."

"Yes," said Enid, "but his happiness will last," and she wept.

"I understand," said Joan, and kissed her cousin, not without tears of her own.

The Trees of Pride

I

The Tale of the Peacock Trees

Squire Vane was an elderly schoolboy of English education and Irish extraction. His English education, at one of the great public schools, had preserved his intellect perfectly and permanently at the stage of boyhood. But his Irish extraction subconsciously upset in him the proper solemnity of an old boy, and sometimes gave him back the brighter outlook of a naughty boy. He had a bodily impatience which played tricks upon him almost against his will, and had already rendered him rather too radiant a failure in civil and diplomatic service. Thus it is true that compromise is the key of British policy, especially as effecting an impartiality among the religions of India; but Vane's attempt to meet the Moslem halfway by kicking off one boot at the gates of the mosque, was felt not so much to indicate true impartiality as something that could only be called an aggressive indifference. Again, it is true that an English aristocrat can hardly enter fully into the feelings of either party in a quarrel between a Russian Jew and an Orthodox procession carrying relics; but Vane's idea that the procession might carry the Jew as well, himself a venerable and historic relic, was misunderstood on both sides. In short, he was a man who particularly prided himself on having no nonsense about him; with the result that he was always doing nonsensical things. He seemed to be standing on his head merely to prove that he was hard-headed.

He had just finished a hearty breakfast, in the society of his daughter, at a table under a tree in his garden by the Cornish coast. For, having a glorious circulation, he insisted on as many outdoor meals as possible, though spring had barely touched the woods and warmed the seas round that southern extremity of England. His daughter Barbara, a good-looking girl with heavy red hair and a face as grave as one of the garden statues, still sat almost motionless as a statue when her father rose. A fine tall figure in light clothes, with his white hair and mustache flying backwards rather fiercely from a face that was good-humored enough, for he carried his very wide Panama hat in his hand, he strode across the terraced garden, down some stone steps flanked with old ornamental urns to a more woodland path fringed with little trees, and so down a zigzag road which descended the craggy cliff to the shore, where he was to meet a guest arriving by boat. A yacht was already in the blue bay, and he could see a boat pulling toward the little paved pier.

And yet in that short walk between the green turf and the yellow sands he was destined to find, his hard-headedness provoked into a not unfamiliar phase which the world was inclined to call hot-headedness. The fact was that the Cornish peasantry, who composed his tenantry and domestic establishment, were far from being people with no nonsense about them. There was, alas! a great deal of nonsense about them; with ghosts, witches, and traditions as old as Merlin, they seemed to surround him with a fairy ring of nonsense. But the magic circle had one center: there was one point in which the curving conversation of the rustics always returned. It was a point that always pricked the Squire to exasperation, and even in this short walk he seemed to strike it everywhere. He paused before descending the steps from the lawn to speak to the gardener about potting some foreign shrubs, and the gardener seemed to be gloomily gratified, in every line of his leathery brown visage, at the chance of indicating that he had formed a low opinion of foreign shrubs.

"We wish you'd get rid of what you've got here, sir," he observed, digging doggedly. "Nothing'll grow right with them here."

"Shrubs!" said the Squire, laughing. "You don't call the peacock trees shrubs, do you? Fine tall trees—you ought to be proud of them."

"Ill weeds grow apace," observed the gardener. "Weeds can grow as houses when somebody plants them." Then he added: "Him that sowed tares in the Bible, Squire."

"Oh, blast your—" began the Squire, and then replaced the more apt and alliterative word "Bible" by the general word "superstition." He was himself a robust rationalist, but he went to church to set his tenants an example. Of what, it would have puzzled him to say.

A little way along the lower path by the trees he encountered a wood-cutter, one Martin, who was more explicit, having more of a grievance. His daughter was at that time seriously ill with a fever recently common on that coast, and the Squire, who was a kind-hearted gentleman, would normally have made allowances for low spirits and loss of temper. But he came near to losing his own again when the peasant persisted in connecting his tragedy with the traditional monomania about the foreign trees.

"If she were well enough I'd move her," said the woodcutter, "as we can't move them, I suppose. I'd just like to get my chopper into them and feel 'em come crashing down."

"One would think they were dragons," said Vane.

"And that's about what they look like," replied Martin. "Look at 'em!"

The woodman was naturally a rougher and even wilder figure than the gardener. His face also was brown, and looked like an antique parchment, and it was framed in an outlandish arrangement of raven beard and whiskers, which was really a fashion fifty years ago, but might have been five thousand years old or older. Phoenicians, one felt, trading on those strange shores in the morning of the world, might have combed or curled or braided their blue-black hair into some such quaint patterns. For this patch of population was as much a corner of Cornwall as Cornwall is a corner of England; a tragic and unique race, small and interrelated like a Celtic clan. The clan was older than the Vane family, though that was old as county families go. For in many such parts of England it is the aristocrats who are the latest arrivals. It was the sort of racial type that is supposed to be passing, and perhaps has already passed.

The obnoxious objects stood some hundred yards away from the speaker, who waved toward them with his ax; and there was something suggestive in the comparison. That coast, to begin with, stretching toward the sunset, was itself almost as fantastic as a sunset cloud. It was cut out against the emerald or indigo of the sea in graven horns and crescents that might be the cast or mold of some such crested serpents; and, beneath, was pierced and fretted by caves and crevices, as if by the boring of some such titanic worms. Over and above this draconian architecture of the earth a veil of gray woods hung thinner like a

vapor; woods which the witchcraft of the sea had, as usual, both blighted
and blown out of shape. To the right the trees trailed along the sea
front in a single line, each drawn out in thin wild lines like a caricature.
At the other end of their extent they multiplied into a huddle of hunch-
backed trees, a wood spreading toward a projecting part of the high
coast. It was here that the sight appeared to which so many eyes and
minds seemed to be almost automatically turning.

Out of the middle of this low, and more or less level wood, rose
three separate stems that shot up and soared into the sky like a lighthouse out of the waves or a church spire out of the village roofs. They
formed a clump of three columns close together, which might well be
the mere bifurcation, or rather trifurcation, of one tree, the lower part
being lost or sunken in the thick wood around. Everything about them
suggested something stranger and more southern than anything even
in that last peninsula of Britain which pushes out farthest toward Spain
and Africa and the southern stars. Their leathery leafage had sprouted
in advance of the faint mist of yellow-green around them, and it was
of another and less natural green, tinged with blue, like the colors of a
kingfisher. But one might fancy it the scales of some three-headed
dragon towering over a herd of huddled and fleeing cattle.

"I am exceedingly sorry your girl is so unwell," said Vane shortly.
"But really—" and he strode down the steep road with plunging strides.

The boat was already secured to the little stone jetty, and the boatman, a younger shadow of the woodcutter—and, indeed, a nephew of
that useful malcontent—saluted his territorial lord with the sullen formality of the family. The Squire acknowledged it casually and had soon
forgotten all such things in shaking hands with the visitor who had just
come ashore. The visitor was a long, loose man, very lean to be so
young, whose long, fine features seemed wholly fitted together of bone
and nerve, and seemed somehow to contrast with his hair, that showed
in vivid yellow patches upon his hollow temples under the brim of his
white holiday hat. He was carefully dressed in exquisite taste, though
he had come straight from a considerable sea voyage; and he carried
something in his hand which in his long European travels, and even
longer European visits, he had almost forgotten to call a gripsack.

Mr. Cyprian Paynter was an American who lived in Italy. There was
a good deal more to be said about him, for he was a very acute and

cultivated gentleman; but those two facts would, perhaps, cover most of the others. Storing his mind like a museum with the wonder of the Old World, but all lit up as by a window with the wonder of the New, he had fallen heir to some thing of the unique critical position of Ruskin or Pater, and was further famous as a discoverer of minor poets. He was a judicious discoverer, and he did not turn all his minor poets into major prophets. If his geese were swans, they were not all Swans of Avon. He had even incurred the deadly suspicion of classicism by differing from his young friends, the Punctuist Poets, when they produced versification consisting exclusively of commas and colons. He had a more humane sympathy with the modern flame kindled from the embers of Celtic mythology, and it was in reality the recent appearance of a Cornish poet, a sort of parallel to the new Irish poets, which had brought him on this occasion to Cornwall. He was, indeed, far too well-mannered to allow a host to guess that any pleasure was being sought outside his own hospitality. He had a long standing invitation from Vane, whom he had met in Cyprus in the latter's days of undiplomatic diplomacy; and Vane was not aware that relations had only been thus renewed after the critic had read Merlin and Other Verses, by a new writer named John Treherne. Nor did the Squire even begin to realize the much more diplomatic diplomacy by which he had been induced to invite the local bard to lunch on the very day of the American critic's arrival.

Mr. Paynter was still standing with his gripsack, gazing in a trance of true admiration at the hollowed crags, topped by the gray, grotesque wood, and crested finally by the three fantastic trees.

"It is like being shipwrecked on the coast of fairyland," he said,

"I hope you haven't been shipwrecked much," replied his host, smiling. "I fancy Jake here can look after you very well."

Mr. Paynter looked across at the boatman and smiled also. "I am afraid," he said, "our friend is not quite so enthusiastic for this landscape as I am."

"Oh, the trees, I suppose!" said the Squire wearily.

The boatman was by normal trade a fisherman; but as his house, built of black tarred timber, stood right on the foreshore a few yards from the pier, he was employed in such cases as a sort of ferryman. He was a big, black-browed youth generally silent, but something seemed now to sting him into speech.

"Well, sir," he said, "everybody knows it's not natural. Everybody knows the sea blights trees and beats them under, when they're only just trees. These things thrive like some unholy great seaweed that don't belong to the land at all. It's like the—the blessed sea serpent got on shore, Squire, and eating everything up."

"There is some stupid legend," said Squire Vane gruffly. "But come up into the garden; I want to introduce you to my daughter."

When, however, they reached the little table under the tree, the apparently immovable young lady had moved away after all, and it was some time before they came upon the track of her. She had risen, though languidly, and wandered slowly along the upper path of the terraced garden looking down on the lower path where it ran closer to the main bulk of the little wood by the sea.

Her languor was not a feebleness but rather a fullness of life, like that of a child half awake; she seemed to stretch herself and enjoy everything without noticing anything. She passed the wood, into the gray huddle of which a single white path vanished through a black hole. Along this part of the terrace ran something like a low rampart or balustrade, embowered with flowers at intervals; and she leaned over it, looking down at another glimpse of the glowing sea behind the clump of trees, and on another irregular path tumbling down to the pier and the boatman's cottage on the beach.

As she gazed, sleepily enough, she saw that a strange figure was very actively climbing the path, apparently coming from the fisherman's cottage; so actively that a moment afterwards it came out between the trees and stood upon the path just below her. It was not only a figure strange to her, but one somewhat strange in itself. It was that of a man still young, and seeming somehow younger than his own clothes, which were not only shabby but antiquated; clothes common enough in texture, yet carried in an uncommon fashion. He wore what was presumably a light waterproof, perhaps through having come off the sea; but it was held at the throat by one button, and hung, sleeves and all, more like a cloak than a coat. He rested one bony hand on a black stick; under the shadow of his broad hat his black hair hung down in a tuft or two. His face, which was swarthy, but rather handsome in itself, wore something that may have been a slightly embarrassed smile, but had too much the appearance of a sneer.

Whether this apparition was a tramp or a trespasser, or a friend of some of the fishers or woodcutters, Barbara Vane was quite unable to guess. He removed his hat, still with his unaltered and rather sinister smile, and said civilly: "Excuse me. The Squire asked me to call." Here he caught sight of Martin, the woodman, who was shifting along the path, thinning the thin trees; and the stranger made a familiar salute with one finger.

The girl did not know what to say. "Have you—have you come about cutting the wood?" she asked at last.

"I would I were so honest a man," replied the stranger. "Martin is, I fancy, a distant cousin of mine; we Cornish folk just round here are nearly all related, you know; but I do not cut wood. I do not cut anything, except, perhaps, capers. I am, so to speak, a jongleur."

"A what?" asked Barbara.

"A minstrel, shall we say?" answered the newcomer, and looked up at her more steadily. During a rather odd silence their eyes rested on each other. What she saw has been already noted, though by her, at any rate, not in the least understood. What he saw was a decidedly beautiful woman with a statuesque face and hair that shone in the sun like a helmet of copper.

"Do you know," he went on, "that in this old place, hundreds of years ago, a jongleur may really have stood where I stand, and a lady may really have looked over that wall and thrown him money?"

"Do you want money?" she asked, all at sea.

"Well," drawled the stranger, "in the sense of lacking it, perhaps, but I fear there is no place now for a minstrel, except nigger minstrel. I must apologize for not blacking my face."

She laughed a little in her bewilderment, and said: "Well, I hardly think you need do that."

"You think the natives here are dark enough already, perhaps," he observed calmly. "After all, we are aborigines, and are treated as such."

She threw out some desperate remark about the weather or the scenery, and wondered what would happen next.

"The prospect is certainly beautiful," he assented, in the same enigmatic manner. "There is only one thing in it I am doubtful about."

While she stood in silence he slowly lifted his black stick like a long black finger and pointed it at the peacock trees above the wood. And a queer feeling of disquiet fell on the girl, as if he were, by that mere gesture, doing a destructive act and could send a blight upon the garden.

The strained and almost painful silence was broken by the voice of Squire Vane, loud even while it was still distant.

"We couldn't make out where you'd got to, Barbara," he said. "This is my friend, Mr. Cyprian Paynter." The next moment he saw the stranger and stopped, a little puzzled. It was only Mr. Cyprian Paynter himself who was equal to the situation. He had seen months ago a portrait of the new Cornish poet in some American literary magazine, and he found himself, to his surprise, the introducer instead of the introduced.

"Why, Squire," he said in considerable astonishment, "don't you know Mr. Treherne? I supposed, of course, he was a neighbor."

"Delighted to see you, Mr. Treherne," said the Squire, recovering his manners with a certain genial confusion. "So pleased you were able to come. This is Mr. Paynter—my daughter," and, turning with a certain boisterous embarrassment, he led the way to the table under the tree.

Cyprian Paynter followed, inwardly revolving a puzzle which had taken even his experience by surprise. The American, if intellectually an aristocrat, was still socially and subconsciously a democrat. It had never crossed his mind that the poet should be counted lucky to know the squire and not the squire to know the poet. The honest patronage in Vane's hospitality was something which made Paynter feel he was, after all, an exile in England.

The Squire, anticipating the trial of luncheon with a strange literary man, had dealt with the case tactfully from his own standpoint. County society might have made the guest feel like a fish out of water; and, except for the American critic and the local lawyer and doctor, worthy middle-class people who fitted into the picture, he had kept it as a family party. He was a widower, and when the meal had been laid out on the garden table, it was Barbara who presided as hostess. She had the new poet on her right hand and it made her very uncomfortable. She had practically offered that fallacious jongleur money, and it did not make it easier to offer him lunch.

"The whole countryside's gone mad," announced the Squire, by way of the latest local news. "It's about this infernal legend of ours."

"I collect legends," said Paynter, smiling.

"You must remember I haven't yet had a chance to collect yours. And this," he added, looking round at the romantic coast, "is a fine theater for anything dramatic."

"Oh, it's dramatic in its way," admitted Vane, not without a faint satisfaction. "It's all about those things over there we call the peacock trees—I suppose, because of the queer color of the leaf, you know, though I have heard they make a shrill noise in a high wind that's supposed to be like the shriek of a peacock; something like a bamboo in the botanical structure, perhaps. Well, those trees are supposed to have been brought over from Barbary by my ancestor Sir Walter Vane, one of the Elizabethan patriots or pirates, or whatever you call them. They say that at the end of his last voyage the villagers gathered on the beach down there and saw the boat standing in from the sea, and the new trees stood up in the boat like a mast, all gay with leaves out of season, like green bunting. And as they watched they thought at first that the boat was steering oddly, and then that it wasn't steering at all; and when it drifted to the shore at last every man in that boat was dead, and Sir Walter Vane, with his sword drawn, was leaning up against the tree trunk, as stiff as the tree."

"Now this is rather curious," remarked Paynter thoughtfully. "I told you I collected legends, and I fancy I can tell you the beginning of the story of which that is the end, though it comes hundreds of miles across the sea."

He tapped meditatively on the table with his thin, taper fingers, like a man trying to recall a tune. He had, indeed, made a hobby of such fables, and he was not without vanity about his artistic touch in telling them.

"Oh, do tell us your part of it!" cried Barbara Vane, whose air of sunny sleepiness seemed in some vague degree to have fallen from her.

The American bowed across the table with a serious politeness, and then began playing idly with a quaint ring on his long finger as he talked.

"If you go down to the Barbary Coast, where the last wedge of the forest narrows down between the desert and the great tideless sea, you will find the natives still telling a strange story about a saint of the Dark Ages. There, on the twilight border of the Dark Continent, you feel the Dark Ages. I have only visited the place once, though it lies, so to speak, opposite to the Italian city where I lived for years, and yet you would hardly believe how the topsy-turvydom and transmigration of this myth somehow seemed less mad than they really are, with the wood loud with lions at night and that dark red solitude beyond. They say that the hermit St. Securis, living there among trees, grew to love them like companions; since, though great giants with many arms like Briareus, they were the mildest and most blameless of the creatures; they did not devour like the lions, but rather opened their arms to all the little birds. And he prayed that they might be loosened from time to time to walk like other things. And the trees were moved upon the prayers of Securis, as they were at the songs of Orpheus. The men of the desert were stricken from afar with fear, seeing the saint walking with a walking grove, like a schoolmaster with his boys. For the trees were thus freed under strict conditions of discipline. They were to return at the sound of the hermit's bell, and, above all, to copy the wild beasts in walking only to destroy and devour nothing. Well, it is said that one of the trees heard a voice that was not the saint's; that in the warm green twilight of one summer evening it became conscious of some thing sitting and speaking in its branches in the guise of a great bird, and it was that which once spoke from a tree in the guise of a great serpent. As the voice grew louder among its murmuring leaves the tree was torn with a great desire to stretch out and snatch at the birds that flew harmlessly about their nests, and pluck them to pieces. Finally, the tempter filled the tree-top with his own birds of pride, the starry pageant of the pea-cocks. And the spirit of the brute overcame the spirit of the tree, and it rent and consumed the blue-green birds till not a plume was left, and returned to the quiet tribe of trees. But they say that when spring came all the other trees put forth leaves, but this put forth feathers of a strange hue and pattern. And by that monstrous assimilation the saint knew of the sin, and he rooted that one tree to the earth with a judg-ment, so that evil should fall on any who removed it again. That, Squire, is the beginning in the deserts of the tale that ended here, almost in this garden."

"And the end is about as reliable as the beginning, I should say," said Vane. "Yours is a nice plain tale for a small tea-party; a quiet little bit of still-life, that is."

"What a queer, horrible story," exclaimed Barbara. "It makes one feel like a cannibal."

"Ex Africa," said the lawyer, smiling. "It comes from a cannibal country. I think it's the touch of the tar-brush, that nightmare feeling that you don't know whether the hero is a plant or a man or a devil. Don't you feel it sometimes in 'Uncle Remus'?"

"True," said Paynter. "Perfectly true." And he looked at the lawyer with a new interest. The lawyer, who had been introduced as Mr. Ashe, was one of those people who are more worth looking at than most people realize when they look. If Napoleon had been red-haired, and had bent all his powers with a curious contentment upon the petty lawsuits of a province, he might have looked much the same; the head with the red hair was heavy and powerful; the figure in its dark, quiet clothes was comparatively insignificant, as was Napoleon's. He seemed more at ease in the Squire's society than the doctor, who, though a gentleman, was a shy one, and a mere shadow of his professional brother.

"As you truly say," remarked Paynter, "the story seems touched with quite barbarous elements, probably Negro. Originally, though, I think there was really a hagiological story about some hermit, though some of the higher critics say St. Securis never existed, but was only an allegory of arboriculture, since his name is the Latin for an ax."

"Oh, if you come to that," remarked the poet Treherne, "you might as well say Squire Vane doesn't exist, and that he's only an allegory for a weathercock." Something a shade too cool about this sally drew the lawyer's red brows together. He looked across the table and met the poet's somewhat equivocal smile.

"Do I understand, Mr. Treherne," asked Ashe, "that you support the miraculous claims of St. Securis in this case. Do you, by any chance, believe in the walking trees?"

"I see men as trees walking," answered the poet, "like the man cured of blindness in the Gospel. By the way, do I understand that you support the miraculous claims of that—thaumaturgist?"

Paynter intervened swiftly and suavely. "Now that sounds a fascinating piece of psychology. You see men as trees?"

"As I can't imagine why men should walk, I can't imagine why trees shouldn't," answered Treherne.

"Obviously, it is the nature of the organism," interposed the medical guest, Dr. Burton Brown; "it is necessary in the very type of vegetable structure."

"In other words, a tree sticks in the mud from year's end to year's end," answered Treherne. "So do you stop in your consulting room from ten to eleven every day. And don't you fancy a fairy, looking in at your window for a flash after having just jumped over the moon and played mulberry bush with the Pleiades, would think you were a vegetable structure, and that sitting still was the nature of the organism?"

"I don't happen to believe in fairies," said the doctor rather stiffly, for the *argumentum ad hominem* was becoming too common. A sulphurous subconscious anger seemed to radiate from the dark poet.

"Well, I should hope not, Doctor," began the Squire, in his loud and friendly style, and then stopped, seeing the other's attention arrested.

The silent butler waiting on the guests had appeared behind the doctor's chair, and was saying something in the low, level tones of the well-trained servant. He was so smooth a specimen of the type that others never noticed, at first, that he also repeated the dark portrait, however varnished, so common in this particular family of Cornish Celts. His face was sallow and even yellow, and his hair indigo black. He went by the name of Miles. Some felt oppressed by the tribal type in this tiny corner of England. They felt somehow as if all these dark faces were the masks of a secret society.

The doctor rose with a half apology. "I must ask pardon for disturbing this pleasant party; I am called away on duty. Please don't let anybody move. We have to be ready for these things, you know. Perhaps Mr. Treherne will admit that my habits are not so very vegetable, after all."

With this Parthian shaft, at which there was some laughter, he strode away very rapidly across the sunny lawn to where the road dipped down toward the village.

"He is very good among the poor," said the girl with an honorable seriousness.

"A capital fellow," agreed the Squire. "Where is Miles? You will have a cigar, Mr. Treherne?"

And he got up from the table; the rest followed, and the group broke up on the lawn.

"Remarkable man, Treherne," said the American to the lawyer conversationally.

"Remarkable is the word," assented Ashe rather grimly. "But I don't think I'll make any remark about him."

The Squire, too impatient to wait for the yellow-faced Miles, had betaken himself indoors for the cigars, and Barbara found herself once more paired off with the poet, as she floated along the terrace garden; but this time, symbolically enough, upon the same level of lawn. Mr. Treherne looked less eccentric after having shed his curious cloak, and seemed a quieter and more casual figure.

"I didn't mean to be rude to you just now," she said abruptly.

"And that's the worst of it," replied the man of letters, "for I'm horribly afraid I did mean to be rude to you. When I looked up and saw you up there something surged up in me that was in all the revolutions of history. Oh, there was admiration in it too! Perhaps there was idolatry in all the iconoclasts."

He seemed to have a power of reaching rather intimate conversation in one silent and cat-like bound, as he had scaled the steep road, and it made her feel him to be dangerous, and perhaps unscrupulous. She changed the subject sharply, not without it movement toward gratifying her own curiosity.

"What *did* you mean by all that about walking trees?" she asked. "Don't tell me you really believe in a magic tree that eats birds!"

"I should probably surprise you," said Treherne gravely, "more by what I don't believe than by what I do."

Then, after a pause, he made a general gesture toward the house and garden. "I'm afraid I don't believe in all this; for instance, in Elizabethan houses and Elizabethan families and the way estates have been improved, and the rest of it. Look at our friend the woodcutter now." And he pointed to the man with the quaint black beard, who was still plying his ax upon the timber below. "That man's family goes back for ages, and it was far richer and freer in what you call the Dark Ages than it is now. Wait till the Cornish peasant writes a history of Cornwall."

"But what in the world," she demanded, "has this to do with whether you believe in a tree eating birds?"

"Why should I confess what I believe in?" he said, a muffled drum of mutiny in his voice. "The gentry came here and took our land and took our labor and took our customs. And now, after exploitation, a viler thing, education! They must take our dreams!"

"Well, this dream was rather a nightmare, wasn't it?" asked Barbara, smiling; and the next moment grew quite grave, saying almost anxiously: "But here's Doctor Brown back again. Why, he looks quite upset."

The doctor, a black figure on the green lawn, was, indeed, coming toward them at a very vigorous walk. His body and gait very much younger than his face, which seemed prematurely lined as with worry; his brow was bald, and projected from the straight, dark hair behind it. He was visibly paler than when he left the lunch table.

"I am sorry to say, Miss Vane," he said, "that I am the bearer of bad news to poor Martin, the woodman here. His daughter died half an hour ago."

"Oh," cried Barbara warmly, "I am *so* sorry!"

"So am I," said the doctor, and passed on rather abruptly; he ran down the stone steps between the stone urns; and they saw him in talk with the woodcutter. They could not see the woodcutter's face. He stood with his back to them, but they saw something that seemed more moving than any change of countenance. The man's hand holding the ax rose high above his head, and for a flash it seemed as if he would have cut down the doctor. But in fact he was not looking at the doctor. His face was set toward the cliff, where, sheer out of the dwarf forest, rose, gigantic and gilded by the sun, the trees of pride.

The strong brown hand made a movement and was empty. The ax went circling swiftly through the air, its head showing like a silver crescent against the gray twilight of the trees. It did not reach its tall objective, but fell among the undergrowth, shaking up a flying litter of birds. But in the poet's memory, full of primal things, something seemed to say that he had seen the birds of some pagan augury, the ax of some pagan sacrifice.

A moment after the man made a heavy movement forward, as if to recover his tool; but the doctor put a hand on his arm.

"Never mind that now," they heard him say sadly and kindly. "The Squire will excuse you any more work, I know."

Something made the girl look at Treherne. He stood gazing, his head a little bent, and one of his black elf-locks had fallen forward over his forehead. And again she had the sense of a shadow over the grass; she almost felt as if the grass were a host of fairies, and that the fairies were not her friends.

II

The Wager of Squire Vane

It was more than a month before the legend of the peacock trees was again discussed in the Squire's circle. It fell out one evening, when his eccentric taste for meals in the garden that gathered the company round the same table, now lit with a lamp and laid out for dinner in a glowing spring twilight.

It was even the same company, for in the few weeks intervening they had insensibly grown more and more into each other's lives, forming a little group like a club. The American aesthete was of course the most active agent, his resolution to pluck out the heart of the Cornish poet's mystery leading him again and again to influence his flighty host for such reunions. Even Mr. Ashe, the lawyer, seemed to have swallowed his half-humorous prejudices; and the doctor, though a rather sad and silent, was a companionable and considerate man. Paynter had even read Treherne's poetry aloud, and he read admirably; he had also read other things, not aloud, grubbing up everything in the neighborhood, from guidebooks to epitaphs, that could throw a light on local antiquities. And it was that evening when the lamplight and the last daylight had kindled the colors of the wine and silver on the table under the tree, that he announced a new discovery.

"Say, Squire," he remarked, with one of his rare Americanisms, "about those bogey trees of yours; I don't believe you know half the tales told round here about them. It seems they have a way of eating things. Not that I have any ethical objection to eating things," he continued, helping himself elegantly to green cheese. "But I have more or less, broadly speaking, an objection to eating people."

"Eating people!" repeated Barbara Vane.

"I know a globe-trotter mustn't be fastidious," replied Mr. Paynter. "But I repeat firmly, an objection to eating people. The peacock trees seem to have progressed since the happy days of innocence when they only ate peacocks. If you ask the people here—the fisherman who lives on that beach, or the man that mows this very lawn in front of us— they'll tell you tales taller than any tropical one I brought you from the Barbary Coast. If you ask them what happened to the fisherman Peters, who got drunk on All Hallows Eve, they'll tell you he lost his way in that little wood, tumbled down asleep under the wicked trees, and then— evaporated, vanished, was licked up like dew by the sun. If you ask them where Harry Hawke is, the widow's little son, they'll just tell you he's swallowed; that he was dared to climb the trees and sit there all night, and did it. What the trees did God knows; the habits of a vegetable ogre leave one a little vague. But they even add the agreeable detail that a new branch appears on the tree when somebody has petered out in this style."

"What new nonsense is this?" cried Vane. "I know there's some crazy yarn about the trees spreading fever, though every educated man knows why these epidemics return occasionally. And I know they say you can tell the noise of them among other trees in a gale, and I dare say you can. But even Cornwall isn't a lunatic asylum, and a tree that dines on a passing tourist—"

"Well, the two tales are reconcilable enough," put in the poet quietly. "If there were a magic that killed men when they came close, it's likely to strike them with sickness when they stand far off. In the old romance the dragon, that devours people, often blasts others with a sort of poisonous breath."

Ashe looked across at the speaker steadily, not to say stonily.

"Do I understand," he inquired, "that you swallow the swallowing trees too?"

Treherne's dark smile was still on the defensive; his fencing always annoyed the other, and he seemed not without malice in the matter.

"Swallowing is a metaphor," he said, "about me, if not about the trees. And metaphors take us at once into dreamland—no bad place, either. This garden, I think, gets more and more like a dream at this corner of the day and night, that might lead us anywhere."

The yellow horn of the moon had appeared silently and as if suddenly over the black horns of the seaweed, seeming to announce as night something which till then had been evening. A night breeze came in between the trees and raced stealthily across the turf, and as they ceased speaking they heard, not only the seething grass, but the sea itself move and sound in all the cracks and caves round them and below them and on every side. They all felt the note that had been struck—the American as an art critic and the poet as a poet; and the Squire, who believed himself boiling with an impatience purely rational, did not really understand his own impatience. In him, more perhaps than the others—more certainly than he knew himself—the sea wind went to the head like wine.

"Credulity is a curious thing," went on Treherne in a low voice. "It is more negative than positive, and yet it is infinite. Hundreds of men will avoid walking under a ladder; they don't know where the door of the ladder will lead. They don't really think God would throw a thunderbolt at them for such a thing. They don't know what would happen, that is just the point; but yet they step aside as from a precipice. So the poor people here may or may not believe anything; they don't go into those trees at night."

"I walk under a ladder whenever I can," cried Vane, in quite unnecessary excitement.

"You belong to a Thirteen Club," said the poet. "You walk under a ladder on Friday to dine thirteen at a table, everybody spilling the salt. But even you don't go into those trees at night."

Squire Vane stood up, his silver hair flaming in the wind.

"I'll stop all night in your tomfool wood and up your tomfool trees," he said. "I'll do it for twopence or two thousand pounds, if anyone will take the bet."

Without waiting for reply, he snatched up his wide white hat and settled it on with a fierce gesture, and had gone off in great leonine strides across the lawn before anyone at the table could move.

The stillness was broken by Miles, the butler, who dropped and broke one of the plates he carried. He stood looking after his master with his long, angular chin thrust out, looking yellower where it caught the yellow light of the lamp below. His face was thus sharply in shadow, but Paynter fancied for a moment it was convulsed by some passion passing surprise. But the face was quite as usual when it turned, and Paynter realized that a night of fancies had begun, like the cross purposes of the "Midsummer Night's Dream."

The wood of the strange trees, toward which the Squire was walking, lay so far forward on the headland, which ultimately almost overhung the sea, that it could be approached by only one path, which shone clearly like a silver ribbon in the twilight. The ribbon ran along the edge of the cliff, where the single row of deformed trees ran beside it all the way, and eventually plunged into the closer mass of trees by one natural gateway, a mere gap in the wood, looking dark, like a lion's mouth. What became of the path inside could not be seen, but it doubtless led round the hidden roots of the great central trees. The Squire was already within a yard or two of this dark entry when his daughter rose from the table and took a step or two after him as if to call him back.

Treherne had also risen, and stood as if dazed at the effect of his idle defiance. When Barbara moved he seemed to recover himself, and stepping after her, said something which Paynter did not hear. He said it casually and even distantly enough, but it clearly suggested something to her mind; for, after a moment's thought, she nodded and walked back, not toward the table, but apparently toward the house. Paynter looked after her with a momentary curiosity, and when he turned again the Squire had vanished into the hole in the wood.

"He's gone," said Treherne, with a clang of finality in his tones, like the slamming of a door.

"Well, suppose he has?" cried the lawyer, roused at the voice. "The Squire can go into his own wood, I suppose! What the devil's all the fuss about, Mr. Paynter? Don't tell me you think there's any harm in that plantation of sticks."

"No, I don't," said Paynter, throwing one leg over another and lighting a cigar. "But I shall stop here till he comes out."

"Very well," said Ashe shortly, "I'll stop with you, if only to see the end of this farce."

The doctor said nothing, but he also kept his seat and accepted one of the American's cigars. If Treherne had been attending to the matter he might have noted, with his sardonic superstition, a curious fact—that, while all three men were tacitly condemning themselves to stay out all night if necessary, all, by one blank omission or oblivion, assumed that it was impossible to follow their host into the wood just in front of them. But Treherne, though still in the garden, had wandered away from the garden table, and was pacing along the single line of trees against the dark sea. They had in their regular interstices, showing the sea as through a series of windows, something of the look of the ghost or skeleton of a cloister, and he, having thrown his coat once more over his neck, like a cape, passed to and fro like the ghost of some not very sane monk.

All these men, whether skeptics or mystics, looked back for the rest of their lives on that night as on something unnatural. They sat still or started up abruptly, and paced the great garden in long detours, so that it seemed that no three of them were together at a time, and none knew who would be his companion; yet their rambling remained within the same dim and mazy space. They fell into snatches of uneasy slumber; these were very brief, and yet they felt as if the whole sitting, strolling, or occasional speaking had been parts of a single dream.

Paynter woke once, and found Ashe sitting opposite him at a table otherwise empty; his face dark in shadow and his cigar-end like the red eye of a Cyclops. Until the lawyer spoke, in his steady voice, Paynter was positively afraid of him. He answered at random and nodded again; when he again woke the lawyer was gone, and what was opposite him was the bald, pale brow of the doctor; there seemed suddenly something ominous in the familiar fact that he wore spectacles. And yet the vanishing Ashe had only vanished a few yards away, for he turned at that instant and strolled back to the table. With a jerk Paynter realized that his nightmare was but a trick of sleep or sleeplessness, and spoke in his natural voice, but rather loud.

"So you've joined us again; where's Treherne?"

"Oh, still revolving, I suppose, like a polar bear under those trees on the cliff," replied Ashe, motioning with his cigar, "looking at what an older (and you will forgive me for thinking a somewhat better) poet called the wine-dark sea. It really has a sort of purple shade; look at it."

Paynter looked; he saw the wine-dark sea and the fantastic trees that fringed it, but he did not see the poet; the cloister was already empty of its restless monk.

"Gone somewhere else," he said, with futility far from characteristic. "He'll be back here presently. This is an interesting vigil, but vigil loses some of its intensity when you can't keep awake. Ah! Here's Treherne; so we're all mustered, as the politician said when Mr. Colman came late for dinner. No, the doctor's off again. How restless we all are!" The poet had drawn near, his feet were falling soft on the grass, and was gazing at them with a singular attentiveness.

"It will soon be over," he said.

"What?" snapped Ashe very abruptly.

"The night, of course," replied Treherne in a motionless manner. "The darkest hour has passed."

"Didn't some other minor poet remark," inquired Paynter flippantly, "that the darkest hour before the dawn—? My God, what was that? It was like a scream."

"It was a scream," replied the poet. "The scream of a peacock."

Ashe stood up, his strong pale face against his red hair, and said furiously: "What the devil do you mean?"

"Oh, perfectly natural causes, as Dr. Brown would say," replied Treherne. "Didn't the Squire tell us the trees had a shrill note of their own when the wind blew? The wind's beating up again from the sea; I shouldn't wonder if there was a storm before dawn."

Dawn indeed came gradually with a growing noise of wind, and the purple sea began to boil about the dark volcanic cliffs. The first change in the sky showed itself only in the shapes of the wood and the single stems growing darker but clearer; and above the gray clump, against a glimpse of growing light, they saw aloft the evil trinity of the trees. In their long lines there seemed to Paynter something faintly serpentine and even spiral. He could almost fancy he saw them slowly revolving as in some cyclic dance, but this, again, was but a last delusion of dreamland, for a few seconds later he was again asleep. In dreams he toiled through a tangle of inconclusive tales, each filled with the same stress and noise of sea and sea wind; and above and outside all other voices the wailing of the Trees of Pride.

When he woke it was broad day, and a bloom of early light lay on wood and garden and on fields and farms for miles away. The comparative common sense that daylight brings even to the sleepless drew him alertly to his feet, and showed him all his companions standing about the lawn in similar attitudes of expectancy. There was no need to ask what they were expecting. They were waiting to hear the nocturnal experiences, comic or commonplace or whatever they might prove to be, of that eccentric friend, whose experiment (whether from some subconscious fear or some fancy of honor) they had not ventured to interrupt.

Hour followed hour, and still nothing stirred in the wood save an occasional bird. The Squire, like most men of his type, was an early riser, and it was not likely that he would in this case sleep late; it was much more likely, in the excitement in which he had left them, that he would not sleep at all. Yet it was clear that he must be sleeping, perhaps by some reaction from a strain. By the time the sun was high in heaven Ashe the lawyer, turning to the others, spoke abruptly and to the point.

"Shall we go into the wood now?" asked Paynter, and almost seemed to hesitate.

"I will go in," said Treherne simply. Then, drawing up his dark head in answer to their glances, he added:

"No, do not trouble yourselves. It is never the believer who is afraid."

For the second time they saw a man mount the white curling path and disappear into the gray tangled wood, but this time they did not have to wait long to see him again.

A few minutes later he reappeared in the woodland gateway, and came slowly toward them across the grass. He stopped before the doctor, who stood nearest, and said something. It was repeated to the others, and went round the ring with low cries of incredulity. The others plunged into the wood and returned wildly, and were seen speaking to others again who gathered from the house; the wild wireless telegraphy which is the education of countryside communities spread it farther and farther before the fact itself was fully realized; and before nightfall a quarter of the county knew that Squire Vane had vanished like a burst bubble.

Widely as the wild story was repeated, and patiently as it was pondered, it was long before there was even the beginning of a sequel to it. In the interval Paynter had politely removed himself from the house of mourning, or rather of questioning, but only so far as the village inn; for Barbara Vane was glad of the traveler's experience and sympathy, in addition to that afforded her by the lawyer and doctor as old friends of the family. Even Treherne was not discouraged from his occasional visits with a view to helping the hunt for the lost man. The five held many counsels round the old garden table, at which the unhappy master of the house had dined for the last time; and Barbara wore her old mask of stone, if it was now a more tragic mask. She had shown no passion after the first morning of discovery, when she had broken forth once, speaking strangely enough in the view of some of her hearers.

She had come slowly out of the house, to which her own or some one else's wisdom had relegated her during the night of the wager; and it was clear from her face that somebody had told her the truth; Miles, the butler, stood on the steps behind her; and it was probably he.

"Do not be much distressed, Miss Vane," said Doctor Brown, in a low and rather uncertain voice. "The search in the wood has hardly begun. I am convinced we shall find—something quite simple."

"The doctor is right," said Ashe, in his firm tones; "I myself—"

"The doctor is not right," said the girl, turning a white face on the speaker, "I know better. The poet is right. The poet is always right. Oh, he has been here from the beginning of the world, and seen wonders and terrors that are all round our path, and only hiding behind a bush or a stone. You and your doctoring and your science—why, you have only been here for a few fumbling generations; and you can't conquer even your own enemies of the flesh. Oh, forgive me, Doctor, I know you do splendidly; but the fever comes in the village, and the people die and die for all that. And now it's my poor father. God help us all! The only thing left is to believe in God; for we can't help believing in devils." And she left them, still walking quite slowly, but in such a fashion that no one could go after her.

The spring had already begun to ripen into summer, and spread a green tent from the tree over the garden table, when the American visitor, sitting there with his two professional companions, broke the silence by saying what had long been in his mind.

"Well," he said, "I suppose whatever we may think it wise to say, we have all begun to think of a possible conclusion. It can't be put very delicately anyhow; but, after all, there's a very necessary business side to it. What are we going to do about poor Vane's affairs, apart from himself? I suppose you know," he added, in a low voice to the lawyer, "whether he made a will?"

"He left everything to his daughter unconditionally," replied Ashe. "But nothing can be done with it. There's no proof whatever that he's dead."

"No legal proof?" remarked Paynter dryly. A wrinkle of irritation had appeared in the big bald brow of Doctor Brown; and he made an impatient movement.

"Of course he's dead," he said. "What's the sense of all this legal fuss? We were watching this side of the wood, weren't we? A man couldn't have flown off those high cliffs over the sea; he could only have fallen off. What else can he be but dead?"

"I speak as a lawyer," returned Ashe, raising his eyebrows. "We can't presume his death, or have an inquest or anything till we find the poor fellow's body, or some remains that may reasonably be presumed to be his body."

"I see," observed Paynter quietly. "You speak as a lawyer; but I don't think it's very hard to guess what you think as a man."

"I own I'd rather be a man than a lawyer," said the doctor, rather roughly. "I'd no notion the law was such an ass. What's the good of keeping the poor girl out of her property, and the estate all going to pieces? Well, I must be off, or my patients will be going to pieces too."

And with a curt salutation he pursued his path down to the village.

"That man does his duty, if anybody does," remarked Paynter. "We must pardon his—shall I say manners or manner?"

"Oh, I bear him no malice," replied Ashe good-humoredly, "But I'm glad he's gone, because—well, because I don't want him to know how jolly right he is." And he leaned back in his chair and stared up at the roof of green leaves.

"You are sure," said Paynter, looking at the table, "that Squire Vane is dead?"

"More than that," said Ashe, still staring at the leaves. "I'm sure of how he died."

"Ah!" said the American, with an intake of breath, and they remained for a moment, one gazing at the tree and the other at the table.

"Sure is perhaps too strong a word," continued Ashe. "But my conviction will want some shaking. I don't envy the counsel for the defense."

"The counsel for the defense," repeated Paynter, and looked up quickly at his companion. He was struck again by the man's Napoleonic chin and jaw, as he had been when they first talked of the legend of St. Securis.

"Then," he began, "you don't think the trees—"

"The trees be damned!" snorted the lawyer. "The tree had two legs on that evening. What our friend the poet," he added, with a sneer, "would call a walking tree. Apropos of our friend the poet, you seemed surprised that night to find he was not walking poetically by the sea all the time, and I fear I affected to share your ignorance. I was not so sure then as I am now."

"Sure of what?" demanded the other.

"To begin with," said Ashe, "I'm sure our friend the poet followed Vane into the wood that night, for I saw him coming out again."

Paynter leaned forward, suddenly pale with excitement, and struck the wooden table so that it rattled.

"Mr. Ashe, you're wrong," he cried. "You're a wonderful man and you're wrong. You've probably got tons of true convincing evidence, and you're wrong. I know this poet; I know him as a poet; and that's just what you don't. I know you think he gave you crooked answers, and seemed to be all smiles and black looks at once; but you don't understand the type. I know now why you don't understand the Irish. Sometimes you think it's soft, and sometimes sly, and sometimes murderous, and sometimes uncivilized; and all the time it's only civilized; quivering with the sensitive irony of understanding all that you don't understand."

"Well," said Ashe shortly, "we'll see who's right."

"We will," cried Cyprian, and rose suddenly from the table. All the drooping of the aesthete had dropped from him; his Yankee accent rose high, like a horn of defiance, and there was nothing about him but the New World.

"I guess I will look into this myself," he said, stretching his long limbs like an athlete. "I search that little wood of yours to-morrow. It's a bit late, or I'd do it now."

"The wood has been searched," said the lawyer, rising also.

"Yes," drawled the American. "It's been searched by servants, policemen, local policeman, and quite a lot of people; and do you know I have a notion that nobody round here is likely to have searched it at all."

"And what are you going to do with it?" asked Ashe.

"What I bet they haven't done," replied Cyprian. "I'm going to climb a tree."

And with a quaint air of renewed cheerfulness he took himself away at a rapid walk to his inn.

He appeared at daybreak next morning outside the Vane Arms with all the air of one setting out on his travels in distant lands. He had a field glass slung over his shoulder, and a very large sheath knife buckled by a belt round his waist, and carried with the cool bravado of the bowie knife of a cowboy. But in spite of this backwoodsman's simplicity, or perhaps rather because of it, he eyed with rising relish the picturesque plan and sky line of the antiquated village, and especially the wooden square of the old inn sign that hung over his head; a shield, of which the charges seemed to him a mere medley of blue dolphins, gold crosses, and scarlet birds. The colors and cubic corners of that painted board pleased him like a play or a puppet show. He stood staring and straddling for some moments on the cobbles of the little market place; then he gave a short laugh and began to mount the steep streets toward the high park and garden beyond. From the high lawn, above the tree and table, he could see on one side the land stretch away past the house into a great rolling plain, which under the clear edges of the dawn seemed dotted with picturesque details. The woods here and there on the plain looked like green hedgehogs, as grotesque as the incongruous beasts found unaccountably walking in the blank spaces of mediaeval maps. The land, cut up into colored fields, recalled the heraldry of the signboard; this also was at once ancient and gay. On the other side the ground to seaward swept down and then up again to the famous or infamous wood; the square of strange trees lay silently tilted on the slope, also suggesting, if not a map, or least a bird's-eye view. Only the triple centerpiece of the peacock trees rose clear of the sky line; and these stood up in tranquil sunlight as things almost classical, a triangular temple of the winds. They seemed pagan in a newer and more placid sense; and he felt a newer and more boyish curiosity and courage for the consulting of the oracle. In all his wanderings he had never walked so lightly, for the connoisseur of sensations had found something to do at last; he was fighting for a friend.

He was brought to a standstill once, however, and that at the very gateway of the garden of the trees of knowledge. Just outside the black entry of the wood, now curtained with greener and larger leafage, he came on a solitary figure.

It was Martin, the woodcutter, wading in the bracken and looking about him in rather a lost fashion. The man seemed to be talking to himself.

"I dropped it here," he was saying. "But I'll never work with it again I reckon. Doctor wouldn't let me pick it up, when I wanted to pick it up; and now they've got it, like they've got the Squire. Wood and iron, wood and iron, but eating it's nothing to them."

"Come!" said Paynter kindly, remembering the man's domestic trouble. "Miss Vane will see you have anything you want, I know. And look here, don't brood on all those stories about the Squire. Is there the slightest trace of the trees having anything to do with it? Is there even this extra branch the idiots talked about?"

There had been growing on Paynter the suspicion that the man before him was not perfectly sane; yet he was much more startled by the sudden and cold sanity that looked for an instant out of the woodman's eyes, as he answered in his ordinary manner.

"Well, sir, did you count the branches before?"

Then he seemed to relapse; and Paynter left him wandering and wavering in the undergrowth; and entered the wood like one across whose sunny path a shadow has fallen for an instant.

Diving under the wood, he was soon threading a leafy path which, even under that summer sun, shone only with an emerald twilight, as if it were on the floor of the sea. It wound about more shakily than he had supposed, as if resolved to approach the central trees as if they were the heart of the maze at Hampton Court. They were the heart of the maze for him, anyhow; he sought them as straight as a crooked road would carry him; and, turning a final corner, he beheld, for the first time, the foundations of those towers of vegetation he had as yet only seen from above, as they stood waist-high in the woodland. He found the suspicion correct which supposed the tree branched from one great root, like a candelabrum; the fork, though stained and slimy with green fungoids, was quite near the ground, and offered a first foothold. He put his foot in it, and without a flash of hesitation went aloft, like Jack climbing the Bean stalk.

Above him the green roof of leaves and boughs seemed sealed like a firmament of foliage; but, by bending and breaking the branches to right and left he slowly forced a passage upward; and had at last, and suddenly, the sensation coming out on the top of the world. He felt as if he had never been in the open air before. Sea and land lay in a circle below and about him, as he sat astride a branch of the tall tree; he was almost surprised to see the sun still comparatively low in the sky; as if he were looking over a land of eternal sunrise.

"Silent upon a peak in Darien," he remarked, in a needlessly loud and cheerful voice; and though the claim, thus expressed, was illogical, it was not inappropriate. He did feel as if he were a primitive adventurer just come to the New World, instead of a modern traveler just come from it.

"I wonder," he proceeded, "whether I am really the first that ever burst into this silent tree. It looks like it. Those—"

He stopped and sat on his branch quite motionless, but his eyes were turned on a branch a little below it, and they were brilliant with a vigilance, like those of a man watching a snake.

What he was looking at might, at first sight, have been a large white fungus spreading on the smooth and monstrous trunk; but it was not.

Leaning down dangerously from his perch, he detached it from the twig on which it had caught, and then sat holding it in his hand and gazing at it. It was Squire Vane's white Panama hat, but there was no Squire Vane under it. Paynter felt a nameless relief in the very fact that there was not.

There in the clear sunlight and sea air, for an instant, all the tropical terrors of his own idle tale surrounded and suffocated him. It seemed indeed some demon tree of the swamps; a vegetable serpent that fed on men. Even the hideous farce in the fancy of digesting a whole man with the exception of his hat, seemed only to simplify the nightmare. And he found himself gazing dully at one leaf of the tree, which happened to be turned toward him, so that the odd markings, which had partly made the legend, really looked a little like the eye in a peacock's feather. It was as if the sleeping tree had opened one eye upon him.

With a sharp effort he steadied himself in mind and posture on the bough; his reason returned, and he began to descend with the hat in his teeth. When he was back in the underworld of the wood, he studied the hat again and with closer attention. In one place in the crown there was a hole or rent, which certainly had not been there when it had last lain on the table under the garden tree. He sat down, lit a cigarette, and reflected for a long time.

A wood, even a small wood, is not an easy thing to search minutely; but he provided himself with some practical tests in the matter. In one sense the very density of the thicket was a help; he could at least see where anyone had strayed from the path, by broken and trampled growths of every kind. After many hours' industry, he had made a sort of new map of the place; and had decided beyond doubt that some person or persons had so strayed, for some purpose, in several defined directions. There was a way burst through the bushes, making a short cut across a loop of the wandering path; there was another forking out from it as an alternative way into the central space. But there was one especially which was unique, and which seemed to him, the more he studied it, to point to some essential of the mystery.

One of these beaten and broken tracks went from the space under the peacock trees outward into the wood for about twenty yards and then stopped. Beyond that point not a twig was broken nor a leaf disturbed. It had no exit, but he could not believe that it had no goal. After some further reflection, he knelt down and began to cut away grass and clay with his knife, and was surprised at the ease with which they detached themselves. In a few moments a whole section of the soil lifted like a lid; it was a round lid and presented a quaint appearance, like a flat cap with green feathers. For though the disc itself was made of wood, there was a layer of earth on it with the live grass still growing there. And the removal of the round lid revealed a round hole, black as night and seemingly bottomless. Paynter understood it instantly. It was rather near the sea for a well to be sunk, but the traveler had known wells sunk even nearer. He rose to his feet with the great knife in his hand, a frown on his face, and his doubts resolved. He no longer shrank from naming what he knew. This was not the first corpse that had been thrown down a well; here, without stone or epitaph, was the grave of Squire Vane. In a flash all the mythological follies about saints and peacocks were forgotten; he was knocked on the head, as with a stone club, by the human common sense of crime.

Cyprian Paynter stood long by the well in the wood, walked round it in meditation, examined its rim and the ring of grass about it, searched the surrounding soil thoroughly, came back and stood beside the well once more. His researches and reflections had been so long that he had not realized that the day had passed and that the wood and the world round it were beginning already to be steeped in the enrichment of evening. The day had been radiantly calm; the sea seemed to be as still as the well, and the well was as still as a mirror. And then, quite without warning, the mirror moved of itself like a living thing.

In the well, in the wood, the water leapt and gurgled, with a grotesque noise like something swallowing, and then settled again with a second sound. Cyprian could not see into the well clearly, for the opening, from where he stood, was an ellipse, a mere slit, and half masked by thistles and rank grass like a green beard. For where he stood now was three yards away from the well, and he had not yet himself realized that he had sprung back all that distance from the brink when the water spoke.

III
The Mystery of the Well

Cyprian Paynter did not know what he expected to see rise out of the well—the corpse of the murdered man or merely the spirit of the fountain. Anyhow, neither of them rose out of it, and he recognized after an instant that this was, after all, perhaps the more natural course of things. Once more he pulled himself together, walked to the edge of the well and looked down. He saw, as before, a dim glimmer of water, at that depth no brighter than ink; he fancied he still heard a faint convulsion and murmur, but it gradually subsided to an utter stillness. Short of suicidally diving in, there was nothing to be done. He realized that, with all his equipment, he had not even brought anything like a rope or basket, and at length decided to return for them.

As he retraced his steps to the entrance, he recurred to, and took stock of, his more solid discoveries. Somebody had gone into the wood, killed the Squire and thrown him down the well, but he did not admit for a moment that it was his friend the poet; but if the latter had actually been seen coming out of the wood the matter was serious. As he walked the rapidly darkening twilight was cloven with red gleams, that made him almost fancy for a moment that some fantastic criminal had set fire to the tiny forest as he fled. A second glance showed him nothing but one of those red sunsets in which such serene days sometimes close.

As he came out of the gloomy gate of trees into the full glow he saw a dark figure standing quite still in the dim bracken, on the spot where he had left the woodcutter. It was not the woodcutter.

It was topped by a tall black hat of a funeral type, and the whole figure stood so black against the field of crimson fire that edged the

421

sky line that he could not for an instant understand or recall it. When he did, it was with an odd change in the whole channel of his thoughts.

"Doctor Brown!" he cried. "Why, what are you doing up here?"

"I have been talking to poor Martin," answered the doctor, and made a rather awkward movement with his hand toward the road down to the village. Following the gesture, Paynter dimly saw another dark figure walking down in the blood-red distance. He also saw that the hand motioning was really black, and not merely in shadow; and, coming nearer, found the doctor's dress was really funereal, down to the detail of the dark gloves. It gave the American a small but queer shock, as if this were actually an undertaker come up to bury the corpse that could not be found.

"Poor Martin's been looking for his chopper," observed Doctor Brown, "but I told him I'd picked it up and kept it for him. Between ourselves, I hardly think he's fit to be trusted with it." Then, seeing the glance at his black garb, he added: "I've just been to a funeral. Did you know there's been another loss? Poor Jake the fisherman's wife, down in the cottage on the shore, you know. This infernal fever, of course."

As they both turned, facing the red evening light, Paynter instinctively made a closer study, not merely of the doctor's clothes, but of the doctor. Dr. Burton Brown was a tall, alert man, neatly dressed, who would otherwise have had an almost military air but for his spectacles and an almost painful intellectualism in his lean brown face and bald brow. The contrast was clinched by the fact that, while his face was of the ascetic type generally conceived as clean-shaven, he had a strip of dark mustache cut too short for him to bite, and yet a mouth that often moved as if trying to bite it. He might have been a very intelligent army surgeon, but he had more the look of an engineer or one of those services that combine a military silence with a more than military science. Paynter had always respected something ruggedly reliable about the man, and after a little hesitation he told him all the discoveries.

The doctor took the hat of the dead Squire in his hand, and examined it with frowning care. He put one finger through the hole in the crown and moved it meditatively. And Paynter realized how fanciful his own fatigue must have made him; for so silly a thing as the black finger waggling through the rent in that frayed white relic unreasonably displeased him. The doctor soon made the same discovery with professional acuteness, and applied it much further. For when Paynter began to tell him of the moving water in the well he looked at him a moment through his spectacles, and then said:

"Did you have any lunch?"

Paynter for the first time realized that he had, as a fact, worked and thought furiously all day without food.

"Please don't fancy I mean you had too much lunch," said the medical man, with mournful humor. "On the contrary, I mean you had too little. I think you are a bit knocked out, and your nerves exaggerate things. Anyhow, let me advise you not to do any more to-night. There's nothing to be done without ropes or some sort of fishing tackle, if with that; but I think I can get you some of the sort of grappling irons the fishermen use for dragging. Poor Jake's got some, I know; I'll bring them round to you tomorrow morning. The fact is, I'm staying there for a bit as he's rather in a state, and I think is better for me to ask for the things and not a stranger. I am sure you'll understand."

Paynter understood sufficiently to assent, and hardly knew why he stood vacantly watching the doctor make his way down the steep road to the shore and the fisher's cottage. Then he threw off thoughts he had not examined, or even consciously entertained, and walked slowly and rather heavily back to the Vane Arms.

The doctor, still funereal in manner, though no longer so in costume, appeared punctually under the wooden sign next morning, laden with what he had promised; an apparatus of hooks and a hanging net for hoisting up anything sunk to a reasonable depth. He was about to proceed on his professional round, and said nothing further to deter the American from proceeding on his own very unprofessional experiment as a detective. That buoyant amateur had indeed recovered most, if not all, of yesterday's buoyancy, was now well fitted to pass any medical examination, and returned with all his own energy to the scene of yesterday's labors.

It may well have brightened and made breezier his second day's toil that he had not only the sunlight and the bird's singing in the little wood, to say nothing of a more scientific apparatus to work with, but also human companionship, and that of the most intelligent type. After leaving the doctor and before leaving the village he had bethought himself of seeking the little court or square where stood the quiet brown house of Andrew Ashe, solicitor, and the operations of dragging were worked in double harness. Two heads were peering over the well in the wood: one yellow-haired, lean and eager; the other redhaired, heavy and pondering; and if it be true that two heads are better than one, it is truer that four hands are better than two. In any case, their united and repeated efforts bore fruit at last, if anything so hard and meager and forlorn can be called a fruit. It weighed loosely in the net as it was lifted, and rolled out on the grassy edge of the well; it was a bone.

Ashe picked it up and stood with it in his hand, frowning. "We want Doctor Brown here," he said. "This may be the bone of some animal. Any dog or sheep might fall into a hidden well." Then he broke off, for his companion was already detaching a second bone from the net.

After another half hour's effort Paynter had occasion to remark, "It must have been rather a large dog." There were already a heap of such white fragments at his feet.

"I have seen nothing yet," said Ashe, speaking more plainly. "That is certainly a human bone." "I fancy this must be a human bone," said the American.

And he turned away a little as he handed the other a skull.

There was no doubt of what sort of skull; there was the one unique curve that holds the mystery of reason, and underneath it the two black holes that had held human eyes. But just above that on the left was another and smaller black hole, which was not an eye.

Then the lawyer said, with something like an effort: "We may admit it is a man without admitting it is—any particular man. There may be something, after all, in that yarn about the drunkard; he may have tumbled into the well. Under certain conditions, after certain natural processes, I fancy, the bones might be stripped in this way, even without the skill of any assassin. We want the doctor again."

Then he added suddenly, and the very sound of his voice suggested that he hardly believed his own words.

"Haven't you got poor Vane's hat there?"

He took it from the silent American's hand, and with a sort of hurry fitted it on the bony head.

"Don't!" said the other involuntarily.

The lawyer had put his finger, as the doctor had done, through the hole in the hat, and it lay exactly over the hole in the skull.

"I have the better right to shrink," he said steadily, but in a vibrant voice. "I think I am the older friend."

Paynter nodded without speech, accepting the final identification. The last doubt, or hope, had departed, and he turned to the dragging apparatus, and did not speak till he had made his last find.

The singing of the birds seemed to grow louder about them, and the dance of the green summer leaves was repeated beyond in the dance of the green summer sea. Only the great roots of the mysterious trees could be seen, the rest being far aloft, and all round it was a wood of little, lively and happy things. They might have been two innocent naturalists, or even two children fishing for eels or tittlebats on that summer holiday when Paynter pulled up something that weighed in the net more heavily than any bone. It nearly broke the meshes, and fell against a mossy stone with a clang.

"Truth lies at the bottom of a well," cried the American, with lift in his voice. "The woodman's ax."

It lay, indeed, flat and gleaming in the grasses by the well in the wood, just as it had lain in the thicket where the woodman threw it in the beginning of all these things. But on one corner of the bright blade was a dull brown stain.

"I see," said Ashe, "the woodman's ax, and therefore the Woodman. Your deductions are rapid."

"My deductions are reasonable," said Paynter, "Look here, Mr. Ashe; I know what you're thinking. I know you distrust Treherne; but I'm sure you will be just for all that. To begin with, surely the first assumption is that the woodman's ax is used by the Woodman. What have you to say to it?"

"I say 'No' to it," replied the lawyer. "The last weapon a woodman would use would be a woodman's ax; that is if he is a sane man."

"He isn't," said Paynter quietly; "you said you wanted the doctor's opinion just now. The doctor's opinion on this point is the same as my own. We both found him meandering about outside there; it's obvious this business has gone to his head, at any rate. If the murderer were a man of business like yourself, what you say might be sound. But this murderer is a mystic. He was driven by some fanatical fad about the trees. It's quite likely he thought there was something solemn and sacrificial about the ax, and would have liked to cut off Vane's head before a crowd, like Charles I's. He's looking for the ax still, and probably thinks it a holy relic."

"For which reason," said Ashe, smiling, "he instantly chucked it down a well."

Paynter laughed.

"You have me there certainly," he said. "But I think you have something else in your mind. You'll say, I suppose, that we were all watching the wood; but were we? Frankly, I could almost fancy the peacock trees did strike me with a sort of sickness—a sleeping sickness."

"Well," admitted Ashe, "you have me there too. I'm afraid I couldn't swear I was awake all the time; but I don't put it down to magic trees—only to a private hobby of going to bed at night. But look here, Mr. Paynter; there's another and better argument against any outsider from the village or countryside having committed the crime. Granted he might have slipped past us somehow, and gone for the Squire. But why should he go for him in the wood? How did he know he was in the wood? You remember how suddenly the poor old boy bolted into it, on what a momentary impulse. It's the last place where one would normally look for such a man, in the middle of the night. No, it's an ugly thing to say, but we, the group round that garden table, were the only people who knew. Which brings me back to the one point in your remarks which I happen to think perfectly true."

"What was that?" inquired the other.

"That the murderer was a mystic," said Ashe. "But a cleverer mystic than poor old Martin."

Paynter made a murmur of protest, and then fell silent.

"Let us talk plainly," resumed the lawyer. "Treherne had all those mad motives you yourself admit against the woodcutter. He had the knowledge of Vane's whereabouts, which nobody can possibly attribute to the woodcutter. But he had much more. Who taunted and goaded the Squire to go into the wood at all? Treherne. Who practically prophesied, like an infernal quack astrologer, that something would happen to him if he did go into the wood? Treherne. Who was, for some reason, no matter what, obviously burning with rage and restlessness all that night, kicking his legs impatiently to and fro on the cliff, and breaking out with wild words about it being all over soon? Treherne. And on top of all this, when I walked closer to the wood, whom did I see slip out of it swiftly and silently like a shadow, but turning his face once to the moon? On my oath and on my honor—Treherne."

"It is awful," said Paynter, like a man stunned. "What you say is simply awful."

"Yes," said Ashe seriously, "very awful, but very simple. Treherne knew where the ax was originally thrown. I saw him, on that day he lunched here first, watching it like a wolf, while Miss Vane was talking to him. On that dreadful night he could easily have picked it up as he went into the wood. He knew about the well, no doubt; who was so likely to know any old traditions about the peacock trees? He hid the hat in the trees, where perhaps he hoped (though the point is unimportant) that nobody would dare to look. Anyhow, he hid it, simply because it was the one thing that would not sink in the well. Mr. Paynter, do you think I would say this of any man in mere mean dislike? Could any man say it of any man unless the case was complete, as this is complete?"

"It is complete," said Paynter, very pale. "I have nothing left against it but a faint, irrational feeling; a feeling that, somehow or other, if poor Vane could stand alive before us at this moment he might tell some other and even more incredible tale."

Ashe made a mournful gesture.

"Can these dry bones live?" he said.

"Lord Thou knowest," answered the other mechanically. "Even these dry bones—"

And he stopped suddenly with his mouth open, a blinding light of wonder in his pale eyes.

"See here," he said hoarsely and hastily. "You have said the word. What does it mean? What can it mean? Dry? Why are these bones dry?"

The lawyer started and stared down at the heap.

"Your case complete!" cried Paynter, in mounting excitement. "Where is the water in the well? The water I saw leap like a flame? Why did it leap? Where is it gone to? Complete! We are buried under riddles."

Ashe stooped, picked up a bone and looked at it.

"You are right," he said, in a low and shaken voice: "this bone is as dry—as a bone."

"Yes, I am right," replied Cyprian. "And your mystic is still as mysterious as a mystic."

There was a long silence. Ashe laid down the bone, picked up the ax and studied it more closely. Beyond the dull stain at the corner of the steel there was nothing unusual about it save a broad white rag wrapped round the handle, perhaps to give a better grip. The lawyer thought it worth noting, however, that the rag was certainly newer and cleaner than the chopper. But both were quite dry.

"Mr. Paynter," he said at last, "I admit you have scored, in the spirit if not in the letter. In strict logic, this greater puzzle is not a reply to my case. If this ax has not been dipped in water, it has been dipped in blood; and the water jumping out of the well is not an explanation of the poet jumping out of the wood. But I admit that morally and practically it does make a vital difference. We are not faced with a colossal contradiction, and we don't know how far it extends. The body might have been broken up or boiled down to its bones by the murderer, though it may be hard to connect it with the conditions of the murder. It might conceivably have been so reduced by some property in the water and soil, for decomposition varies vastly with these things. I should not dismiss my strong prima facie case against the likely person because of these difficulties. But here we have something entirely different. That the bones themselves should remain dry in a well full of water, or a well that yesterday was full of water—that brings us to the edge of something beyond which we can make no guess. There is a new factor, enormous and quite unknown. While we can't fit together such prodigious facts, we can't fit together a case against Treherne or against anybody. No; there is only one thing to be done now. Since we can't accuse Treherne, we must appeal to him. We must put the case against him frankly before him, and trust he has an explanation—and will give it. I suggest we go back and do it now."

Paynter, beginning to follow, hesitated a moment, and then said: "Forgive me for a kind of liberty; as you say, you are an older friend of the family. I entirely agree with your suggestion, but before you act on your present suspicions, do you know, I think Miss Vane ought to be warned a little? I rather fear all this will be a new shock to her."

"Very well," said Ashe, after looking at him steadily for an instant. "Let us go across to her first."

From the opening of the wood they could see Barbara Vane writing at the garden table, which was littered with correspondence, and the butler with his yellow face waiting behind her chair. As the lengths of grass lessened between them, and the little group at the table grew larger and clearer in the sunlight, Paynter had a painful sense of being part of an embassy of doom. It sharpened when the girl looked up from the table and smiled on seeing them.

"I should like to speak to you rather particularly if I may," said the lawyer, with a touch of authority in his respect; and when the butler was dismissed he laid open the whole matter before her, speaking sympathetically, but leaving out nothing, from the strange escape of the poet from the wood to the last detail of the dry bones out of the well. No fault could be found with any one of his tones or phrases, and yet Cyprian, tingling in every nerve with the fine delicacy of his nation about the other sex, felt as if she were faced with an inquisitor. He stood about uneasily, watched the few colored clouds in the clear sky and the bright birds darting about the wood, and he heartily wished himself up the tree again.

Soon, however, the way the girl took it began to move him to perplexity rather than pity. It was like nothing he had expected, and yet he could not name the shade of difference. The final identification of her father's skull, by the hole in the hat, turned her a little pale, but left her composed; this was, perhaps, explicable, since she had from the first taken the pessimistic view. But during the rest of the tale there rested on her broad brows under her copper coils of hair, a brooding spirit that was itself a mystery. He could only tell himself that she was less merely receptive, either firmly or weakly, than he would have expected. It was as if she revolved, not their problem, but her own. She was silent a long time, and said at last: "Thank you, Mr. Ashe, I am really very grateful for this. After all, it brings things to the point where they must have come sooner or later." She looked dreamily at the wood and sea, and went on: "I've not only had myself to consider, you see; but if you're really thinking *that*, it's time I spoke out, without asking anybody. You say, as if it were something very dreadful, 'Mr. Treherne was in the wood that night.' Well, it's not quite so dreadful to me, you see, because I know he was. In fact, we were there together."

"Together!" repeated the lawyer.

"We were together," she said quietly, "because we had a right to be together."

"Do you mean," stammered Ashe, surprised out of himself, "that you were engaged?"

"No, no," she said. "We were married."

Then, amid a startled silence, she added, as a kind of afterthought: "In fact, we are still."

Strong as was his composure, the lawyer sat back in his chair with a sort of solid stupefaction at which Paynter could not help smiling.

"You will ask me, of course," went on Barbara in the same measured manner, "why we should be married secretly, so that even my poor father did not know. Well, I answer you quite frankly to begin with; because, if he had known, he would certainly have cut me off with a shilling. He did not like my husband, and I rather fancy you do not like him either. And when I tell you this, I know perfectly well what you will say—the usual adventurer getting hold of the usual heiress. It is quite reasonable, and, as it happens, it is quite wrong. If I had deceived my father for the sake of the money, or even for the sake of a man, I should be a little ashamed to talk to you about it. And I think you can see that I am not ashamed."

"Yes," said the American, with a grave inclination, "yes, I can see that."

She looked at him thoughtfully for a moment, as if seeking words for an obscure matter, and then said:

"Do you remember, Mr. Paynter, that day you first lunched here and told us about the African trees? Well, it was my birthday; I mean my first birthday. I was born then, or woke up or something. I had walked in this garden like a somnambulist in the sun. I think there are many such somnambulists in our set and our society; stunned with health, drugged with good manners, fitting their surroundings too well to be alive. Well, I came alive somehow; and you know how deep in us are the things we first realize when we were babies and began to take notice. I began to take notice. One of the first things I noticed was your own story, Mr. Paynter. I feel as if I heard of St. Securis as children hear of Santa Claus, and as if that big tree were a bogey I still believed in. For I do still believe in such things, or rather I believe in them more and more; I feel certain my poor father drove on the rocks by disbelieving, and you are all racing to ruin after him. That is why I do honestly want the estate, and that is why I am not ashamed of wanting it. I am perfectly certain, Mr. Paynter, that nobody can save this perishing land

and this perishing people but those who understand. I mean who understand a thousand little signs and guides in the very soil and lie of the land, and traces that are almost trampled out. My husband understands, and I have begun to understand; my father would never have understood. There are powers, there is the spirit of a place, there are presences that are not to be put by. Oh, don't fancy I am sentimental and hanker after the good old days. The old days were not all good; that is just the point, and we must understand enough to know the good from the evil. We must understand enough to save the traces of a saint or a sacred tradition, or, where a wicked god has been worshiped, to destroy his altar and to cut down his grove."

"His grove," said Paynter automatically, and looked toward the little wood, where the sunbright birds were flying.

"Mrs. Treherne," said Ashe, with a formidable quietness, "I am not so unsympathetic with all this as you may perhaps suppose. I will not even say it is all moonshine, for it is something better. It is, if I may say so, honeymoonshine. I will never deny the saying that it makes the world go round, if it makes people's heads go round too. But there are other sentiments, madam, and other duties. I need not tell you your father was a good man, and that what has befallen him would be pitiable, even as the fate of the wicked. This is a horrible thing, and it is chiefly among horrors that we must keep our common sense. There are reasons for everything, and when my old friend lies butchered do not come to me with even the most beautiful fairy tales about a saint and his enchanted grove."

"Well, and you!" she cried, and rose radiantly and swiftly. "With what kind of fairy tales do you come to me? In what enchanted groves are *you* walking? You come and tell me that Mr. Paynter found a well where the water danced and then disappeared; but of course miracles are all moonshine! You tell me you yourself fished bones from under the same water, and every bone was as dry as a biscuit, but for Heaven's sake let us say nothing that makes anybody's head go round! Really, Mr. Ashe, you must try to preserve your common sense!"

She was smiling, but with blazing eyes; and Ashe got to his feet with an involuntary laugh of surrender.

"Well, we must be going," he said. "May I say that a tribute is really due to your new transcendental training? If I may say so, I always knew you had brains; and you've been learning to use them."

The two amateur detectives went back to the wood for the moment, that Ashe might consider the removal of the unhappy Squire's remains. As he pointed out, it was now legally possible to have an inquest, and, even at that early stage of investigations, he was in favor of having it at once.

"I shall be the coroner," he said, "and I think it will be a case of 'some person or persons unknown.' Don't be surprised; it is often done to give the guilty a false security. This is not the first time the police have found it convenient to have the inquest first and the inquiry afterward."

But Paynter had paid little attention to the point; for his great gift of enthusiasm, long wasted on arts and affectations, was lifted to inspiration by the romance of real life into which he had just walked. He was really a great critic; he had a genius for admiration, and his admiration varied fittingly with everything he admired.

"A splendid girl and a splendid story," he cried. "I feel as if I were in love again myself, not so much with her as with Eve or Helen of Troy, or some such tower of beauty in the morning of the world. Don't you love all heroic things, that gravity and great candor, and the way she took one step from a sort of throne to stand in a wilderness with a vagabond? Oh, believe me, it is she who is the poet; she has the higher reason, and honor and valor are at rest in her soul."

"In short, she is uncommonly pretty," replied Ashe, with some cynicism. "I knew a murderess rather well who was very much like her, and had just that colored hair."

"You talk as if a murderer could be caught red-haired instead of red-handed," retorted Paynter. "Why, at this very minute, you could be caught red-haired yourself. Are you a murderer, by any chance?"

Ashe looked up quickly, and then smiled.

"I'm afraid I'm a connoisseur in murderers, as you are in poets," he answered, "and I assure you they are of all colors in hair as well as temperament. I suppose it's inhumane, but mine is a monstrously interesting trade, even in a little place like this. As for that girl, of course I've known her all her life, and—but—but that is just the question. Have I known her all her life? Have I known her at all? Was she even there to be known? You admire her for telling the truth; and so she did, by God, when she said that some people wake up late, who have never lived before. Do we know what they might do—we, who have only seen them asleep?"

"Great heavens!" cried Paynter. "You don't dare suggest that she—"

"No, I don't," said the lawyer, with composure, "but there are other reasons.... I don't suggest anything fully, till we've had our interview with this poet of yours. I think I know where to find him."

They found him, in fact, before they expected him, sitting on the bench outside the Vane Arms, drinking a mug of cider and waiting for the return of his American friend; so it was not difficult to open conversation with him. Nor did he in any way avoid the subject of the tragedy; and the lawyer, seating himself also on the long bench that fronted the little market place, was soon putting the last developments as lucidly as he had put them to Barbara.

"Well," said Treherne at last, leaning back and frowning at the signboard, with the colored birds and dolphins, just about his head; "suppose somebody did kill the Squire. He'd killed a good many people with his hygiene and his enlightened landlordism."

Paynter was considerably uneasy at this alarming opening; but the poet went on quite coolly, with his hands in his pockets and his feet thrust out into the street.

"When a man has the power of a Sultan in Turkey, and uses it with the ideas of a spinster in Tooting, I often wonder that nobody puts a knife in him. I wish there were more sympathy for murderers, somehow. I'm very sorry the poor old fellow's gone myself; but you gentlemen always seem to forget there are any other people in the world. He's all right; he was a good fellow, and his soul, I fancy, has gone to the happiest paradise of all."

The anxious American could read nothing of the effect of this in the dark Napoleonic face of the lawyer, who merely said: "What do you mean?"

"The fool's paradise," said Treherne, and drained his pot of cider.

The lawyer rose. He did not look at Treherne, or speak to him; but looked and spoke straight across him to the American, who found the utterance not a little unexpected.

"Mr. Paynter," said Ashe, "you thought it rather morbid of me to collect murderers; but it's fortunate for your own view of the case that I do. It may surprise you to know that Mr. Treherne has now, in my eyes, entirely cleared himself of suspicion. I have been intimate with several assassins, as I remarked; but there's one thing none of them ever did. I never knew a murderer to talk about the murder, and then at once deny it and defend it. No, if a man is concealing his crime, why should he go out of his way to apologize for it?"

"Well," said Paynter, with his ready appreciation, "I always said you were a remarkable man; and that's certainly a remarkable idea."

"Do I understand," asked the poet, kicking his heels on the cobbles, "that both you gentlemen have been kindly directing me toward the gallows?"

"No," said Paynter thoughtfully. "I never thought you guilty; and even supposing I had, if you understand me, I should never have thought it quite so guilty to be guilty. It would not have been for money or any mean thing, but for something a little wilder and worthier of a man of genius. After all, I suppose, the poet has passions like great unearthly appetites; and the world has always judged more gently of his sins. But now that Mr. Ashe admits your innocence, I can honestly say I have always affirmed it."

The poet rose also. "Well, I am innocent, oddly enough," he said. "I think I can make a guess about your vanishing well, but of the death and dry bones I know no more than the dead; if so much. And, by the way, my dear Paynter"—and he turned two bright eyes on the art critic— "I will excuse you from excusing me for all the things I haven't done; and you, I hope, will excuse me if I differ from you altogether about the morality of poets. As you suggest, it is a fashionable view, but I think it is a fallacy. No man has less right to be lawless than a man of imagination. For he has spiritual adventures, and can take his holidays when he likes. I could picture the poor Squire carried off to elfland whenever I wanted him carried off, and that wood needed no crime to make it wicked for me. That red sunset the other night was all that a murder would have been to many men. No, Mr. Ashe; show, when next you sit in judgment, a little mercy to some wretched man who drinks and robs because he must drink beer to taste it, and take it to drink it. Have compassion on the next batch of poor thieves, who have to hold things in order to have them. But if ever you find *me* stealing one small farthing, when I can shut my eyes and see the city of El Dorado, then"—and he lifted his head like a falcon— "show me no mercy, for I shall deserve none."

"Well," remarked Ashe, after a pause, "I must go and fix things up for the inquest. Mr. Treherne, your attitude is singularly interesting; I really almost wish I could add you to my collection of murderers. They are a varied and extraordinary set."

"Has it ever occurred to you," asked Paynter, "that perhaps the men who have never committed murder are a varied and very extraordinary set? Perhaps every plain man's life holds the real mystery, the secret of sins avoided."

"Possibly," replied Ashe. "It would be a long business to stop the next man in the street and ask him what crimes he never committed and why not. And I happen to be busy, so you'll excuse me."

"What," asked the American, when he and the poet were alone, "is this guess of yours about the vanishing water?"

"Well, I'm not sure I'll tell you yet," answered Treherne, something of the old mischief coming back into his dark eyes. "But I'll tell you something else, which may be connected with it; something I couldn't tell until my wife had told you about our meeting in the wood." His face had grown grave again, and he resumed after a pause:

"When my wife started to follow her father I advised her to go back first to the house, to leave it by another door and to meet me in the wood in half an hour. We often made these assignations, of course, and generally thought them great fun, but this time the question was serious, and I didn't want the wrong thing done in a hurry. It was a question whether anything could be done to undo an experiment we both vaguely felt to be dangerous, and she especially thought, after reflection, that interference would make things worse. She thought the old sportsman, having been dared to do something, would certainly not be dissuaded by the very man who had dared him or by a woman whom he regarded as a child. She left me at last in a sort of despair, but I lingered with a last hope of doing something, and drew doubtfully near to the heart of the wood; and there, instead of the silence I expected, I heard a voice. It seemed as if the Squire must be talking to himself, and I had the unpleasant fancy that he had already lost his reason in that wood of witchcraft. But I soon found that if he was talking he was talking with two voices. Other fancies attacked me, as that the other was the voice of the tree or the voices of the three trees talking together, and with no man near. But it was not the voice of the tree. The next moment I knew the voice, for I had heard it twenty times across the table. It was the voice of that doctor of yours; I heard it as certainly as you hear my voice now."

After a moment's silence, he resumed: "I left the wood, I hardly knew why, and with wild and bewildered feelings; and as I came out into the faint moonshine I saw that old lawyer standing quietly, but staring at me like an owl. At least, the light touched his red hair with fire, but his square old face was in shadow. But I knew, if I could have read it, that it was the face of a hanging judge."

He threw himself on the bench again, smiled a little, and added: "Only, like a good many hanging judges, I fancy, he was waiting patiently to hang the wrong man."

"And the right man—" said Paynter mechanically. Treherne shrugged his shoulders, sprawling on the ale bench, and played with his empty pot.

IV
THE CHASE AFTER THE TRUTH

Some time after the inquest, which had ended in the inconclusive verdict which Mr. Andrew Ashe had himself predicted and achieved, Paynter was again sitting on the bench outside the village inn, having on the little table in front of it a tall glass of light ale, which he enjoyed much more as local color than as liquor. He had but one companion on the bench, and that a new one, for the little market place was empty at that hour, and he had lately, for the rest, been much alone. He was not unhappy, for he resembled his great countryman, Walt Whitman, in carrying a kind of universe with him like an open umbrella; but he was not only alone, but lonely. For Ashe had gone abruptly up to London, and since his return had been occupied obscurely with legal matters, doubtless bearing on the murder. And Treherne had long since taken up his position openly, at the great house, as the husband of the great lady, and he and she were occupied with sweeping reforms on the estate. The lady especially, being of the sort whose very dreams "drive at practice," was landscape gardening as with the gestures of a giantess. It was natural, therefore, that so sociable a spirit as Paynter should fall into speech with the one other stranger who happened to be staying at the inn, evidently a bird of passage like himself. This man, who was smoking a pipe on the bench beside him, with his knapsack before him on the table, was an artist come to sketch on that romantic coast; a tall man in a velvet jacket, with a shock of tow-colored hair, a long fair beard, but eyes of dark brown, the effect of which contrast reminded Paynter vaguely, he hardly knew why, of a Russian. The stranger carried his knapsack into many picturesque corners; he obtained permission to set up his easel in that high garden where the late Squire had held his *al*

437

fresco banquets. But Paynter had never had an opportunity of judging of the artist's work, nor did he find it easy to get the artist even to talk of his art. Cyprian himself was always ready to talk of any art, and he talked of it excellently, but with little response. He gave his own reasons for preferring the Cubists to the cult of Picasso, but his new friend seemed to have but a faint interest in either. He insinuated that perhaps the Neo-Primitives were after all only thinning their line, while the true Primitives were rather tightening it; but the stranger seemed to receive the insinuation without any marked reaction of feeling. When Paynter had even gone back as far into the past as the Post-Impressionists to find a common ground, and not found it, other memories began to creep back into his mind. He was just reflecting, rather darkly, that after all the tale of the peacock trees needed a mysterious stranger to round it off, and this man had much the air of being one, when the mysterious stranger himself said suddenly:

"Well, I think I'd better show you the work I'm doing down here."

He had his knapsack before him on the table, and he smiled rather grimly as he began to unstrap it. Paynter looked on with polite expressions of interest, but was considerably surprised when the artist unpacked and placed on the table, not any recognizable works of art, even of the most Cubist description, but (first) a quire of foolscap closely written with notes in black and red ink, and (second), to the American's extreme amazement, the old woodman's ax with the linen wrapper, which he had himself found in the well long ago.

"Sorry to give you a start, sir," said the Russian artist, with a marked London accent. "But I'd better explain straight off that I'm a policeman."

"You don't look it," said Paynter.

"I'm not supposed to," replied the other. "Mr. Ashe brought me down here from the Yard to investigate; but he told me to report to you when I'd got anything to go on. Would you like to go into the matter now?

"When I took this matter up," explained the detective, "I did it at Mr. Ashe's request, and largely, of course, on Mr. Ashe's lines. Mr. Ashe is a great criminal lawyer; with a beautiful brain, sir, as full as the Newgate Calendar. I took, as a working notion, his view that only you five gentlemen round the table in the Squire's garden were acquainted with the Squire's movements. But you gentlemen, if I may say so, have a way of forgetting certain other things and other people which we are rather taught to look for first. And as I followed Mr. Ashe's inquiries through the stages you know already, through certain suspicions I needn't discuss because they've been dropped, I found the thing shaping after all toward something, in the end, which I think we should have considered at the beginning. Now, to begin with, it is not true that there were five men round the table. There were six."

The creepy conditions of that garden vigil vaguely returned upon Paynter; and he thought of a ghost, or something more nameless than a ghost. But the deliberate speech of the detective soon enlightened him.

"There were six men and five gentlemen, if you like to put it so," he proceeded. "That man Miles, the butler, saw the Squire vanish as plainly as you did; and I soon found that Miles was a man worthy of a good deal of attention."

A light of understanding dawned on Paynter's face. "So that was it, was it!" he muttered.

"Does all our mythological mystery end with a policeman collaring a butler? Well, I agree with you he is far from an ordinary butler, even to look at; and the fault in imagination is mine. Like many faults in imagination, it was simply snobbishness."

"We don't go quite so fast as that," observed the officer, in an impassive manner. "I only said I found the inquiry pointing to Miles; and that he was well worthy of attention. He was much more in the old Squire's confidence than many people supposed; and when I cross-examined him he told me a good deal that was worth knowing. I've got it all down in these notes here; but at the moment I'll only trouble you with one detail of it. One night this butler was just outside the Squire's dining-room door, when he heard the noise of a violent quarrel. The Squire was a violent gentleman, from time to time; but the curious thing about this scene was that the other gentleman was the more violent of the two. Miles heard him say repeatedly that the Squire was a public nuisance, and that his death would be a good riddance for everybody. I only stop now to tell you that the other gentleman was Dr. Burton Brown, the medical man of this village.

"The next examination I made was that of Martin, the woodcutter. Upon one point at least his evidence is quite clear, and is, as you will see, largely confirmed by other witnesses. He says first that the doctor prevented him from recovering his ax, and this is corroborated by Mr. and Mrs. Treherne. But he says further that the doctor admitted having the thing himself; and this again finds support in other evidence by the gardener, who saw the doctor, some time afterward, come by himself and pick up the chopper. Martin says that Doctor Brown repeatedly refused to give it up, alleging some fanciful excuse every time. And, finally, Mr. Paynter, we will hear the evidence of the ax itself."

He laid the woodman's tool on the table in front of him, and began to rip up and unwrap the curious linen covering round the handle.

"You will admit this is an odd bandage," he said. "And that's just the odd thing about it, that it really is a bandage. This white stuff is the sort of lint they use in hospitals, cut into strips like this. But most doctors keep some; and I have the evidence of Jake the fisherman, with whom Doctor Brown lived for some time, that the doctor had this useful habit. And, last," he added, flattening out a corner of the rag on the table, "isn't it odd that it should be marked T.B.B.?"

The American gazed at the rudely inked initials, but hardly saw them. What he saw, as in a mirror in his darkened memory, was the black figure with the black gloves against the blood-red sunset, as he had seen it when he came out of the wood, and which had always haunted him, he knew not why.

"Of course, I see what you mean," he said, "and it's very painful for me, for I knew and respected the man. But surely, also, it's very far from explaining everything. If he is a murderer, is he a magician? Why did the well water all evaporate in a night, and leave the dead man's bones dry as dust? That's not a common operation in the hospitals, is it?"

"As to the water, we do know the explanation," said the detective. "I didn't tumble to it at first myself, being a Cockney; but a little talk with Jake and the other fisherman about the old smuggling days put me straight about that. But I admit the dried remains still stump us all. All the same—"

A shadow fell across the table, and his talk was sharply cut short. Ashe was standing under the painted sign, buttoned up grimly in black, and with the face of the hanging judge, of which the poet had spoken, plain this time in the broad sunlight. Behind him stood two big men in plain clothes, very still; but Paynter knew instantly who they were.

"We must move at once," said the lawyer. "Dr. Burton Brown is leaving the village."

The tall detective sprang to his feet, and Paynter instinctively imitated him.

"He has gone up to the Trehernes possibly to say good-by," went on Ashe rapidly. "I'm sorry, but we must arrest him in the garden there, if necessary. I've kept the lady out of the way, I think. But you"—addressing the factitious landscape painter— "must go up at once and rig up that easel of yours near the table and be ready. We will follow quietly, and come up behind the tree. We must be careful, for it's clear he's got wind of us, or he wouldn't be doing a bolt."

"I don't like this job," remarked Paynter, as they mounted toward the park and garden, the detective darting on ahead.

"Do you suppose I do?" asked Ashe; and, indeed, his strong, heavy face looked so lined and old that the red hair seemed unnatural, like a red wig. "I've known him longer than you, though perhaps I've suspected him longer as well."

When they topped the slope of the garden the detective had already erected his easel, though a strong breeze blowing toward the sea rattled and flapped his apparatus and blew about his fair (and false) beard in the wind. Little clouds curled like feathers, were scudding seaward across the many-colored landscape, which the American art critic had once surveyed on a happier morning; but it is doubtful if the landscape painter paid much attention to it. Treherne was dimly discernible in the doorway of what was now his house; he would come no nearer, for he hated such a public duty more bitterly than the rest. The others posted themselves a little way behind the tree. Between the lines of these masked batteries the black figure of the doctor could be seen coming across the green lawn, traveling straight, as a bullet, as he had done when he brought the bad news to the woodcutter. To-day he was smiling, under the dark mustache that was cut short of the upper lip, though they fancied him a little pale, and he seemed to pause a moment and peer through his spectacles at the artist.

The artist turned from his easel with a natural movement, and then in a flash had captured the doctor by the coat collar.

"I arrest you—" he began; but Doctor Brown plucked himself free with startling promptitude, took a flying leap at the other, tore off his sham beard, tossing it into the air like one of the wild wisps of the cloud; then, with one wild kick, sent the easel flying topsy-turvy, and fled like a hare for the shore. Even at that dazzling instant Paynter felt that this wild reception was a novelty and almost an anticlimax; but he had no time for analysis when he and the whole pack had to follow in the hunt; even Treherne bringing up the rear with a renewed curiosity and energy.

The fugitive collided with one of the policemen who ran to head him off, sending him sprawling down the slope; indeed, the fugitive seemed inspired with the strength of a wild ape. He cleared at a bound the rampart of flowers, over which Barbara had once leaned to look at her future lover, and tumbled with blinding speed down the steep path up which that troubadour had climbed. Racing with the rushing wind they all streamed across the garden after him, down the path, and finally on to the seashore by the fisher's cot, and the pierced crags and caverns the American had admired when he first landed. The runaway did not, however, make for the house he had long inhabited, but rather for the pier, as if with a mind to seize the boat or to swim. Only when he reached the other end of the small stone jetty did he turn, and show them the pale face with the spectacles; and they saw that it was still smiling.

"I'm rather glad of this," said Treherne, with a great sigh. "The man is mad."

Nevertheless, the naturalness of the doctor's voice, when he spoke, startled them as much as a shriek.

"Gentleman," he said, "I won't protract your painful duties by asking you what you want; but I will ask at once for a small favor, which will not prejudice those duties in any way. I came down here rather in a hurry perhaps; but the truth is I thought I was late for an appointment." He looked dispassionately at his watch. "I find there is still some fifteen minutes. Will you wait with me here for that short time; after which I am quite at your service."

There was a bewildered silence, and then Paynter said: "For my part, I feel as if it would really be better to humor him."

"Ashe," said the doctor, with a new note of seriousness, "for old friendship, grant me this last little indulgence. It will make no difference; I have no arms or means of escape; you can search me if you like.

I know you think you are doing right, and I also know you will do it as fairly as you can. Well, after all, you get friends to help you; look at our friend with the beard, or the remains of the beard. Why shouldn't I have a friend to help me? A man will be here in a few minutes in whom I put some confidence; a great authority on these things. Why not, if only out of curiosity, wait and hear his view of the case?"

"This seems all moonshine," said Ashe, "but on the chance of any light on things—well, from the moon—I don't mind waiting a quarter of an hour. Who is this friend, I wonder; some amateur detective, I suppose."

"I thank you," said the doctor, with some dignity. "I think you will trust him when you have talked to him a little. And now," he added with an air of amiably relaxing into lighter matters, "let us talk about the murder.

"This case," he said in a detached manner, "will be found, I suspect, to be rather unique. There is a very clear and conclusive combination of evidence against Thomas Burton Brown, otherwise myself. But there is one peculiarity about that evidence, which you may perhaps have noticed. It all comes ultimately from one source, and that a rather unusual one. Thus, the woodcutter says I had his ax, but what makes him think so? He says I told him I had his ax; that I told him so again and again. Once more, Mr. Paynter here pulled up the ax out of the well; but how? I think Mr. Paynter will testify that I brought him the tackle for fishing it up, tackle he might never have got in any other way. Curious, is it not? Again, the ax is found to be wrapped in lint that was in my possession, according to the fisherman. But who showed the lint to the fisherman? I did. Who marked it with large letters as mine? I did. Who wrapped it round the handle at all? I did. Rather a singular thing to do; has anyone ever explained it?"

His words, which had been heard at first with painful coldness were beginning to hold more and more of their attention.

"Then there is the well itself," proceeded the doctor, with the same air of insane calm. "I suppose some of you by this time know at least the secret of that. The secret of the well is simply that it is not a well. It is purposely shaped at the top so as to look like one, but it is really a sort of chimney opening from the roof of one of those caves over there; a cave that runs inland just under the wood, and indeed *is* connected by tunnels and secret passages with other openings miles and miles away. It is a sort of labyrinth used by smugglers and such people for ages past. This doubtless explains many of those disappearances we have heard of. But to return to the well that is not a well, in case some of you still don't know about it. When the sea rises very high at certain seasons it fills the low cave, and even rises a little way in the funnel above, making it look more like a well than ever. The noise Mr. Paynter heard was the natural eddy of a breaker from outside, and the whole experience depended on something so elementary as the tide."

The American was startled into ordinary speech.

"The tide!" he said. "And I never even thought of it! I guess that comes of living by the Mediterranean."

"The next step will be obvious enough," continued the speaker, "to a logical mind like that of Mr. Ashe, for instance. If it be asked why, even so, the tide did not wash away the Squire's remains that had lain there since his disappearance, there is only one possible answer. The remains had *not* lain there since his disappearance. The remains had been deliberately put there in the cavern under the wood, and put there *after* Mr. Paynter had made his first investigation. They were put there, in short, after the sea had retreated and the cave was again dry. That is why they were dry; of course, much drier than the cave. Who put them there, I wonder?"

He was gazing gravely through his spectacles over their heads into vacancy, and suddenly he smiled.

"Ah," he cried, jumping up from the rock with alacrity, "here is the amateur detective at last!"

Ashe turned his head over his shoulder, and for a few seconds did not move it again, but stood as if with a stiff neck. In the cliff just behind him was one of the clefts or cracks into which it was every-where cloven. Advancing from this into the sunshine, as if from a narrow door, was Squire Vane, with a broad smile on his face.

The wind was tearing from the top of the high cliff out to sea, passing over their heads, and they had the sensation that everything was passing over their heads and out of their control. Paynter felt as if his head had been blown off like a hat. But none of this gale of unreason seemed to stir a hair on the white head of the Squire, whose bearing, though self-important and bordering on a swagger, seemed if anything more comfortable than in the old days. His red face was, however, burnt like a sailor's, and his light clothes had a foreign look.

"Well, gentlemen," he said genially, "so this is the end of the legend of the peacock trees. Sorry to spoil that delightful traveler's tale, Mr. Paynter, but the joke couldn't be kept up forever. Sorry to put a stop to your best poem, Mr. Treherne, but I thought all this poetry had been going a little too far. So Doctor Brown and I fixed up a little surprise for you. And I must say, without vanity, that you look a little surprised."

"What on earth," asked Ashe at last, "is the meaning of all this?"

The Squire laughed pleasantly, and even a little apologetically,

"I'm afraid I'm fond of practical jokes," he said, "and this I suppose is my last grand practical joke. But I want you to understand that the joke is really practical. I flatter myself it will be of very practical use to the cause of progress and common sense, and the killing of such superstitions everywhere. The best part of it, I admit, was the doctor's idea and not mine. All I meant to do was to pass a night in the trees, and then turn up as fresh as paint to tell you what fools you were. But Doctor Brown here followed me into the wood, and we had a little talk which rather changed my plans. He told me that a disappearance for a few hours like that would never knock the nonsense on the head; most people would never even hear of it, and those who did would say that one night proved nothing. He showed me a much better way, which had been tried in several cases where bogus miracles had been shown up. The thing to do was to get the thing really believed everywhere as a miracle, and then shown up everywhere as a sham miracle. I can't put all the arguments as well as he did, but that was the notion, I think."

The doctor nodded, gazing silently at the sand; and the Squire resumed with undiminished relish.

"We agreed that I should drop through the hole into the cave, and make my way through the tunnels, where I often used to play as a boy, to the railway station a few miles from here, and there take a train for London. It was necessary for the joke, of course, that I should disappear without being traced; so I made my way to a port, and put in a very pleasant month or two round my old haunts in Cyprus and the Mediterranean. There's no more to say of that part of the business, except that I arranged to be back by a particular time; and here I am. But I've heard enough of what's gone on round here to be satisfied that I've done the trick. Everybody in Cornwall and most people in South England have heard of the Vanishing Squire; and thousands of noodles have been nodding their heads over crystals and tarot cards at this marvelous proof of an unseen world. I reckon the Reappearing Squire will scatter their cards and smash their crystals, so that such rubbish won't appear again in the twentieth century. I'll make the peacock trees the laughing stock of all Europe and America."

"Well," said the lawyer, who was the first to rearrange his wits, "I'm sure we're all only too delighted to see you again, Squire; and I quite understand your explanation and your own very natural motives in the matter. But I'm afraid I haven't got the hang of everything yet. Granted that you wanted to vanish, was it necessary to put bogus bones in the cave, so as nearly to put a halter round the neck of Doctor Brown? And who put it there? The statement would appear perfectly maniacal; but so far as I can make head or tail out of anything, Doctor Brown seems to have put it there himself."

The doctor lifted his head for the first time.

"Yes; I put the bones there," he said. "I believe I am the first son of Adam who ever manufactured all the evidence of a murder charge against himself."

It was the Squire's turn to look astonished. The old gentleman looked rather wildly from one to the other.

"Bones! Murder charge!" he ejaculated. "What the devil is all this? Whose bones?"

"Your bones, in a manner of speaking," delicately conceded the doctor. "I had to make sure you had really died, and not disappeared by magic."

The Squire in his turn seemed more hopelessly puzzled than the whole crowd of his friends had been over his own escapade. "Why not?" he demanded. "I thought it was the whole point to make it look like magic. Why did you want me to die so much?"

Doctor Brown had lifted his head; and he now very slowly lifted his hand. He pointed with outstretched arm at the headland overhanging the foreshore, just above the entrance to the cave. It was the exact part of the beach where Paynter had first landed, on that spring morning when he had looked up in his first fresh wonder at the peacock trees. But the trees were gone.

The fact itself was no surprise to them; the clearance had naturally been one of the first of the sweeping changes of the Treherne regime. But though they knew it well, they had wholly forgotten it; and its significance returned on them suddenly like a sign in heaven.

"That is the reason," said the doctor. "I have worked for that for fourteen years."

They no longer looked at the bare promontory on which the feathery trees had once been so familiar a sight; for they had something else to look at. Anyone seeing the Squire now would have shifted his opinion about where to find the lunatic in that crowd. It was plain in a flash that the change had fallen on him like a thunderbolt; that he, at least, had never had the wildest notion that the tale of the Vanishing Squire had been but a prelude to that of the vanishing trees. The next half hour was full of his ravings and expostulations, which gradually died away into demands for explanation and incoherent questions repeated again and again. He had practically to be overruled at last, in spite of the respect in which he was held, before anything like a space and silence were made in which the doctor could tell his own story. It was perhaps a singular story, of which he alone had ever had the knowledge; and though its narration was not uninterrupted, it may be set forth consecutively in his own words.

"First, I wish it clearly understood that I believe in nothing. I do not even give the nothing I believe a name; or I should be an atheist. I have never had inside my head so much as a hint of heaven and hell. I think it most likely we are worms in the mud; but I happen to be sorry for the other worms under the wheel. And I happen myself to be a sort of worm that turns when he can. If I care nothing for piety, I care less for poetry. I'm not like Ashe here, who is crammed with criminology, but has all sorts of other culture as well. I know nothing about culture, except bacteria culture. I sometimes fancy Mr. Ashe is as much an art critic as Mr. Paynter; only he looks for his heroes, or villains, in real life. But I am a very practical man; and my stepping stones have been simply scientific facts. In this village I found a fact—a fever. I could not classify it; it seemed peculiar to this corner of the coast; it had singular reactions of delirium and mental breakdown. I studied it exactly as I should a queer case in the hospital, and corresponded and compared notes with other men of science. But nobody had even a working hypothesis about it, except of course the ignorant peasantry, who said the peacock trees were in some wild way poisonous.

"Well, the peacock trees were poisonous. The peacock trees did produce the fever. I verified the fact in the plain plodding way required, comparing all the degrees and details of a vast number of cases; and there were a shocking number to compare. At the end of it I had discovered the thing as Harvey discovered the circulation of the blood. Everybody was the worse for being near the things; those who came off best were exactly the exceptions that proved the rule, abnormally healthy and energetic people like the Squire and his daughter. In other words, the peasants were right. But if I put it that way, somebody will cry: 'But do you believe it was supernatural then?' In fact, that's what you'll all say; and that's exactly what I complain of. I fancy hundreds of men have been left dead and diseases left undiscovered, by this suspicion of superstition, this stupid fear of fear. Unless you see daylight through the forest of facts from the first, you won't venture into the wood at all. Unless we can promise you beforehand that there shall be what you call a natural explanation, to save your precious dignity from miracles, you won't even hear the beginning of the plain tale. Suppose there isn't a natural explanation! Suppose there is, and we never find it! Suppose I haven't a notion whether there is or not! What the devil has that to do with you, or with me in dealing with the facts I do know? My own instinct is to think there is; that if my researches could be followed far enough it would be found that some horrible parody of hay fever, some effect analogous to that of pollen, would explain all the facts. I have never found the explanation. What I have found are the facts. And the fact is that those trees on the top there dealt death right and left, as certainly as if they had been giants, standing on a hill and knocking men down in crowds with a club. It will be said that now I had only to produce my proofs and have the nuisance removed. Perhaps I might have convinced the scientific world finally, when more and more processions of dead men had passed through the village to the cemetery. But I had not got to convince the scientific world, but the Lord of the Manor. The Squire will pardon my saying that it was a very different thing. I tried it once; I lost my temper, and said things I do not defend; and I left the Squire's prejudices rooted anew, like the trees. I was confronted with one colossal coincidence that was an obstacle to all my aims. One thing made all my science sound like nonsense. It was the popular legend.

"Squire, if there were a legend of hay fever, you would not believe in hay fever. If there were a popular story about pollen, you would say that pollen was only a popular story. I had something against me heavier and more hopeless than the hostility of the learned; I had the support of the ignorant. My truth was hopelessly tangled up with a tale that the educated were resolved to regard as entirely a lie. I never tried to explain again; on the contrary, I apologized, affected a conversion to the common-sense view, and watched events. And all the time the lines of a larger, if more crooked plan, began to get clearer in my mind. I knew that Miss Vane, whether or no she were married to Mr. Treherne, as I afterward found she was, was so much under his influence that the first day of her inheritance would be the last day of the poisonous trees. But she could not inherit, or even interfere, till the Squire died. It became simply self-evident, to a rational mind, that the Squire must die. But wishing to be humane as well as rational, I desired his death to be temporary.

"Doubtless my scheme was completed by a chapter of accidents, but I was watching for such accidents. Thus I had a foreshadowing of how the ax would figure in the tale when it was first flung at the trees; it would have surprised the woodman to know how near our minds were, and how I was but laying a more elaborate siege to the towers of pestilence. But when the Squire spontaneously rushed on what half the countryside would call certain death, I jumped at my chance. I followed him, and told him all that he has told you. I don't suppose he'll ever forgive me now, but that shan't prevent me saying that I admire him hugely for being what people would call a lunatic and what is really a sportsman. It takes rather a grand old man to make a joke in the grand style. He came down so quick from the tree he had climbed that he had no time to pull his hat off the bough it had caught in.

"At first I found I had made a miscalculation. I thought his disappearance would be taken as his death, at least after a little time; but Ashe told me there could be no formalities without a corpse. I fear I was a little annoyed, but I soon set myself to the duty of manufacturing a corpse. It's not hard for a doctor to get a skeleton; indeed, I had one, but Mr. Paynter's energy was a day too early for me, and I only got the bones into the well when he had already found it. His story gave me another chance, however; I noted where the hole was in the hat, and made a precisely corresponding hole in the skull. The reason for creating the other clews may not be so obvious. It may not yet be altogether apparent to you that I am not a fiend in human form. I could not substantiate a murder without at least suggesting a murderer, and I was resolved that if the crime happened to be traced to anybody, it should be to me. So I'm not surprised you were puzzled about the purpose of the rag round the ax, because it had no purpose, except to incriminate the man who put it there. The chase had to end with me, and when it was closing in at last the joke of it was too much for me, and I fear I took liberties with the gentleman's easel and beard. I was the only person who could risk it, being the only person who could at the last moment produce the Squire and prove there had been no crime at all. That, gentlemen, is the true story of the peacock trees; and that bare crag up there, where the wind is whistling as it would over a wilderness, is a waste place I have labored to make, as many men have labored to make a cathedral.

"I don't think there is any more to say, and yet something moves in my blood and I will try to say it. Could you not have trusted a little these peasants whom you already trust so much? These men are men, and they meant something; even their fathers were not wholly fools. If your gardener told you of the trees you called him a madman, but he did not plan and plant your garden like a madman. You would not trust your woodman about these trees, yet you trusted him with all the others. Have you ever thought what all the work of the world would be like if the poor were so senseless as you think them? But no, you stuck to your rational principle. And your rational principle was that a thing must be false because thousands of men had found it true; that *because* many human eyes had seen something it could not be there."

He looked across at Ashe with a sort of challenge, but though the sea wind ruffled the old lawyer's red mane, his Napoleonic mask was unruffled; it even had a sort of beauty from its new benignity.

"I am too happy just now in thinking how wrong I have been," he answered, "to quarrel with you, doctor, about our theories. And yet, in justice to the Squire as well as myself, I should demur to your sweeping inference. I respect these peasants, I respect your regard for them; but their stories are a different matter. I think I would do anything for them but believe them. Truth and fancy, after all, are mixed in them, when in the more instructed they are separate; and I doubt if you have considered what would be involved in taking their word for anything. Half the ghosts of those who died of fever may be walking by now; and kind as these people are, I believe they might still burn a witch. No, doctor, I admit these people have been badly used, I admit they are in many ways our betters, but I still could not accept anything in their evidence."

The doctor bowed gravely and respectfully enough, and then, for the last time that day, they saw his rather sinister smile.

"Quite so," he said. "But you would have hanged me on their evidence."

And, turning his back on them, as if automatically, he set his face toward the village, where for so many years he had gone his round.

Coachwhip Publications

CoachwhipBooks.com

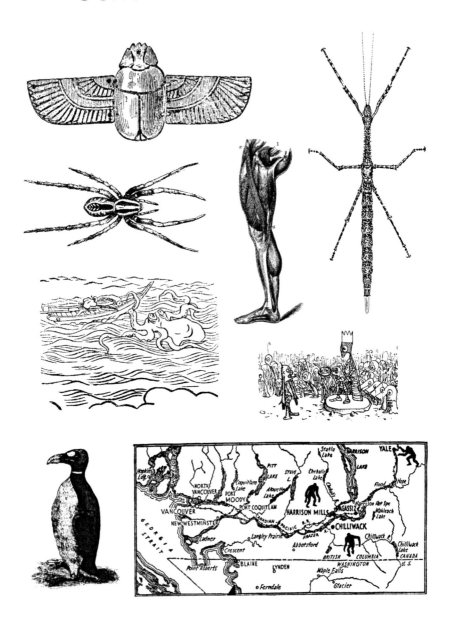

ALSO AVAILABLE

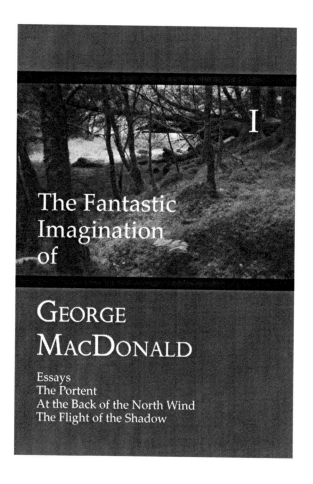

THE FANTASTIC IMAGINATION OF GEORGE MACDONALD

Three Volumes

ISBN 1-930585-61-6

ISBN 1-930585-62-4

ISBN 1-930585-63-2

ALSO AVAILABLE

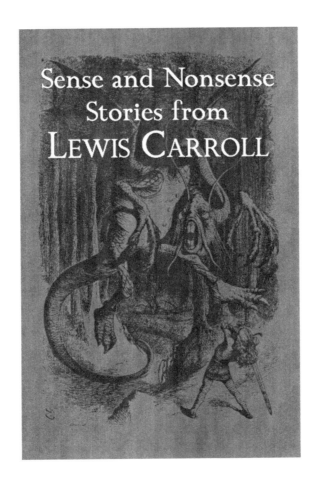

SENSE AND NONSENSE STORIES WITH LEWIS CARROLL

Alice, Sylvie and Bruno, and More...

ISBN 1-930585-75-6

ALSO AVAILABLE

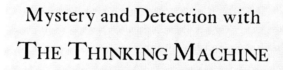

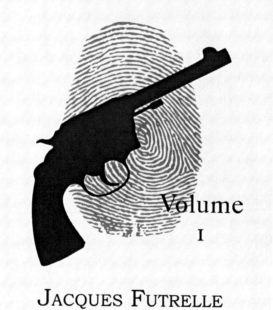

Mystery and Detection with

THE THINKING MACHINE

Volume

I

JACQUES FUTRELLE

MYSTERY AND DETECTION WITH THE THINKING MACHINE

Two Volumes

ISBN 1-930585-70-5

ISBN 1-930585-71-3

Lightning Source UK Ltd.
Milton Keynes UK
UKOW04f2022020714

234463UK00001B/17/P

9 781930 585805